SHW

NOBODY
TRUE

NOBODY TRUE

JAMES HERBERT

A TOM DOHERTY ASSOCIATES BOOK

NEW YORK

NOBODY TRUE

Copyright © 2003 by James Herbert

Originally published in London in 2003 by Macmillan, an imprint of Pan Macmillan, Ltd.

A Tor Book
Published by Tom Doherty Associates, LLC
175 Fifth Avenue
New York, NY 10010

www.tor.com

Tor® is a registered trademark of Tom Doherty Associates, LLC.

Library of Congress Cataloging-in-Publication Data

Herbert, James, 1943–
    Nobody true / James Herbert.—1st ed.
        p. cm.
    "A Tom Doherty Associates book."
    ISBN 0-765-31212-3 (acid-free paper)
    EAN 978-0-765-31212-9
    1. Murder victims—Fiction. 2. Serial murderers—Fiction. 3. Astral projection—Fiction. 4. Murder victims' families—Fiction. I. Title.

PR6058.E62N63 2005
823'.914—dc22

                                                                2005040586

First U.S. Edition: September 2005

Printed in the United States of America

0 9 8 7 6 5 4 3 2 1

NOBODY
TRUE

. . . So that this I, that is to say the soul by which I am what I am, is entirely distinct from the body, is even easier to know than the body, and furthermore would not stop being what it is, even if the body did not exist.

RENÉ DESCARTES

Cogito, ergo sum—I think, therefore I am.

RENÉ DESCARTES

I think therefore am I?

JAMES TRUE

It's not that I'm afraid to die. I just don't want to be there when it happens.

WOODY ALLEN

I wasn't there when I died.

Really. I wasn't. And finding my body dead came as a shock. Hell, I was horrified, lost, couldn't understand what the fuck had happened.

Because I'd been away, you see, away from my physical body. My mind—spirit, soul, psyche, consciousness, call it what you will—had been off on one of its occasional excursions, to find on its return that my body had become a corpse. A very bloody and mutilated corpse.

It took me a long time to absorb what lay spread before me on the hotel's blood-drenched bed—*much* longer, as you'll come to appreciate—to get used to the idea. I was adrift, floating in the ether like some poor desolate ghost. Only I wasn't a ghost. Was I? If that were the case, shouldn't I have been on my way down some long black tunnel toward the light at the end? Shouldn't my life have flashed before me, sins and all? Where was my personal Judgment Day?

If I were dead why didn't I *feel* dead?

I could only stand—hover—over the empty shell that once was me and moan aloud.

How did this come about? I'll give no answers just yet, but instead will take you through a story of love, murder, betrayal, and revelation, not quite all of it bad.

It began with a hot potato . . .

TWO

I was six or seven years old at the time (I died aged thirty-three) and on holiday with my mother, having dinner in a Bournemouth boarding house. It was just the two of us because my dad had run out on us before I made my third birthday; I was told he'd gone off with another lady—my mother made no bones about it, despite my tender years I was always the sounding board for her vexations and rages, especially when they concerned my errant father. The nights were many when my bedtime story was a denunciation of marriage and cheap "tarts." The topic of breakfast conversation often had a lot to do with the failings of men in general and the iniquities of wayward husbands in particular. I must have been at least ten before I realized that the equation "men = bad, women (specifically wives) = good but put-upon," was a mother-generated myth, and that was only because I had several friends whose fathers were terrific to their sons and their sons' friends, as well as loving toward their own wives. I got to know about marriages built on firm foundations and I have to admit to an envy of the other boys and girls who had normal home lives. Why did my dad betray me, why did he abandon us for this "tart"? It bugged me then, but now I understand. The icon of worship that was Mother eventually lost some of its shine. Yes, in later years I still loved her, but no, I didn't turn into Norman Bates and murder Mother, stow her bones away in the fruit cellar. Let's say my view of men in general, and my father in particular, became more balanced. Lord, in my teens I even began to understand how some wives—the nagging, abusive kind—could drive their husbands off. No disrespect, Mother, but you certainly had a mouth on you.

Back to the potato.

We'd had, my mother and I, a wet morning on the beach and a damp afternoon in the seaside town's cinema. I rustled sweet papers and my mother wept her way through what must have been a matinee rerun of *Love Story*. Having only just got dry, we got wet again walking through the drizzle back to the boarding house. I remember how starved I was that evening when we sat down for dinner in the bright, yet inexplicably dreary dining room, the sweets during the film not enough to fill a growing boy's belly (the burger was by now a mouth-watering memory), and I tucked into my meat, veg, and potatoes without any of the normal blandishments or threats from my mother. The boiled potatoes were smallish but steamy hot and in my enthusiasm I forked a whole one into my mouth. I'd never realized until then that potatoes could get so scorching—that certainly wasn't the way Mother served them up—and I burned the roof of my mouth as well as my tongue on the blistering gob-stopper. Aware that spitting it out onto the plate in front of a room full of strangers would get me into a whole heap of trouble with Mother, who liked to maintain a "refined" (one of her favorite words) demeanor in public, I swallowed.

She looked up in surprise, then horror, as I sucked air to cool the potato, the horror having nothing to do with concern for her distressed son but because of the spectacle I was making of myself. Heads turned in our direction, forks froze mid-air, and the low buzz of conversation ceased as my breath squeezed through whatever vents it could find around the blockage in my throat. I'm pretty certain that my watery eyes were bulging and my face a torrid red. The noise I made was like a discordant flute played by some tone-deaf jackass, and when the offending vegetable was drawn further into my throat by air pressure the pitch became even higher, developing into a peculiar wheezing. I was panicking, the option of hawking out the obstruction already missed because it was now lodged just behind my tonsils. My only choice was to swallow and hope for the best.

I could feel the lump searing its way down my gullet and I'm not sure which was worse, the agony or air deprivation. Anyway, I fainted. Just keeled off my chair, Mother liked to tell me for years afterward in long-standing disapproving tones. One moment I was sitting opposite her and making funny sounds and even funnier faces—eyes popping, cheeks as red as red peppers, mouth thin-lipped oval as I tried to quaff air—then I was gone, vanished from view. There was little reaction from the other diners—they merely cranked their heads to look at my still body on the floor, because I'd passed out in a dead faint. Mother probably apologized to everyone present before running round the table to tend me. Fortunately, I was no longer choking; I'd swallowed the hot potato during my fall, or when I'd landed with a hard thump.

Now this is what I remember about lying on the cheap lino flooring: I had found myself observing from above as my mother sank to her knees beside me and lifted my head onto her lap. She lightly slapped my cheek with four fingers, but I didn't feel a thing, although I knew it was me stretched out there on the dining room floor, with six or seven pairs of strangers' eyes paying attention as Mother frantically—and, it has to be said, with some embarrassment—tried to revive me. It was as if I were watching another unconscious person who just happened to look exactly like me.

I recall that I enjoyed the sensation before I became frightened of it. Young as I was, I was aware that this self-observation and the floating above my own body was not the natural order of things; I soon began to wonder if I would be able to get back into myself. And as that anxiety occurred, I was inside my body once more, eyes flickering open, the burning deep down in my gullet now mellowed. Mother gave one small gasp of relief, then immediately began apologizing to the other diners, whose raised forks resumed the journey from plates to open mouths as if someone had switched their power back on. Dazed as I was I understood that all interest in me had been lost: the clatter of cutlery and mumble of conversation had resumed. Only Mother remained concerned, but even that was tempered by her flushed self-consciousness.

She had helped me to my feet, and then rushed me to the communal bathroom upstairs to flannel my face with cold water. I was okay though: the potato had already cooled inside my belly. I was mystified and not a little excited about what had happened to me—not the fainting, but the floating near the ceiling above my own body. I tried to tell my mother of the experience, but she shushed me, saying it was all imagined, only a dream while I was insensible from eating too fast. I soon gave up trying to convince her, because she was getting more and more cross by the moment. As you'll have gathered Mother didn't like public scenes.

So that was the very beginning of my out-of-body experiences—OBEs, as they are generally referred to.

Of course, it's not something that most sensible people can believe in.

THREE

I didn't have another OBE for a good few years and by the time I was in my teens—I was seventeen, to be precise—I had all but forgotten about it. I suppose I eventually had come to believe that it had been a dream as Mother had said, so it played no important part in my thinking as I grew up; I didn't *quite* forget about the experience, because when it happened again I immediately related the two events. This time the circumstances were far more serious.

As a kid I'd always loved drawing and painting*—drawing in pencil or pen and ink mainly, because tubes of paint were a bit expensive for a single-parent family (and, being dead, my father discontinued the alimony payments, which were never official anyway because my parents hadn't actually divorced. Apparently, he'd died—I don't know what killed him—when I was twelve years old, but I didn't learn about it until a couple of years later). I'd spend most of my free time sketching, even creating my own comic books—graphic novels, as they're grandly called nowadays—writing my own adventures to go with the action frames. Some of those comics were not so bad, unless my memory is gilding them a little; I'll never know anyway, because Momma Dearest threw away the

---

*Art and English: they were my top subjects at school. In fact, so certain was I that my future career was going to be drawing and painting, making up advertisements—I called it advert-*ie*-sements those days—to go in newspapers and on wall posters (this was "commercial art" I soon learned, now "graphic design"), that other lessons didn't concern me very much. Math I hated—I think I'm "dyslexic" as far as numbers go—history was okay because it was stories, although I could never remember the dates of all those historic events (unnecessary in these reforming and "new-ideology" times, I gather). Geography was dull, RI—religious instruction—not too bad because, again, it was about stories. Between art and English, I enjoyed art the most. Sure, I loved writing tales and essays, but I got more satisfaction from pen, pencil, and paint. Eventually, I began to appreciate the masterpieces, initially the works of Rembrandt, Michelangelo, Leonardo da Vinci, all the great but obvious guys, later moving on to artists as diverse as Turner and Picasso (I loved the latter's earlier stuff, before he started taking the piss), from Degas to Sir Lawrence Alma-Tadema—yep, I know, all the populist stuff, but so what? Only later, when I enrolled in art college, did I learn to value the trickier and more imaginative works.

big cardboard box I'd kept them in, along with the few paintings I'd done and short stories I'd written, when we downgraded and moved to a poky flat in a less reputable part of town. No room here for all that junk, she'd told me when I complained that my box of valuables hadn't turned up. I could appreciate the problem, but it would have been nice to be consulted. Maybe then I could have at least saved some of my favorite stuff. Pointless to blame her—she had enough worries coping with life itself and the day-to-day expense of existing.

She used to take in sewing at home and was pretty good at it too, until too much working in inadequate lighting ruined her eyes. She received some income support, although it wasn't much, and the old man had a small life insurance policy, which she claimed as they were still legally married. It wasn't a lot, but I'm sure it helped a little, and I suppose it was the best thing my father had done for us. As soon as I was old enough I got a job stacking shelves in a local supermarket and collecting wayward wire trolleys from nearby streets and car parks—they might escape the store's boundary but they couldn't run forever. Another problem with Mother was that the more she worked alone, often through the night, the more neurotic she became about people. I think she became a bit agoraphobic—she was, and still is, something of a recluse. She began to stay at home all the time, weekdays and weekends. The clothes stitching and repairs she did for chainstore tailors was delivered and collected, and by the age of eleven I was doing most of the shopping. Two summers before that was the last time we took our annual holiday at the same old boarding house (the proprietors of which had never forgotten my fainting spell over dinner and liked to remind me affectionately of it the moment we arrived). Partly it was because Mother could no longer afford it, but mostly because she couldn't handle people anymore. Everyone, she maintained, was out to cheat her, from the milkman to the employers who used her sewing skills. According to her, all men were like my father, undependable, had questionable habits, and were not very nice. Regarding this last judgment, I guess the bad poison worked on me, for I never had the least curiosity about my dad, and certainly no desire ever to meet him. At least, not until later in life, when curiosity did finally kick in; before that he was just a cold-hearted bastard who had no love for me and Mother, just as I had no interest in him.

Eventually I managed to get a smallish grant that would allow me to go to art college and study graphic design (I never had the luxury of studying fine art like many of the students who had nice rich daddies—my sole aim was to get all the training I could for a career in advertising) as long as I had a proper weekend job and could pick up the occasional evening work. God bless supermarkets, bars, and restaurants—there's always employment out there if you're able and willing, most of it paying cash-in-hand.

At art college I learned about photography, printing, model-making, typography, and design itself—news and magazine ads, posters, brochures, that kind of thing—and I met and mixed with some good people from varied backgrounds (not all had rich daddies). There were also plenty of attractive girls around, many of whom were pioneers of free spirit living—and, importantly (to us boys), free loving. I had one or two girlfriends during my time at the place and there were no hassles when we broke up; the barrel was too full to get heavily involved with just one person, and that applied to both sides. My only problem—my only *big* problem, that is—was transport.

The art college was on the other side of London and the daily journey by tube and bus was eating away at both my grant money and earnings from those weekend and late-night shifts. So, ignoring near-hysterical objections from Mother—*those machines are death-traps, you'll kill yourself within a week*—I bought myself an old secondhand Yamaha 200cc motorbike. Not much of a machine really—a *mean* machine by no means—but good enough to get me from A to B, and cheap to run too. I'd had to save and scrape together every penny I made, working double-shifts most weekends, but because of that labor I cherished the old two-wheeled hornet even more. Trouble is, Mother was almost right.

I'd moved away from home—I admit it: Mother, who had become a little crazy by then, was driving me crazy too—and into a run-down apartment with three fellow students, two guys and a girl. It was closer to the art college and saved me a small fortune on tube and bus fares. I still needed the bike though for buzzing around town.

The accident happened on a wet, drizzly day, a typical winter city day, and the air was chilled, the streets greasy. I'd skipped a model-making class (it was an unnecessary part of the curriculum as far as I was concerned: I had no intention of making a career out of fiddling with glue and little sticks of wood and cardboard) so it was late afternoon, four o'clockish. The kids were coming out of school, mothers collecting them in four-wheel-drives and hatchbacks. Aware there were school gates up ahead, I'd slowed down considerably (and thank God for that), but as I said, the street surface was slippery and visibility in the early winter evening none too good. I was about to pass a parked Range

Rover when a kid of about five or six ran out from behind it. I learned later that the boy had seen his mother parked on the other side of the road and, in his eagerness to get to her (her and the little white Scottie yapping in the back of the car), he had raced out without looking.

I remember I had two choices, but nothing at all after that: I could run straight into him, or swerve to my right, across to the other side of the road. The only trouble with the second option was that there was a van coming from the opposite direction.

I liked to think afterward that I made the decision quickly and rationally, but it could be it was merely a reflex action. I steered to the right, the machine began to slide under me on the slippery tarmac (so I was told later) and headed into the path of the oncoming van. It seemed the van was braking hard already, because the driver had seen the boy about the same time as I had and had guessed he might run out. But of course, the wheels beneath him had trouble with the road surface too and both van and motorcycle slithered toward each other.

It was fortunate that the van had also reduced speed, otherwise the crash would probably have been lethal to me. As it was, the impact was hard enough to break one of my legs and send me skittering across the road using my helmet as a skateboard. As well as the damaged limb, I sustained massive bruising and a hairline fracture of the skull—the crash helmet saved it from cracking like an egg.

The kid's sunny little face, blue eyes sparkling as he ran toward the yapping dog in the car, blond curls peeking out from beneath his infant school cap, the bright blazer two sizes too big for him, is still imprinted on my mind as if the accident occurred only yesterday, even though the resulting crash was a complete blank to me. I just know that if I'd injured that small boy—or, God forbid, if I'd *killed* him—then I would never have forgiven myself.

But here's the thing of it: although hitting the van and its immediate aftermath have no place in my memory bank, the moments that followed are still very vivid to me, because I left my body for the second time, and on this occasion it was for a lot longer. It was as if my other side, my mind, my consciousness, my spirit—I had no idea what it was at the time—had been jolted from my physical form by the van's impact. As if the psyche, or whatever, had taken a leap from its host.

No doubt you've heard or read about the debates concerning whether the human body is merely the shell that contains the soul, but hell, I was just a teenager at that time, a callow youth who was fairly lucky with the girls, was reasonably good-looking, was healthy, and loved what I was studying and looking forward to a successful career because of it; what did I care for spiritual and religious concepts and theories? I'd hardly given the conundrum a second thought. I have now though. I've given it a lot of thought now.

I suddenly found myself standing by the roadside, on the pavement. And I was looking down at my own body, which had ended up in the gutter by my feet. For a few moments, nobody moved; everything was eerily silent. Then the little boy I'd just avoided knocking down began to bawl. His distraught mother left her car and ran across the road to him, gathering him up in her arms and squeezing him tight. When she whirled around to look at my motionless body in the gutter, her son's head buried into her shoulder, I saw her face was white with shock. I could only imagine the emotions she was going through, the relief mixed with the fear and concern for the unmoving body lying a few meters away, one leg sticking out from the knee at a ludicrous angle, a trickle of dark blood seeping out from beneath the bashed crash helmet. Other kids, tiny boys and girls in scarlet and green blazers, who had witnessed the accident, began to wail and clutch their mummies, a daddy or two also comforting their offspring. The van driver was still sitting in his van, a dull look of incomprehension on his moon-shaped face.

As for me, well, I was no longer me, but something aloof from my own self. I felt no pain whatsoever and, for the moment, no confusion either. I was just there, looking down at myself, completely emotionless right then. Soon though, very soon, reason began to kick in.

Although there was not yet fear, I became curious, then anxious. Was I dead? Was I now in the state that followed death? What was I supposed to do? Hang around, wait for someone—*something*—to come and fetch me? If so, where was I going? And how would I explain this to Mother? Shit, she'd be cross.

I bent down to get a better look at myself. My body was lying face up and I appeared quite peaceful, almost serene, as if I were taking a nap. The only thing that spoiled the picture was the awkward-angled leg and that thin trail of blood seeping from beneath the yellow crash helmet and forming a puddle on the hard gray surface of the road. I felt no alarm, unlike the majority of the onlookers, the kids and their mums, maybe a teacher or two, but I *was* surprised. And did I say curious? Yeah, I was very curious.

How could this be? Why was I suddenly two persons? I *had* divided into two, hadn't I? Something caught my eye. The fingers of one of my hands were twitching, so there was some kind of reaction, if not life itself, still going on. I don't know why but the movement caused me to examine the hand attached to whatever I had become.

And I could see it, just as if it was properly made of flesh and blood.

I wriggled my fingers, a more vigorous effort than those other twitching fingers in the road, and was satisfied that I could both see myself and move myself. My head snapped up as onlookers hesitantly approached the unconscious other me—the *real* me—as if I were a bomb that might explode at any moment and I was disappointed when no one seemed to notice the other self, the upright one who could wriggle his fingers at will, not by reflex.

I said something, I don't know what—maybe I was telling them that I really was all right—but none of them so much as glanced my way. Their attention was directed entirely toward the damaged figure lying in the gutter.

They gathered round so that my body was blocked from view and I spoke again, but was ignored as before. Then a weird thing happened—well, something peculiar on peculiar: I began to float in the air.

It was an easy, fluid rise and, or so I thought at the time, completely unintentional. I found myself hovering over the gathering crowd, my own crumpled figure coming into view once more. (Later, I came to realize—once I'd begun to get used to this strange state that is—that the floating had, in fact, been quite deliberate: subconsciously I was afraid of losing sight of my own body even for a moment, probably because I sensed it was my only anchor to reality and normal earthbound life.) I could hear the people murmuring, someone shouting for an ambulance, a man kneeling beside my body, the van driver lurching unsteadily toward the crowd to see the damage, all the while saying over and over again like a mantra to anyone who would listen, "It wasn't my fault, it wasn't my fault, he came straight at me . . ."

And curiouser and curiouser, there were filmy shapes on the edge of the crowd, human figures that were not quite focused (not to me anyway), forms that you could see right through and which shimmered occasionally like unsettled holograms. They were just standing by watching the action, no different from the other onlookers except they were transparent. One looked up at me—I was pretty sure it was a man, although the shape was difficult to define—and he opened his mouth as if speaking to me. I heard nothing though, apart from the anxious mumbles of the real crowd. But there was something familiar about the spectral man and I didn't know why. Something . . . No, I had no idea. There was something benevolent about him though.

Often in dreams one situation can swiftly and easily meld into another, the shift seamless but illogical in the cold light of dawn. Well, that's how it seemed to me.

From floating above the scene, I was suddenly and fluidly inside an ambulance where my physical body was strapped to a cot and covered by a red blanket, an ambulance man (who would be called a paramedic these days) easing off my battered helmet to examine the wound in my skull. This, quickly and fluidly again, changed into a hospital emergency theater where people in white gowns and masks calmly tended my body. I assumed my head and other parts had been X-rayed before the surgeon got to work on me, but I must have missed that bit because I have no recollection of it at all. I hung around the ceiling of the operating room for a time, watching over the medics with concern: if I wasn't dead already, then I certainly didn't want to be. Too young to die, I assured myself.

Next thing I knew I was in an intensive care unit, standing by a bed in which I lay unconscious with a swathe of bandages around the top part of my head. There were three other beds around the room, these filled with patients fitted with IVs and tubes and wires hooked up to little machines. Fade into Mother weeping at my bedside. A nurse lifting an eyelid to check my pupil. A doctor giving me the once-over. My mother again, weeping as before. Then complete fade-out until I woke up.

I think what had actually happened during this, my second out-of-body experience, is that the other me, the one with no flesh and blood form, had returned to my body from time to time. To my *unconscious* body, that is. And because I was in a coma for a couple of days, with no conscious thought, I had no natural memories of that period.

When I finally came round, much to the relief of my mother and my friends, I kept quiet about the odd experiences, a) because I didn't understand them myself and b) because I didn't want everybody to think the head trauma had short-circuited the wires in my brain.

I recovered quickly, you do when you're young. My leg took a little while to mend (still had the occasional twinge up until my death), but the hairline fracture in my skull soon healed with due care and attention of the medics and nurses (I dated one of the nurses for a while when I got out, a pretty redhead of Irish descent but no accent). Despite heavy bruising there was no internal damage. In short, I'd been bloody lucky; and so had that little boy, thank God.

Physically, I was soon back to normal. Mentally? That was something else.

Oh, and the motorbike was wrecked, by the way, and I never bought another one. Death or injury comes too easily on those things.

FOUR

Figure this . . .

A woman walks into a London police station, her step awkward, slow, kind of stiff. Much of her face is covered with dark drying blood. Blood also ruins her blouse and jacket just below her left breast.

In faltering words, she speaks to the duty sergeant, who is more than a little surprised, maybe nervous too—the visitor's face (the part that could be seen) is chalky white in stark contrast to the burned umber bloodstains. And her clothes are a mess, stockings or tights laddered, dirt on her knees and hands. She is wearing no shoes.

The woman's voice is somewhat forced and gargled, as if internal blood has risen and is congealing inside her throat, and the policeman struggles to make out the words she says. But he understands enough to catch the meaning.

The deathly pale woman is telling him that she wishes to report a murder. Her own. A name is almost spat out, but it is coherent. Then the woman drops dead. Or so the policeman thinks.

A police doctor is called, who quickly examines the body and asserts that the woman is, indeed, dead. But the doctor is puzzled and adds another diagnosis.

The corpse is taken away and because there is some confusion, if not mystery, about her condition, a post-mortem is swiftly carried out.

The pathologist confirms the doctor's first conclusion: at the time the woman had walked into the police station, her body was already in the first stages of rigor mortis, indicating she had been dead for at least forty-five minutes.

How so? Later.

FIVE

I continued to have those OBEs. Sometimes they were vague, like a partially re-membered dream, while at other times they were perfectly clear yet somewhat unreal in their flow, like movies that have been badly producer-edited. There were gaps in the order, you see, as if I'd reverted to my sleeping body for a while where even my subconscious seemed to be in repose.

The thing is, they no longer needed to be sparked off by any sort of trauma, they started to happen of their own volition when I was near to sleep, body and mind completely relaxed. They occurred only perhaps once or twice a year at first, but then I began to control them—at least, I *tried* to control them. I'd lie in bed alone and concentrate on leaving my body at will, but nothing tran-spired at those first clumsy attempts, either because I wasn't relaxed enough, or was trying *too* hard. I learned that OBEs are not something that can be con-trolled entirely at will.

I also realized that between the hot potato incident when I was seven and the motorbike accident when I was seventeen, there had, in fact, been a few other OBEs, when I'd wandered through empty darkened school classrooms, visiting my own desk, or flights when I seemed to be high over the city, with thousands of lights below, many of them moving traffic headlights. I'd put these down to dreams, very, very clear dreams. What did I know? I was just a kid. But dreams always fade with time, if not on awakening, and these excur-sions or "flights" never did. I nearly always remembered them.

As I got older I began trying consciously to put myself into the OBE state, lying in bed at night and imagining I was looking down at myself from a cor-ner of the ceiling. At first, I'd choose a point above me, think of a small bright light glowing there, then I'd will myself to join it. Nothing really happened though, at least not for a long while. I even used dope—marijuana only, noth-ing hard—to see if it would help, you know, put me into a relaxed state, free my mind, transcend the norm, but it never worked. I almost gave up until one day in my last year at art college I was bored and listless—a hand-lettering class,

I seem to remember, always a drag for me—when suddenly and without warning I was gone.

This was a weird phenomenon (I agree, it must always sound weird to anyone—which means most people—who has never been through it themselves) because it was daytime, the sun shining gloriously through a window—maybe its warmth enhanced my drowsiness—and nothing physical had jolted me; no trauma and certainly no accident. One moment I was trying to get the curve on a Century Old Style cap "S" right with my 3A cable paintbrush, next I felt a kind of shifting within me, as if I were being gently hoovered out of my skin, and then I was floating above my own head.

Now on this occasion and after the initial surprise—oddly, there was no apprehensive shock involved—I decided I was going to examine the experience rather than just live it. It was as calculating as that. No alarm, no concern that I might not be able to re-enter my body again, no panicky thoughts about death. I could see myself with exquisite clarity, my figure and everything around it finely defined. I noticed the tip of my paintbrush was poised about a millimeter above the letter "S" and my arm—my whole body, in fact—was perfectly still, as if I'd been frozen there. Other people in the artroom were moving: the girl student next to me was wiping her T-square with a clean rag, while on another table, a friend of mine was carefully dipping his brush into an inkpot as our tutor, a thin dandified Swiss with a wispy blond mustache and slicked-back hair, was turning the page of a typeface book opened out before him on the desk top, unconsciously tucking an overspilling cream handkerchief back into his breast pocket with his free hand as he did so. A round clock with a dark-wood frame ticked on the wall. Someone sneezed. Someone else said, "Bless you." A putty rubber fell off a table and a student bent to retrieve it. All was normal. No one was taking any notice of me.

I wasn't scared. I guess I was too curious for that. I just felt cool about the whole situation. And because of that lack of anxiety I was able to examine my situation calmly.

I decided to see if I could move about and instantly I could. Just by willing myself I floated to the other side of the artroom, observing the heads and hunched shoulders of the students at work as I did so. I half-expected some of them to look up as I passed over, perhaps disturbed by the breeze I must be creating, skimming along like that. I thought my tutor might bark, "You there, True, *come down from zat ceiling and get back to your pless!*" in that prissy accent of his, but he continued to study his book, one finger of his hand dipped deeply into his breast pocket as he settled the silk hanky. I could see myself—I'd stretched both hands out in front of me like some ethereal Superman and they were plainly visible—so why couldn't the teacher and students see me? (At that time, of course, I hadn't yet come to understand that it was my mind filling in what it expected to see.)

Hovering over a bright window, I turned back to the class. The notion of passing through the window glass had occurred to me, but while remaining perfectly level-headed, I was a little anxious about wandering too far from my natural body. I really did not want to lose sight of it, and I think that was quite reasonable. What if I got lost outside? What if there was a point where the spirit (or whatever I was up there hovering inches away from the ceiling) became *too* separated from the physical body and something, some invisible connection, snapped, making re-entry impossible?

Anyway, during that time in the artroom I was, as mentioned, pretty cool about the situation, even if I was reluctant to let my material self out of sight. I looked around, took notice of things, considered how I felt about my condition, then, and only after several minutes, I became eager to get back into my body. (It was like resisting one last chocolate from the box because you've already had too many.) And the moment I felt that way I *was* back.

I don't recall any journey across the room, nor dipping myself into my natural form; I was just there, looking at the world through my physical eyes once more. Only then did I begin to feel some panic, but it was mild. I think I was too stunned to experience overwhelming anxiety. Soon I was plain curious as well as elated. I'd gone through something rare—at least I thought it was rare, because I'd never heard of this sort of thing happening to anyone on a regular basis, although I'd read of one-off dream-flying and of survivors who claimed they had left their bodies while close to death.

I sat there bemused, worrying that my cracked skull had its aftermath, that the impact had messed with my brain and was creating hallucinations, fantasy trips. But I'd been too passive during the experience and observed too much too clearly for this to have been an illusion. Besides, everything else in the room had been quite ordinary and the other students' behavior perfectly normal.

Laying my paintbrush down, I sank back into my chair. What the hell was going on? I remembered the hot potato incident, then the immediate consequences of the motorcycle accident. I'd told the doctors of my out-of-body experience and they'd just smiled benevolently and explained that when the head—the brain, more specifically—took such a hard knock, it often went into some kind of seizure, perhaps losing control for a short time, so that visions in the unconscious state might seem like reality. Nothing to worry about, but a few tests would be in order.

Scans showed nothing amiss as far as my head was concerned; fortunately, the fracture had been minimal, the bone barely penetrated, and the brain itself revealed no evidence of swelling or injury. Rest up, give yourself time for the leg to heal and the skull's light fracture to knit together. Any trauma to the head could be dangerous and cause concern, no matter how light the blow, but in this case, there appeared to be no such problem. A little surgery on the leg was all that was required.

It was some months after the artroom OBE that I began to think back and re-examine some of the "dreams" I'd had from the age of seven onward, dreams that had not gradually faded from memory as they were supposed to, those that had lingered in my thoughts because of their extreme clarity and almost rational content. In them, I'd visited places I'd only heard or read about, art galleries (paintings and sculptures had fascinated me from an early age), playgrounds, and homes of schoolfriends. I'd spied on my mother as she sewed the lapels of handmade suits while pausing every so often to watch her precious soaps and game shows on the small television we owned and which lit up an otherwise dreary corner of the room. There was no sense of adventure with these dream excursions, nothing exciting about them at all really, and this was what eventually made me realize they were something other than natural dreams.

That's when I started reading up on the phenomenon and discovered it was more common than I had first thought. I learned that certain curious and dedicated people had achieved by research and perseverance what came naturally to me. Even so, nothing I read compared exactly to my own experiences. Others, apparently, had not attained such clearness of vision or logical continuity; their OBEs were more dreamlike and lacked control, and generally were broken up by blank periods of unconsciousness so that their flow was interrupted, to be remembered later only in vague episodes. However, I did pick up some useful techniques for putting myself into a receptive state, not quite a trance-like mode, but a kind of open responsiveness that encouraged the phenomenon to occur. Things like alert relaxation, where the body is in repose, but the mind is acutely aware of *itself* rather than the physical body; or the method of loosening the body completely, resting it limb by limb, piece by piece from head to toe; or the perception of outside from within, as if my eyes were merely portals through which I could observe the outer world; or shrinking inside my-self, so that my skin and flesh were like an ill-fitting suit, loose enough to es-cape from. Then there was the mirror image method, whereby a person thinks of themselves floating about their own body, just a foot or two away; the image is clear, an exact replica of himself or herself wearing the same clothes, sport-ing the same five-o'clock shadow or make-up; the person then imagines he or she is now looking *down* at their own body from above, that now it's the phys-ical self that is being viewed. It's supposed to make the transition easier, but it never worked for me.

In fact, all I had to do was make myself as relaxed as possible, relieve my mind of extraneous thoughts, and will myself to leave my body, sometimes looking at some particular spot on the ceiling or far corner of the room so that my "spirit" had a destination. Then I'd wait for it to happen.

Which it didn't, more often than not. But sometimes I was successful and the more I was, the more I started to control my "flight." Initially, I never left the room I occupied, but gradually I began to venture further to other rooms in the flat, cautiously graduating to outside locations, so that ultimately I was able to fly above rooftops, explore places I'd never physically visited—Buckingham Palace was dull, while the homes of some complete strangers could be interesting, even scary. It seemed I was limited only by my own boldness (I have to admit that in those early days I was somewhat timid; the fear of being unable to find my way back to my body was too strong. I was also afraid that the further afield I trav-eled, the easier it would be to break the psychic link to my physical self.)

I slowly learned though that I only had to think of myself back inside my flesh and blood form for it to be so. It would happen in a rush, a dizzying race through space that took no longer than a second or so, and always I'd arrive back safely, with no hitches whatsoever.

I can't say that I explored this thrilling new state to the full. For one, it didn't work every time, and for two, after the original excitement, I began to lose in-terest. I don't know why, it was just the way it was. Maybe deep down I was really afraid of the capability, some part of my subconscious feeling it was an unnatural state to be in, and that sooner or later something would go wrong, and I'd be punished.

In a way, I was right.

SIX

Did I ever tell anyone about these OBEs? And if I didn't, then why not?

Simple answer is, no, I didn't tell a soul. The reason why is not quite that simple, but you've a right to know.

I've always been a private person, never one for sharing all my deep-seated angst or emotions. Something I learned from Mother, I guess.

She brought me up to hide my feelings, to put on a face in front of others, particularly strangers. It was all to do with her pride and her shame at being deserted by her husband. Our reduced circumstances embarrassed her and when we moved into our little flat on the rougher side of London, she cut off all contact with friends and acquaintances. You know, I never knew if I had any other living relatives when I was growing up and eventually it didn't matter to me anyway; Mother and me, we kept to ourselves. I was content enough. I spent most of my time drawing, sometimes painting (when I had the paints, which were usually Christmas or birthday gifts), writing little stories, and reading—God, I'd read anything that came my way, from comics to books to the back of cornflake packets. I loved movies too, and Mother and I went at least twice a week, sometimes twice in one day. For me it was all escapism, I suppose, all these things taking me out of both my environment and my circumstances; it must have been the same for Mother as far as the movies and TV soaps were concerned.

I think that in her mind she lived in some kind of dream world, a place the ugly realities of life could not touch. She was fooling herself, of course, life itself isn't that easy to shut out.

Now you might imagine that all this would have turned me into a mother's boy, but nothing could have been further from the truth. I was always independent as a kid, self-contained you might say; I loved my mother, but I could never understand her, couldn't be the doting son she so much wanted. Just as she disappeared into her film world where everything had a tendency to turn out okay in the end (there were romantic magazines and novels also to keep her dreams occupied), so I retreated into my own small planet, which was a whole deal more exciting than the real one. Although I could never bring them home because of Mother's strict rule that outsiders were never welcome, never allowed to be "insiders," I had many good friends at school and later at art college, and as soon as I realized I was capable of taking care of myself I was rarely at home, despite Mother's accusatory pleas to stay with her. I was no rebel, but I was aware that there was something more, and something better, going on out there and I wanted some of it for myself. Guilt always dogged me though— I did truly love my mother—but I soon learned to accommodate it. Besides, I'd discovered football, which I became pretty good at, and not too long after that, I discovered girls.

But still, the growing-up years are always influenced by your parents and home background, so Mother's insistence on privacy where all things personal were concerned stuck with me. By the time I was twelve, I couldn't even tell *her* things; I'd learned from her to keep my thoughts and emotions to myself and I think, ultimately, she was kind of pleased about that herself—other people's emotions (yes, even her son's) could be a "rotten nuisance." She was complex: she wanted me to love her and be her "best friend in all the wide world," but she'd been too badly hurt by my father's desertion to trust any other man, perhaps even any other person; she didn't really want to hear my troubles or concerns, because that always brought her back to the real world, and the real world had let her down badly. I can admit it now, and I half-knew it then: Mother was a little screwy. If I did upset her by, say, coming home late, or deliberately disobeying her wishes (I can't say orders, because she was never strong enough to give orders as such—they were always suggestions and sometimes pleadings, rather than dictates), she would regale me with the sins of my father, how he'd left us, been untrue to both of us, run off with some floozy, didn't care if we starved to death, or were put out on the streets. Eventually, I closed my mind to all this, but even so, the guilt somehow transferred itself to me.

There I go getting off the point. The thing of it is, I'd learned from an early age to keep personal matters to myself, initially because that was the way Mother wanted it, and ultimately, perhaps inevitably, I became embarrassed about life with Mother. In some ways it worked well for me when I reached my older teens, because the girls seem to like that slight air of mystery that hung on me like a dark cloak, made me seem deeper than probably I was. It was something I used to my advantage anyway.

So, enough of all that. I'm still uncomfortable about our mother–son relationship, but it just might help explain why I kept quiet about the OBEs. I'd learned to keep such things to myself.

Another reason was that I was scared of being laughed at. Or misunderstood, thought to be out of my skull. The pragmatic side of my nature also figured: easier for me to put the experiences down to lurid dreaming, no matter how real they seemed to be. By talking about them, I was admitting their fundamental reality to myself and, frankly, they were a distraction I didn't need in my life. Besides, the OBEs were infrequent enough not to be a problem.

One more reason, and I think this was as important as the others in its way. Say you were a friend of mine—or, maybe even more significantly, a girlfriend of mine—and I told you I could travel invisibly sometimes, mostly at night when my body was totally relaxed, that my mind could leave my body to go on excursions. Say I told you that and you didn't think I was *totally* crazy, you half-believed me. How would you feel about me being able to spy on you at any time, that I could be watching you in your most private moments? You wouldn't like the idea. In fact, I don't think you'd ever trust me again. Everyone needs their privacy, their own space. It's what makes us civilized.

Now and again, I felt the overwhelming need to confide in a close friend or special girl, but common sense always prevailed, something—call it instinct, if you like—always shut me up before I said too much. Later, even marriage could not persuade me to disclose my little secret; maybe I'd kept it to myself so long it had become unimportant.

In truth though, it was never an issue.

SEVEN

Something else for you to consider:

You're physically near to someone, a person you love more than any other in the world, more than life itself. That person is about to be murdered.

That person you love so much is helpless.

And so are you, even though you're present at the scene and you're free to move around. You cannot protect your loved one no matter how hard you try.

You have to watch as death slowly, and oh so painfully, begins to claim its victim.

EIGHT

My name is—*was*—James True. Anyone who knew me called me Jim: James was just for passports and tax returns. I was pretty average, five-eleven tall, slim-mish, good mid-brown hair, blue eyes, not bad-looking. Like I said, average, quite ordinary. I did have a lively imagination though, which was just as well given the career choice I'd made at an early age.

I dreamed a lot. I don't mean daydreams, reveries; I mean sleep dreams. Always lucid, full color, Dolby sound. Reality dreams, but not too logical. Busy, wear-you-down dreams. The medical profession deny the possibility, but often I wake mornings more exhausted than when I've gone to sleep. Hard day's night, and all that. I always figured I was putting in another seven or eight hours labor when I slumbered.

Content was anything from fantasy to mundane everyday stuff. Usually a fair bit of angst in most of them. I'd lose something, couldn't quite reach something, would be placed in an embarrassing situation—you know the kind: in a crowded room or at a bus stop wearing only my vest. Nothing abnormal though, nothing any different from the dreams of other dreamers; it was their lucidity, I suppose, that made them special, plus the fact that I could always remember them. I've no idea if any had particular significance, because I rarely tried to analyze them. Except for one that was recurring.

In this dream, which came maybe once or twice a year, I could kind of fly. I say kind of, because it was more like long floating hops: I could rise from the ground, sometimes high over buildings, or zoom along several feet above the surface, pushing myself off with my hands every fifty yards or so, gaining altitude whenever it was necessary to rise above people or obstructions. I always thought that these particular dreams were informing me that I *was* a dreamer, that I had high expectations, perhaps wanted to break away from reality, aspired to things that could only be fantasy, that my own pragmatism, which was tempered by the realities of life itself, unfailingly brought me back down to earth—literally, in the dreams. The way I saw it this was no bad thing.

It meant I was *grounded*. And that was a plus in my eventual profession, where the ideal was advanced—the best soap powder, the finest lager, the greatest value—all of which claims had to stay within the realms of possibility and true to the advertising standards code (I admit that often—no, most times—we pushed those selling virtues to the limit, but we never quite lied).

I soon got over my motorbike accident at seventeen—the hairline skull fracture had been caused by my crash helmet having been dented by the edge of the kerb but it was one of those lucky fractures (if such a break could ever be deemed lucky) that cause no pressure on the brain and it healed itself within weeks. No surgery was required. Headaches for a few weeks afterward were the only penalty, and mercifully even these were not severe. My broken leg took longer to mend and I hobbled into college on crutches for a couple of months, but there were no long-lasting effects, no permanent limp, just those periodic twinges.

Because my bike was wrecked I had to stick to London Transport after that, despite high fares and shit services. At least Mother was relieved. It was a drain on my cash, but it only made me take on more evening and weekend work. In fact, day college became a bit of a rest period until my principal hauled me into his office and threatened expulsion if I didn't get my act together again. Fortunately, one of my flatmates was given the money by his father to buy a secondhand car, which turned out to be an old American army Jeep that we all loved—it might have been cold in winter, because it had no canvas top, but boy, the Jeep gave us great kudos at the college when we rode in together. Despite its lack of comfort, it was babe bait, and we took full advantage.

After completing the three-year course and gaining my national diploma in design, I started looking for a job in advertising. It took me a year of living on social security, hawking my work round one agency after another (same excuse always: come back when you've had more experience. So how the hell do you gain experience if nobody's willing to take you on?). Anyway, I finally struck lucky—if you could call it that—by getting a job with a finished art studio and minor agency. I started as a paint-pot washer, coffee maker, errand runner, art filer—all this after three years art school training—but I was glad to be employed and I made the most of it. It took a while to work my way up to the drawing board, but once there, my training finally kicked in. It was a cheapskate company though and once I felt I'd gained the initially elusive and hard-earned experience, I moved on to a big advertising agency.

Employed at first as a typographer because I'd exaggerated my qualifications a little, I quickly worked my way up to art director on some pretty big accounts. I was used to the work ethic, you see; all those years working through art college as well as evenings and weekends had instilled in me a discipline that could only be for the good. I enjoyed hard work and now, when it was bringing with it substantial financial reward, I found my enthusiasm for the job was even greater. You're under great pressure in advertising because of its high turnover of fresh ideas, campaigns and ads always wanted yesterday, constant meetings both internal and with client, briefings from clients, your own briefings to photographers, artists, and commercials directors and producers. Long working weekends again, late nights too. Then there's the social side of the business. Smart, attractive girls, intelligent colleagues, long, boozy lunches balanced out with long and sober bouts of overtime. Add the humor. There's a *lot* of humor in advertising, a lot of wit, much of it against the client, although they could never be aware of that. And to top it all, there are the politics. Outside politics itself, the advertising game must be the most political business of all. Unless you can avoid it, it's dog-eat-dog, all inspired by vanity and insecurity in equal doses, envy, ambition, suspicion, and the quest for money and power.

I always tried to steer clear of it, mainly because it was all too time-consuming and petty; but that didn't mean I didn't have to watch my back. Some knives were pretty lethal. The two good things I had going for me were ability (to get on with the work) and talent.

Lucky happenstance brought me in contact with a dream copywriter. Oliver Guinane was brilliant with words and ideas, totally secure in himself, and he loved to work as a team. We were around the same age, had the same enthusiasm for the job, agreed on what was "in," what was "out," and what was plain garbage. Best of all, we admired and appreciated each other's flair for the job.

I'm not sure that in the correct order of things I would have chosen Oliver as a best buddy—he was a little bit brash for me and didn't always treat everyone as an equal; but he had many other qualities that more than made up for the, well, the deficiencies. Oliver was generous to a fault, had great charm and wit, frequently produced wonderful copy and ideas, and was unselfish with the latter; he also had great energy. With his handsome face, light-brown eyes, and full reddish-brown hair that curled around his ears and over his brow, he was also a female magnet, much like that old Jeep, which often meant that I could leave him to the chatlines while I played the quiet interesting one. Occasionally we'd switch and I'd take on the gregarious role, but Oliver could never stay quiet and interesting for long; his natural boisterousness—and vanity—would eventually take over. He was no good playing stooge. Didn't matter though, we were a great team both professionally and socially.

We had good times together and through our teamwork we produced some memorable campaigns for accounts as diverse as banking and hair products, alcohol and automobiles. Our reputation grew, as did our salaries, and soon we were being headhunted by other reputable agencies.

We only moved twice though, once to J. Walter Thompson, then to Saatchi & Saatchi, as it was then called. After that, with quite a bit of soul-searching, some sleepless nights, and earnest debates (with Oliver as the prime mover in this new and risky plan), we took the plunge and started up our own outfit.

We were lucky. The economy was healthy, house prices were booming, and a lot of money was coming in from abroad. Bank managers (as they still were at the time) were not quite throwing money at businessmen who wanted to expand or start up new companies but, encouraged by their own banking grandees, were generous toward new ventures that had legs. Oliver and I gave a polished presentation to our friendly city bank manager, as if we were pitching for a new account, with my copywriter doing most of the talking while I showed some of our better award-winning work (yep, we were that good) and the manager bought it all.

We approached an excellent account director we knew from another agency and poached a good fresh junior copywriter and art director from Saatchi's. Oliver had a girlfriend at that time (foolishly, I'd introduced her to him at the old agency) who was a rep for a high-blown and high-priced photographer whose food and product stills were as good as his people work. She was a clever, beautiful brunette, fashionable, and keen with big brown eyes and a slim, leggy body most women would die for and most men would kill for. Her name was Andrea Dodds and eventually I married her. But now's not the time to go into that. We hired Andrea to be our office manager and second to Sydney Presswell, our financial manager and third partner, who looked after the business side of things (he was the account director we picked up from another agency). She was presentable, good at handling clients (I used to *be* one of her clients), and stood no bullshit. Did I say she was beautiful? Well, she was—and still is.

We took on just one secretary, Lynda, to begin with, who also acted as receptionist and telephone operator; a runaround junior, a young kid named Raymond who aspired to be an art director, but who'd had no art school training;

a typographer called Peter; and the young creative team I mentioned, Paul and Mark. Finding the right premises wasn't that easy, but after a lot of searching and a lot of rejections, we stumbled upon premises with two vacant floors slap in the middle of Covent Garden. It had just come on the market and it was pricey—actually, too pricey for us—but we knew instantly it was exactly what we were looking for.

We set about the hardest part of the whole venture: acquiring clients. Legally we had contracts with our ex-employers which forbade Oliver and I approaching our existing clients for the next three years. Of course, that did not prevent those clients approaching *us* once the news got out that we were quitting and branching out on our own. So one or two who trusted our abilities, solicited us instead. We gained two quite big accounts that way, but we needed a third large one to make us viable.

We went after new business with a passion, toiling day and night to come up with outstanding presentations and better marketing strategies than the companies already had. Media buying was handled by Sydney for a while, until we were established enough to bring someone in on a full-time basis. We ruthlessly targeted any business that we felt was right for us and whom we considered was receiving less than perfect service—mediocre advertising, poor media choices, etc.—from their existing agency, and we failed to win them over more times than we succeeded. Nevertheless, through sheer nerve, perseverance, and, I like to think, talent, we gained three new clients, one medium-sized and two smaller, but easily making up for the third biggie we thought we needed. Heady days, and you know what? I miss them. Yeah, I miss a lot of things . . . We called it gtp in the fashion of the day, the acronym for Guinane, True, Presswell, of course, set in Baskerville lower case, letters touching. It looked pretty cool.

The agency did take off. Around town we became known as a creative hot shop and we began pitching for and acquiring more and more accounts, some blue chip but mainly clients who wanted that little bit of extra creativity in selling their products, clients who were not afraid to take fresh marketing leaps that would not go unnoticed by the public or the trade. You'd be surprised how many big budget spenders could only live with the known, concepts without risk, strategies that dared not stray from formula or jeopardize the marketing manager's position. Internal politics are always rife in both small corporations and big ones (the bigger the worse, in fact) and they're third only to advertising, which, as I've said, is second only to politics itself.

The companies that came to us were already aware of our reputation for risk taking and they were usually primed for something different. Maybe nothing truly off the wall, but at least something individual. We didn't win everything we pitched for by any means—easy to say you're looking for something "different," but not always easy to go with it once it's presented—but we acquired enough business to expand our offices and staff. We even managed to win a few advertising awards along the way, all voted for by our peers in the industry itself.*

Oliver and I were in our element, working like dogs, our enthusiasm never diminishing. Often we'd book a hotel suite for a weekend and work day and night to produce a fresh and sometimes even original advertising campaign. We used hotel rooms because now and again we needed new surroundings, different venues somehow helping with an objective approach to the brief. Frankly, it's not unknown in the business for some agencies to lock their creative team away in a five-star hotel for a couple of nights and feed them cocaine

---

*Interestingly, now that Oliver and I were joint bosses, we actually felt more responsibility toward our clients. A long-standing joke in advertising circles is how an art director is constantly devising ways of including a palm tree in the left-hand corner of his layout no matter what the product might be because it meant a photo-shoot somewhere in the Bahamas, a beautiful excursion for himself (and possibly, but not necessarily, for the copywriter) accompanied by glamorous models, plus photographer and his assistants (you couldn't sell dog food this way, you might insist, but don't think it hasn't been tried). Another and even more heavily disguised objective is the DA&D award for best advertising, when fabulous— and very expensive—film or TV commercials (or brilliantly smart ones, but a little oblique as far as selling the product is concerned) are proposed by the agency. These litter the whole media range, great concepts that fail to do their job because the brand name either goes unnoticed, or is never remembered (I'm sure you could mention one or two wonderful TV commercials without recalling the brand they were selling).

It's a vanity that reveals a lack of respect for the client, but then, more fool the client who allows it to happen. The answer is simple, although often not easy: the truly great advertising always combines a clever (and often amusing) idea with distinct branding (and I don't mean a large company logo); GREAT COPY, GREAT VISUAL, CLEAR PRODUCT IDENTIFICATION, is the legend that should be pinned to every marketing manager or company advertising director's office wall, and creative teams should constantly be reminded of it. So, this was our company philosophy and no headlined layout or storyboard ever left our office for client presentation without it being fulfilled. Okay, I won't pretend we did it every time. Rush or panic jobs, copy deadlines, overnight work, client procrastination, together with their insecurity and occasional inability to recognize a superb concept, all are inherent and expected in the advertising business, so we could not always deliver of our best, but hell, we tried, oh how we tried.

for inspiration and to keep them going. It isn't *standard* practice, but it does happen sometimes when agencies are desperate, out of time, and the great ideas aren't coming. We didn't do that though, because I for one just couldn't get into drugs of any sort. Sure, I did some hash at art college, and later, when finances started to allow, I tried coke, but it never seemed to work for me, only made me hyper-tense. Same with alcohol to some extent; it took a lot to get me smashed. I don't know why—something in my metabolism, I suppose—but I was glad. Drugs are bad news, as I later found out. Besides, I didn't need any chemical substances to stimulate my imagination; that could take care of itself, and anyway, there's nothing quite like the high you get through creative brainstorms.

Maybe we worked *too* hard in those early years, took too much on, but Oliver and I, and to some extent Sydney, were overly ambitious and we ran on adrenaline. We seemed to have unlimited energy—although when we crashed we really crashed—which is great to begin with, but too much of it could easily have led to early burn-out. As well as producing the creative work, we had the responsibility—the *burden*—of running our own company even though Sydney took much of the administration side of things onto his own shoulders. We still had to attend too many meetings, many with clients—oh God, those bloody long lunches—but we always made important decisions as a threesome.

So, we worked hard and we played hard, and possibly it was the pressure of both that instigated the first cracks in the partnership. The fact that I stole Oliver's live-in lover didn't help either.

NINE

I'd known Andrea Dodds for several months before I introduced her to Oliver, because I'd worked with two of her lensmen on a couple of jobs. She was tall-ish, slim and, as I told you earlier, had fantastic legs. At that time she wore her dark-brown hair long and straight so that it fell over her narrow shoulders (these days she has it cut short, urchin-style, the sides flicked away from her face). I'd learned that she was single, had no current man in her life, lived in a tiny flat near Dolphin Square, Pimlico, and I was just priming myself to make a move on her. It wouldn't usually have taken me so long to ask her out—it certainly didn't with other girls—but Andrea was an exception. Why? Because I'd already half-fallen in love with her and I was terrified of rejection. Funny how easily you can lose your confidence when something matters too much. Of course, Oliver's charm antenna was at full alert the moment he spotted her talking to our art buyer in the corridor of our old agency. He asked me who she was and, stupidly, I hauled her in to our office to make introductions.

I groaned inwardly as soon as I saw his eyes light up and he held onto her hand for much too long. I knew I was whipped before I'd even started, but I bore no grudges. It served me right for being so boneless.

Soon she had moved in with him. So soon, in fact, that I was stunned. I hadn't quite given up hope for myself as far as she was concerned, because there still seemed to be something going on whenever she and I made eye contact. Andrea was no flirt, but she made me feel special when we spoke together or arranged times and dates for photography. She could have merely been do-ing her job, massaging the ego of an important client, but I didn't think so; there was something incredibly sincere about her, and something very, very sweet.

Still, I had to accept the situation and I couldn't be mad at Oliver for having the boldness to jump in first whereas, like some lame fool, I'd hung back, too cautious to make my move.

Ollie and Andrea. They made a hot couple. I couldn't begrudge him, even though secretly I continued to pine for her. Get over it, I eventually told myself. Oliver was more her league. Besides, there were plenty of other fish, so go fish. And I did for a while, but I never quite got over my original crush. It was when Oliver and I were in the first exciting but anxious throes of setting up our own agency that he suggested bringing Andrea on board as an account manager and assistant to Sydney.

It took me all of two seconds to agree: from experience I knew she was more than just competent and I had no doubt she'd be an asset to our fledgling company; she might have been soft in the looks and attitude department, but believe me, she was shrewd as far as business was concerned and had always driven a hard bargain for the photographers she represented (and I was no pushover—I always treated my clients' money as if it were my own).

So, initially on a lowish salary but with the promise it would grow as quickly as the agency itself—we were all working on spec those days—she joined gtp. And took to it like a duck might take to Evian, charming both prospective and existing clients, selling our talents as passionately as she'd previously sold the skills of her photographers.

Our team expanded as the client list grew and all seemed well but, like I said, maybe we worked and played a little too hard, because eventually the cracks began to appear. And most of the problems were to do with Oliver.

We'd both stretched ourselves to the limit, Ollie and I, but the relentless grind took a greater toll on my friend and colleague than me. After a while he seemed to be running on empty, becoming irritable with staff members (especially Sydney, who did his best to keep us all sane), going to the edge with clients (most of whom were good and intelligent people—although even those who were not had to be treated with a modicum of respect). Sydney Presswell came into his own on such occasions, smoothing things over, turning any acid observations Oliver might have made into nothing more than humorous banter.

Nevertheless, the work was always good; Oliver never let the agency down on that score. He usually managed to pull some little creative gem out of the bag at the last possible moment, when timing was crucial and we had to present an ad or campaign that the client could run with. And if he didn't, then I did. We were still a great team, but I was beginning to grow anxious about my buddy. Couple of times I took Oliver aside and told him of my concerns—you're cracking, pal, you've got to ease up on the playtime, grab a break, somewhere warm and sunny, pay Andrea a bit more attention maybe . . . He just shrugged it off, gave me the Ollie-grin that said everything was cool. He wasn't sleeping too well lately, he would indeed cut out extra-curricular activities, and anyway, mood swings were part of his nature. Often on these occasions, he would also remind me that it was his creative input that had won us many clients, a fact I couldn't deny. Sure, I told him, but we're more worried about your health nowadays, not your input. You don't look good, sport, and those mood-swings are affecting Andrea in a bad way.

Shouldn't have said it. Oliver exploded, told me to keep my nose out of his personal business, then stormed out of the office we shared. We didn't see him for the rest of the day and I regretted having spoken out. Still it seemed to do the trick—for a while, at least. Ollie arrived back at the agency early the next day, bright and shiny and with a box of expensive cigars as a gift for me. Andrea, who had looked a little flaky for some time now, was with him and she seemed almost as chirpy as he was. I assumed they'd had a heart-to-heart and a new leaf had been turned by Oliver. Both looked refreshed, as if they'd had a good night's sleep, hopefully in each other's arms.

It couldn't last though; Oliver's jittery moods soon swung back and forth like a personality pendulum and I began to suspect it was more than just over-work and booze that was the problem. But it was Sydney who finally put me wise by pointing out the symptoms.

Insiders call it either the curse or the crutch of the trade, but I subscribe to neither view; sure, coke and cannabis are popular in the business—speed, too—but they're more of an occupational hazard than a prevalence, recre-ational rather than obligatory. Creativity can often extend itself to taking mind-expanding substances, and advertising must be one of the most pressur-izing careers one could choose. There's always the exhaustion factor too, when both your brain and body become so fatigued they require a little charge now and again. I'm not advocating drugs as a prop—far from it—I'm merely ex-plaining how the trap is set. I've known good people who have succumbed to its lure, and now I was concerned that my best friend and business partner had become yet another victim.

To cut it short, Ollie's condition grew steadily worse, the pendulum becom-ing caught on the downswing. One evening I was pigged out on a sofa in my apartment—only a slim triangle of pizza left in its shallow box, bare feet resting over one arm of the sofa, my head propped up by a couple of cushions at the other end, half-empty can of Stella resting on my stomach, cigarette butt smoking in a crowded ashtray on the floor—when the annoying chime of the doorbell roused me from my mindless vigil over a docu-soap on the TV. With a groan, I dropped the lager can beside the ashtray and swung my feet to the carpet. Hitching up my jeans beneath the loose sweatshirt I wore, I grumbled my way to the door.

Andrea was outside, her face wet with tears, mascara staining her fair skin. She threw herself into my arms, blurting out her woes as she did so: she'd had enough, Oliver was out of control, he'd lashed out at her, hurt her, sworn at her; she had fled and this time it was for good. I hadn't even known there'd been other occasions and I felt a rising anger as she told me her sad tale.

Apparently, Oliver's coke habit had reached critical mass, one of the results being his physical abuse of Andrea, and she had left him and had no intention of ever going back. I hadn't realized that their relationship was anywhere near this sorry state so good was their cover-up at the agency. I was stunned.

To cut the story even shorter, she stayed with me.

I'm not proud of it, but I was incredibly angry with Oliver at the time, because not only had he stolen my girl (okay, she hadn't actually been my girl at the time) but he was now physically—and mentally, I soon learned—abusing her. Just having her there in my own home, distressed and desperate, revived all those feelings toward her that I'd suppressed since I'd lost out to my side-kick. I admit, I'm a sucker as far as women or girls are concerned. I offered to ring him, or to go and see him personally, tell him face-to-face what a jerk he was being, but Andrea wouldn't allow it. We collapsed onto the sofa together and she begged me to let her stay, if only for the night.

She never went back to Oliver. Again, I'm not proud of it, but we made love that very first evening. All those emotions, those frustrated desires, burst out of me like floodwater from a breached dam.

Oliver didn't show up at the office for two days, but when he did, he was perfectly calm and reasonable. In truth, he was almost arrogant as far as Andrea's departure was concerned and I think that hurt her more than anything else. His indifference was a shock for us both, but it helped us overcome the guilt Andrea and I were feeling. He'd had space to think, he told us, and realized he was screwing up Andrea's life, not to mention his own. He might also be screwing up the business we had all worked so hard for. And he was definitely screwing up his long friendship with me. All that had to change and he knew this might be his last chance.

From now on the drugs and the booze were out, hard work and sobriety were in. He wasn't going to ask Andrea to come back to him until she felt she wanted to (to be honest, he didn't seem to care too much on this point; it was as if the ball was entirely in her court) and I felt it wasn't the appropriate time to explain how she had already moved in with me. That could come later.

Things were awkward between us for a few weeks, but Oliver made the effort. I don't know how he fought—and *conquered*—his demons, but he managed to. He came off the drugs and the difference in him was quickly apparent. He became my old, true friend once more and although it took a while to get his creative juices flowing again, eventually the magic returned. We became like the team of old, a regular Lennon and McCartney of the advertising game. I don't know how it came out that Andrea had moved in with me, but it seemed to happen naturally and there was certainly no overt resentment on Ollie's part. Maybe he had already begun to tire of their relationship before the big upset—never in the past had Oliver been one for long-term relationships—and so he accepted the new situation without apparent rancor. Perverse though it might sound, I thought he was genuinely pleased for me, because I'd never been able to disguise my attraction to Andrea in the past; now, at last, I'd found someone with whom I could settle down. Oh, now and again, I caught him giving me an odd, reflective stare, but I thought it was remorse.

Everything soon got back to normal and we became frantically busy, pitching for new accounts as well as maintaining those we already had. We employed more staff, creating two new art director / copywriter teams, hiring a couple more secretaries and another account executive, and eventually took over the whole building to allow for our expansion. We were a terrific, young creative hot shop and more than a few advertising awards came our way, either for press and poster campaigns or television commercials.

Within a year Andrea was pregnant with our child (so left the agency in her seventh month) and we were married—in that order. Time went by and, bar a few downsides not worth mentioning at this point, life was pretty good. Or so I thought.

Seven years later I was still enjoying my career, was happily married, and had a wonderful daughter called Primrose. (Yeah, I know. Advertising people, eh? In fact, it took only three months to call her Prim—Primrose seemed such a heavy handle for such a squirt, pretty as she was.) I still had OBEs, which

I was learning to control more as well as initiate. They remained my secret and continued to fascinate me.

Little did I know it was those OBEs that would lead to my premature demise.

Hopefully, you've stayed with me so far. It's just that I thought it important that you knew some of my history—it's pertinent to all I'm about to tell you. Believe me, I've left out heaps of personal stuff because I didn't want you to lose interest along the way.

But now I'm ready and—hopefully again—you're primed to hear my tale. Everything I've told you leads to the horrendous event that was to change my life—or I should say, my *existence*—forever . . .

TEN

"It's too big for us," I said, keeping my voice steady, avoiding Oliver's glare. The debate—all right, the *argument*—between Sydney, Ollie, and myself had been going on for over an hour at least. "We're just not ready." I leaned back in my chair, arms folded across my chest, staring at my outstretched feet, ankles also crossed.

"Not if we expand." Oliver was leaning forward in his seat, wagging a finger at me.

"The time isn't right for us to take on more staff. We just don't have the capacity here."

Oliver slapped his thigh hard and I winced; the slap must have made his leg smart.

"Then we move!" was his reply.

"Are you kidding? It was difficult enough taking over these premises. We're too busy for the disruption anyway."

"There is another way." Sydney Presswell was sitting behind his broad but minimalist desk, and his voice, as usual, was quietly soothing. Sydney had always been a good advocate between myself and Ollie, whose interaction these days was becoming more and more volatile; we barely agreed on anything lately, particularly when creative work was involved.

We both turned our heads toward our finance director/manager.

Sydney had piled on the weight over the years—too many drawn-out client lunches—but still managed to look dapper with his gray receding hair and gray suits, the latter always worn with deep blue or red ties. The flesh of his neck puffed out over his shirt collar a little, but his aquiline nose and soft gray eyes beneath finely arched eyebrows gave him the appearance of a benevolent patriarch. He wore those understated glasses, no frames, just plain lenses supported by hinges and plastic nose pads. Although now going through his third divorce, no lines furrowed his smooth brow and only slight bags hung beneath those pale-gray eyes.

We waited for him to speak again, perhaps both of us relieved that our increasingly angry confrontation had been interrupted.

"We could merge," he said simply, leaning forward and interlacing his fingers on the desktop before him.

Neither Oliver nor I reacted. I just stared.

Sydney's pale face was impassive. "Blake & Turnbrow have been chasing us for some time, as you know. They're much larger than us and have offices worldwide. Together we could easily manage our respective clients and any more we might care to pitch for. Blake & Turnbrow are keen to amalgamate with us."

"To take us over, you mean, don't you?" I said, my annoyance now focused on him. That in itself was unusual, because Sydney was the easiest person in the world to get along with.

"No, I don't mean that," he said, his retort mild, not at all offended. "If getting into bed with a prestigious global agency will help us expand and find bigger clients, why should we balk at the idea?"

"Because, Sydney," I said with disguised impatience, "it means giving up control of our own business."

"Wait a minute, Jim," Ollie put in. "It doesn't have to mean that at all. Let's take the helicopter view."

It irritated me further when my copywriter used ad-speak: "overview" wasn't good, but "*helicopter* view?" And a "takeover" was a "takeover," not the sharing of a bed. A suspicion struck me: was Oliver really surprised at the suggestion, or had he and Sydney already discussed the prospect in my absence (I was often away from the office on photographic shoots or making TV commercials, allowing plenty of opportunities for cozy get-togethers for my partners)? Or was I just being paranoid?

"Obviously Blake & Turnbrow like our client list, as well as the creative talent in this agency," Oliver went on. "But then don't we envy their client list and some of their creative teams?"

"If we get taken over—" I began to say.

"Merge," Sydney insisted.

I didn't drop a beat. "—there's no guarantee that some of our accounts won't leave us. They signed up with Guinane, True, Presswell, not with Blake, Turnbrow, Guinane, True, Presswell . . ."

"BTGTP has a nice ring to it." Oliver smiled and I wasn't sure if he was deliberately winding me up.

Before I could respond, Sydney cut in once more. "Companies rarely switch agencies unless they've been let down by bad marketing strategies, mediocre creative work, or poor servicing: we're guilty of none of those. However, we might fall down on the first and last points if we pitch for and win this new account."

"I'm still not sure why such a large corporate bank should approach us," I muttered, a little sourly I think. "The agency they have now is one of the biggest and best."

"Yes, and it's become complacent. The bank has been with them for twenty years or more and I think they've both become tired of each other. It happens to every account eventually, no matter how solid the relationship has been."

Sydney unlocked his fingers and rested back in his chair. "Fortunately, the bank's marketing director is a very old acquaintance of mine and for the past year I've been rekindling our friendship. We belong to the same club and more than once I've let him thrash me at golf."

"This is the first time you've mentioned it to us," I said grudgingly.

"Because I've had nothing to report until now. Geoff tipped me the wink only a few months ago and I've been working on him since. He's well aware of my interest, of course, and I think he's enjoyed the little game between us. I want the carrot and he loves to dangle it before me. Naturally, I've allowed him to enjoy himself at our expense—and I mean that literally." He looked meaningfully at me, and then at Oliver.

"British Allied Bank is beginning to lose out in the market place," Sydney went on. "Its competitors, the other big banks, are regarded as more friendly toward small businesses and more trendy as far as the younger market is concerned. Certainly British Allied is banker to many vast corporations, but never underestimate how important the smaller businesses are. What they lack fiscally as individuals, they more than make up in quantity. Not quite as important, but certainly worth considering are the young non-account holders, the upwardly mobile C2s, who have to be encouraged—or enticed—to open a bank account. Like the small businesses their numbers are incredibly high and well worth bringing in. Catch 'em while you're young is the motto of all the banks, because they rarely change banks during their lifetimes."

"So we're seen as more cutting edge than British Allied's present agency? Is that why they want us to pitch?" Oliver was jigging a foot on the carpet, a habit of his when his energy was running high.

"Precisely," Sydney replied. "But naturally, there will be other agencies pitching, including their present one, which has to be given a chance. I've learned from Geoff, though, that we're the only hot shop; all the others are good and well established, but don't have our reputation for high-concept campaigns. I think, provided we come up with the right pitch, if we hinted that we could possibly be associated with another much larger agency in the near future, it might be to our advantage. Of course, if we did win it, it would be the biggest single account we'd held financially. The advertising budget would be phenomenal."

"Are you saying both deals go hand-in-hand?" I asked, frowning.

"Not at all. But a merger would help in regard to back-up. It's all very well having wonderfully innovative ideas, but if we can't service the account fully, then what's the point? The bank will be all too aware of our limitations as much as I know they'll like our ideas."

I turned to Oliver. "What do you think?"

He grinned, and his foot was still tapping. "I say let's take it to the max. Let's burn the blacktop, go for both."

He spoke in precise, clipped tones, an "elitist" accent he'd never even tried to modify for street-cred purposes; estuary-speak had become the norm in our game, but he was having none of it. I liked him for that, even though he had an irritating penchant for jargoneze. He never tried to hide his wealthy, upper-class background and, with his shortish brown-almost-auburn hair, loose strands of which hung over his forehead, and military-straight back, intelligent brown eyes, home-counties accent, he would never have succeeded in doing so anyway. Even though his clothes were casual, they had a sharp neatness to them, a kind of preciseness that matched his clipped voice.

"I think we've a good chance of winning the account," he went on, "particularly if they're tired of the old staid bank advertising they've become used to and are looking for something fresher and more original."

"And the takeover?"

"Merger," Sydney persisted.

Oliver shrugged. "Whatever. It might be an extremely beneficial move."

"You'd give up everything we've worked for?" I was beginning to simmer.

"It wouldn't necessarily mean that, chum. Try seeing it from the north."

I hated it when he called me chum, especially when it was coupled with the jargon.

"Sydney and I already more or less agreed it would be a smart way for us to expand."

Ah, so Sydney and Oliver *had* already discussed the matter without me.

"Beside which," Oliver put in, resting his elbows on the cushioned arms of his leather swivel chair and making a steeple under his chin with his fingers, "we three would each receive quite a large sum for the company."

"That sounds like a buyout to me," I said.

"Not at all. Financial remuneration for the partners would be merely part of the deal . . ."

There was a light tap on the door and it opened a little. Lynda, our receptionist/switchboard girl, poked her head through the gap. She looked directly at me.

"Phone call for you, Jim. Your wife."

"Did you tell her I was in a meeting?"

"She said you're always in a meeting."

I couldn't argue with that: over the last couple of years, my whole life seemed to revolve around meetings, which was frustrating for someone who wanted to work only on the drawing board. I knew Oliver felt the same as far as copywriting was concerned, but somehow he was better than me on such occasions, especially where clients were concerned. Ollie was also terrific at presentations and his social skills were excellent, whereas I tended to be too stiff and was hopeless at cozying up to the clients, particularly those I didn't like.

"Ah, tell her I'll ring back in a couple of minutes, will you?"

Lynda smiled and retreated, quietly drawing the door closed after her.

Ollie was looking at his wristwatch. "Look, Jim, I've got something on tonight so I have to get away," he said, his foot stopping its tattoo on the carpet.

I breathed a loud sigh. "Okay with me," I said. "But I still think we should take things one step at a time."

"You think we should pitch though?" Sydney leaned forward over his desk again.

"You two would outvote me anyway, wouldn't you?"

"Oh no, Jim," said Oliver, standing up and brushing an imaginary crease from the knee of his trousers. "Also, I want to think on bedding down with Blake & Turnbrow myself. Let's touch base again tomorrow morning when we're fresher. I have to admit, though, right now I'm inclined to push the envelope. We could all benefit from a paradigm shift."

I assumed Sydney understood the lingo; I did, just about.

"If we're going for the new account we have to start work right away." Despite the warning, there was no impatience in Sydney's manner, nor in his gray eyes. There was only his usual impassiveness.

"We wouldn't start on it tonight anyway," said Oliver to Sydney. "Let's sleep on it, okay?"

Sydney nodded and I got to my feet, still wondering if I'd been left out of the loop somewhere along the way. Ollie hadn't seemed very surprised by either of the two propositions, nor by the possible linking between them. I followed my copywriter out of Sydney's office back to the one we shared as the agency's creative directors, Oliver switching on the light as we entered.

Moving behind my desk and picking up a long steel cutting rule that rested there, slapping the flat side against my open palm, a habit of mine when I was tense, I began to say, "We oughta talk . . ."

"Ring Andrea first, Jim," he interrupted. "It might be something urgent."

Reluctantly, I placed the heavy rule back on the desk and picked up my phone, pressing 9 for an outside line. We needed to discuss things, Ollie and I. I dialed my home number.

"Hello, please?"

It was Prim's breathy little voice.

"Hey, squirt, it's Daddy."

"Daddy! Are you coming home now?"

I smiled as I thought of her standing in the sitting room, phone clutched in both hands, her curly hair kept away from her face with an Alice-band. Lush brown hair like her mother's, a few shades lighter though, with a reddish hue when the sun lightened it; tawny brown eyes full of innocence and fun.

"Soon, Prim," I told her.

"You got to, Daddy. You're looking after me tonight. Don't you 'member?"

Uh-oh. Sure I remembered. Andrea was meeting two of her girlfriends this evening for a quietish girlie night out and I was the appointed childminder.

"Did you think I'd forgotten? Anything special you want to do?"

"Lots and lots. And cards."

Seven years old and I'd already taught her how to gamble. Taught her to cheat a little too.

"No DVDs you want to watch?" I needed some thinking time tonight.

"Just games, please."

I laughed. "Okay." Plenty of time to think once I'd put her to bed. "Now run and get Mummy for me, will you?"

"Love you!"

She was gone and I pictured her running to the kitchen—she was of an age when kids are always in a hurry, rushing from one interest to the next. A snapshot view of her came to mind, a holiday photo, the sun directly behind her so that the curls around her face were orangey red, a halo of fire, her features softened even more because they were in light shadow, her brown eyes deepened so that they were like Andrea's. I wanted to eat her.

"Jim?"

Andrea's voice, low-pitched, even now seductive to me.

"Hi. You rang me," I told her.

"You haven't forgotten I'm out tonight."

"No, I'll be home in plenty of time."

"No last-minute meetings. You know what you're like."

In truth, I did want to discuss Sydney's proposal some more with him and Oliver, but maybe a breather would be useful at this point: I was getting just a bit rankled with this talk of a merger—it still sounded like a sell-out to me—and needed time to think on it to calm myself.

"I'll be home within the hour," I assured Andrea. "Where are you meeting the girls?" The dinner with two girlfriends of old, was a bi-monthly get-together to yak and catch up on the latest gossip.

"San Lorenzo's."

I was impressed. "Hope you're not paying."

"We always go Dutch. You don't mind, do you?"

Of course I didn't; we both needed own-time every so often. "No, you have a good dinner, order the best on the menu." She deserved it; I was always ringing home at the last moment to tell her I was going to be stuck in yet another meeting, or that I'd be working till late. "Tell you what, I'll cover the whole bill. You can treat your friends."

"No, Jim, that's not necessary. I don't want to start a precedent."

"Up to you, but really, I don't mind."

"Thanks anyway. Prim's already eaten, but can you fix something for yourself. There's plenty of easy stuff in the fridge."

"No prob. I'll see you soon. Oh, and Andrea . . .?"

"Yes."

"I need to talk to you later."

I caught the faint rush of anxiety in her voice. "Is something wrong?" she asked.

"No, no. Just things going on here that I'd like your opinion on. Nothing that can't wait till later."

"Okay, Jim. I'll see you soon, then?"

"Almost on my way. Bye for now."

I replaced the receiver and sat at my desk for a while. Oliver had left the office during my telephone conversation and I was alone. People leaving for home were passing by the open door, some of them calling in a brief "G'night" on their way. Preoccupied, I waved a casual hand.

Something was making me uneasy and at the time I thought it was due to both the suggested merger and the pitch for the new account (which I didn't think the agency was quite ready for).

Only much, much later did I realize I was intuitively troubled over something that had nothing to do with business.

But then, I'd understand a lot of things once I was dead.

ELEVEN

The hotel was one we'd used before for brainstorming sessions. Rooms and service were top-grade and we'd hired a suite with two bedrooms, one for me, the second one, across the large lounge, for Oliver.

This was a week or so after my meeting with Oliver and Sydney in which we'd discussed the possibility of "merging" with a bigger advertising agency and whether or not to pitch for the British Allied Bank account. I'd reluctantly agreed to the latter, but the idea of amalgamating with Blake & Turnbrow—a sell-out as far as I was concerned—was still in abeyance. My partners knew my view, which was in the negative, but I guess they thought I'd come round eventually. They were wrong: I wouldn't. I'd worked too bloody hard—we all had—building our own creative shop to let it be gobbled up by a rival agency, no matter how global and how many blue chip accounts it carried. I suppose ego came into it somewhere—I didn't want to lose control of our company, which inevitably would happen despite Sydney's assurances that it wouldn't be the case.

The point of booking into the hotel for the weekend was to keep us away from telephones—unless we wanted to ring out—and all the other nuisance stuff of running a company. Also, and I'm not quite sure why this is true, getting away from our normal surroundings somehow led to fresher ideas; strange how a different environment can promote new concepts. As well as that, everything was on tap for us, room service ruled. We only had this one weekend to come up with a brand new press poster, and television campaign for the British Allied Bank, an advertising campaign with a budget of several million pounds.

The team was just Oliver and me, and I must admit that, despite my reservation about the account possibly being too big for us to handle, I had become more and more excited as the preceding week had worn on. It's called the Buzz, and there's nothing quite like it.

On this Saturday night, the second night of the weekend—we'd be working all day Sunday as well—the hotel room's thick-carpeted floor was covered with sheets of thin layout paper, rough-scamp ideas on every leaf. And there were some good thoughts on those sheets, pithy copy lines with strong visuals, and I was pretty pleased with most.

But there was a problem. I wanted to go with the idea of humanizing the bank by simply informing the public that human beings were running the individual accounts, not computerized automatons, and all had names, families, and other interests, but were experts in their particular fields of finance, always with the customer's interest at heart. Oliver, however, wanted to try a much more grandiose approach, showing how grand and mighty the corporation was, how its network spread throughout the world, and how it employed superior specialists in all matters of finance. I saw the latter as far too anonymous for the ordinary people who would use the bank's services; and Oliver saw my concept as too limited, even though I explained that the advertising would be good for bank staff as well as prospective customers, putting staff on a plateau, letting them know they were appreciated by their employers while still trying to hook new customers. We even argued over the media, because I wanted newspaper ads along with television whereas Ollie wanted to use glossy color supplements, forty-eight-sheet posters, and enormously expensive sixty-second commercials.

The answer, of course, was to split the budget on different campaigns, using the bank's size and grandeur as an umbrella under which all aspects were covered, but neither of us saw that at the time. I think by that second night we were both too wired for compromise—literally, in Oliver's case, as I was soon to find out.

What was missing was a mediator, a cool voice of reason that would argue both cases, then come up with a compromise solution suitable to both parties. That was the role Sydney usually played, but although he'd looked in on us earlier that day he'd long gone by now. If he could, he had told us, he would call in later when we'd both had the chance to cool off a bit.

But now it was almost 11 P.M. and I didn't think he would return at this time of night. Probably wanted to catch us when we were refreshed the following day, Sunday.

I stared at the layouts scattered around me on wall-to-wall carpet and, whether it was sheer weariness or I'd been half-convinced by Oliver's persuasive reasoning, I was about to give in. Too much time and energy was being wasted on useless yatter and not enough on getting the job done. I'd work up Ollie's idea with visuals, then together we'd see how it would run as a TV commercial. Maybe we could show how huge the bank's network was by showcasing real individuals . . . Anyway, that's the way my thoughts were heading and I could just see the glimmer of a satisfactory solution up ahead and not too far away.

I heard the toilet flush and soon after the bathroom door opened, Oliver sweeping through. His shirtsleeves were rolled to his elbows, his silk tie at half-mast, shirt collar unbuttoned.

"Right, let's just harmonize on this fucking thing," he said without looking at me. His voice was angry and, when he took the chair at the suite's desk bureau, the toe of his shoe began its familiar drumbeat on the carpet.

"Chill out, Ollie," I said, not rising to the bait. "I think—"

"Chill . . .?"

It was snapped out and I stiffened, taken aback.

"We've got until Monday morning to come up with the goods," he went on. "Presentation's at the end of the week, and you're telling me to chill out! What is it with you? Doesn't anything ever puncture your cool?"

"Hey. C'mon," I began to protest.

"Finished layouts, full-color posters, storyboards—Jim, we've got to get our shit together on this, we've got to ink the paper! But no, as usual, you've got to have your own way. *Your* idea has to be the one we go with." The *your* came as a sneer.

I was, well, I was astonished. Oliver and I had had our spats over the years, always about work, but on balance it was generally his ideas that went through. The split was about sixty–forty in his favor.

"This is stupid . . ." I said, beginning to lose some of that cool just a little bit.

"Don't call me stupid!" he came back. "You're the one who's stupid." His eyes were wide; he was staring at me in a way that was somehow familiar. His knee jerked as the heel of his toe-cap continued to punish the carpet.

"Ollie, I'm not calling you anything. Look, let's just ease up, give ourselves a break. Maybe carry on early tomorrow morning after a good night's sleep."

"Fuck you," he said, reaching behind him for his cigarettes on the bureau top.

As he looked away I suddenly remembered why that wildness in his eyes had seemed familiar. Without another word, I rose and strode toward the shared bathroom.

Cigarette halfway to his lips, he noticed I'd left my chair. "Where the fuck are you going?" I heard him say.

Ignoring him I went into the bathroom and did not bother to close the door behind me. A black-marble shelf containing two basins ran beneath the full length of the long wall mirror and I squatted so that its surface was at eye level. I moved over to the second basin, studying the smooth, flecked marble beside it and saw exactly what I feared might be present: a small amount of scattered granules of fine powder and smears where Oliver had gathered up some of the residue with a damp finger to wipe into his gums.

Just to make perfectly sure, I licked the tip of my own finger and dabbed it on the hard marble surface, then tasted it. Although rarely one for any kind of drugs, I had tasted cocaine before, and this was the real McCoy. Oliver was doing blow again.*

I stormed from the bathroom to confront my friend.

"You silly bastard!" I told him.

His turn to freeze for a moment. The flame from his lighter hovered a couple of inches away from the cigarette, then was extinguished without completing the job. He glared back at me, but said nothing.

"You told us you were finished with drugs. Didn't you learn your lesson last time?"

"All right, all right, okay, okay. So what if I am back off the wagon? Where's the harm?"

"It nearly broke the partnership before!"

"You remember what Sinatra said: A nip every now and again pulls you through the day."

"I saw the movie; he was talking about booze, for fuck's sake."

"Same thing, chum."

---

*Sydney had taught me how to spot this years ago when we first suspected Oliver was a user. Unlike the cokeheads and their habits you might see in Hollywood movies, addicts who bend over glass tables or flat mirrors to snort cocaine, one finger closing a nostril while the other provides passage to the nose's inner membranes, leaving a slight residue of fine powder like dandruff on a dark suit, coke is never wasted this way. It's too expensive to leave even the smallest spillage. No, true addicts will always tongue-damp a finger so that it picks up whatever's left. They will either lick their finger again as though it was some kind of narcotic lollipop, or will rub the substance into the gums. Where drugs are concerned there is no wastage. Doesn't happen.

"The hell it is."

"Same thing and no hangover."

"It'll ruin you." I shook my head in dismay.

"So will constant work overload. Besides it sharpens me up."

"Sometimes," I told him, "it makes you think the crappiest idea is awesome."

"Hey, I give you good copy."

"No, Oliver, you don't. Trouble is, you don't know it when you're high. Don't you remember how strung out you were before?"

"You're exaggerating, chum. I can handle it."

"Don't fucking call me *chum*." Maybe it was the "chum" usage that made me a little bit cruel. "You lost Andrea, remember that?"

I didn't like the dark grin he gave me. Nevertheless, I softened my tone.

"You promised you'd quit, Oliver. You're letting us all down, but mostly yourself."

"Ah, fuck it!" An ugly snarl accompanied the curse. "It's my problem, not yours."

"No, it's *our* problem. We're the ones who have to deal with it."

Anger spoiling his good looks, he jumped to his feet, shoving the lighter back into his pocket and tossing the unlit cigarette onto the carpet.

"You know what you can do with the agency."

"Hey, c'mon." Even though I was more than a little annoyed I raised both hands placatingly. "You don't mean that. See, this is what happens when you're doing coke. It makes you bloody schizophrenic."

"At least I'm not the one that's holding the agency back. You were frightened to pitch for this account until Sydney and I persuaded you. Even worse, you're scared of tying in with a bigger agency so that we can expand."

I felt the skin of my face tighten. "Let's leave it there, okay? I don't want to get into this right now."

"No, Jim, 'course you don't. Let's face it, *chum,* you don't like change, you never have."

I could have pointed out that we'd built the agency together, account by account, and I was equally a prime mover in everything we had achieved; but it wasn't worth it—it was no good talking common sense to him when he was in one of these stupid moods. He had been hitting the bottle all evening, first emptying the miniature whiskies from the minibar, then ordering a bottle of Black Label from room service, while slipping into the bathroom every so often for cocaine hits. And I'd thought he had a bladder problem.

"We're both tired," I said evenly, grimly aware that there was no point in trying to reason with him. Alcohol and coke were a bad combination. "Let's call it a day, carry on tomorrow morning when I'm fresher and you're straight."

"Why? You think that's going to change anything? You'll still be holding me back, as ever."

"You don't know what you're saying, Oliver." I refused to rise to the bait, suspecting the bitterness of his words had more to do with whiskey than powder. "Enough for tonight, okay? We'll start again in the morning."

"You won't change your mind though, will you? You still won't agree to a merger."

"This isn't the time to discuss it!" I shouted back at him. I wanted to give him a smack, wipe the supercilious smirk from his face. Instead, I said through suppressed anger, "I'm turning in and I think you should do the same."

"What?" he raised his arm and peered at his wristwatch. "Going to bed at half-past eleven. Well I've got better things to do."

He grabbed his jacket hanging over the back of a chair and tramped across the sheets of layout paper toward the door, crumpling them, leaving scuff marks over my Pentel visuals.

"Oliver, don't," I called after him. "This is bloody silly."

"Fuck you," he said as he pulled open the door to the long hallway beyond and turned to give me a contemptuous look. Never before had he regarded me with that kind of expression and I was shocked. He looked as if he could kill me.

Then he was gone, slamming the door behind him, and that was the last time I saw Oliver while I was alive.

TWELVE

Maybe it was the vodka, then the brandy, then the gin I'd consumed from the mini-bar that made my OBE so confusing; I'd downed them all in rapid succession after Oliver had left the suite.

Now on my own, surrounded by trampled layouts, I'd grown more and more angry. Trust Ollie to walk out on me when there was so much work to be done by Monday. And trust the fool to go back on his word that he'd keep off drugs for good. Now our partnership was in jeopardy all over again. I needed a copywriter who could judge what was good and what was awful. I needed a business partner who could think clearly when important decisions had to be made. I thought Ollie had learned his lesson from last time around.

It was past midnight when I went through to the room next door and threw myself onto the bed, an almost empty miniature of gin clutched in one hand. I supported myself on an elbow and drank the last dregs (shit, I *hated* gin) and let the tiny bottle drop to the floor as I flopped onto my back. Oliver, Oliver, why did you have to do it? Why now at this crucial time? The bank was probably one of the most significant accounts we'd ever take on and once we became committed, we couldn't be seen to blow it. Okay, it might not seriously knock us back in the industry, but it could damage our reputation as a winning hot shop a little. As for the so-called "merger" with Blake & Turnbrow, we needed to talk about it coolly and rationally without internecine disputes even before negotiations had begun.

Man, I was tired. Sick and tired, I guess. I'd never liked arguments and this one was a dinger. Ollie and I used to be tight, but now the relationship appeared to be over. For good? Who could say?

Closing my eyes I felt the room shift around me; by no means a seismic shift, but a smooth displacement that had more to do with exhaustion than the alcohol I'd consumed. I opened my eyes again and stared at the ceiling. Orange light came through the windows from the street below, this occasionally brightened by a whiter light, traffic approaching from a side street opposite, so that shadows moved around the darkened room like playful ghosts, growing then waning as headlights outside moved on.

I wasn't drunk—I'm *sure* I wasn't drunk—but anxiety, mental weariness, and booze were never a good mix. For a moment I was disorientated, but the room soon settled itself again. The hum of late-night traffic that filtered through the windows' double glazing was almost soothing. We would get through this I told myself, and things eventually would go back to the way they were. Compromise was all that was needed here, and Sydney was good at smoothing over difficulties and offering solutions to disputes. I'd give him a call in the morning, get him over here, let him sort things out. Sydney had always been the perfect middleman, the soother of awkward situations. Hopefully, he would back down once he saw how anti-"merger" I really was and, in turn, he would help dissuade Oliver from such a drastic course.

My eyes closed again and this time they remained closed. Within seconds I was gone.

It was as easy and as quickly as that. One moment I was drowsy, sinking into sleep, the next I was out of body, hovering near the ceiling, gazing down at myself.

Sometimes—in fact, most times—I had to work at it, consciously putting myself into a state of relaxation, imagining myself outside of my own physical form, seeing myself lying below in my imagination only, until the image became sharper, clearer, and suddenly I would actually *be* there, some other place watching myself, no longer confined to the shell of my physical body. Usually, a great sense of freedom accompanied egression, a feeling of limitless space around my spirit form, a knowledge that I could fly to any destination I chose without constraint; but tonight, I was confused, my mind not as liberated as my spirit. It was as if a thick yet invisible harness held me to my body, the bondage of reality perhaps. It could have been that my body, the part of me that was permanently chained to the physical world, sensed more than my spiritual self did and so was reluctant to release me, somehow afraid of the parting.

This state did not last long though, because a moment or two later my body dwindled below me as I zoomed away, through the ceiling, then the ceiling of the room above, swifter and swifter until I was out into the night sky.

It's difficult to describe the feeling accurately, because it involves so much that is unknowable to most people. To begin with there is an incredible sense of wellbeing, for there are no physical torments such as pain, weariness, hunger, or hangover anymore and, although there is some initial apprehension, this quickly vanishes with familiarity and you begin to enjoy the sensation. Most of the time you're not in control of your destination but sometimes, if your mind is clear and compliant enough, you can direct yourself, you can choose a place and suddenly you will zoom off to it. Same thing if you envisage a particular person. It's a bit like those rare times when you realize you are dreaming and so for a while can direct your own actions in the dream. Usually this interesting state doesn't last long, because a little consciousness soon encourages full consciousness, and you find yourself awake again, annoyed you hadn't made more of the experience.

On this night though, I was unable to govern my journey and found myself inside a kind of kaleidoscope of images, none of which appeared relevant to me. I seemed to travel back in time, because I saw myself as a little boy, skateboarding down a hill, picking up speed, shouting both with glee and fear as I increased speed, and then I watched myself sailing through the air, because the skateboard had hit some obstruction in its path (I wasn't sure, but I thought it was my mother's handbag lying in the roadway, and that was ridiculous, because why should her handbag be lying there?) and the board I had been standing on clattered over and over on the hard concrete while I glided smoothly through the air, screaming because I knew I was going to hit solid ground before too long. But instead of smashing into concrete, I found myself lying on cheap lino flooring, gazing up at a ring of faces that stared down at me, one of which was my mother's, embarrassment as well as anxiety written across her plump features, and I remembered I'd just swallowed a steaming hot potato, a potato whose fire singed the inside walls of my chest, and then I was in another place, in a room filled with oldish-looking furniture, and I was watching a little boy, an even younger me, playing with a plastic Skywalker and Darth Vader on a rug in front of an electric fire, only two of its bars working, and I was desperately trying to ignore a row that was going on between a man and a woman who shared the room with me, and I could see that the woman was my mother, only she was much younger than she was today and she was almost pretty, despite the roundness of her face, and she was shouting at the man who, for some reason, had no face, his image masked beneath one of those pixel cover-ups, you know, little squares of different hues technically superimposed on screens so that the person being filmed cannot be identified, and he was silent as my mother screeched into his face, only occasionally uttering some kind of weak protest, and the more I stared at him the more the pixels disintegrated, square by square, while he was turning to me and saying *"Jimmy,"* until—

—until I was off again, flying over rooftops, winging through darkness, skimming through shadowed canyons, until, until . . .

. . . until I found myself descending worn stone steps that led down from the street, then passing through a battered, paint-chipped door. I was inside a dingy, dank room, its only light source an angle-poise lamp on a table covered with newspaper clippings, the dusty naked lightbulb hanging from the ceiling switched off.

A figure was seated there, back to me, long-bladed scissors in one hand, snipping away at a newspaper. The cuttings already taken from other newspapers were set out neatly, without one piece overlapping another, the lines in between precise in their parallels. (I could tell it was a man by the size of his hands and the heavy set of his hunched shoulders.) I was puzzled by the sounds he made, a kind of wet snuffling. Every so often he would reach for a soiled, wrinkled rag lying on the desk and bring it to his face as if to wipe away mucus. Perhaps he had a heavy cold.

I was suddenly very afraid.

Why I had been drawn to this place I couldn't tell, yet somehow I knew there had to be a reason. Certainly, I didn't want to be here in this somber room. Through an open doorway I could just make out a narrow cot bed against a wall, its sheets rumpled, unmade. In there the window's grubby curtains were closed tight, as if to discourage snoopers, even though the flat itself was below street level. Well-thumbed magazines lay untidily on an old sofa, barely leaving a place to sit. There was no cheer here, no welcome; the place seemed filled with threat.

Snip-snip-snip.

The metallic cutting sound was eerily loud in the room's stillness and, if I'd had a heartbeat, I'm sure I would have heard that too.

I drew nearer, but not willingly. It was a compulsion, an undeniable curiosity, that drove me.

Even though I was of no physical substance, I was afraid as I peered over the man's shoulder to read the large print of newspaper headlines.

POLICE ADMIT SERIAL KILLER AT LARGE.
MURDER VICTIM MUTILATED.
WHY THESE VICTIMS? POLICE BAFFLED.
HUNT FOR MUTILATOR CONTINUES.

I straightened in shock. These murders had been happening for the past six weeks and the newspapers were full of lurid stories; even the broadsheets seemed to have lost their sense of decorum in their gory descriptions of the crimes. According to these stories all the victims were chosen at random, there was no connection between them. Also, the killings appeared to be motiveless, the unfortunate victims had no known enemies and apparently were not involved in any kind of criminal activity. In fact, the only similarity between the victims was that all three were professional people: the first had been a lawyer, the second an insurance broker, and the third, a woman this time, was a radiologist in the Royal London Hospital in Whitechapel.

I was no more than a few inches away from the man's head as he snipped away at a copy of the *Daily Telegraph* and I became even more disturbed by his odd breathing. It was somehow coarse, guttural, as if his throat were clogged, and I was repulsed by the sound.

I backed away a step and stared at the back of his bowed head. His scrappy hair was badly cut, bald patches visible even in the poor light from the low lamp that threw his back into dark shadow; what hair there was looked lank and dirty and I was sure that if I had a sense of smell in my altered state, the man himself would be rank, unwashed.

I realized what else made me feel so uneasy about this person: the perception had never before been this clear as far as others were concerned, but now I could just make out this man's aura, the glow that emanates from every living thing. Some claim it's a person's soul shining from within, while others, more pragmatic, say it's merely the normal radiation emitted from any material form. Nowadays, I tend to go for the former.

It was nasty, this aura around him, thick with muddy grays and blacks, their range short, shallow, extending only here and there beyond half-an-inch, and it seemed to me that the phenomenon exuded something foul, something rotten. I backed further away and that was when the man stiffened, the scissors stopping mid-snip. His head lifted and I became still, almost afraid to breathe (not that I needed to breathe at all).

It was as if he had sensed my presence.

Yet I'd made no noise—I couldn't, not in this form.

He seemed to have felt my gaze on the back of his neck.

But, of course, I wasn't there in person, there could be no presence to feel.

He lifted the scissors and clicked the blade shut. He changed his grip and held them like a knife.

Then he slowly began to turn my way.

I retreated even further, hoping to become lost in the shadows. Ridiculous, I know, because I was invisible. In all my out-of-body excursions nobody had ever been able to observe me in this immaterial state.

Yet he was turning toward me with purpose and I felt terribly exposed.

And then his black bulbous eyes were looking into mine.

I screamed. I fled.

THIRTEEN

It was horrible, ugly, and suddenly the world was spinning around me.

I don't know if it was the shock, or my natural abhorrence that took over and whisked me away from harm, but I left the room fast. I didn't run away, of course, I merely zoomed off as if yanked by a hook, images and sounds whirling around me. I was out of the darkened room, heading skyward, and then I knew nothing more for a while. It was as if my spiritual form had passed out.

I "awoke," if that could be the word, in the living room of my own house. There were no lights on, but I could see my location by the street light flooding through the window. I've since reasoned that it was instinct that brought me there, that I'd fled to where I felt safest—doesn't everyone feel safest in the sanctity of their own home? What I didn't realize though, not until I inadvertently glanced at the clock on the mantelpiece, was that a few hours had passed since I'd entered the OBE.

I remembered the horribly dingy basement room and the man inside snipping away at the newspapers, and I remembered him slowly turning round as if he'd become aware of me. I remembered . . . I remembered . . . no, I *couldn't* remember the face that had looked directly at me. Somehow the image had been frightened from my mind. I tried to recall what had scared me so, but I couldn't, I just could not bring it into focus. But I knew I'd witnessed something awful, something that my brain had no wish to recollect. Perhaps later . . .

It was good to be home, oh, it was *so* good. Familiar furniture, framed pictures, comfortable sofa and armchair, thick wall-to-wall carpet—home, sweet home. A natural response had brought me here, of that I had no doubt: I guess self-preservation has a homing instinct all its own. But where had I been during the intervening hours? It took me some time to work this out, but eventually

I realized that my mind—and hence my "spirit"—had just closed down. Panic had set it to flight, and when I was safely away from that . . . that . . . *thing* in the dark room, my mind had sought sanctuary in oblivion. Why I had not simply returned to my body, I had no idea, but now the impulse to do so was immense.

As a rule, just the thought was enough to send me gliding back, a journey never more than a second or two no matter how far I had journeyed. But this time I resisted the impulse. Maybe it was the recent threat of danger that had me seeking the assurance of everything familiar and ordinary—what could be more commonplace than your own house? Or maybe I just had to touch base with reality for a while—again, what's more real than your own place? Before I went back to my body, I had to reassure myself that my loved ones were safe and secure for the night.

Just that thought sent me gliding into the hall and up the stairs to the bedrooms. Now you have a choice when out of body, in that you can move exactly as you would in real life—one step at a time, that sort of thing—or you can kind of sail or glide everywhere. I usually chose to do both, sometimes taking steps, other times pushing myself along as in those dreams I spoke of earlier. On this fretful occasion I glided up the stairs, using my hands to propel myself upward as though I were beneath the ocean, almost weightless, exploring some undersea wreck. Normally, it was a wonderful feeling, but this night I was too agitated to enjoy the experience.

Up I went, for some reason terribly afraid for my family. It made no sense at all—the man had only felt my presence, hadn't actually seen me. And so what? What could the man do? He didn't know me, could have no idea of where I lived. But still the anxiety sent me gliding purposely up the stairs. I *had* understood that the man I'd witnessed collecting clippings from various newspapers was wicked, because it was evil that seemed to ooze from his very pores, manifesting itself in the ugly monochromed aura. Yes, he seemed to sweat badness and I'd sensed that even if I could not physically smell it.

Why should he have been cutting out those particular news stories of a serial killer? My absent heart turned cold, a peculiar experience, I must admit. Foolish too, because there was no way I could be traced back here to my home. Even *if* the man had actually seen me, even *if* he had some psychic sense that made it possible, he would not know me from Adam, and therefore could not know my home address. Yet his threat seemed very real.

I paused at the top of the stairs, unsettled, now definitely afraid for my wife and daughter. What if this person had the ability to follow me? What if he was capable of OBEs? No, not possible. Certainly I, myself, had caught glimpses of spirit people, a kind of faded print of moving images, but nothing I could connect with. If I approached, they merely melted away. They were sometimes picked up only in the periphery of my vision, to evaporate when looked at directly.

I got a grip of myself and went on.

Primrose's bedroom door, as always, was open wide so that we could hear her if she had a bad dream and called out during the night, and I sped through. I hovered over her and regarded her lovely little face, her lips slightly parted, the soft drone of baby-snores assuring me she was safe and well. Her arms were thrown back, small clenched fists resting on the pillow, and her brown curls framed her sweet face. Leaning down I planted a gentle kiss on her cheek and she wrinkled her nose and turned her head aside as though something had tickled her. Without thought I tried to tuck the bedcovers up around her neck, but of course, my hands merely went through the soft material. I lingered for a few moments and imagined I could actually hear the small *thud-ups* of her heartbeat; imagined or not, it was reassuring.

Backing away cautiously as if I might make a sound and wake her, I tiptoed out (silly, I know) onto the landing. Again I paused, this time to listen for any extraneous sounds, anything foreign to the domestic peace, and only when satisfied there was nothing to be anxious about did I move along the landing to the bedroom I normally shared with Andrea.

The lamplight outside the window allowed me to see her lying on one side of our large double bed—she once told me that, out of habit, she never invaded my side when I was away—and she, too, looked peaceful. Her skin was pale in the cold glow from the street, and her features were beautiful and unlined. We'd had our problems during the marriage, particularly over the past year—I was the guilty party, work had eaten up so much of my time that Andrea was entitled to feel neglected—but I'd never stopped loving her and I hoped it was the same for her. I still found her exquisite and inwardly, and constantly, blessed her for giving me such a wonderful daughter. Her naked arm was above the bedclothes and I ran invisible fingers along the smooth white skin. I had watched her before like this, my own body lying empty beside her with my spirit form hovering over us both, wondering at the unique experience. You might think that it was spying, but truthfully, it doesn't feel like that. Maybe it's because you're existing in your purest form and bodily desires are not present.

It doesn't mean you can't appreciate the beauty before you, but there is no lust involved, no sexual pruriency whatsoever (otherwise I guess most out-of-body practitioners would turn into voyeurs and sex surfers). I had once caressed Andrea's naked sleeping body on a hot summer's night when the bedsheets had been tossed aside, but because there was no physical contact involved, there was no arousal (and certainly not for my sleeping beauty). You can't have it all ways, I suppose.

I sat next to her on the bed (no, there's no strain in standing—weariness only comes with the length of time you're in OBE—but you tend to follow the normal life patterns), just watching her sleep, making up my mind to pay her and Prim more attention once this new client presentation was out of the way, resolving to take more time off in future, delegate more of the creative work to my up-and-coming art directors and copywriters, when suddenly I was jolted by some awful, sickening dread.

It seemed to hit me like a sledge-hammer, a sudden powerful shock that had me collapsed over the bed, where I stayed, stunned and gasping for unnecessary air. A memory—a scene—flashed through my mind: I seemed to be very small, for I was looking up, looking up at two figures. I recognized one. Mother, smiling down at me. She was different though and for a moment—no, it must have been a nanosecond, because it was all happening so fast, so fast yet so ridiculously drawn out, as if I had conquered time itself—I wondered why. Then I realized it was because she was so much younger than the woman I now knew, than the image that I had held within my head, the present-day woman. As in the vision earlier that night, she was younger, her smile was sweeter, and she was pretty in a plumpish, round-faced way. Now she was making noises at me, but I heard no sound; somehow—perhaps it was because of the O shape of her lips—I knew she was making cooing sounds at me, baby sounds.

I turned to the figure standing next to her, a man who was also gazing down at me although I could not see his face, only his clothes, his long thin legs, a woolen jumper. I tried, I really tried, to see his face, because I knew he was important to me; all I saw was a blur this time, a soft pink-grayness as if the head had lost focus, but I knew it was the pixel-disguised person I'd seen with Mother before.

The couple dissolved and I was still low to the ground, for once again I was looking upward and figures were bending over me, a circle of curious heads, and I was choking, something was burning my throat, something was stopping my breath. It was hot-potato time all over again. And there was Mother, older than a moment ago, her expression inexplicably overridden with embarrassment rather than concern.

Dissolve, very quick, fade-in scenes coming thick and fast. I was surrounded by other kids, in a schoolyard I could tell, for the buildings rose around us like brick canyon walls and a bell was ringing somewhere, calling us all to assembly, but I was otherwise engaged, me and another boy, a bit bigger than me but with a bloody nose and tears in his eyes as he rained punches at me. I knew I had given him the bloody nose and I was feeling good because of it, even though I also knew I was now going to take a hammering. I felt pain, nasty, powerful pain, but it didn't last long, for I was in another scene, the story of my life revealed in incidents rather than episodes, and I was watching a girl, a beautiful, dark-haired girl of about fifteen, and my whole body seemed wracked with emotion that I think was first-time love, and this did not last either, but the scenes—the incidents—were changing even more rapidly, becoming a kind of vortex of images, speedy but perfectly clear and in their encapsulated way, perfectly presented with beginnings and ends. It was thrilling, but at the same time so bloody scary.

And I had to wonder why it was happening.

On it went, more scenes—sorry, *incidents, episodes*—from the past came and went, and I saw them all as an observer, not a participant. Weird, unsettling, some events leaving me steeped in guilt, while others were totally joyous.

It occurred to me with some dismay that this must be like the death experience some people spoke of, the retelling of their life in all-embracing flashback. But there appeared to be no judgment, only a subliminal and non-specific weighing-up of good and bad deeds committed by me. And anyway, I wasn't dead, only out-of-body, so whatever was happening was merely some freakish phenomenon I'd never experienced before.

Through the years of practicing the out-of-body state, I had read up on the subject and tried to learn as much as I could about the theory, the control, and other people's personal experiences, and had been surprised to learn that the spirit essence never quite leaves the body, that there is a kind of silver thread (some preach that it's golden) always connecting you to your physical form, that no matter how far you leave your body behind, this thread or cord stretches but never breaks the link. This, according to the theories, is why you can never lose your physical self, that nothing can destroy the connection. Well

I'd never observed this so-called silver or gold thread or cord, although I'd always felt some kind of invisible bond. But now I felt it break.*

I could not see it, I could not feel the link, but somehow I sensed that it had snapped like a long, finely drawn rubber band and the result was that I had been propelled forward, my invisible head almost smacking my invisible knees. It was a terrible, fear-inducing jolt and I was suddenly cast free of myself, the metaphorical umbilical cord that held both parts of me together, body and soul, had been sundered.

I had an equally sudden vision of that man in the darkened room cutting the cord with his long-bladed scissors. Impossible, of course, but somehow I couldn't shake the image from my mind. I began to panic.

Could you lose the connection with your own body? Could you be cast adrift? I had no idea—I was a lone pioneer as far as OBEs were concerned; I certainly had no knowledge of others who practiced it, although I'd read the few books written by people who claimed they had mastered the technique of leaving their own bodies to become entirely spirit; but nothing they'd said covered this eventuality. I was scared, terribly scared, and I wanted to get back to my body without delay.

Normally, that very thought would have effortlessly sent me home to my body within moments; but this time I had to will myself deliberately to return. I flew from the house and along streets rapidly enough, but I had to negotiate the route, will myself along, whereas before there was no conscious effort, I just arrived back in my body without thought or direction. A couple of times now I even got lost, became confused, had to force myself to slow down and

---

*There is no visible link, although without doubt there is a *psychic* link. While separated from the host body, the bond between soul and body is too strong and yet too delicate to be broken (think of some of those deep-sea creatures whose flesh is so fine it's transparent, yet they withstand constant unbelievably intense physical pressure without being crushed; or think of finely spun spiders' webs that can bear comparatively heavy loads without tearing. I'd say the psychic link between body and itinerant spirit—let's call this other self that for the moment—is even stronger). This, of course, is not a fact, but something I've rationalized as time has gone by and certainly—and this is the important part—I've kind of *sensed* from the beginning; so much in that incorporeal state is *sensing,* which is considerably heightened in the out-of-body state. Maybe bodiless you're closer to life's mysteries. Or maybe it's some kind of compensation for the absence of one of your other senses: I mean touch, because there *is* no physical contact anymore, you just cannot *feel* anything at all material. And believe me, that's hard to get used to. Your fingers just merge into anything you touch, your body can move through anything solid like liquid through a fine sieve.

think of where I was and where I had to get to. Luckily, I knew the city well, so it was no great problem to return to the Knightsbridge hotel; the difficulty was having to *think* my way there.

And then I arrived, gliding upward to the tenth floor, through the thick wall, into a lengthy corridor, sinking through the closed door to the suite I shared with Oliver, coming to a jerky halt in the lounge where all my layouts and Ollie's copy ideas littered the floor. I felt more fear as I glanced toward the open doorway to my bedroom, wary of going in, deeply anxious about what I might find.

I suppose some kind of homing instinct had brought me here, but now I felt nothing. No, I did feel something—I felt adrift . . . dispossessed. I moved toward the open doorway.

I'd left the two wall lights on above the bed when I'd half-drunkenly collapsed onto the large double bed and I could see what remained of my body lying there on top of the covers. The blood was horrendous. I mean the amount of it. The human body holds, what? Eight and a half pints or thereabouts, and it looked like most of it had spilt out of me. You know how it is when you drop a bottle of milk? It seems to spread everywhere. In the bottle it doesn't look that much, but on the floor? It's like a dam just broke.

My blood soaked the quilt on which I lay and what wasn't absorbed ran over the edge of the bed to puddle the floor. There was even blood on the wall behind the headboard, great arcs of it, drooling streams, as well as dramatic splatters. It resembled art from a Jackson Pollock red period.

My eyes were slightly open in the scarlet mess that once had been my face and the pupils were like unpolished marble, frozen and lacklustre. I was dead, well and truly dead.

FOURTEEN

Whoever had murdered me had left me unrecognizable; if not for the hair and blood-soiled clothes I wouldn't have known myself. Wait, I got that wrong: it wasn't the hair or clothes—I just *knew* the body was mine; although the link had been broken, I wanted to get back inside myself, pure instinct overriding logical thought. I wanted to put life back into my body no matter how mutilated it had become.

Usually, intention did not come into it; I just arrived back, kind of slipping inside like a hand into a glove, a foot into a shoe. But now I had to force my spiritual-self to step into the mess and gore that was my former self, into the clumps of sliced flesh.

Squatting over my remains, I lowered my spiritual butt into my physical pelvis; then, after a moment's hesitation, lay back like a vampire into a coffin.

Unfortunately, whereas at other times I'd merely melded with myself, returning to flesh and bone an easy and smooth accommodation, I now seemed alien to my own substance. I fitted okay, but I did not adhere, did not *become* myself again.

I found myself lying loose inside an empty desecrated vessel. And every time I tried to move, I failed to stir my flesh; my spiritual self just parted company with its host. Frustrated and in deep despair, I began to moan.

I had no idea how long I'd stayed there, endlessly sitting, then lying down, trying to "think" my way back into my body, because in the OBE time has no proper meaning, no value at all, unless you related to a living event played out before you, but I think my endeavors went on through the night and into the morning.

One of the strange things among all these other strange things was that there was still a residue of thought left inside my battered brain; or maybe it came from my body as a whole, as if all that was experienced through life etched itself into the very meat and bone of our being, perhaps even ingraining memories into our tissue and sinews, the very texture of our bodies. Maybe the brain isn't the *all* of our thinking.

I caught glimpses of other moments in my life, never fast, yet not clear images as before, almost reflections of events and people, some from long ago, most more recent. The strongest were of Primrose and Andrea, but Oliver was also there among them, and so was Mother. But they were all too insubstantial and I was too distressed to pay them much attention.

I was panicking by now, desperate to fill myself and having no success at all. No matter how mutilated, I wanted my body back. I wanted to be *me* again. I began to pray and pray in earnest, even though I'd never been religious during my lifetime—my God, my *lifetime:* I'd already given it time span—but that didn't prevent the hypocrisy now; I prayed as if I'd been a devout religionist all my days. Help me, Lord, I begged, beseeched—*whined*—and I made outrageous promises about my future actions should my existence so kindly be extended. Church would be my second home, good deeds my second nature. Just another chance, dear Lord, I'm really not ready for this. And remember, dear God, I'm a Catholic.

Yet I kept asking myself through the blathering, was I truly dead?

I didn't *feel* dead. But what would I know? It was a first-time experience. Why couldn't I see the talked-about bright light at the end of the dark tunnel? Where were the deceased relatives and friends who were supposed to welcome me over to the other side? Where were the angels?

All I saw was the walls and furniture of a luxurious but impersonal bedroom in a hotel suite, a TV inside an open cupboard in one corner, a built-in wardrobe in another, long windows with fancy heavy drapes to the left. Neither heaven nor hell. Purgatory then? Could be, I supposed. I'd learned about purgatory in my junior school, which had been run mainly by nuns (I'd attended a Catholic school, even though my mother aspired to no particular religion, and learned that purgatory—if the place existed, which I always very much doubted—was an intermediate place where the soul sweated for purification of sin. But nobody had told me it might be a hotel room).

No, that couldn't be it, because I wasn't really dead. If I were, I'd know it, right? Anybody would know it. I mean, there'd be no doubt, would there? Unless, of course, I was a ghost. A lost, confused ghost. Wasn't that what ghosts were meant to be, the lonely spirits of those who couldn't accept that their bodies had ceased to function and they were now adrift from it? Troubled souls who didn't realize they were outstaying their welcome in this world? Nah, not me. That was stupid. Death had never bothered me either as a concept or a reality: when your time came, that was it, no sense in complaining. Move on. Don't look back. Time was up. Yeah, easy to be pragmatic when it was just a notion for the future. We all know we're not immortal, so how come death rarely figures in our plans?

This was the kind of pointless argument I was having with myself as I tried desperately over and over again to win back the flesh and I guess it could have gone on endlessly had not the telephone next to the bed rung.

I made a lunge for it, forgetting I had no substance, and my hand went straight through the plastic and interior workings so that I unbalanced (yep, you can still do that even without a body) and ended up on the blood-soaked carpet. I swore—under my breath if I'd had a breath—and held up my arms in despair.

Although I had no sense of time, I knew it was still late night or early morning because it was dark outside save for the street lights. Besides, when I looked, the digital radio/alarm clock on the bedside cabinet told me it was 1:55 A.M. So who could be ringing me at that hour? Oliver, phoning to apologize for his behavior earlier? I doubted it. My copywriter's strops could last for days, sometimes weeks when he was really in a sulk. So who then?

Andrea. Her and Prim's images leaped into my mind. Andrea would certainly ring if something was up at home. Or maybe she had expected me to ring her last night, as I always did when I was away. I invariably checked if things were okay with Prim and Andrea before dinner or around bedtime (my daughter's bedtime), but tonight—last night, to be accurate—I'd been too engaged in hassles with Ollie to remember. There might not be a problem at home, I thought, calming myself to a degree, because my wife was aware that I'd probably still be working late into the night, so she wouldn't be disturbing my sleep. I hoped that was the case as I studied the still-ringing phone.

It stopped abruptly, but I continued to stare. She'd given up, but would be worried that I hadn't answered. What the hell could I do? I certainly couldn't phone her back. One more try at the body. You never know, it could just work this time.

I rose and knelt on the bed, gazing down at my mashed face and the sight made me feel sick to my nonexistent stomach. I didn't avert my gaze though. Even if I could get back inside and take control, tap out my number on the phone despite blood-drenched and now misaligned real eyes, how could I speak to Andrea without a discernible mouth? I'd only spit gore and loose teeth into the mouthpiece.

Shit in a bubble bath, what the fuck was I supposed to do? I roared my anguish, a sound no living person could ever hear, and I sobbed into my hands. What had happened to me? *Why* had it happened to me?

Understand that the thing which makes you a person is not the flesh and blood, but the mind—not the brain—that lives within the shell. It forms the personality, the philosophy, the instinct and perception, the very nature of the man or woman or child themselves and I've learned over the years that this is what you take with you when you leave the body. It *is* you, and when you're in spirit or OBE you perform just as though you're in the physical. You close your eyes, you weep, you feel fear, you feel joy, you feel all emotions as usual; and you dress yourself as you would in life, your mind creates the phantom material; as mentioned before, you can experience desire, but because your mind is aware there can be no physical expression, it necessarily becomes unimportant. Your mind also reconciles other senses, so that you can hear, touch (but not actually feel—it's all to do with perception), obviously see and you can speak, although no one else will hear you (in fact, all those senses are inexplicably heightened, because no longer are there physical defects or dulling limitations). I guess it's all to do with the mind convincing itself—no, wait, it has to be stronger than that. Possibly it's because the mind *is* the reality, all other material things nonexistent or irrelevant, unless accepted by the mind itself. I'm no philosopher, never was, but it makes some kind of sense to me. Let's just say I existed in the sixth sense, which does not preclude all of the other five. Taste is missing and so is smell. Just like in dreams, in fact.

But the main point I'm making is that even in my spirit form I acted exactly as if I were occupying my body as normal. I could sit, lie down, walk, run, jump. And on top of this, I knew I could fly, float, pass through walls, and *think* myself to other locations.

So now I kneeled on the bed and wailed. I was frightened and lost and had no idea where I was supposed to go from here. I was homeless; I had no body and no tangibility.

I cried for Primrose and Andrea, and I cried for myself. God, I even cried for Oliver and Sydney, my friends and business partners: what were *they* going to do without me, who would get the work done? I cried for my mother. We didn't get along anymore, but what was she to do with me gone? She'd lost one man already, her husband, and now me, her son. Self-pity mingled with commiseration for my friends and family as I hugged my *self* there on the big, blood-ruined bed, rocking backward and forward on my knees, and all the while the demolished face of my old self watched me with crooked glazed eyes.

It took some time, but eventually I began to calm down. I wasn't all-cried-out just yet—I knew more tears would be shed later—but I gradually became aware that staying here with the wrecked meat and bone that once was my human form was pointless. Besides, I felt an urgent need to see my wife and daughter once more, because maybe there would be no other chance; if I *was* dead (and let's face it, all the signs indicated that I was) I might have only this last chance before I went on to the place where all souls go (I began truly hoping there was a heaven after all).

Before my life expired, merely the imagined picture of a location was enough to get me there almost immediately; I was always aware of my flight, but it usually went by so swiftly it hardly felt like a journey. This time, however, I consciously had to make the effort of leaving the hotel room by passing through the thick outside wall into the night. Once outside I had to follow a route to my home that I knew, transportation now a considered thing rather than just a wish-fulfillment. I was strangely chilled as I traveled, as if a breeze was flowing through me, even though I had no physical outline to capture its draft, and my journey was by short body-hopping movements, casting off with either hands or feet to float some distance before sinking to the ground again. It was like the recurring dreams I used to have where I never could quite fly above the earth completely, my own pragmatism allied with gravity drawing me back to solid ground each time. Those astronauts who had walked the moon must have shared the same experience.

The London streets were quiet, the occasional lonely lorry or all-night bus passing me by; only a few cars were about, their headlights dipped. There were people here and there, sometimes in small groups as if they had left late-night parties or clubs together (this was the weekend, I reminded myself) and I avoided them without knowing why. But on turning a corner and briefly grounded at the time, I ran straight through a person who had been about to make the turn from the other direction.

It was the weirdest feeling, because for an instant I was almost part of the stranger. Alien thoughts poured through me, not quite visions and certainly not manifestations, but thoughts, representations of people the person must have known. There was a fraction of a situation too, an altercation between two women, neither of whom were particularly attractive, over the person—a man, I assumed, the guy whose body I'd trespassed on—himself. There were other things too, as if this pedestrian was carrying the baggage of his whole life around with him, but these were confusing and easily relegated by the two-women scenario. Then it was gone and I was in open space again.

I felt suddenly drained, slightly nauseated, as if my invasion was punishable—or perhaps too much to handle—and I came to a halt. Turning my head to watch the man's retreating back, I saw that he also had stopped and was looking behind him toward me, a bewildered expression on his lamp-lit face. I thought he might even see me and I unconsciously raised a hand in salutation, but of course he stared right through me (literally).

He shuddered, a jerky spasm, a feeling of someone walking over his grave, I guessed. And I felt the same way too, although I didn't give a shudder. The man turned and went on his way, disappearing round the next corner, leaving me perplexed and no less afraid for myself. It was an unpleasantness I intended to avoid in the future. If there was some kind of future for me.

Resuming my journey, I discovered I could no longer float quite so easily. I realized much later that I was becoming used to my situation, my state-of-being, and the familiarity appeared to set its own limitations. You see, this was not entirely the OBE of before, when I had a proper life. No, I was now in some kind of limbo, unattached but still linked with the former life. Somehow, this condition imposed certain restrictions and I was yet to learn what they were. I guessed that the more I accepted and adapted, the less freedoms I would have, reasoned thought perhaps setting its own boundaries, if only to a certain extent.

The journey home was one of the worst I'd ever undertaken; I was in grief and I was frightened and confused. Only the image of my loved ones, Prim and Andrea, kept me from sinking into an invisible whimpering heap on the pavement. This can't be death, I repeatedly told myself, this can't be the consequence of dying, the next stage, the step through the door; this couldn't be the after-death existence most of us hoped for. If it was, where were all the other souls? If I was a ghost, where were all those who had preceded me? Anyway, I didn't *feel* like a ghost. Disembodied maybe, but I certainly had not left this place on earth. Where was the Big Judgment those nuns in junior school had promised me (or, more truthfully, threatened me with)? Where was the eternal peace and joy we were supposed to expect, and where was God's all-embracing love? Or was *He* having a laugh? (Yep, by now a little anger was creeping in and that was no bad thing—somehow it gave me a bit more focus.)

I went on, at one moment boiling with rage, the next tearful with despair. Never had I felt so alone. I longed to be with my wife and daughter again and I kept willing myself to be home, hoping that the willing would work as it always had before, so that just the thought of Prim and Andrea inside our house would take me there instantly as though the mere desire would act like some futuristic transporter vehicle, a *Star Trek* machine without the electronics and dazzling light particles. It wasn't to be though and I wandered the streets like (literally again) some lost soul.

Nevertheless, I arrived home more swiftly than if I'd been plodding along with real legs and feet, and no tiredness accompanied the effort. I stood by the stone post at the bottom of our short driveway and looked at the house, waiting, not to catch my breath, which was totally unnecessary, but to relish the moment. I felt relieved and at the same time flushed with anticipation.

Oddly, there was a light on in an upstairs window despite the hour. It came from Prim's bedroom.

FIFTEEN

It must have been the *non*-thinking, the sheer reaction, that got me into my daughter's bedroom so swiftly. One moment I was standing by the wall post, the next I was gliding up the driveway to the entrance (my feet skimming inches above the ground) and had passed through the sturdy wooden barrier that was the front door and in a flash was on my way upstairs.* I didn't so much as climb the stairs as sail right up them, finding myself outside Prim's open bedroom door without further thought.

I have no idea why I paused there—perhaps I was preparing myself for another shock—but pause I did. No, now I think about it, it was more of an involuntary hesitation than a deliberate halt, for I could hear a familiar soothing voice. It could be that I expected both Prim and my wife to glimpse me in this new and surprising state, for I hadn't yet learned enough about my condition to know how it might affect others. In OBE I'd always been invisible to people, but now the rules might have changed dramatically. Some people do see ghosts, don't they? Especially when they've had some physical connection. I truly did not want to scare my wife and daughter. But then, was I a ghost? True enough, I appeared to be dead, my body wasn't breathing anymore (despite its incredibly ruined state I had checked for any signs of breathing or heartbeat back in the hotel room), but I really *did . . . not . . . feel . . . dead!* It was becoming a mantra for me.

Andrea's soft-spoken words encouraged me to enter. The room was lit by a colorful *Winnie the Pooh* lamp, a gentle glow that only tempered the shadows,

---

*Let me just tell you about going through a closed door or wall:

You don't just flow through in an easy, fluid movement like a ghost does it in a movie. What happens is that for an instant you are part of that substance, be it wood, stone or cloth. With the last you become part of the fabric itself, a piece of the weave; with wood you're the very grain; with stone you're part of the dust that makes it. You mix with the atoms, integrate with them, become unified until you move beyond. It's more or less the same when you pass through a living body, only then you also become part of its memories and metaphysical nature; but more of that later.

rather than banishing them completely. Beneath the lamp on the pretty bedside cabinet stood Prim's little blue puffer, placed on the very edge so that it was within easy reach. Our daughter had suffered her first asthma attack more than a year ago and it almost broke my heart to know she was always so afraid of having another (she'd had four more since the first one) that the Ventolin spray was always close at hand, especially during the night. Some kids had their own personal security blanket; my little girl had her inhaler. I stood in the doorway watching for a long difficult moment. Andrea was sitting on the bed, with Primrose cradled in one arm, pillows propped up behind them. Her other hand stroked our daughter comfortingly as Andrea continued to speak in that low, calming voice.

"It was just a nasty old dream, darling," she was saying. "Nothing's happened to Daddy, I promise you."

In her arms, Prim clutched Snowy, her favorite teddy bear whose fur used to be pure white but was now faded to a light yellowish gray. I'd given her Snowy on her third birthday.

"But he didn't answer the phone, Mummy." Light glistened off cheeks that were still not dry from earlier tears.

"I know, but it was very late and Daddy has been working very hard. He was probably sound asleep."

"You tried his mobile too."

"Yes, but it was switched off."

"He always keeps it by the bed."

"The hotel would already have a phone right next to the bed. He wouldn't need his mobile."

"Then why didn't he hear the hotel phone?"

"Because he must be exhausted. You know how hard Daddy is to wake up when he's been working too hard."

"But I'm afraid, Mummy."

"I know, Prim, but there's no need. I'll ring again first thing in the morning. You'll see, he'll answer it then and wonder what the fuss is about."

"In the dream he was very lost."

"You always get anxious when Daddy's away. Remember when you cried because you thought he'd fallen down some stairs? That was a long time ago, wasn't it? And when he got home, nothing at all had happened to him, had it?"

I remembered the incident. While it was true that nothing had happened to me physically, it was an afternoon when I'd spontaneously gone out-of-body while sitting at my desk and half-falling asleep. I'd been surprised to find myself in this other realm without any warning and had had no control whatsoever. In the OBE I was at the top of a tall building, standing on the very edge of the roof (it was a familiar building some miles away from my office and I had no idea how I'd got there) and about to take a step forward. Well, whereas if in control I would have glided to a safer place, this time I fell. Really it was no more than what sometimes occurs in a normal dream, where you seem to take a wrong step off a pavement and the sudden jolt wakes you, but in this instance the location was a little more serious. And, as if in a normal dream, I was instantly awake, my whole body no doubt jerking with surprise, and I almost *did* fall off my chair, but I managed to save myself in time. Fortunately, I was alone in the office I shared with Oliver, or I would have had to endure his laughter and teasing for the rest of the afternoon. My heart was beating a little faster than usual, but otherwise I was okay; it was only later I learned that around the same time—about four in the afternoon—Primrose, who was belted up in the back of Andrea's little Peugeot on their way home from school, had given a small scream and burst into tears, proclaiming that her daddy had fallen down some stairs and hurt himself.

I hadn't revealed what had actually happened to me when I got home that evening, because I really didn't grasp the connection when Prim ran down the hallway to tell me of her outburst and to make sure I wasn't hurt. I laughed and reassured her that I was fine, there had been no accident earlier, and it was only when I was in bed that night that I related the two incidents. Even so, I dismissed it as coincidence, but now, in the doorway, I began to wonder.

"Can't you phone again now, Mummy?" Prim was persistent.

"No, darling. Daddy would be cross if we woke him. It's not long till morning, so we'll call him together then. Perhaps if his work has gone well he'll be coming home." She leaned down to kiss Prim's freckled nose, then said, "Time for you to go to sleep too. You'll be in a grumpy state all day if you don't."

"Andrea," I said, stepping further into the room. "I'm here. I'm fine. There's nothing wrong."

I don't know why I made that last remark: maybe I wanted to believe it myself. In fact, I don't know why I even spoke: previous experience in out-of-body had taught me I couldn't be heard. Nevertheless, the practice of a lifetime was hard to break. Besides, if my daughter had the insight or intuition to sense something bad had happened to me, then perhaps she might see and hear me now.

"Something's happened to my body," I told them both, "but I'm all right. I'm not dead, you must believe me."

"Come on now." Andrea eased her arm from Prim's back and laid the pillows flat. "Lie down and go to sleep." She bent to kiss the top of Prim's head then pulled the flower-patterned duvet up to our daughter's chin. Primrose wasn't pacified, but she was tired, her eyelids drooping even though she fought to keep them open.

"I won't sleep, Mummy," she said.

"Ssssh. You will. Think nice things."

Prim pulled a disgruntled face, but it was half-hearted. I knew she'd be asleep within moments.

Andrea switched off the bedside lamp before standing, then walked soft-toed to the door. She stepped through to the landing, turned to look back at our child once more, and then half-closed the door behind her. I lingered a while by Prim's bed and sure enough, she had already fallen asleep. I tried to brush a stray curl from her closed eyes and my fingers made no contact. With a last, regretful stare at her innocent shadowy face, I turned away and followed my wife.

I found her sitting on the edge of our own bed, her eyes fixed on the phone on the small bedside cabinet, one hand resting beside it. Her bedside lamp was switched on. I could tell she wanted to ring the hotel again, her anxiety plain to see but, sensibly enough—although I clenched my fists tightly in anticipation—she let her hand fall away, obviously deciding it was too late to disturb me. She slipped beneath the covers and switched the lamp off.

"No," I cried, almost in tears. "No, Andrea. Ring the hotel, get someone to check my room. It's not too late, it can't be too late!"

I wondered if somehow she could hear my distant voice, because for a moment she rested on one elbow as if still pondering, wondering what she should do. But then, she laid down, one arm above the covers, and closed her eyes. In the pale-orange light from outside I could see the frown that disturbed her features. Soon though, the worry-lines eased and her face was smooth again. Andrea, too, was asleep.

In abject misery, I sank down beside her. I closed my own invisible eyes.

SIXTEEN

It was a strange gagging sound that roused me. I don't say "woke me up," because I didn't know if I'd been sleeping; I didn't know if it was possible to sleep in my condition (what a joy it would have been if I'd been woken from a nightmare).

I just opened my eyes at the noise and there I was, back in the hotel suite, lying on the bed beside my own butchered carcass. I didn't have time to consider whether or not some kind of instinct had drawn me back to the site of my own annihilation, an unconscious determination to rejoin my soul's host while my mind was blanked, because the uniformed waitress with the breakfast trolley was now standing in the doorway staring, gawping at the bloody, chopped thing on the bed with horrified eyes. Her jaw flapped and closed as she tried to summon up a scream.

It finally erupted in a piercingly high-pitched, bloodcurdling shriek, which was immediately followed by a series of wheezing staccatos of half-stifled, breath-catching screeches that scared the hell out of me. For a moment I thought she might suffer a seizure and I raised my hands, palms forward, as if to calm her.

She was the same sallow-skinned, dark-haired girl who had brought my breakfast the previous morning. Her instructions were to let herself directly into my bedroom if her knock failed to wake me (my bedroom had two doors, one of which led to the suite's sitting room, the other out into the hotel corridor. Oliver had a large bedroom on the opposite side of the sitting room). I'd tipped her generously the day before and although she seemed to understand little English, I think she was eager to please me with her efficiency; unfortunately, this morning she got something more than just a tip.

The poor girl, smart in her white shirt, green waistcoat and tight black skirt, fell back against the doorframe and for a second I thought she might pass out. Her pupils rolled back inside her head for a fleeting moment and her whole body swooned, but the doorframe itself kept her upright and she recovered enough to stagger out of sight. I heard her lumbering down the hallway (she was a heavyish girl) on unsteady legs, the semi-screams still struggling to reach full-voice again, and then it was quiet.

I turned my head and looked at my blood-coated remains. Oh dear God . . .

Early daylight coming through the open curtains did nothing to improve the scene. In the cold light of day, as it were, the sight was even more appalling. Last night the immediate shock must have numbed me from the full horror, because not everything had sunk in. I was now noticing more details without hysteria blanking me.

The blood was already coagulating, its color turning coppery, and my disorganized eyes were still gazing flatly outward, matt crescents between their lids. My nose was nothing more than shattered pulp resting within the bloody valley of flesh and bone that was my indented face. Just inside the lopsided rictus grin of a mouth I could see broken stumps of teeth resembling vandalized gravestones against their inky backdrop and, if I had been capable of vomiting, then I think I would have; I certainly felt nauseous. My chin was a crooked peak, but otherwise okay, the worst of the facial damage just above it.

It occurred to me that somebody would have to identify my body and a fresh revulsion swept through me. My God, it might have to be Andrea. I groaned silently at the thought.

The rest of me had been battered too, both my arms broken, one at the wrist, the other at the elbow—maybe I had tried to fight off the attacker (but how could I if *I* wasn't there?)—and one of my legs was twisted awkwardly at the knee, the kneecap itself pulped, my ripped trouser leg messy with glutinous, hardening blood. There were deep cuts all over my body and my head was almost severed as if the neck had been sliced by some sort of small chopper or axe. Whoever had attacked me *really* wanted me dead.

The wounds were crude and a great flow of viscous-looking blood ruined the pale-green bedspread, overspilling its sides and running down onto the carpet below. Its edges had hardened, the color very dark.

"Oh God . . ." I whispered, still contemplating my lifeless form with tear-blurred eyes, I shuddered at the damage done to my chest and stomach, where blood had poured copiously, even now small bubbles forming every few seconds or so, as though pockets of air were escaping the wound. I noticed something protruding from below my left ribcage, blood almost covering it. It was small and round, but before I could inspect it, something else distracted me. The zip of my trousers was open. Because of the thickness of blood that had welled there, I could not tell—nor did I honestly want to know—exactly what damage had been done. In fact, I didn't even have to guess, because something lay between my outstretched legs, a mound of bloody meat that had been removed from my groin and slapped down on the soft bedcover, an abstract genital pile, the sight of which now had me retching again.

As I bent over my knees I heard heavy footsteps hurrying along the hall outside my room. Still retching, pointlessly because I had nothing to bring up, I retreated into the corner of the room.

Oh, it was a long day. A terribly *long* day. And I stuck around for most of it.

Where else would I go? What else could I do?

I hunkered down in the corner in abject misery and watched the comings and goings, the shock and utter dismay of the hotel's under-manager and concierge, who had rushed to the room after the room-service waitress' hysterical alert, then the horror of the manager himself and the small posse of staff he'd brought with him, later the calm reaction of the first uniformed police officer to arrive. By the time two plainclothed detectives bustled in I was just a traumatized wreck.

"Help me," I croaked pitifully, not even bothering to rise to my feet because I knew there was no chance of being seen, let alone heard.

Eventually the room was cleared of everybody save the detectives, who reprimanded the first cop for not having cleared the crime scene immediately. The professionals soon arrived and took over. Some wore all-in-one white shell suits and I assumed they were the forensic scientists. The police surgeon, careful not to get blood on his civilian clothes and shoes, examined my body. With an ironic grin he pronounced me dead. One of the guys in white took photographs before another one took measurements of blood splatters and drifts. Yet another used a camcorder, and all the while the two detectives conferred in hushed tones, as if they didn't want the corpse to overhear.

An extremely tall gray-haired man with a jet-black mustache and matching eyebrows entered and the two detectives acknowledged him with respectful nods. The uniformed policeman at the door saluted him.

His stature was impressive, his back ramrod straight, his charcoal-gray suit immaculately pressed. He went immediately over to the police surgeon, who was making notes on a pad.

"Detective Superintendent Sadler," the newcomer announced without extending a hand to shake.

The medic just gave him a curt nod. "Dr. Breen," he said, looking back at his notes. "Too early to give you anything."

"Hazard a guess at time of death?" DS Sadler asked, his tone implying little hope.

"You'll need a proper autopsy for that."

"Do your best."

"Well, the body—what's left of it—is still warmish, but then the room temperature is quite high. I could take a quick rectal reading, but I imagine you don't want anything disturbed at this stage."

The policeman grunted something that must have been agreement and the police surgeon went on.

"Lividity is underway as far as I can tell—and the state of the body itself doesn't help—but the pathologist will have a clearer time of death after the post-mortem."

"But rigor mortis . . .?"

"Oh yes, that's certainly begun, but you're aware of how unreliable that can be when determining these things."

The detective superintendent's impatience was made apparent. "Good God, man, I only asked for a rough estimation," he said gruffly.

"Eyelids frozen, muscles of what's left of the jaw stiff. Same with neck and upper chest, but the corpse's disarray and loss of blood make it difficult to assess."

Dr. Breen caught the grimness and steely-eyed severity of the tall policeman's gaze and hurriedly proffered his informal judgment.

"Death definitely occurred more than three hours ago and I'd guess it was closer to six, maybe a bit more than that."

DS Sadler wasn't quite finished with him yet.

"And . . .?" he demanded brusquely.

"And? And what?" The police surgeon obviously wasn't used to blunt interrogation and it showed in his irritated frown.

"Is it another one?" asked Sadler.

"We think it is, Sir," Simmons, one of the detectives, put in, stepping forward and carefully avoiding a glob of thick blood on the carpet as he did so.

"Through the heart?" queried the detective superintendent.

"Yep. You can just see it under the ribs if you look closely."

The senior policeman took his detective's word for it.

"So we have yet another victim."

"Could be a copycat," suggested the second detective.

"Don't be bloody daft, Coates," Sadler said crossly. "Actual cause of death is not public knowledge."

Coates' face reddened. "Yes, Sir."

I looked up and stared at them all, almost but not quite shaken out of my torpor. What did he mean, "Actual cause of death is not public knowledge?" I was confused for a moment, but then it began to come together. The tall man had asked if it—*it* being me, my stone-dead corpse—was another one, obviously meaning another *victim*. And one of the detectives, the one called Coates, had suggested it could be a *copycat murder* implying I was one of a series. I might be dead, but I was still alert.

What was it that the public didn't know, though? I began to pay even more attention.

"It's there all right." It was the police surgeon, Breen, who spoke up.

All eyes, including mine, turned toward him.

"Hole through the heart?" said Sadler.

A grave nod of the doctor's head. "Yes. Underneath the left side of the ribcage and straight up. As in all the other cases. Hard to find at first, with all the blood. But the flat end of the needle is there all right."

I remembered the blood-covered bump I'd noticed earlier.

"And that's what killed him?"

"Well, I hope the mutilation came afterward, for the victim's sake, but I don't think so. The pathologist will let you know for sure. If already dead, the blood flow would have been heavy, but not as fierce as it would have been if the victim were still alive.

"Look." He pointed with his pen. "The thigh's femoral artery has been cut through. If the victim had still been alive at the time, the blood would have escaped in a spurt that might even have reached the ceiling." The three men looked up: the high ceiling was pure white. "But, as you can see, it gushed in a great arc that reached well beyond the bed, almost as far as the wall, which suggests to me the victim's face was cleaved first, killing him instantly, the other weapon used afterward. The main flows have soaked the carpet, and there are splatters everywhere, some quite a distance from the general spillage, although they were probably caused by the action of the first weapon itself, sinking into the body and jerked out again with considerable force. Looks to me as if the instrument used, by the way, was a butcher's chopper, or something similar. I've seen their kind of deep wounds before. Forensics will let you now for sure."

"Whoever did this must also be covered in blood. Surely someone on the staff had to see the killer leave."

Simmons shook his head resignedly. "Night porter and the lobby reception guy, who were still on duty, spent most of the time in the office behind the counter, saw no one suspicious and certainly no one with blood on their clothes. In fact, not one guest arrived or left."

Coates spoke up. "There is a back entrance to the place. For staff and workmen, small deliveries, that kind of thing."

"Unattended?" snapped Sadler.

" 'Fraid so," Coates told him. "At least, some of the time. There is night security, an open cubicle near the door, but the guard on duty frequently leaves it to do his rounds."

"Wasn't the door locked?"

"No, Sir," Simmons replied. "Night staff and early morning cleaners are using it all the time."

"There has to be a bigger delivery area."

"It's in the basement. Heavy vehicles get to it by a ramp leading from the road outside."

"Locked though, Sir," added Coates. "It's a big roll-up door and it was closed for the night. No deliveries were expected."

Sadler considered all he had been told for a few moments, then: "Right, I want you to interview every person who was on duty during the night and early hours. No doubt the manager or the under-manager will supply a list of personnel. Question the night porter and the receptionist again. They may remember something they've forgotten. Oh, and the security man also. Prompt him—he might just come up with something useful."

There were raised voices in the next-door room, the lounge area, and I thought I recognized one of them. Hurried footsteps, the rustle of my layouts from yesterday being trampled on, a sharp, "You can't go in there," followed by scuffling noises, and then Oliver was in the bedroom doorway.

"Oh . . ." is all he said, but it was an agonized sound, a soul-wrenching sound. Horror, shock, disbelief whitened his face and highlighted the few faint scattered freckles on either side of his nose. He stared at my blood-drenched remains on the bed.

"Jim . . .?" I heard him say in a breathless whisper.

I realized he could only assume it was me lying there.

"Who are you?" Sadler barked at him.

Another uniformed policeman was behind Oliver, holding his arm to drag him away. "I couldn't stop him, Sir," the annoyed policeman grumbled. "He pushed past me."

"Leave it for a moment," his superior ordered. The PC released his grip.

"What . . . what's happened?" Oliver's voice was hoarse now, strained, as if he could barely force the question.

One of the detectives moved toward him to block his view.

"It's all right, Simmons," said the chief. "Let's hear what he's got to say." He addressed Oliver directly. "I'm Detective Superintendent Sadler from New Scotland Yard, and this is Detective Sergeant Simmons and Detective Constable Coates. Now will you please tell me your name?"

Oliver raised both hands to his face to block out the sight on the bed. Somehow he couldn't quite cover his eyes, though, and he continued to stare over Simmons' shoulder through slightly spread fingers at my blood-covered carcass.

"Okay, get him back into the other room," Sadler ordered, striding toward my distraught friend.

The uniformed policeman took him by the arm again and Simmons gently guided Oliver backward. Sadler disappeared next door with them and I followed.

My campaign layouts, scuffed and in disarray, lay on the thick-carpeted floor and Oliver was led through them toward an armchair; he was carefully helped to sit.

"Will you tell me your name, Sir?" repeated Sadler, his voice less harsh this time, but still authoritative.

"What?" was all Oliver could utter. He was staring back at the doorway to the bedroom, but his eyes were unfocused.

"Your name," Sadler said again.

I settled in a corner by one of the long windows as if to be unobtrusive.

"Oliver Guinane," my copywriter managed to say.

"And do you know who the dead person in the other room is?" he was asked.

No doubt the detective superintendent knew my name already. They would have been told who occupied the suite by the management and, as Oliver was sitting in front of him, it was a fairly safe bet to assume the corpse was James True. Nevertheless he watched Oliver closely.

"It's Jim . . . James True. He . . . he was my partner."

"Life partner or business partner?"

Ollie's attention was finally distracted from the open doorway and he peered up at Sadler, incomprehension masking the shock for a moment.

"Did you work together or did you live together?" the senior policeman asked patiently.

"We worked together." Ollie was too dazed to be offended. "He was my art director. We have our own advertising agency, gtp—Guinane, True, Presswell." He looked at the faces around him as if expecting them to know of our company. Nobody said a word, but I did notice one of the detectives, the one called Coates, give Ollie an odd look.

"We hired the suite so we could spend the weekend working on a pitch for a new client without being interrupted. We do that now and again, you know, when it's important."

Now he was gabbling too much. Still in shock, I assumed.

Sadler cut through it. "How do you know it's James True lying there. The face is unrecognizable."

Oliver cringed; the image of the chopped heap next door had almost overwhelmed him once more.

"I . . ." He paused, gathering himself. "It has to be Jim. It's his room. And the clothes . . ."

"They're shredded and bloodstained."

"The shoes. Jim always wears . . ." He shook his head. "I mean, always wore old Nikes when we brainstormed; they were comfortable, familiar. Jim said he'd had his best ideas wearing them and it was true. They're old and worn, but they were a good-luck kind of thing to him."

"Despite the mess the body's in, you managed to notice the shoes?" It was Simmons who asked the question.

"Yes. Yes. They were the only part of him that wasn't covered in blood."

"When did you last see Mr. True?" It seemed Sadler was satisfied with the identification.

"Uh . . ." Oliver blinked at the senior officer. "Uh, late last night. We . . ." He stopped mid-sentence as if suddenly aware of the implication.

"One of the hotel staff heard loud shouts coming from this room last night," said the detective called Coates.

"Uh, yeah. Yes, that was us." Ollie returned his attention to the superintendent. "We had a bit of an argument. Nothing serious," he quickly added. "Just a normal disagreement about work. Happens all the time."

"Does it really," Sadler remarked dryly.

"Yes, yes it does. It's never serious."

"Is that why you left the hotel? I'm informed that you were both guests here."

"That's right. If we hadn't had a row I'd have just gone off to my own bedroom. Things would have been resolved more easily after a good night's sleep. We were both incredibly tired, we'd been working non-stop since Friday."

"You said your argument wasn't serious, yet you stormed out of the hotel. You didn't just go to bed."

They all watched him silently.

"Look, if you're implying . . ." Some of the old Oliver was finally breaking through. He was getting angry.

"I'm not implying anything, Mr. Guinane. I'm merely trying to establish the facts. You left the hotel, so where did you go?"

There was just a beat before Oliver replied. "I went home, of course. I'd had enough. I was exhausted, stressed—I had to have a break."

"Did your . . ." Sadler considered for a moment, "*words* with Mr. True lead to violence?"

"Good God, no! Jim and I are friends. We're friends. There was nothing serious in what we said to each other."

"The porter collecting breakfast cards outside another door claims the argument he heard sounded violent."

"He's exaggerating. Jim and I would never come to blows. God, we've known one another for years." He looked up appealingly at the tall policeman. "I would never hurt Jim."

Sadler gave a slight nod of his head as if absorbing all he'd heard. He turned away from Oliver and went to the window where he nudged back one side of the lace curtains to study the street below. He was only a couple of feet away from me and I could tell there was a lot more deliberation going on beyond those cold blue eyes.

"Tell me precisely what the argument was about," he said, still looking through the glass.

Ollie shook his head in frustration. "It's complicated. Primarily it was about the creative work for a prospective client, but it went on from there."

"Oh?" Sadler turned back to Oliver and I caught the other detectives glance at each other.

"Another company, a big agency, wanted to merge with us."

"*Swallow us up, Ollie!*" I wanted to shout.

"Jim was against it, I was for. But look, it wasn't serious enough to kill him over. It would have been resolved, just as all our little spats are."

"So you often argued, then," said Simmons.

"God, no." Oliver shook his head vehemently. "That is, yes, but it was never serious, it was always over small things."

"Merging with another company?" said Simmons with scorn in his voice. "Sounds serious enough to me."

"That'll do, Simmons," Sadler said curtly. He looked as if he had other things on his mind now. "Mr. Guinane, we could take your home address and phone number from the hotel register, but I'd appreciate it if you gave it to one of my officers before you leave."

Oliver nodded anxiously, as though he were eager to please. You'd have thought he had something to feel guilty about.

"Also, before you go," Sadler added, "can you tell me a little more about James True?"

"You're certain it is him, then?" Oliver almost looked hopeful that there might be some mistake. "I mean, his face . . ."

"You assured us it was a few moments ago. Why would you think otherwise now?"

"I don't." Oliver lowered his head into his hands and his voice was muffled. "It was just . . . just . . ."

"I know it's hard to accept, but we have no reason to believe the body belongs to anyone else but James True. His name was in the hotel register, along with yours. Despite the facial damage, his dental records will confirm his ID because the lower jaw is almost intact. I'd imagine some reconstruction work could be done on the upper jaw without too much trouble. What I'd like you to tell me is, what kind of man was he? You must have known him very well."

Oliver lifted his head again and his hands flapped limply over his knees. "He was a good friend. He was just, you know, a regular guy. A bit self-contained, I suppose, he never really gave much of himself away. But he had a good sense of humor and, of course, he was very talented."

"A very successful man, I would expect," surmised Sadler while one of his officers made notes.

"Yes, very. Together we were a great team. Although I'm the copywriter and Jim is . . . Jim *was* the art director, we interchanged a lot. Generally we both came up with ideas, but sometimes he thought up good copy lines while I had layout ideas. Our track record speaks for itself."

Oliver paused, as if it were difficult to continue. He stared blankly at the carpet.

"Was he married?" Sadler persisted.

My friend nodded.

"Did he have any children?"

At that, Oliver finally broke down and wept.

The chief superintendent stepped toward him and placed a hand on Ollie's shoulder. "Please try and answer my questions, Mr. Guinane. Then you're free to go."

"Jim had a daughter. Primrose. She's only seven years old." Now he *really* broke down. The two younger detectives seemed embarrassed by his sobs.

"Just one more thing, Mr. Guinane. One more question for now, and then it's over. Try to answer me."

"Yeah . . . okay." Ollie found a handkerchief in his trouser pocket and dabbed at his eyes with it. "I'm sorry," he said, his voice shaking. "What did you want to know?"

"Just one thing." Sadler's somber tone had all the quality of an undertaker's. "Was James True a handsome man?"

SEVENTEEN

It was a lousy day for me, as you'd expect.

I spent the best part of it chained to the hotel room, not because I wasn't free to go, but because I didn't want to leave. I couldn't face going away from my body, bloody and cleaved though it might be.

I slunk into different corners whenever someone came near, generally just keeping out of the way. Silly, I know, but it was hard to come to terms with the phantom I'd become: I still imagined people would bump into me. Besides, I didn't like that feeling I had when someone brushed through me, which they did twice when I went from the lounge into the bedroom, and *vice versa*. I got a weird sensation of assorted thoughts and feelings when it happened, a jumble of emotions that were entirely alien to me. A certain amount of chemical electricity was involved, much milder but similar to touching the wire of an exposed light switch. No more than a brief but uncomfortable buzz.

At one point in the proceedings, the bedroom telephone together with the one in the lounge rang and it was DC Coates who picked it up. He listened, then turned to his superior, who was watching.

"Hotel switchboard, Sir," Coates said quietly, as if in deference to my corpse. "Mrs. True is on the line, wants to speak to her husband."

"Tell them to say he can't take the call right now," advised Sadler. "I'll be leaving here soon to go to True's home address. I want to break the bad news to his wife myself."

I jumped to my feet and kind of glided across the room to reach the phone, but Coates had already given instructions and was replacing the receiver when I reached it. I had no idea what I'd have done if I'd got there in time. Andrea would have been unable to hear me and what would I have told her anyway? "Hey, honey, I'm a ghost." Nonexistent heart twice as heavy, I slunk back into my corner.

More white-clad figures appeared, then left. More photos were taken, more video-filming done, including the lounge and Ollie's bedroom. Blood splatters and even minute spots were measured in relation to my corpse. A Home Office pathologist arrived and, together with the superintendent, examined me more closely, their conversation kept to a low murmuring.

Finally, the pathologist, who was a woman, straightened and I heard her say, "The autopsy will tell us a whole lot more."

Sadler said, "Make it priority," and the pathologist organized my body's removal. A polythene body bag was brought in and I was carefully loaded into it. I admit, I turned away at that point, and I groaned with self-pity when the bag's zipper was pulled up over my head so that my defiled carcass was completely hidden from view. The ratchet sound seemed so final. I only heard myself being carried from the bedroom because I refused to watch.

The police chief (I'd heard him referred to as SIO, which presumably means Senior Investigating Officer) conferred with his two detectives, then gave further instructions to the forensic team. Fibers from the bedroom's carpet and the blood-soaked quilt were to be taken and a close inch-by-inch search of not just this room, but the lounge area and second bedroom, was to be undertaken. Of course blood samples would be used to ensure they all matched (the sick bastard who had even chopped off my genitals might have bled too if there had been a struggle, although the best guess was that my heart was pierced while I lay zonked out on the bed), and naturally everything was to be dusted for fingerprints (of which there would be many—mine, the maid's, workmen's, previous guests' . . . the list would be extensive). Apparently satisfied, Sadler departed from the crime scene and I wondered if he would go straight to my home with the awful news.

Oh, dear God, I thought. *How will she take it? And how will she tell Primrose? They'd both be devastated. No, worse than that, much worse.* This time I didn't bawl: I wept. I wept quietly for my wife and daughter.

The tears fell until I finally ran out of them. I drifted through to the lounge and found a different corner to mourn in. Dropping to the floor I raised my knees, wrapped my arms around my shins, and rested my forehead on my kneecaps. I've no idea how much time went by,* but eventually I found myself

---

*Time is a funny thing in this strange dimension I'd found myself inhabiting. There are kind of blank-outs, whole bits go missing, like in dreams; or like in movies, where every scene is usually relevant to the plot rather than following a natural linear, moment-by-moment progression. Maybe you sink so far down into your own psyche that you reach the subconscious level, which might preclude any tangible thoughts and images. I mean, even if you're big on dreams, you never ever spend the whole night dreaming; there are long gaps from which you emerge into different scenarios once more.

alone. It wasn't dark outside, but shadows were long and the streets below were filled with even more traffic and pedestrians. Obviously it was rush hour, which lasted a couple of hours, sometimes more as this was London.

I cursed myself. I should have left with the senior cop, followed him to my home, maybe even hitched a lift in his car so that I could be there when he broke the news. It was time to go home: I was desperate to be with my family.

I suppose I could have passed through the building's thick outer wall and floated down to the busy street below, but for some reason that I couldn't quite fathom, I opted to take the normal route. I kind of walked/drifted through the suite's closed door and the blue-and-white exclusion tape strung across it, past the uniformed cop on guard duty, then along the high-ceiling hallway to the stairs. I could have taken the lift, but how would I have pressed the buttons? I passed one or two people along the way and did my best to avoid contact with them, just as if my body was solid.

There were a lot of journalists and photographers in the reception area, those by the lifts being held at bay by the frustrated under-manager and a surly porter. I slunk by them all like a celeb trying to avoid paparazzi—irrational, I know, because I was perfectly aware that I could not be seen, but I was not as yet used to the condition.

Outside, the street was full of bustle: traffic, commuters hurrying by, pretty girls in short skirts, long skirts, or sexy trousers. Every one of them had a place to go and lived inside their own bodies. Me, I'd become a bodiless nomad. Rudely disinterred from my own host body. A mystery even to myself. *Especially* to myself.

On this fine autumn evening, imbibers from the pub across the road spilled out onto the pavement and tables were set outside a nearby café, with several occupied by customers who, no doubt, were familiar with the Continental practice, a custom that never worked well when one of our winters came along. Despite the chill in the air they all seemed happy enough, which seemed particularly cruel to me. Illogically, I wanted them to share my misery, needed them to empathize with my acute loneliness. I think really I just yearned for them to be aware of my plight. Or maybe I wanted to be among them in human form.

Uhhh! Someone had walked straight through me. It was most definitely imaginary, but I thought I felt myself sucked along with the person for a brief moment, a sensation so slight, so subtle, that I wondered if it had really happened.

I gave a little shiver and pushed away the memory of his sour visions; yet I experienced an unexpected regret at having left him. The man walked on, unaffected it seemed, save for the sudden familiar "someone-walking-over-my-grave" shudder he gave.

Pulling myself together, I moved away from the hotel steps and drifted along the pavement, catching a shoulder or arm now and again, passing through any body when it could not be avoided. But then I became aware of something new that was weird and a little worrying: I seemed to be tuning in to the collective consciousness. By that I mean I was beginning to experience the unspoken words of these rush-hour people, their intellections: their imaginings, notions, perceptions, cogitations, deliberations and reflections, together with their shared apprehensions, *all* their cerebral musing suddenly breaking through and coming at me like a great tidal wave of mass thought, so that I had to squat against a wall and cover my ears as if it was their *noise* tormenting me, piercing my mind, not their conjoined brain yammerings. Almost overwhelmed, I crouched against the brickwork, pressing my hands against my ears even harder and yelling at the top of my own soundless voice to mute their cacophony.

Dear God, my mind screamed, *this is going to drive me crazy.*

Then, within seconds, something in me started to take control. It was as if I had some inbuilt protection unit that could nullify the "sound." This was my first lesson in asserting some governance over my new status—I think the mere wish to rebuff the assault, coupled with the "physical" act of blocking my ears and "yelling loudly" was the catalyst that exerted my own will and saved me from going loco. Ultimately, it was instinctive, just as many actions in real life are.

Eventually, I got to my feet and moved cautiously onward. I realized it would probably take the best part of an hour to reach home at this rate (had it taken that long to get back to the hotel last night? I couldn't remember) and I became impatient. Experimentally, I tried leaping into the air, arms and legs straight in superhero mode, and kicking off with my toes. I could have been a normal human being for all the good it did. I rose about ten inches before settling down on concrete again. Cursing, I tried once more and the result was the same. I thought of those floating dreams again, and as I did, I was back in the air, just a couple of feet for sure, but learning another lesson about myself.

On the pavement once more, I willed myself to float—no, I *imagined* myself floating—and that was when I rose anew. The earth still had some gravitational pull, because I sunk yet again, although I now had some idea of how it was done. Just as in the old dreams, I thought of myself in the air, launched myself, and there I was riding high.

Whooping with glee, despite the dull heaviness in my heart, I pushed—*imagined*—myself a little further this time, and further I went. In spite of my troubled mind, I gloried in this small achievement. In truth, it was exhilarating, a tiny oasis of delight in a wretched day. I was airborne, had risen above mere mortals—*that sudden conceit caused me to think on.* Was I truly lost to this world, then?

Traffic and people passed beneath me and I gazed down at both with wonderment and trepidation. I asked myself the same question, but in different ways: *Was I really dead?* I mean, do *ghosts* get excited?

"Couldn't be dead," I said to myself as I sank back to earth. I just didn't *feel* dead, I kept reminding myself. But I'd stood over my own vandalized corpse, so I *had* to be dead. Then why was I here, gliding through the air, invisible to my fellow-men in human form, but aware of everything around me? *I think, therefore I am,* said Descartes, and he was a clever guy. Well, I thought, but did I exist?

I touched concrete without feeling a bump and immediately two young girls passed right through me. Just a *frisson* of alien incursion—a fleeting vision of a good-looking young guy, obviously the topic of the girls' giggly conversation. Something more though, a covert, brooding envy underlying the pleasure. Within the blink of an eye, I understood that one of the hurrying girls had a date with a new boyfriend, while the other girl, who pretended to share her companion's anticipation, secretly harbored a nasty streak of jealousy deep within her heart. The insight was quickly gone, but a sour memory lingered with me. I shivered, because the residue of bad will was slow to fade and tainted my own temporary lightness. I resolved to pay even more attention to oncoming strangers—these partial absorptions were way too unsettling. (Interestingly, the one with the new boyfriend was the plainer of the two girls—I had caught a glimpse of their faces just before they walked straight through me—and it was the attractive one who was burdened with the envy.)

I stepped into the gutter and continued my journey, sweeping along the streets, making better progress when all I had to avoid was jaywalkers and cyclists. Once, at a road junction, I came down in the path of a single-decker bus and I couldn't help but scream as I cowered and covered my head with my arms. It was bad, but not as bad as I expected it to be.

For a start, there was no impact (obviously, not in my state) and the sense of metal, engine parts, oil, and people's lower bodies washing through me like fluid through a sieve (well, *something* like that) was no big deal. It happened so fast and there were so many passengers on board that their every perception dimmed the next, or mixed with it so none was clear. As a round color chart filled with different color samples will become completely white when spun, so the individual concerns and considerations melded into one, and were reduced to a senseless but subdued intrusion. It could be handled and that new lesson came as a relief: a mass assault would have quickly sent me crazy.

It became impossible to take any more pleasure in my flight, because primary concerns soon overwhelmed anything else. Anxiety became my driving force. I had to get to Andrea and Primrose, I wanted to be with them when they heard the news of my demise. Somehow—God only knew how—I had to offer them some comfort. If there was a way of letting them know I wasn't gone, that I was still around . . .

Minor incidents along the route are not worth mentioning here; suffice to say, that by the time I reached journey's end I'd learned more rules of my condition and was beginning to adapt. People passing through me, something that couldn't always be evaded every time, was something akin to a cold shiver, or sometimes, when it happened very swiftly, like a cerebral sneeze, a mild shock that shook me for only an instant.

Even so, by the time I reached home I was an emotional wreck, because pernicious traveling companions—fear, doubt, curiosity, bewilderment, apprehension—had accompanied me all the way. But finally I was there and I paused—hesitated?—at the entrance to the short drive as I had last time I'd journeyed home, but now for a different reason.

I suddenly felt completely inadequate.

As previously noted, time appeared to have little relevance in the new dimension I occupied, but the autumn sun was sinking behind buildings on the false horizon, leaving night and lengthening shadows to settle in. I was dimly aware that the trip from the heart of London into the near-suburbs shouldn't have taken *that* long, but at the moment other concerns took precedence.

My home stood in a broad, tree-lined avenue and was one of the rewards of my success, although I wasn't wealthy by any means, just comfortably off. Detached from its neighbors, with two cars inside the double garage—my BMW and Andrea's small new runaround, a green VW—the house comprised four bedrooms (one of them converted into a study/studio for me, another used as an exercise room for Andrea, and the other two as normal bedrooms), two bathrooms, downstairs cloakroom, a well-spaced hall, long lounge area with patio doors to the rear garden at the far end, dining room and fair-sized kitchen. At the front was the short drive I now lingered in, a small, neat lawn with a couple of flowerbeds to one side, and at the rear of the house another, larger garden.

I noticed there was no police car, liveried or unmarked, parked at the curbside.

I stood watching my home, emotionally but obviously not physically weary, until the sun was just an orange glow behind the distant buildings. I don't know why I stayed there—I think I was just afraid. Something within nagged at me, told me that when I confronted my wife and daughter and they neither heard nor saw me, then it would be final confirmation of my death. And that *really* scared me.

I'm not sure how long it was before I stirred myself—as I said, time had little meaning to me now and could be judged only by the actions of mortals—but eventually I resolved to face the truth.

I approached the heavy front door to my home.

EIGHTEEN

A second's obliteration of sight, the briefest sense of being inside, even being part of the wood grain itself, that's what I experienced when I passed through the front door. I became kin to its texture, its essence, and somehow I understood its growth as well as its roots (yes, literally; I had knowledge of the tree itself, when the oak was planted in the ground and drawing life from the earth and sky). But it *was* only an instant (by now you'll have caught the drift that time isn't quite what it seems to be).

Even as I emerged from the door into the hallway, stairs dead ahead leading to the bedrooms, a feeling of dread pushed oaks and grainy textures from my mind.

The place seemed empty. Certainly there was a coldness of atmosphere to it that I'd never experienced here before. One of my greatest pleasures in life had been stepping over the threshold of my own home after a good and fruitful day's work at the office and knowing someone was waiting for my return. Especially when it was Primrose waiting for me. But it was only at this precise moment that I appreciated just how *much* it meant to me, for now there was nothing. No sound of voices, no music, no small running footsteps. Nothing. But no, that wasn't quite right. It was the feeling of something *missing* that held me there.

I was suddenly afraid to move.

Surely the police, the detective superintendent called Sadler, should be here breaking the tragic news to Andrea, commiserating with her, asking questions about me? Had I got here ahead of him? But the place was quiet.

Maybe it had taken only minutes for me to reach here, I told myself. Maybe the journey was quicker than I thought and my timing was all askew. My family was not at home and the policeman hadn't yet arrived. Yes, that was it. There was no strange car parked by the roadside or in the drive, and perhaps Prim was being collected from school at this very moment. But then, outside, the blood-orange sun was already settling behind the spread of buildings to the west and I'd left the hotel when it was high and brighter in the sky. I checked my wristwatch.

Yes, it was there all right, although I had to pull my shirtcuff back to see its face.* It was a reflex action because *I did not feel dead.* The digits told me it was 1:32 A.M. But that was impossible. It was not yet dark enough outside. And anyway I couldn't have lost that amount of time getting here from the hotel. It wasn't possible! Then it struck me: 1:32 A.M. was the time of my death. That was the precise moment natural things stopped for me. The shirt and trousers I was wearing (I had no jacket) and the watch on my wrist accompanied me into this other existence because they were an intrinsic part of me. Somehow I knew that the digits on the watch would always be set at the same time unless I concentrated hard to make them change, and the clothes I wore would never need cleaning or ironing as long as I didn't "see" them as disheveled. This awareness seemed to come as naturally to me as other realizations surely would.

The digression was quickly over with and my thoughts returned to the house's emptiness. And that was when at last I heard the small sniffling sounds, then the murmur of a soft, soothing voice. Andrea's voice, Prim's sniffles. I hadn't heard them until now because I was too out of my mind with anxiety to take in much else.

I moved fast. I walked or glided, I don't know which, through the open door to my left, following the sounds. They were sitting cuddled together on the long sofa in the lounge, arms entwined round each other, Prim's small head buried into her mother's chest. It was such a heart-rending sight that my own eyes stung with tears.

I rushed to them and tried to smother them in my embrace, but of course, there was no contact, only an unintended sinking into their flesh. I pulled away, startled, even though by now I should have known what could happen. But I'd been caught off guard and I guess, under the circumstances, it was

---

*This is just one of the many peculiar things about being out-of-body. You assemble everyday clothes and accessories upon yourself, your hair is combed the way you usually comb it and it can become mussed when you mess with it; you even wear shoes when walking isn't essential. I knew if I put a hand in my pocket I could pull out a handkerchief, because I existed in a state of false normalcy, so subconsciously I equipped myself with normal paraphernalia, even though those things and I have no substance. I think it's just a way of preventing your mind from going AWOL; you cling to things that are familiar in order to maintain some kind of reality you can work with.

understandable. I backed off: the utter misery I'd partially absorbed from them was even worse than my own. I could only gaze at them.

While journeying through the streets, and even as early as back there in the hotel suite, I'd been aware of a kind of fuzziness around individuals, shallow halos that had not quite impressed themselves upon me enough to give them any thought—let's face it, I'd had plenty to think about at the time. When I inadvertently got too close to people (and remember I was doing my best to avoid them) I could see those halos more clearly, softish, but often bright vignettes surrounding each figure. I had accepted that these were each person's aura* and I had neither the time nor inclination to give it further consideration. Now I was witnessing it around my wife and daughter, a miserable dull gray that was dense in places. At this time I was not strongly attuned to the phenomenon, but it was definitely present and somehow it revealed their depths of misery even more clearly than Prim's sniffles and Andrea's tears. Obviously they'd been told the dreadful news and by the state they were in it must have been some time ago, because there was no hysteria in their grief, and no denial either, only resigned, sorrowful acceptance. It seemed they had come to terms with the reality of my death already, although I suspected that the full, unexpected horror of it would crush them again and again over the next few weeks, perhaps the next few months. If I'd had a heart, it would have bled for them, but as things were, I could only join in their pain.

Andrea was repeating the same soft mantra to Prim: "It's all right, baby, Daddy just passed away, he didn't feel a thing."

It seemed that, wisely, the whole story was being kept from Primrose, and I was grateful for that. I mean, how *do* you tell a little seven-year-old girl that her father was murdered and mutilated in the worst possible way by some sick maniac? Which words do you use? I prayed right there and then that she would never be told the full truth, not even when she was a grown woman.

I dropped to my knees on the plush carpet and whispered that I loved them both and that I had not left, I was still around, that I'd find some way to let them know.

---

*You've probably heard of Kirlian photography, by which rays emitted by any living thing are recorded on film. The process reveals that we are all surrounded by a kind of high-frequency electric field whose color range or level of brightness can indicate a person's state of health or wellbeing. Tumours and diseases, as well as damage to certain parts of the body, can be detected by the dullness or unhealthy murkiness of certain patches in the field. This "halo" can also be influenced by moods and imbalances of the mind.

What? Haunt my own family? Had disembodiment driven me crazy so soon? I'd seen the mangled state of my corpse. There was *no* coming back. But there had to be a way of making myself known. It happened in movies didn't it? What was that big hit several years ago, the one with Whoopi Goldberg and the two actors whose stars never rose as high again? The one where the husband or boyfriend is murdered but comes back and contacts his girlfriend through a medium. *Ghost,* that was it. Yeah, *big* hit at the time, but hardly rated at all in retrospect. Okay, that was pure Hollywood, but grieving widows and widowers visited mediums all the time, searching for some word from their lost loved ones. I'd always thought that that kind of thing was hokum, sheer nonsense, the greedy feeding off the needy, but hey, today I was clutching at straws. I'd try anything to make my family aware that I was okay, not the same, but generally okay. I know it was desperation, but I just could not bear their suffering. I had to do *something.*

I knelt, my hands touching but not feeling their shoulders (I was already learning ways to make my condition just a little more tolerable: I'd reach out and touch, and although I made no physical contact, by leaving my hands where they would normally have rested on the other person, I *imagined* I could feel. It was better than nothing).

"Don't worry for me," I said as if they could hear. "I'm fine, really. I didn't feel any pain, I didn't even know I was going to die." Maybe it wasn't helping them, but in a strange way it was helping me. What better way to go than when you're not there? No suffering, no fear—just, well, just oblivion. Only it wasn't quite oblivion, was it? No, it was discovery, *then* fear, this followed by all kinds of angst.

I was about to blubber, so I forced myself to snap out of it. Withdrawing my hands, I got to my feet and made a resolution. There was a reason for my condition and I was going to find out what it was. I was an enigma, a mystery to myself, and I determined to find the answer. And while I was at it, I'd discover a way to contact my precious wife and daughter. Hell, spirits spoke to the living through mediums all the time, didn't they?

Unfortunately, it was precisely at that point that Andrea gently nudged Primrose away from her and said: "I have to phone Nanny True, darling. I have to let her know about Daddy."

And my new resolve crashed.

While I hadn't felt close to Mother for many years now (if ever, in fact), the grief I knew my sudden death would cause her almost overwhelmed me with sadness. What's the old Chinese saying? *The torment of the gods is for your children to die before you.* It goes something like that. Anyway, that day I understood the adage perfectly. Despite her detachedness, she would be devastated at losing a second man in her life, my father being the first (despite her apparent disdain of him, there had to have been some love at the beginning). She had no close friends—she'd never courted friendship, for that matter—and although there was still Andrea and her granddaughter Primrose, she hardly ever saw them before my death, so I was pretty certain she wouldn't after.

I sat with Prim and tried not to listen to the one-sided conversation coming from the phone. Fortunately, Andrea kept her voice low, only the gravity of its tone reaching Prim and I on the sofa. My daughter had slumped with one cheek pressed against the back of the sofa, her brown eyes glittering with tears. Small catches of breath jerked her chest and shoulders every few seconds and her solitary sobs had become dry with repetition. I'd have given anything to hold and reassure her Daddy was okay, he was right there beside her and feeling no pain—no physical pain, at least. But I had nothing to give. What could a bodiless person possibly possess *to* give? Even a future was in serious doubt. So I used the new trick I'd learned: I put my arms around her and imagined they were making contact. I whispered loving things into her ear and hoped they would, in some mysterious way, get through to her. Oh God, I could feel her hurt and it was terrible to bear.

Andrea returned and her face was ashen. I saw that she was going to sit in the place I already occupied and I moved away, reluctantly relinquishing my imagined hold on Prim, but just as unwilling to undergo the added trauma of being "invaded" by my wife.

Prim snuggled into her mother's arms once again and looked up into Andrea's face. "What . . . did . . . Nanny . . . say?" Each word had had to be forced.

A child's question and perhaps the only way she could express concern for her grandmother.

Andrea's reply was as grim as her face was pallid. "Not much," she said.

Kneeling on the floor in front of them, I let go a deep sigh. No, it was more of a silent groan. I should have known Mother would deal with my death in her own remote way. Any wayward emotion would be kept in check in another's presence. Maybe she'd burst into tears once she put the phone down. Maybe. I wondered if she had even inquired how I'd died. Well, could be I was judging my mother too harshly, but it had taken a lifetime for that judgment to be formed. Let it go, I told myself without bitterness. Mother was Mother. Her self-preservation took its own line. I returned to my wife and daughter, who had no such hangups.

I don't know how long we remained there in that gloom-laden room, all of us weeping and scarcely moving—it could've been an hour or half an hour—but finally it was the sound of a car door slamming on the drive, then the doorbell ringing, that roused us.

Andrea gave Prim one last hug before rising and walking right through me as she went to answer the door. Briefly I felt that now-familiar disorientation as her psyche mixed with mine and misery piled on misery. But I'd also caught a curious hint of anticipation, a kind of reflex lightening of her mood which, while hardly shifting the grief, at least interrupted it for a moment.

I heard the front door open, then a loud sob that came from Andrea. The silence that followed was broken only by a few more muffled sobs. Rising smoothly—at least I had acquired a certain grace of movement in my new state—I went through to the hallway.

Andrea was in Oliver's arms, one of his hands in her hair, holding her head against his shoulder. His eyes were closed and there was nothing in his expression.

NINETEEN

I hung around the house for three days—I think (time continued to baffle me)—full of self-pity and anguish for my family. Outside, the weather had turned gray and drizzly, suitable for the general mood, I suppose.

I think I must have been afraid to leave everything that was familiar to me; somehow the contact helped maintain my own reality. Nothing could be mundane for me anymore, but at least the familiar offered a kind of sanctuary.

It was terrible to witness the suffering of my family and I searched for ways of letting my presence be known to them (I wasn't yet ready to leave the house and find a spiritualist). I tried to move objects, anything from ornaments on the mantelpiece to lace curtains; I spoke directly and loudly into Andrea's ear; I tried writing my name on a steamed-up bathroom mirror; I willed cups to rattle in saucers; I tried rapping on table-tops, kitchen counters, any hard surface that came to hand. Nothing, though. I made no sound, I caused no disturbance. I could only watch as a stream of visitors offering condolences came to the house—friends, neighbors, and of course my business partners, Oliver (again) and Sydney. Surprisingly, it had been Sydney who had formally identified my body, I learned—eavesdropping was a cinch when you couldn't be seen. Or maybe it wasn't surprising after all. It would have killed Andrea to view my mutilated corpse and my mother was out of the question. Oliver? To be honest, I'm not sure how he would have handled it. Badly, I'd guess, given his reaction when he arrived back at the hotel suite to see what was left of me on the bed. Underneath his bravura persona, he was quite a sensitive soul. Despite police suspicion he'd have been an awful choice of murderer. In fact, I think he would have been a disaster as a murderer.

The police came twice, asking the same old questions about dodgy acquaintances and outright enemies, but Andrea had nothing to give. The worst were the Press and television journalists who rang the doorbell night and day—*how does it feel to know that your husband was the fourth victim of a serial killer, are you satisfied that the police are doing their job efficiently, do you fear for your own life knowing that the murderer is still at large, do you have photographs of your husband we could take copies of?* It was intrusive and it was cruel. I would have done anything in my power to keep them away, but of course, I was helpless. The frustration and the sense of inadequacy were hard to bear.

Eventually, I became restless within myself. I don't feel I've ever been one for self-pity (never much cause before anyway), but I'd indulged too much in the aftermath of my death. Okay, maybe I had good reason, but basically I've always been an optimist and it seems to me that death should not necessarily erase the character you've developed during your lifetime. It wasn't exactly optimism that got me moving, though, more like curiosity, a compelling urge to discover more about myself and this dimension in which I existed. Also, I felt the need to find my murderer, and certain ideas were pushing their way through this great fog of misery and woe that had engulfed me.

First things first, though. I had a duty to call in on Mother. All right, it was more than duty—I wanted to see her, she was my only parent, after all. Yes, and I did love her. How can a son not love his mother? I made up my mind to leave my house and visit her. Besides, arrangements for my funeral and kind eulogies from well-meaning visitors (my canonization was due any day, I began to feel) were unsettling. I needed to get into the world again before I turned into a morose, reclusive ghost.

So I bade silent farewells to Andrea and Prim, whom I'd followed around during the day just to be near her (understandably she was being kept away from school for a while), sitting on the floor beside her bed at night when she slept; later I'd drift off to my own bedroom and lie down next to Andrea, throwing an arm over her, imagining I was real and could feel her. Purposely, I set out into my strange new world.

It was late afternoon as far as I could tell and the traffic flow from the city was already beginning to swell as I made my way to the wide main road. Prepared for a long haul—my mother lived close to the river on the east side of London—something happened that both surprised and pleased me.

My mother's image and the low-rent flat she lived in were strong in my mind, because I was thinking of her sitting in her old lumpy armchair, the curtains behind her possibly drawn closed so she would be in shadow (that was her usual mode of mourning, and by mourning I don't necessarily mean grieving for someone just passed away; any slight or upset that involved altercation with other people—might be the milkman delivering late, or a neighbor making too much noise—would send her off into one of her sulky moods). Just my staying out late when I was a teen—which I did a lot, I admit—was enough to send her into a grumpy retreat for a few days. Sunshine was never allowed into the room during that time, but the gap between the curtains would open an inch or so usually about the third day, widening from then little by little as the mood drained from her. It was irritating, but eventually I learned to take no notice. I'd carry on talking to her as normal and sometimes, if there was no response, I'd reply for her. I had many such self-conversations and I'm afraid it never improved the situation. In the end I'd begin to annoy myself, so I'd make an apology and finally—after the third or fourth one that is—it would be accepted. Full daylight returned to our front sitting room.

So that was what I was thinking of, except I saw Mother in a more distraught state, because this time my death would be the culprit. I usually endeavored to visit my mother at least once a week and the reception was always frosty if I was late, or had missed the previous week. Drawn curtains in summer, single lamplight only in winter. I pictured her there now, shriveled in her armchair, tear-stains blotching her plumpy face. Maybe she'd be holding a photograph of me in her trembling hands, possibly me as a boy and more manageable. *Just you and me, Jimmy,* she used to say then, grasping my small hand in hers and squeezing. *We don't need anybody else—and especially not him* (she meant my father, the absconded husband). *Just the two of us against the whole world.* Well that was fine when I was little, but when I grew up I got wiser and realized the whole world and its residents had a lot to offer. Eventually—around twelve, I guess—I rebelled and started to become my own person. Sure, I still loved her, but I wasn't certain that I liked her that much anymore.

Yet again, I digress. There I was, three (?) days after my body's death, breezing along—not quite gliding, but not quite walking either—with Mother's image and environment sharp in my mind, when suddenly, everything became *rushed.* That is, *I* was rushing, leaving my own surroundings far behind.

This was how I mostly arrived at places in my previous *living* OBEs. I'd think of a location that was known to me, or a familiar person, then with a blurred kind of flight, I'd be there. It was a bewildering but exhilarating experience, a "Beam me up, Scotty" affair without the dazzling column of starlights. For an instant, when I appeared before the person I'd had in mind, I was always sure that I could be seen, or that my sudden arrival had at least been sensed. I felt so real myself, you see. It took a beat for me to realize that my body had not come along for the ride.

And that's how it was again soon after my death. One moment I was moving along a main road, then everything kind of blurred and rushed, and I found myself in an unfamiliar part of the city. However, I was aware that I'd been brought closer to my mother's address. Concentrating hard this time, rather than just thinking of her, I experienced another blurred rush. Whatever had been accomplished instinctively in my previous dream-states, I realized, now had to be considered.

I found myself even closer to my mother's address, in a side street where the houses were run-down and the gutters littered. This time I knew exactly where I was and it took only a mental picture of Mother and her surrounds for the rush to start again and the journey to be completed.

Only a few inches of daylight shone through the narrow gap in the curtains, but at least she had the small table lamp on, which cast as many shadows as it defeated. And, yes, sure enough she was in her lumpy old armchair, sitting forward, leaning toward the low coffee table I'd bought her years ago. There were three photographs on its small surface, one of them black-and-white and torn into four pieces, the other two in color, both of me. The first, a shot when I was no more than ten or eleven years old, the other as a young man, when I'd graduated from art college with an NDD—National Diploma of Design. I looked good—smiling, happy, kind of confident in myself.

The torn monochrome was of an older man, but although the four pieces had been roughly assembled, they had not been tightly joined, the gaps between distorting the subject's features. It was a small photograph too, which didn't help; I couldn't recognize the man. Yet he—I could see that his hair was gray at the temples and that he was smiling—was somehow familiar to me.

I turned my attention to Mother and whispered to her that I was there but, naturally, there was no reaction. Her poor face was puffy, and the redness around her eyes indicated that a multitude of tears had been shed. Unusually for her, she looked untidy: the collar-less blouse beneath her thin beige cardigan was wrinkled, unfresh, and her skirt was rumpled too; she wore old carpet slippers and her tights or stockings were crimped around the ankles. Even her gray-brown hair was slightly messy; normally it was tightly set and not a single hair moved when she shook her head. Now it fell over her forehead in untidy locks while the rest was a confused tangle of curled snake-like clumps all over her head. Rarely had I seen her in a state like this. In fact, the last time she had been almost as distraught was on the day I told her I wanted to find my father (I was seventeen, if I recollect correctly, and it was shortly before my motor-bike accident). He might—according to her—have been a bad man, an awful husband and father, a person who drank too much and was obsessive about things that decent people did not mention aloud (I took it that she meant sex), but I'd insisted, told her, it was my right to know my own father no matter what kind of scumbag he might be. That was it: curtains closed, sitting in a sulk for the next five days, with a blotchy, tear-stained face, accusations that I was becoming just like him, didn't care for her anymore, that I was obstinate, bullheaded, and disrespectful—all this thrown at me, wearing me down bit by bit until I figured that finding my long-lost dad was more trouble than it was worth. I admit it—as far as women were concerned, whether they be Mother, girlfriends, or wife, I took the easy way. Can't stand moods, never could. Maybe because Mother always seemed to be in one. Anyway, like that time, when I was seventeen, this was just as heavy. Heavy, but at least understand-able. She'd lost her only son, hadn't she? And in the most awful way any mother could imagine.

I noticed her pinkish, transparent-framed spectacles were lying on the cof-fee table behind the photographs. I also noticed a bundle of letters on the car-pet by her feet. Curiosity taking over from the pity I felt for her, I went down on my knees beside the low table so that I could get a closer look at those let-ters. At first I thought they were letters of condolences for her recent bereave-ment, but now I saw that some of the envelopes were battered and old-looking. Peering even closer, I saw that the one on the top said: Master James True, with our old address beneath the name.

It was a jolt. *Why would someone have written to me at our previous address?* Leaning forward so that my head almost touched Mother's knees, I tried to dis-cern the postmark, but it was smudged. The envelope itself was light blue and the stamp was one I hadn't seen for many years. The other envelopes were of various sizes and mostly white; frustratingly, I could not riffle through them.

A tearful sigh, not quite a sob, came from Mother. I toppled over as she stretched forward, a reflex because I thought she might touch me and I didn't want to scare her. Silly, but I still hadn't become accustomed to my present state; there were all kinds of things yet to learn and, until I did, involuntary ac-tions or reactions would continue.

She reinstated her glasses on her nose, then picked up the most recent pho-tograph of me.

"*Traitor,*" she hissed with some venom.

I was shocked. I stared at her.

"*Just like him!*"

The "*him*" was almost spat out.

She took the color shot by its top edge, then slowly and deliberately tore it down the center. Putting one side over the other, she turned the picture and tore it down the center again. Because of the double-thickness, this was not quite as easy as the first tear, and she breathed an oath as she gripped it, her face as white as her knuckles.

I was shocked again. I'd never heard Mother swear before.

Scooping up the pieces, she mixed them with the other torn photo before leaning over and dropping them into the yellow metal bin on the other side of the armchair. Their sound as they hit the bottom was louder than it should have been because of the stillness of the room itself, the noise of traffic outside muffled by the curtains.

"*Bastard!*" Mother said again and I couldn't be sure if she meant me or the man in the black-and-white. "*Both bastards!*" she said as if to put me right.

I could not believe it. She was acting as if I had deliberately left her. In fact, the same stiff-faced expression that she'd used when I announced that I was leaving home to flat-share with friends, then when I told her I was getting married, now hardened her features. I'd witnessed similar solidifying countenances many times in the past, particularly when I inquired after my father, but they had never been quite as severe, nor as furious, as this one. This was bloody scary! This was Medusa on a bad-hair day.

I shuddered and wondered if it was my hideous death that had sent her over the edge. Then I reconsidered. She'd always been a *little* crazy, hadn't she? I mean, not outright, frothing-mouthed kind of crazy, but . . . disturbed. A hoarder of hurt feelings, a miser as far as warm regard was concerned. *Why did she hate me? What had I done? It wasn't my fault that I got killed. I had problems dealing with it myself. Did she think I'd deliberately deserted her? Did she assume I was just following my father's example? No, it didn't make sense. No sane person would blame a son for being killed. Not unless they really were insane . . .*

It came back to that again. I refused to admit it. She couldn't have been mad. But tearing up my picture . . . ? What was that all about? And I was beginning to guess who the gray-haired man in the black-and-white was.

In the meantime, as I was assessing the state of my mother's mind, she was reaching down for the letters on the floor. Several of them slipped through her podgy fingers as she picked them up and I was in like a dog whose supper bowl is ready. I quickly scanned the names and checked the addresses.

Every one of the aged envelopes bore my name and our old address except for two which still had my name, although the "Master" had been dropped, and this current address. What the hell was Mother doing with them and why hadn't she passed them on to me? It didn't make sense. What reason could she have for keeping them to herself? They hadn't even been opened.

Call me thick, but it did eventually dawn on me who had written and had kept on writing to me over the years. The old black-and-white photograph, torn but not thrown away—until now, that is, the letters addressed to our previous home, and then to Mother's current one, the house I had shared with her through the early teenage years. You didn't need to be a rocket scientist to work it out. The picture was of my father; the unopened letters were from him.

Oddly, I didn't feel rage toward my mother. A huge sadness descended on me, though. How could she do it? All right, even if he had deserted us, run off with some other woman for all I knew—Mother would never speak of it, preferring to let my own imagination do its worst—he was still my dad. Even if he was the vilest man on Earth, I still had the right to know him and judge for myself. Really, how *could* she do it?

I screamed *"No!"* as she began to tear up the letters, methodically, one by one, dropping the remnants into the bin by her side, and I tried to grab them, but of course, my scrabbling hand touched nothing. I beat on the carpeted floor with the heel of my fist in angry frustration, as if the noise alone would stop her. Naturally, there was no noise. I could have wept, I could have screamed my frustration over and over again. But all I could do in the end was watch.

I remembered the drawings and paintings of mine, the long essays in exercise books, short stories meant for my eyes only, all those personal treasures— treasures to *me!*—which she had blindly, *thoughtlessly,* thrown into the dustbin, never letting me know until it was too late and the refuse had been collected, *never* asking me. I hadn't hated her then, but I did now.

What had I been to her all those years? A son, or her possession? Had she never felt any real true love? If so, she would have talked to me, she would have confided in me. She would never have sulked every time I made plans of my own. It was the natural thing for offspring to stretch their wings, to learn for themselves, and finally to leave the nest, so why had she never accepted that? Why had she never welcomed Andrea as my wife? Why was she so aloof toward her grandchild, Primrose? Was she so selfishly wrapped up in her own ways and woes that there wasn't room for others in her chilly heart? But the prime question kept stalking me.

Was she nuts?

Terrible things to think about your own mother, I know, but remember what I'd been through. Murdered most foully, witness to my wife and daughter's grief, lost and alone without a body to call home. Who could blame me for being in a bitter frame of mind?

Those letters *were* from my father and she had kept them to herself for reasons of her own. Skunk, he might have been, but a kid needs to have some knowledge of its old man. And maybe he wasn't quite as rotten as she'd said. I'd heard only her side of the story. Years of poison. But now a brittle glimmer of doubt had opened up in my mind. Maybe, just maybe, he wasn't the swine she'd always led me to believe.

One by one she gathered up the letters that had fallen from her clutches, tearing each of them with growing vigor—and anger. By now the thunderous look on her face would have turned cream sour, the hateful beam of her eyes would have paralyzed rabbits. Spittle glistened on her lips and there was a drool at one corner of her mouth.

"*Bastard!*" she repeated again and again, and I wasn't quite sure if she meant the author of those letters or me. Better to think she meant the former, but it was still shocking. I wasn't sure what I'd expected visiting Mother—deep mourning or stoic fortitude—but it certainly wasn't this.

"*Bastard!*" Rip.

I stood and gazed down at her hunched shoulders, her spiteful hands, and frighteningly hard face, shaking my head with a different kind of sadness than before. This was a pitying melancholy, the anger in me held tight, restrained by the pity itself. Her head seemed to vibrate with her displeasure, the tangled "snakes" quivering as if truly alive. I wanted to leave, but stayed rooted to the spot. Her behavior was almost mesmerizing.

"*Bastard!*" Rip.

Then a word I would never in a hundred years have imagined my mother using.

"*Cuntcuntcuntcunt . . .*" Over and over.

At least it broke the spell. I'd backed off, over to the other side of the room, my startled eyes fixed on her as she dropped the strewn letters, picking up pieces and tearing them into even smaller pieces. What in God's name had happened to Mother? Had my death driven her over the edge, finally broken through that old, cold reserve she had always worn like a self-protective mantle? Or was this the true Mother, the monster lurking behind the respectable and reserved woman she showed to the rest of the world? Abruptly, I realized I didn't want to witness any more, and with this thought, I left my mother's home . . .

. . . To find myself beside my own corpse.

It was a stark, miserable room, with off-white tiles from floor to ceiling and frosted-glass windows on two sides. There were work counters filled with bottles, jars, bowls, and various kinds of metal instruments all around the walls, with cupboards and single drawers beneath them, glass-fronted cabinets above; these were crammed with more bottles and compounds, most of them brightly labeled and the only cheer in this gloomy place. When I say gloomy, I mean in aspect—two long fluorescent lights hung from the ceiling, but their brightness merely seemed to accentuate the unflinching drabness of the place.

Nearby was a round glass container of pinkish liquid standing on top of a cream-colored box with dials and switches, two clear plastic tubes running from it. It resembled a drinking-fountain, the type you get in American offices, but because of the color of the liquid inside I surmised that it was an embalming machine, because I knew I was in some kind of mortuary. Close to it on the counter was a tray filled with body plugs and eye caps, the latter obviously used to keep eyelids closed, and next to that an open jar with makeup brushes. Further along was a sink and swivel-headed tap, more jars and metal containers filling the worktops alongside and the shelves that ran round two sides of the room. A cushioned stool on wheels stood in one corner, while a small-wheeled utility trolley with two metal shelves, and a drawer beneath the lower shelf, was positioned next to a rectangular white porcelain table with raised lips around its edges and a drainage hole at one end. There was another table a few feet away from the first and both were identical and anchored to the tiled floor by broad central pillars; the only difference between them was that the former also held my cadaver. It was covered up to the hips by a green surgical drape, and my head was supported by a block behind the neck. Behind that was a water tap with a short hose attachment.

I shuddered when I looked down at my patched-up face.

I supposed they'd done as good a job as they were able, but it must have been impossible for the mortician to make me reasonably handsome again. I won't dwell on it, but although an effort had been made to restructure my skull—in other words, to pull the nose and forehead out again (they had been totally bashed in, remember)—it still looked as if it had been hit by a ten-ton truck. God, it was gruesome. Quasimodo's uglier brother. Frankenstein's lesser-known creation. I was a monster, a dead, disfigured monster. No open casket for me then.

The deep cuts over my chest and upper arms had been expertly sewn up with coarse, unfussy stitches; the mauve-to-purplish yellow discolorations of much of my skin resembled hideous body paint. Before I turned my head away in disgust, I noticed one other thing. In fact, I did a double-take. On my left-hand side at a point just below my ribcage was a slightly puckered wound the size of a small bead, a perfectly round puncture that was dark with dried blood.

I was leaning forward for closer inspection when a muted cough from somewhere behind distracted me. Still bent, I looked around and saw the figure of a man sitting at a desk in a small annex room to the mortuary. He was wearing a plain white coat and was busy scribbling notes in a pad on the desk. I wondered if he was writing a post-mortem report on me, but quickly realized he was more likely to be a funeral director than a pathologist, for neither room was excessively large, nor were there any body cabinets. No, I was being prepared for my own funeral, and that realization sent shivers through me.

It made me feel *really* dead.

The third place I visited was the worst.

The first two had disturbed and frightened me, but number three—well, that totally freaked me out. I don't know how I got there, it certainly wasn't intentional, but one moment I was alone with myself in the funeral parlor's drab laboratory, the next I was in a dark, shadowy place that was somehow familiar to me.

I looked around. Yes, I'd been here before, but when? I remembered. I was here the night I was murdered. In this very room. A creepy basement flat. I recognized the desk and the angle-poise lamp, the cupboard against a wall, the dreary curtains. I remembered the shadows.

But why had I come here again? As I asked myself that question, I saw the newspaper clippings on the desk. On the last occasion I'd watched a man—*what was it about that man that made me tremble now?*—cutting up a newspaper, taking the clippings and placing them neatly alongside others. Others whose headlines screamed of murder and mutilation! I knew now and I'm sure I must have known then, even if I hadn't acknowledged it, that the hunched figure was the killer himself. Had to be. Why else would he be cutting out those particular news items if not for his own scrapbook? Why collect them if the stories were not about himself? Actually, this logic meant nothing to me because, you see, I *just knew* that the person who occupied this dingy flat was the killer the police were looking for. Call it instinct, or psychic recognition—call it what you like. I was certain, that's all. I had no doubt whatsoever.

And, I reflected, I had come here because some innate awareness that had nothing to do with logic or calculation had brought me here. After all, I was no longer in the world of reason or normality; I was existing on some other plane where thought—or the psyche—was all. This man (and I wrongly supposed this is why I trembled) was my killer. He murdered and mutilated me!

The trembling ceased. Ceased because in my out-of-body state I had frozen. And I had frozen because I heard heavy footsteps on the stairs outside the window, the stairs that led down to the flat from street level. Then shuffling footsteps as they trod the short passageway.

And stopped outside the door.

TWENTY

I heard the key turning in the lock, nothing smooth about the sound. Then the door was pushed open with some effort, as though its edges were tight or out of skew with the frame. A dark figure shambled through, with hardly any light let into the room from behind him. It was still daylight outside, but it seemed to have difficulty reaching into this place below the street. The door closed with a short grinding noise, wood against perished wood, and once more the deep shadows consumed most of the interior.

A ceiling light flicked on, but its power was belittled by the general gloom, even though the dusty hanging bulb was without a shade.

The figure stood just inside the street door for a moment, as if alerted to my presence, and this gave me a chance to take a better look. I didn't like what I saw, not one bit.

Other than by his strange attire, I don't think his best friend would have recognized him (although I doubted this scruffy individual had *a* friend, let alone a *best* one: apart from his general shoddiness, he seemed to exude unpleasantness. Or maybe my own fragile imagination was doing him a disservice, I thought at the time). He wasn't tall, just kind of bulky, and he wore a dark oversized raincoat that trailed almost to the floor. Covering his head was one of those old-fashioned trilby hats, with the wide brim snapped down in front, shadowing his eyes; and wrapped around his face—*literally* around his face, for it covered everything but his eyes—was a heavy, knitted navy scarf, whose ends were tucked into the breast of the raincoat.

He looked ready to rob a post office.

He didn't move, just stood there inside the threshold, broad but sloping shoulders slouched, and I caught the glimmer of his eyes in their black pits, reflections of the lightbulb that moved from side to side as if they were searching for something. A couple of times they seemed to settled on me, but after a beat, they'd move on, continuing to search. Could he feel my presence? If so, he seemed to be the only person who could. Even Primrose hadn't sensed me, and

I'd always thought kids were particularly susceptible where that kind of thing was concerned. Kids and animals. When he suddenly made a move in my direction, I hurriedly backed away. Dark eyes that were bulging and set wide seemed to stare directly at me from out of the umbra beneath his hat brim. But again, and to my relief, they passed on to stare into the gloom beyond me. This was one person I didn't want to be seen by.

With that same odd snuffling sound he'd made the last time I was here, he turned away and took a rolled-up newspaper from one of the raincoat's deep pockets. He threw it on the table, the draft it caused disturbing the newspaper clippings that remained on the surface from the other night, so that one or two fell lazily to the floor. He unfurled the journal, and laid it on the desk, then, looking again at the headline, he undid the buttons of the coat.

Moving to one side for a better view, I saw that the newspaper was the late edition *Evening Standard* and its headline screamed at me: "AXE KILLER'S 4th VICTIM NAMED."

Without any doubt whatsoever, I knew the fourth victim referred to was me. In whatever dimension I now existed, some kind of psychic gift came with the territory, and that's why I was drawn to this place. My murderer was being shown to me. And I had to wonder why? Was this punishment for past misdemeanors? Was this my own personal hell, my killer revealed with nothing I could do about it? My own torment of the gods? Whatever the reason, I wasn't happy about it.

The man hadn't yet shed the raincoat, although it was unbuttoned; he just stood hunched over the journal, knuckles pressed against the tabletop, his head hung low so that from behind he looked decapitated. He gazed at the headline before him. No, he was reading beyond the headline; he was reading the text. I drew closer to the desk, but well to the side of the bowed figure. I didn't want to be that close to him. Hell, I didn't want to be in the same *room* as him!

I saw the photograph of myself beneath the block type, a company shot, in fact, one showing me a few years younger.* It was weird reading of my own death and heartbreaking to see a smaller, inset picture of Andrea standing on our doorstep, distress evident in her drawn features; next to her, an arm

---

*When we'd started the agency, Oliver, Sydney and I had had to have the standard headshots both for the trade rag *Campaign* and for our own prospectus, so they were formal black-and-white portraits without an inch of personality uncovered. This was one from that bunch and the *Evening Standard* must have poached it from the magazine's photo archives, or from our agency itself.

thrown protectively around her shoulders, was Oliver. In the background, I could make out the figure of Primrose, shyly peeking around her mother's hip. I could have cried for them all.

Without warning, the newspaper was picked up and hurled across the dingy room, its pages separating and falling to the floor in disarray. Still angry, the hunched man swept all the clippings, together with the long-bladed scissors I'd watched him use a few nights ago, off the table. He banged the wood and made another of those horrible snuffling / snorting noises.

I dodged out of his way when he whirled round and took a couple of paces toward me. Foolishly, I felt vulnerable, even though I was sure that I could not be seen. Or maybe it was fear of his body invading my space so that I'd share his feelings. I thought that might somehow be very unhealthy.

He paused, again glancing this way and that, his black eyes searching the oppressive room. Scared, I backed further away, finding a spot in a dim corner and holding my breath in case he heard (although air wasn't necessary for my existence, something in me insisted on carrying on as normal; I was sure if I put a hand over my heart I would still feel it beating). To my relief, the man saw nothing, even if he did stare into my corner for a couple of uncomfortable seconds. He gave a kind of wet growl and I wondered again if he was suffering from a very bad cold, which would explain wearing the raincoat and scarf in the flat. I was soon to learn otherwise.

He turned his back to me again and went to the newspaper now lying in an untidy heap on the floor, shrugging the coat off as he did so, letting it drop from his shoulders. Then he removed the hat and I saw his thin mousy-colored hair was dirty and lank, long strands at the back tucked into the scarf, bald patches showing through, catching the light, such as it was. Leaning forward, the scarf ends dangling in front of him, he shuffled the paper together again in a loose collection, and laid it on the table. He was staring at the front page with its monochrome picture of me and the smaller inset of Andrea, Oliver, and Prim, when he began to unwind the scarf.

I started to panic as he turned and came toward me again, drawing the coarsely knitted scarf from his neck. He paused in front of me and tossed the scarf onto the newspaper- and magazine-cluttered sofa, catching me by surprise, the scarf sailing right through me.

It was at that moment that I looked fully into his face. Or lack of face, I should say.

It must have been shock that made me forget the first time I'd confronted him in this dismal place, because now I remembered instantly. Now I saw it again in all its horribly obscene ugliness.

In fact, this face was not unlike my own after he'd cleaved it down the middle, probably with that axe mentioned in the *Standard,* except mine had had something at least resembling a nose and mouth, whereas here there was only emptiness, a cavern where features should have been, a dark hole with raw gristle around its edges and something fat and black resting inside like a lazy glistening slug.

It was huge, this open wound, a gaping maw with tendrils of saliva drooling inside, the tip of the slug stirring as if roused. Only the eyes appeared normal, but closer inspection showed even they were wide-set, black, and bulging like those of a frog. And there was something in their shine, a madness—no, a *malevolence*—that was more ghastly than the malformation.

If ghosts can faint, then that's what I did.

TWENTY-ONE

Oblivion.

I don't know where I went, what happened to me, unless it was some kind of mind wipeout, engendered by the sight of that man's—that thing's—awful countenance. Or the absence of. I only know that I became lost in some place where neither time *nor* thought had relevance.

What was I but mind? And maybe, as in life, the mind has to close down for periods of time. Maybe even the psyche needs recovery.

Maybe it was just a hint of the true death yet to come to me. Maybe I was in the transient stage, lingering between existence and complete obliteration. Maybe there was no heaven or hell, only a time to reflect before extinction. I had no idea then.

I have now though.

TWENTY-TWO

I surfaced again on the day of my funeral.

I had no idea how long I'd blanked out for, nor could I recollect any dreams from my unconscious state. I could remember that awful dingy basement room though. But now there were other things to occupy my mind.

I loitered in the road outside my house, watching the various vehicles park and people—friends and acquaintances mainly, a few other faces I didn't recognize—emerge to pull raincoat collars tighter around their necks, umbrellas blooming against the cold drizzle. No cars could park directly in front of the house, for a hearse and two dark limousine cars occupied the space.

I observed my mother arrive in a taxi, watched her climb out and walk up the drive, head bowed, but steps taken with a deliberate dignity. Heads turned, following her progress, and I heard the murmurs as the little plump lady in black's identity was passed among the mourners. I don't know why I lingered outside so long, rain passing through me without deflection—perhaps I didn't want to be in a room full of miserable people, absorbing their sadness every time I unavoidably made contact. Eventually though, I felt the overwhelming need to be closer to Andrea and Primrose, but as I moved into the driveway, the front door opened and somber-suited figures began to leave, led by a tall but stooped man dressed in a black long-tailed suit and pin-stripe charcoal trousers, the funeral director I assumed. He was followed by Sydney Presswell, and then Andrea's parents (whom I'd always got on pretty well with), a couple of advertising associates, then Oliver guiding a distraught Andrea, an arm around her shoulders for support, her hand clasping Primrose's. My daughter's face was pale, with dark patches under her red-rimmed eyes, while Andrea's face was covered by a black lace veil. I could see that her eyes were cast downward.

I stifled a sudden sob, even though no one could possibly hear. I wanted to rush forward and embrace them both, tell them there was no pain for me, nor had there been any at my moment of death. I wanted them to know that I was with them now in their time of grief. But just to be near would mean passing through others, so I hung back and watched from a distance as they went to the big limo behind the hearse. On a velvet-covered stand inside the hearse was a big expensive-looking coffin. It was made of beautifully grained yew, my favorite wood.

I was tempted to try claiming my own body one last time, repossess my life—can you imagine the astonished faces of the crowd if the coffin lid pulled aside and a dead man climbed out? I knew it would be pointless, though: my corpse would already be beginning to deteriorate despite the mortician's best efforts to delay the process. Let's face it, I wouldn't be looking my best.

Leave it, I told myself. There *is* no going back.

Primrose, my once oh-so-happy little girl, was helped into the limousine and I fought against a desperate desire to climb in beside her. But, trivial as it might sound, I wondered where I would sit. Andrea had climbed in after Prim, followed by her parents and my mother. And there was Oliver too, occupying the passenger seat beside the driver. Six, plus the driver, was probably full capacity, even if one was only a half-pint.

Others had started to follow, getting into their cars and switching on the engines. Gray vapors were coming from exhaust pipes like swirling ghosts in the cold, damp, morning air. It was no longer raining, but the day was overcast and dull, perfect for a funeral. The hearse pulled away and proceeded slowly along the avenue, Andrea's limo trailing it, more falling in behind, the cortège speeding up only slightly when it turned into the busy main road. I glided alongside the long car carrying Andrea and Primrose, peering into the side windows to catch a glimpse of them. Prim's face was buried into her mother's side, and Andrea's own face remained concealed beneath the veil. I hardly needed prompting, but I realized again how precious your own family was. They are a man's unit. They go beyond parents and siblings; they had to mean so much more to you. They own you and you own them, not in any selfish way, but in terms of responsibility. They are a huge part of you and help define who you are. And mutual trust is the cloth that binds. Remember I said that.

I was struck by the courtesy shown to the funeral procession, both by other road users and pedestrians. On two occasions I witnessed elderly men remove their hats as a mark of respect when the hearse passed them, but the biggest surprise came when a baggy-trousered youth in a camouflage jacket whipped off his reversed baseball cap and made a quick Sign of the Cross as we drew level. Other drivers were remarkably patient with the slow pace, and one bus driver even refused to overtake when there was plenty of room to do so. I have to admit, their regard touched me.

On we went and it was easy for me to glide alongside, my feet touching tarmac only now and again, but the misery bleeding from the limousine carrying my nearest and dearest was palpable and I was beginning to feel sorry again not only for them, but for myself. I suppose all of us have at one time or another wondered what it would be like to be a guest at our own funeral, and I can honestly tell you this: it's no fun at all.

I shouldn't have been shocked, but there you go: I was. Totally. I hadn't expected the funeral cortège to pull into a crematorium.

They were going to burn me.

I really hadn't anticipated that. Why should it matter if I were dead anyway? I don't know. It just did.

Maybe I hadn't entirely given up reclaiming my life, sinking back inside my body and willing it to move. It would scare the hell out of everybody and I'd have to spend years undergoing operations and a lot of plastic surgery, but what did I care? Anything to be flesh and blood again.

No. The burning of my flesh and bones meant the end of me. Possibly I was doomed to roam the earth (or hang around my house) for the rest of eternity as an entity, a shade, wraith or ghost; a lost soul, a spirit, a bogeyman, a specter, a wandering phantom, a disembodied being—there were all kinds of names for what I'd become. Yet I didn't *feel* any one of them was truly me. And now, to have what I was reduced to warm ashes—well it left me without any connection at all to the world I knew, not even the proof that I'd once lived.

Andrea and I had never discussed our individual deaths, had never made any plans for whoever was to go first. I was certain I'd never mentioned cremation at any point in our life together, probably because when you're young and healthy it isn't the kind of thing you want to think about. I suppose I'd just assumed that one day I'd be buried. After all, I was a Catholic, a bad one, I know, but nobody had ever banned me from the club, and Catholics were not meant to be cremated. Or didn't it matter anymore, had the rules changed without my knowledge? Maybe nobody had bothered to tell me. Perhaps it had become like eating meat on a Friday, reduced in the ranks from most grievous sin to no sin at all. Maybe it no longer necessarily meant that my soul would be condemned to the fires of hell throughout eternity. Maybe these things were not as important anymore. Like missing mass on Sunday—a mortal sin I'd been assured by nuns and priests when I was a child. Like masturbation. God, the guilt I'd suffered. Things changed in the more popular religions, centuries-old dogma suddenly modified or just plain recanted because the church had to keep up with the times, had to modify to fit in more easily with today's society in which values had diminished and morality was politically incorrect. We told you that, did we? Sorry, but there's been a change in policy. All those who committed what they thought was mortal sin throughout the centuries agonizing over it, punishing themselves for it. Well, they'd understand when they finally reached nirvana. So what else isn't really a mortal sin anymore? We'll have to get back to you on that one.

And they wondered why people had become cynical about religion these days.

Anyway, none of that really mattered to me right then. It hadn't been a huge revelation to me that I'd found neither heaven nor hell after my death, so why was I bitching now? Oh yeah, I was annoyed that I was going to be cremated.

It was an imposing (imposing while remaining understated) red building set among splendid lawns and gentle rises. A tall tower, which obviously was a chimney stack, rose from the rear of the building, and inside the entrance vestibule was a glass door tastefully marked "Chapel." Everybody alighted from their vehicles, and followed the coffin, which was respectfully carried on the shoulders of four pallbearers, into the red-brick crematorium. There had been other cars waiting when the cortège had arrived, people standing around in groups, making polite and suitably reverential conversation, and I began to feel humbled by the large turnout. I hadn't realized so many people had liked me—there were even some of my business clients among them—and felt the need to pay their respects. I saw familiar faces that I hadn't set eyes on for years; friends, acquaintances, even my lawyer. There were also a lot of faces I didn't know, wives or husbands, partners of people who knew me when I was alive. The sight of all those mourners made me gulp. Again, I wanted to cry.

Into the chapel they filed, voices hushed, movement slow, and I waited for a break to slip through. I could have entered via the red-brick wall itself, but for some reason I wanted to do things as normally as possible. I drifted down to the front pew where I knew I'd find the two people dearest in the world to me.

Andrea and Primrose sat in the middle of the front bench, Andrea's parents by the side of her, my mother next to Prim, whose poor little face was puffy with new tears. My wife had lifted her veil and her face was drawn, her skin ashen. Behind them sat Oliver and Sydney, members of our staff filling the rest of the row. Sydney's expression was grim but passive; Oliver's eyelids looked sore, as if he had wept a lot himself these past few days.

I sat on a raised dais at the center of which was a plain, linen-covered altar bearing a wooden crucifix. I wanted to look at the faces of my friends and family, silently to thank each and every one for attending. There must have been a hundred or more people there and I was filled with a sad warmth, suddenly loving and missing them all. If only I could communicate, let them know that I was fine, that physical pain never followed you into death. In fact, very few physical sensations did, for I was neither warm nor cold, I wasn't hungry or thirsty. And the weariness I felt was of the soul, with nothing physical to it. All other sensations were merely remembered.

I leaned against the lectern.

The service seemed to pass very quickly. No hymns were sung, but Grieg and Beethoven were played through the adequate sound system. It was soft and gentle and almost composed to evoke tears. The priest said a few words, indicating I was a good man if not a particularly religious one. The fact that he'd never actually met me didn't deter him from showering me with praise that I felt I hadn't deserved and was probably attributed to all the deceased, no matter who they were, in every service he conducted. To my surprise, it was Sydney who went to the lectern for the eulogy; I'd expected Oliver to say some kind words about me. When I looked at his wretched face I guessed he had probably been too afraid of breaking down halfway through his speech to take on the responsibility. We'd known each other for a long time and been through many highs and lows together.

I won't repeat Sydney's generous words about me; suffice to say that there were quite a few loud sobs and sniffles here and there among the congregation, as well as much blowing of noses. Andrea kept her head low so that I could not see her face, while Primrose softly cried against her mother's breast throughout, a short length of material, known as her "Bit of Blank," held in her hand so that she could stroke her own cheek with it. The material was all that remained of the pink blanket she had constantly carried around with her since she'd been a toddler. After years and years of wear and washing, the wool had finally disintegrated into tatters, and eventually only the silk trim at one end was left. She clung to the remnant as if the whole blanket, her comfort blanket, still survived, taking it to bed with her every night, nowadays even a little thumb finding its way into her mouth as she softly rubbed the silk fabric against her cheeks and nose. Naturally, she had it with her on this grimmest of days, but I could tell it offered small comfort.

Next to her, my mother sat stony-faced. As usual I felt I'd let her down, but today I didn't give a damn. Today I cared only about those who *truly* loved me.

By the end of Sydney's sentimental eulogy (he praised me for having far too many exemplary qualities) I was at the back of the altar, head in hands, and blubbing like a fool. I guess we've all wondered what our friends would say about us when we were gone and on this miserable autumnal day I was finding out. His words didn't swell me with pride but, as before, they humbled me. Love for my friends, each and everyone of them in that chapel today, expanded within me almost to bursting point. It was both beautiful and an infinitely sad experience.

There was silence for a while as the priest asked the congregation to think of me and how much I had meant to their individual lives. My wails would have filled the chapel if they could have been heard. I would have been an embarrassment. Then the worst part.

Somewhere out of sight, someone pushed a button and the coffin, which was positioned on a unit at the side of the altar, began to trundle backward, velvet curtains behind it smoothly opening. The rumble of small rollers turning was minimal and, in any case, was soon drowned out by the piece of music that accompanied my last journey. It was a modern piece, but head and shoulders above any of its contemporaries, and I'm sure Andrea chose it because she knew it was a favorite of mine, one of the most soulful songs ever sung, REM's "Everybody Hurts." It would bring a lump to my throat and tears to my eyes at any time, but God, at my own funeral—I lost it completely.

I went from one side of the altar to the other, throwing myself at the moving coffin, bawling in despair. *Please don't burn me, please don't burn me! You don't know what you're doing! I'm not dead, I'm not dead!*

Nobody could hear, and nobody would believe it anyway. But by God, *I* believed! At that moment I truly thought that nothing was irreparable, nor irretrievable; I could be saved, it wasn't hopeless!

I beat my fists on the coffin lid (funny, but my fists never went through the wood; it was as if my mind would not allow them to, that I was still clinging to some form of reality as I knew it, and this, in itself, fashioned my abilities) and I called out, crying for them to stop the service, save my body. Naturally, no one took any notice.

The coffin was moving away from me and I didn't like the darkness beyond the curtains. As soon as the coffin was out of view and the drapes closed behind it, it would be placed inside a furnace to be incinerated by gas fires, and I didn't want to be present when that happened. It would be the final confirmation of my bodily demise, after which I'd be completely lost. Irrational, maybe, but as long as my body was still around, I felt I still had some connection to the world I knew and loved.

But it rumbled onward to the raw, emotive voice of Michael Stipe, and so I realized it truly was the end of me as a person. I fell to the floor in utter despair and when I looked pleadingly at my family, all I saw was their faces contorted with grief, their tears flowing freely, shoulders convulsing. Even Mother had silver trickles falling from her eyes. In the second row, Sydney was stoic, while Oliver's head was lowered, his eyes closed. Never had I seen my former business partner and friend look so thoroughly wrecked.

My own head dropped and I was on my hands and knees before the disappearing coffin. I sensed the curtains close and I envisaged the gas jets flaming into life. I didn't want to think about the rest of it.

I was the last one to leave the chapel although, of course, the last *person* to leave didn't know that. I wept copiously, allowing myself the emotion, aware that I would never function properly (however that might be in my present state of being) until I'd shed the worst of my tears. But finally, even I had had enough and I longed for my wife and daughter again.

Moving down the center aisle, I passed an old boy who'd just entered and was collecting the order of service leaflets. He must have been in his late seventies and by the look of him—he was bent and frail, yellow-skinned—he might well have a more serious appointment at the crematorium before too long. Now I might have been wrong, but I'm sure he shuddered as I went by, and as I turned to look back, he seemed to be peering, squinty-eyed, directly at me. He gave a little shrug and continued to pick up the leaflets as I wondered if those close to death themselves could perceive or "sense" things that others could not. It was odd, but I had more immediate thoughts on my mind. Perhaps just my presence by Andrea and Primrose's side would somehow give them subconscious comfort. I could only hope and wish.

Outside, the crowd had fanned out and conversation was rife, although quiet and respectful, some of the mourners examining the tribute wreaths and bouquets that had been carefully arranged against a wall. I even heard subdued laughter break out here and there, no doubt relief that the worst was over.

I hoped it was some funny but affectionate anecdote about me that had caused the merriment. I wanted them to remember the good times, but to my surprise and, I'm embarrassed to admit, to my slight chagrin, hardly any conversations overheard as I drifted among them, careful not to touch, were centered on me and what a great guy I'd been and how much they'd miss me now that I was gone. Sure, I was mentioned, but almost in passing. The weather and the latest government smoke and mirrors fraud got more air time than I did. I didn't expect a great wailing and gnashing of teeth, but I'd have liked a bit more talk about good ol' Jim and his talent and sense of humor, stuff like that. Maybe there'd be more gratifying remembrances later, back at the house. I certainly hoped so.

I noticed there were one or two photographers and persons with notebooks or mini-cassette recorders, no doubt journalists from both the local and national newspapers. It wasn't just my death that was big news; it was to do with the fact that I was one among four suspected of being murdered by the same killer. It was the serial killer who was the real news, but my funeral would help fill extra space. I also spotted another photographer taking shots of the crowd, but he did not look like the other photo-journos—he'd bothered to wear a dark suit and black tie. I realized he was a police lensman, there hopefully to catch a shot of anyone acting suspiciously, a loner, someone who was not part of the general gathering. The police were looking for their killer here and I began to scan the mourners more intensely myself.

Nobody looked out of place to me though. I did spy the two police detectives who had attended the scene of crime at the hotel. Coates and Simmons, if I remembered correctly. Then someone else caught my eye, a lone figure standing on a small grassy knoll beneath a tree, perfectly still as he watched proceedings. Now this was the odd part.

Although he was at least three hundred yards away, somehow I knew he was looking directly at me. He was tall, but his figure was vague, kind of washed out, as if he were a faded color reproduction on thin film. Despite that, there was something familiar about him; I knew I'd seen him somewhere before. Thing was, I couldn't remember where.

And as I observed him, he raised an arm as if waving to me. Then he was gone. Vanished. A true ghost, you might say.

TWENTY-THREE

Andrea didn't hold a proper wake for me. It was more of an exclusive reception back at the house, only a chosen few among the mourners invited. I understood perfectly: what wife would want a big memorial party when her husband had been murdered so vilely? Speaking for myself, I wasn't in the mood for one either. All I wanted to do was get close to Primrose, put my invisible arms around her, and whisper in her ear: "Don't worry about Daddy."

It was a suitably somber affair, and to my relief and, I'm sure, to Andrea's, people soon made their excuses and began to leave. At least now, in the house, I was the subject of most conversations, particularly when they were between my wife and guests. I caught some nice comments about myself and began to wallow in the discovery that I was a pretty good guy, *a brilliant* art director who could also produce slick but smart copy headlines and had a keen sense of humor. I started to like myself a bit more—my former self, that is. Sydney Presswell was one of the first to leave and I had to smile. Typical Sydney; business took precedence over all else, even the death of a friend and colleague. It was a weekday after all (although I had no idea what day it was now) and I kind of admired him for his pragmatism. I wondered if they were still going to pitch for that new banking account and decided no, there wouldn't be time enough to bring in another creative team, brief them, and produce first-rate work. Maybe he and Oliver would let it go out of respect for me. Ollie certainly wouldn't be in any condition to see it through.

Others soon followed and I sat on the stairway outside the lounge and watched them depart. Although not all the mourners who had attended the funeral had been invited back to the house, the lounge had been full to overflowing and some of the guests had spilled into the kitchen. I'd kept my eyes on Primrose through the lounge doorway for most of the time as she sat on her granddad's lap in an armchair; her face wan, cheeks grubby from wiped tears. I noticed that my mother had not returned from the crematorium, obviously having cadged a lift from someone or, more likely, had herself dropped off at the first tube station or taxi rank along the route. Andrea had been a tower of strength, going from group to group, making sure everyone had something to eat—tiny sandwiches and *vol-au-vents*—and enough to drink—sherry or hard liquor, as well as tea and soft stuff. Occasionally, I would see Oliver squeeze her arm for support and I mentally thanked him for being there for her. Our argument seemed so pointless now, so unimportant, and I deeply regretted our parting on such a sour note.

I noticed Andrea now having a quiet word with Primrose, then taking her hand to lead her from the room. Pushing myself against the wall (nearly through it, actually—I still hadn't fully mastered my new-found capabilities) so that they could pass by without touching me, I saw their faint auras close up, and they were dull, grayish in tone, no vibrancy to them. I hadn't known that misery could be so palpable. As soon as they were past, I followed them up to Prim's cheerful little bedroom, with its old *Shrek* and *Little Mermaid* posters on the walls, bookcase full of brightly colored jacket spines, dolls—lots of dolls—arranged in civilized repose on top of a pine cabinet, yellow wallpaper with tiny blue flowers matched with blue-and-yellow curtains. Usually it raised my spirits just to walk in there—not even the small Ventolin inhaler on the bedside cabinet would spoil my mood—but this day was not a normal day. Tears flowed again as soon as Prim lay on the narrow bed and Andrea murmured soothing words as she pulled off our daughter's shoes.

"Why did Daddy have to die, Mummy?" Prim asked in a small, plaintive voice.

I could go on and tell you *all* that Andrea said in reply and more questions asked by Primrose, but I'm not going to. Enough to say they were in this vein: Why did God take away the second-most important person in the world to her? Why is God so cruel? Is Daddy happy where he is now, and if he is, why? Doesn't he miss us? Will he come and get us soon? It's not just heartbreaking to relate, it's soul-wrecking too. And pertinent, you might think. Because there are no good answers to any of those questions, and there's nothing that can remove or even alleviate the pain that those left behind have to endure. I began to get very angry. Not only did I have no satisfactory answers to those questions—and I'd always believed you found out the truth of things once you left this mortal coil—but I could not have reassured Prim even if I did. I was, myself, completely in the dark as to my state, my future, and my purpose. Oh yes, my purpose. I *did* believe there was a reason for my condition—*everything* had a reason, a meaning, call it what you like—but I had no idea what mine was. So, as I say, I began to get angry.

I paced the room, raving to myself, while Andrea tenderly stroked our daughter's forehead. She found Prim's favorite comfort teddy, Snowy, and tucked it into her arms. My raging came to a temporary halt as I embraced both Andrea and Primrose in my own arms, frustrated that I could not hug them tight, squeeze them so hard that they would have lost breath. I don't think I'd ever loved them both as much as I did at that moment. Nevertheless, their mood sank into me and now I had never known such despair.

Finally, Andrea gave Primrose one last hug and kiss, then left her lying on the bed, Snowy (what else would the aged teddy be called? Grayie?) hugged close to her chest, her eyes closed as if ready for sleep. But where was her comfort rag, her "Bit of Blank"? She would need it when she woke or stirred, but as hard as I searched the bedroom with my eyes, I could not find the short length of pink silk anywhere. I remembered she'd had it with her in the chapel and realized it must still be in the pocket of her coat hanging in the cloakroom downstairs. I called out to Andrea, who was tiptoeing toward the door, but of course, she didn't hear me. I couldn't fetch it myself and I groaned in frustration, called to Andrea again to no avail. Never had I felt so useless, so inadequate.

Andrea paused at the door and, one hand on the handle, looked back at Primrose. Our daughter was already asleep, exhausted by the trauma of the past few days. Andrea left the room, quietly closing the door behind her.

I sat on the floor by the bed, pretending to stroke Prim's hair and her back, almost believing I could feel her as I whispered words of comfort, hoping that somehow my words—or at least the sentiment behind them—would get through. Pretty soon, she was giving out tiny snores, but I stayed with her, continuing to whisper, telling her over and over again how much I loved her and that she shouldn't be afraid, Daddy was okay and he was with her even though she could not see him. At one stage, her eyelids flickered and she murmured "Daddy," but she was quickly away again, fast asleep, slowly and unknowingly coming to terms with my death. One day at a time, I told her. It will eventually become all right. You'll always miss me, I hope, but the hurt will lessen and eventually fade. Never completely, but enough for you to carry on with your own life without this debilitating heartache. God, I loved her so much, and the thought of what I was losing almost tore me apart.

Although I wasn't tired myself, I closed my eyes, content just to be with her for a while. Eventually, her chest rose and sank rhythmically and her grasp on Snowy loosened as she fell into a deeper sleep. I opened my eyes and looked out the window: it was getting dark outside.

Rising from the bedside and giving Prim one last simulated kiss, I went to the door and passed through it. There was that fleeting and odd moment of seeping through thin air and atoms (did I actually pass through the air *between* the atoms? I briefly wondered, remembering that nothing in this world of ours—of yours—is truly solid. Maybe that's the secret of insubstantial ghosts walking through apparently substantial walls or doors), the sensation of being part of the door itself, then I was on the landing outside my daughter's bedroom. I could hear the low tones of voices below, the sound indicating that most of the guests had left. Silence followed, then voices again. One was Andrea's. I walked along the landing and turned the bend leading to the stairs. Rather than glide, I took the stairs one at a time, as if my life was normal and I had just finished reading Prim a bedtime story, ready for a vodka tonic, or perhaps a brandy, before dinner. That would have been nice. That would have been *so* nice. But that wasn't the reality. No, surprise, shock, dismay, and misery were the reality. My past life had not quite done with me.

They were kissing. Andrea and Oliver were in each other's arms and they were kissing.

I froze there and gaped.

It wasn't a kiss of condolence. It wasn't a platonic kiss between old friends. It was a ravenous, lustful kind of kiss. The tongue-swallowing kind. The kind Andrea and I hadn't shared for the last three or four years.

I couldn't believe my eyes. I stared through the open door into the lounge and my knees almost gave way. This wasn't happening. This *couldn't* be happening. My wife and my best friend. With me hardly dead five minutes. Was I crazy? Had my loss of body at last driven me crazy? It couldn't be true.

They broke apart and it was only small consolation that Andrea was doing the pushing.

"No, we can't," she said breathlessly. "It isn't right. Not so soon."

Isn't right? Not so soon? What the hell was she saying? It was . . . it was *obscene*!

"I'm sorry, Andrea." He wouldn't release his grip on her though. "I couldn't wait any longer. It's been such a rough few days."

"How the bloody hell do you think it's been for me?" she shouted back. "I never . . . I never wanted anything like this."

His voice was anxious, but relatively calm compared to Andrea's. Still he did not let her go.

She put her hands against his chest. "I loved him, Oliver. You must understand that. I still loved him." There was a slight catch in her throat.

"Yes, I know." He was looking intensely into her eyes. "But it wasn't the same. It was never the way it is with us. Even when you first went to Jim, you still loved me."

He tried to pull her close again, but Andrea resisted. I wished she'd resisted a few minutes ago.

"Primrose might come down," she told him, her efforts to break away feeble.

"She's dead to the world. Sorry, shouldn't have put it that way. But the poor little mite is exhausted. She'll sleep through the night if you'll let her."

Finally, Andrea did manage to free herself. Oliver attempted to grab her back.

"No!" This time her objection was fierce and Oliver took a pace backward.

"All right, Andrea." He kept his voice low, as if he might really wake Primrose. "It's just been difficult keeping away from you when you're going through so much."

"How ironic is that?" She spat out the words contemptuously, but I knew they were directed at herself as much as my so-called friend. "What we're doing is disgusting."

Well, I went along with her there.

"You don't mean it, Andrea. Just because he died in such a terrible way doesn't mean what we have isn't right."

Isn't right? He thought cheating on me was right? Before, I hadn't believed my own eyes; now I couldn't believe my ears. This hypocritical, two-timing bastard was justifying their treachery.

"But . . ."

He shook his head to stop her saying any more. "You needed me a few moments ago. Those were your true feelings, Andrea."

"I need you *now*, but that's not the point. It's too soon, it's too wrong."

"How long do I have to wait?"

"I . . . I don't know, Oliver. We have to give it time. We have to think of Primrose too."

"And our friends? Your mother and father? *His* dreadful mother?"

My dreadful mother? Only I had the right to call her that.

"We have to do the proper thing for now."

"You never stopped loving me, did you?" His eyes were wide, eyebrows raised. That old Oliver little-boy-lost look. Never failed. I'd seen him use it on men as well as women so many times, albeit in different circumstances. Had I ever honestly liked him?

"We shouldn't even be discussing it. He was your best friend—don't you feel any guilt?"

"Of course I do! I always have!" He was angry too. "But you should never have left me in the first place. You used Jim against me."

"Of course I didn't! How can you say that?" Andrea glanced toward the staircase as if afraid her raised voice had roused our daughter. For a moment, she seemed to be looking directly at me.

Then the doorbell rang, making all three of us jump.

Andrea opened the front door. On the doorstep stood DS Simmons and DC Coates. They must have followed the funeral cars back to the house, waiting outside until they thought everybody had left.

The taller of the two, Simmons, appeared to be spokesman. "Sorry to bother you on this sad occasion, Mrs. True, but is Mr. Oliver Guinane still with you? We've been waiting some time for him to leave so that we didn't need to disturb you."

Andrea looked behind her, her mouth open in surprise. Oliver was standing in the doorway of the lounge and only a few feet away from me.

"It's all right, Andrea," he said, "leave this to me." His voice was calm, but I couldn't help noticing there was an edge to it. Natural enough, I suppose, when two unfriendly-looking policemen confront you. "Can I help you?" he asked politely. Now I noticed how pale his face was.

"Yes, Sir. Detective Sergeant Simmons and Detective Constable Coates—we met you at the hotel on Monday."

"Of course." Oliver nodded to them both.

"May we come in?" Simmons asked Andrea courteously.

She hesitated, but only for a moment. "I . . . I suppose so. My daughter is asleep upstairs."

"We'll be very quiet. Just some questions we need to ask Mr. Guinane."

Andrea opened the door wide and stepped to one side to allow the two policemen to enter.

Simmons and Coates stood in the hallway, looking awkward, but their eyes finding Oliver's from time to time.

"As you probably know, Mrs. True, DC Coates and I are working on the case of your husband's murder."

She nodded. "I noticed you at the funeral."

"I hope we weren't obtrusive in any way."

"No. Unlike the Press people."

"Yes." Simmons pondered this for a second or two. "Newspaper people can be a nuisance sometimes. But there was nothing that we, as policemen, could do about it. Free Press, and all that."

"It's okay, I wasn't blaming you." She glanced at Oliver, who was still waiting in the doorway to the lounge. "Why did you want to see Oliver?"

Andrea seemed nervous to me, probably because of what she and my *ex-*friend had been up to a couple of minutes ago.

"Ah, I think that must be between Mr. Guinane and us for now." It was the shorter man, Coates, who had spoken. "It's only a few simple questions, nothing formal. Shouldn't take long."

Andrea looked questioningly at Oliver, who had stepped aside from the door.

"I've no objection to Andrea being present. Shall we go through?" His hand indicated the lounge.

"Uh, no, Mr. Guinane." Simmons again. "Certainly we can talk wherever you suggest, but I don't think it's appropriate for Mrs. True to be in on this."

Quick, anxious looks were exchanged between Andrea and Oliver. Oliver started to protest, but Andrea interrupted.

"That's all right, Sergeant," she said. "I'll check on my daughter and wait with her until you tell me I can come down."

"Shouldn't be too long," Simmons promised this time.

I wasn't prepared for the next moment. Andrea strode straight through me to climb the stairs and I almost sagged with the weight of the emotions that hit me. She was confused and unexpectedly frightened, all beneath a surging undercurrent of terrible grief. Fortunately, she passed on swiftly and mounted the stairs, her step weary.

Both detectives faced Oliver.

"Shall we go through, Sir?" suggested Coates, who had an undisguised glint in his eye as he regarded Oliver.

Oliver allowed them access, then followed into the room. I trailed in after Oliver.

He indicated, inviting both policemen to sit and they duly found places at either end of the sofa. As for me, I was in no mood to sit, because I was raging. I wanted to catch hold of my ex-friend and partner and throttle him there and then. I wanted to beat him to a pulp and, indeed, I took several swings at him, all of them useless, merely swiping through him as though he was nothing more than a hologram. I ranted. I kicked him where it really should have hurt, but he didn't even flinch. *God, I wanted to kill him!*

But I could only wait and listen. The interview went something like this:

DS SIMMONS: Mr. Guinane, the other day you told us that you left the hotel on the night of James True's murder and returned home.

OLIVER: Yes.

DS SIMMONS: Yet a neighbor of yours, an early riser who had a pet dog to let out into the apartment gardens, told us he saw you entering the apartments' foyer around 6 A.M.

OLIVER: *Silence.*

DC COATES: You were empty-handed, so you couldn't have been out to buy milk or the morning papers.

OLIVER: *Uncomfortable silence.*

DS SIMMONS: Do you wish to change your original statement, Sir?

OLIVER: I couldn't sleep. I was kind of wired—you know Jim and I were working on a big campaign for a prospective client? It's hard to relax after you've been dreaming up winning ideas half the night.

DC COATES: So you left the hotel suite quite early, did you? Sunday night, I mean.

OLIVER: Well, not that early. It must've been somewhere around midnight. I didn't check my watch, had no reason to.

DC COATES: You were overheard having a violent argument with James True—

OLIVER: It was hardly violent. There's bound to be creative differences from time to time. It goes with the territory and it's never serious.

DS SIMMONS: The hotel's night porter, who was collecting breakfast order cards, said the row sounded extremely serious when he passed by the room.

OLIVER: He's wrong. We might have been a bit loud, but we didn't come to blows or anything like that.

DC COATES: Isn't it true that there was also a significant business disagreement between you both at this time?

OLIVER: We failed to agree on a forthcoming merger with a larger agency—I was pro, Jim was con—but it was hardly cause for murder, if that's what you're suggesting.

DS SIMMONS: We're not suggesting anything at this time.

DC COATES: You and True's wife were lovers at one time, weren't you?

OLIVER: Good God. Has somebody at the agency been gossiping? Our relationship was years ago, before Jim and Andrea were married. In fact, Andrea was actually my live-in partner before she decided on Jim. There's been nothing between us since.

ME: Huh!

DS SIMMONS: Are you quite certain of that, Mr. Guinane?

OLIVER: Of course I'm bloody certain!

DS SIMMONS: Well, we'll leave that for now.

ME: No, ask him more. He's lying!

DC COATES: A moment ago you mentioned being wired. Was that appertaining to drugs, Sir?

OLIVER: What?

DC COATES: Do you take drugs?

OLIVER: More idle chat at the agency?

DS SIMMONS: We've learned that your drug consumption was bad enough to cause problems more than once over the years, especially as far as Mr. True was concerned.

OLIVER: That was a long time ago. I did marijuana, some coke, nothing really heavy. But now I'm clean. When I said wired, I meant uh, wound up. Wired is just a word we use in the game. You know—in advertising.

DC COATES: You ever heard of a Ruby Red, Mr. Guinane?

OLIVER: What are you talking about?

DC COATES: Ruby Red. Some of my colleagues call it a Rudolph. You know, Rudolph the Red Nose Reindeer.

OLIVER: What's your point?

DC COATES: Well you see, one of the dead giveaways when someone's doing a lot of coke is that the tip of the nose can get slightly sore. Not bright, not loud. You see a few celebs with it on television when their make-up's worn off. Nothing too conspicuous, you understand, just a little redness on the tip. Like on the tip of your nose right now.

OLIVER: That's nonsense! I gave all that up years ago.

ME: Why are you lying, Ollie? What else are you hiding besides having an affair with my wife?

DC COATES: Really?

OLIVER: You may not have noticed, but I lost a good friend this week. I've done some weeping, believe it or not.

DS SIMMONS: Why were you arguing with James True last Sunday night?

OLIVER: Oh, back to that again, is it? It was trivial, a little difference of opinion between friends. Jim thought I was on cocaine again.

DC COATES: Ah, so you are still on drugs.

OLIVER: I didn't say that. I've admitted nothing. But look, do you seriously believe I killed my best friend and business colleague? I thought he was supposed to be the victim of a serial killer?

DS SIMMONS: It could easily have been set up to appear that way. A copycat murder. If someone wanted another person out of the way without becoming an obvious suspect, why not hide the motive among a series of same-such murders, let the serial killer take the blame. Unfortunately for the guilty party, Mr. True's death was not quite the same as in the previous killings. Not quite the same *modus operandi*, you see.

OLIVER: I don't understand.

DS SIMMONS: In the first three cases, all the victims were dead some time before their bodies were mutilated. Although there was a certain amount of blood spilt because of the mutilations, it hadn't traveled far. Their blood didn't gush, for want of a better word. Whereas, in James True's case the mutilation took place either immediately after death, or, more likely, just before, as far as we can tell. That's why there was more blood spillage than with the previous three—his heart was still pumping it through the veins and arteries. It hadn't begun to coagulate.

OLIVER: So presumably the killer would also be covered in blood.

DC COATES: You . . . I mean, the guilty party would have had plenty of time to clean himself. All night, in fact. And of course, he could have been wearing covering clothes—a plastic mac, gloves, things that could easily be hidden or thrown away afterward.

OLIVER: Look, are you charging me with murder? If so, I'm saying nothing more without the presence of my solicitor.

DS SIMMONS: We're not charging you with anything, Mr. Guinane. At least, not for the time being. But we will be questioning you again in the next day or so, probably at New Scotland Yard, so if you feel you will need a solicitor, then I suggest you contact one as soon as possible.

OLIVER: This is preposterous! It's completely insane!

DS SIMMONS: Just make sure you're available to us, Sir. That's all for now.

Finding Oliver and Andrea together in a clinch had devastated me, left me weak (and there was worse to come); now, hearing Oliver more or less accused of my murder left me completely stunned. It wasn't possible! Not Ollie. Not my best friend. No! Couldn't be right! Yet . . . he'd betrayed me with Andrea. There was I, a few days cold, and he was passionately kissing my wife in my own home. How long had their affair been going on? A couple of weeks, a few months—a year? I had no idea, hadn't noticed any signs. Andrea wouldn't do this to me. Would she? She'd loved Oliver before me, so maybe the flame had never truly died. Oh dear God, how much more did I have to take? Had she ever been true to me?

I was literally drooping, my knees bent, shoulders hunched; I would have collapsed had I carried the weight of my physical form. I felt drained, my energy dissipated. But the two detectives were leaving and I wanted to hear more from them. I wanted to hear what they had to say to each other when they were out of earshot of the suspect. I followed them from the house, walking close behind as they made their way to their car parked further down the road.

"How did you know about the drugs?" I heard Simmons ask.

"The old Ruby," Coates replied. His black hair was close-cropped. His frame was stocky and he looked tough, but not quite as hard as his stone-faced companion.

"Come on, Danny. A Ruby? We both know that's rubbish." Simmons, his beaky nose as sharp as a hatchet, was obviously impatient with his lower-ranking officer.

"Inside info," Coates told him. "But I couldn't let Guinane know about that."

"You've been to the advertising agency?"

"You could say."

"Without me? We're supposed to be a team. Shit, we're supposed to be *part* of a team."

"I've got a connection, Nick."

"Don't be playing silly buggers with me. What about this business between Guinane and True's wife? Some more inside gossip?"

"Well I wouldn't call it gossip." They had reached their car and Coates was fumbling inside a trouser pocket for the key. He was grinning across the roof of the Vauxhall at Simmons.

"Okay, that's enough, Danny." Simmons was not at all amused. "You got me to come here after the funeral to talk to Guinane and we've had to hang around for hours. I'm not fucking about now—what's going on?"

"Well it turns out that True's wife used to be Guinane's girlfriend before she married True."

"Yeah, we know that. So?"

"My source tells me the affair took off again shortly after the marriage. And it's still going on."

"Christ. Another reason for Guinane to resent his business partner."

"Right. That and the merger dispute. And, of course, we know that True's murder didn't follow the same pattern as the others."

"What, the weird stuff the first three victims got up to before they were topped?"

"That's it. Two of 'em—the men—visited prostitutes before they died, right? Something that apparently was totally out of character for them. And we got that from close friends of both. We only found out that they had used brasses when we retraced their movements before death."

"A lot of people have dark secrets that nobody else knows about."

"Sure. We can't be certain that neither one had done it before. But both were successful, good-looking guys, professionals, one an insurance broker, the other a lawyer. The first one had a gorgeous-looking wife, remember?"

Simmons nodded as he rested an arm on the car's rooftop.

"Would you wander if you had someone as stunning as her to come home to?"

"Probably not. But y'know, the old adage—a bit of rough now and again. Change is the biggest aphrodisiac."

"Okay. Could happen. But what about the second guy?"

"Again, maybe something different."

"Going off with a rent boy when the guy wasn't even gay?"

"As I said, dark secrets."

"Yeah, but his partner—another great looker, by the way—told us there was nothing bent about her live-in boyfriend. Quite the opposite, as it happens. According to his friends he'd been quite a stud man and only ever looked at women. A bit homophobic, too—and don't tell me that's a sign of latent homosexuality because we both know that's crap."

"All right I know all that. As you say, out of character. But we've both been in the business long enough to know people can do some surprising things."

"Okay. So then there's the third victim, the woman."

"Oh yeah. Now that *was* a bit weird."

"Weird? It was fucking ridiculous. She was an attractive thirty-year-old, married to a wealthy banker, fashionably dressed and, by all accounts, bright and socially gracious. Why the fuck would she suddenly prostitute herself? We found witnesses who said she'd been making a nuisance of herself around Shepherd Market, near where her body was eventually dumped. Shit, the local brasses were complaining because she was trespassing on their turf."

"I know. Makes no sense at all."

"Y'think?" Coates raised his eyebrows in mock surprise.

"Well, they all engaged in some bizarre activities, things that might have put them in danger."

"All except James True."

"Yup, doesn't follow the pattern. He was working for his agency the whole weekend and, as far as we know, he never left the hotel, nor did anything exceptional. And no hookers of either sex went up to his suite—again, as far as we know."

"The only thing that fits the pattern was that he was youngish, good-looking and successful, and the same kinds of murder weapon were used, but in a different order of usage. The point, though, is that his business partner, this Oliver Guinane guy, didn't know about that, nor the peculiar activities of the previous three victims. No one did, we kept it to ourselves."

"SIO's orders. Partly because we didn't want the closest relatives to suffer more over the publicity it would have caused, but mainly because we want to keep the similarities to ourselves for now."

"Right. The public wasn't made aware through the media because we put a block on it. Guinane certainly wouldn't have known. I think that's where he slipped up, not that he could have done anything about it, anyway."

"Because of the theory that the killer either blackmailed or threatened the victims to commit those out-of-character acts. Maybe said he'd kill the victim's family."

"Exactly."

"But he would have had to know about the murder weapons."

"So he found out. We can't keep everything out of the public domain. Loose talk at the Yard got out, spread elsewhere. He could even have picked the info up in a pub. Guinane's a writer, who's to say he doesn't mix with journos? You know how they gab after a couple of drinks."

Simmons shook his head doubtfully. "I dunno, Dan. You're stretching it a bit. Anyway if he knew about the weapons, why wasn't he aware of which one was used first?"

"Trust me on this," Coates said, grinning at his colleague. "Even reporters have a conscience. Maybe they *don't* want it to get out. At least not yet. They're obeying our rules on that."

"We've still got no strong evidence against Guinane. Come on, it's bloody cold out here. Let's get in the car and on the way back you can tell me more about your source."

Coates chuckled as he opened the car door and ducked inside. "You'll believe me when I do," I heard him say.

They were both slamming doors shut before anything else was said. They drove off leaving me standing by the curbside, with nothing to do but stare after them and wonder.

TWENTY-FOUR

Then, for me, there came a time of wandering. I was depressed, confused, afraid—and I felt completely helpless. The police suspected Oliver of my murder, the plan for it to appear as the work of a mad serial killer apparently not wholly successful. I had thought he was my friend, now I knew he had betrayed me. Betrayed me with my wife. How bad could it get? (Funny how often, when you ask yourself that question, things invariably manage to get worse; this was no exception.) I was totally alone, seemingly abandoned by God himself. My body was dead, yet *I* didn't seem to be. No, I didn't even think I was a ghost, because aren't ghosts supposed to see other ghosts? I'd caught weird and fleeting glimpses of things that might once have been living beings (I remembered the almost limpid but familiar face that had lingered at a distance twice now, once when I was in my teens, and then at my funeral) but all were non-communicative and only temporary. So what was my destiny? To walk the earth for all eternity, a kind of spirit nomad that had no purpose? Maybe this was Hell.

I didn't return to the house that afternoon. I didn't want to look at Andrea. I just couldn't. As much as I hungered to be with Prim, I wanted to be as far away from my unfaithful wife as possible. Love should be an honest thing, but how often is it? I wanted to scream with rage, howl in despair, but what would be the point? No one would hear, no one would care.

I drifted away from my home.

Ask yourself how you'd feel if you became invisible. What fun, right? The places you could go, the people you could spy on. And imagine you weren't even solid anymore, that nothing could touch or harm you. A lot more fun, yeah?

Well, you'd be wrong. Doesn't work that way, you see. At least, not if you're traumatized like I was. In my own view, I was the walking dead on a journey of discovery and disillusionment, the main discoveries so far being that in my lifetime I'd been betrayed by my mother (How could she have hidden my father's letters from me? How could she rip up the photograph of her only son with such loathing in her eyes, just because I'd had the audacity to die on her and, to make it worse, in the most public of ways?); by my own father who, despite those unread letters, had run out on me when I was only a child; betrayed by my best friend and business partner, and by the woman I'd loved all these years and who had borne my daughter. People I'd loved and respected during my time on earth (except for my father, for whom I had no feelings whatsoever) had deceived me.

With that heavy load dragging on me, I made my lonely way back to the city.

I visited places: the cinema, theater, bars and hotels, family homes, the zoo (where tigers growled as I went by and monkeys yattered; most animals ignored me as I passed their cages and pens, only a few showing an awareness of me, watching suspiciously as though my presence disturbed them). I became an observer of life, of people, singling out particular individuals who looked interesting, sharing their day or night's routine with them.

I sat at the side of theater stages and watched great actors perform, even stood among the back chorus line of one musical production and sang along with them; I strolled through parks and took bus rides; I watched children in playgrounds and classrooms, and thought of Primrose, yearning for her, desperately wanting to see her again, to hold her, kiss her chubby little cheek, to whisper how much I loved and missed her . . . But I resisted the urge to return home, still consumed with anger and dismay because of Andrea's adultery and Oliver's treachery, telling myself that going back would only worsen my pain. For the best part of one day I traveled on the underground's continuous Circle Line, studying the commuters, listening to their conversations, envying them their physicality, their humanness. Occasionally, I'd meld into one or other unsuspecting passenger, just to get a *feel* of life again, glimpsing his or her thoughts, sensing their emotions. And it was all rather uncomfortable and dull, through no fault of theirs though; the dullness, the disinterest, came from within myself. Even one young guy's lurid reverie of the sexual activity he and his girlfriend had enjoyed the previous night and his daydream of its continuance this coming evening failed to spark anything in me. It was like watching a blue movie with better production values, yet I felt neither desire, nor envy—the images didn't even cause me an erection (although it seemed to work for him okay, but I wasn't part of that). Perhaps if I'd possessed pigment the embarrassment might have colored me red, but as it was, I merely slipped out of him, bored with his private imaginations. My guess is that when you no longer have the power to procreate physically, then your psyche dismisses the arousal instinct, renders such urges redundant. Certain paraplegics might dispute the point, but then they're still flesh and blood; when you are *nothing,* you become detached—*literally*; you don't lose emotions such as love and hatred (witness my resentment), and you certainly can yearn, but sex isn't in the game anymore. Believe me, I've tested myself (you don't forget the *memory* of desire).

You may wonder if any individual I invaded felt my presence and I'd have to answer no, not really, save for a slight shiver each one gave. The merest *frisson* of interrupted energy, the slightest tautness of neck muscles. I had no control over these people, you understand, I wasn't a body-snatcher, I couldn't make them obey my will in any sense; nor did they pick up on *my* thoughts and emotions—it was strictly a one-way street.

Now comes the part that I'm truly embarrassed over and it's about the self-testing I mentioned a moment ago; but, if this is to be an honest account, it has to be told. You see, after the Circle Line disappointment, I was keen to discover the limits my condition had imposed on me. I mean what would any red-blooded male do if he suddenly had the power of invisibility? I still had the memory of desire, I still appreciated beauty, especially when it was to do with the female form, and I still had low inclinations—or I suppose you might be kind and call them human failings.

I followed a beautiful young blonde girl home. And I watched her undress, then take a bath. She was not a natural blonde, I discovered, but even without make-up and stylish clothes, she was gorgeous. I appreciated her great looks well enough, but I was not aroused: it was only the admiration of a dispassionate observer. I suppose I viewed her in the way an octogenarian gentleman might: evaluation without lust. It was how I learned another aspect of my condition, which is why, shaming though the voyeurism was, it had to be mentioned here. A less disheartening example is that although the sight of good food remained pleasant to me, it no longer whetted my appetite, because I didn't feel hungry anymore. And while I trudged the streets and parks, gliding when I wanted to, taking long hops when it pleased me, I suffered no aches or pains or tiredness; rather, my soul became weary and I soon came to understand that this was because of the mental anguish with which I'd been burdened and not the miles I'd traveled. So although I took pleasure from the blonde's nakedness, I was not exhilarated by it, was not turned on in the least. The curves and dips of her flesh were delightful, the sheer graceful length of her thighs delectable, yet in me it led to nothing more than appreciation. So it seems the Pope may have been right when he pronounced several years ago that there is no sex in Heaven.

I had quite a few periods of vacuity, by the way, occasions when I found myself not where I expected to be. If I'd been my mortal self, I would have assumed these were times when I just blanked out, or fell asleep, but if now I never became physically weary, why should that occur? Everybody dreams, we're told, even if we remember nothing upon waking, but we do not dream throughout our slumber. Dreams take up only a small percentage of our unconscious state with longer periods of utter closure in between. Where does our mind go? Our bodies certainly don't shut down entirely—how could our lungs breathe, our hearts beat? But we appear to sink into oblivion and I could only wonder if that was still happening to me even without a functioning body. The mystery intrigued me; but again, there were no answers.

It was mainly because of these blackouts that I began to lose more track of time—as well as any interest in time itself—but I believe several days went by. I walked alone with no purpose, only the occasional cat or dog having some sense of my presence, humans completely unaware of my existence.

But one day an idea occurred to me.

TWENTY-FIVE

Possibly it was because I had that feeling of slowly withdrawing from the world I'd known, observing it more and more objectively rather than subjectively, almost witnessing events, situations, distractedly, very gradually becoming detached from the reality of living, that I became anxious about making some kind of contact with Primrose. I just wanted to reassure her, to let her understand how much I loved and missed her, that there was no pain in this dimension, only emotional suffering (I think it was my unbearable anger that fed the suffering; and maybe, I wondered, it was also the reason I was still tied to this earth). Perhaps most important of all was that I had to say goodbye to her, unlike my own father, who had left without even telling me he was going when I was but a child myself.

What occurred to me is this: if certain animals could sense my presence, then why not spiritualists, mediums, clairvoyants, psychics, whatever they preferred to label themselves? They claimed to be the few people who were able to contact the dead and relate their words and messages to the living. It was worth a try.

But how to find one?

I couldn't exactly thumb through Yellow Pages. So I just kind of wandered around a while, searching.

Don't ask me how it worked, because I don't know. In desperation, I just thought of what I was looking for and within a short time I found myself outside a small terraced house in an unfamiliar part of town. (Strangely, it was nighttime; I'd lost most of the day somewhere, another one of my "blackout" periods I assumed).* My location could have been Camden. Could have been

---

*Time itself seemed not to be having any proper continuum for me. One moment it might be broad daylight, next the deepest—and even lonelier for me—night, my mysterious "blank-outs" filling the hours between. I had the idea of seeking out a medium in the morning, but when I arrived seemingly uncoerced at the house where the séance had begun, guided by nothing more than a self-wish or the medium's dragnet for lost souls, the sun had given over to a half-moon in a cloudy sky.

Peckham—it was of no importance. I just arrived at the place (or was *drawn* to it) and somehow knew the person I sought was inside. On reflection, I think either I tuned into the medium, or she tuned into me. I floated through the brick wall to find myself in a largish, dimly lit parlor, where seven people—five women, two men—were seated around a circular table covered by a burgundy-colored velvet (or something similar) cloth, all their hands splayed on the tabletop, the tips of their fingers connecting them all to one another. It was apparent that the séance had already begun.

The curtains, I noticed, were drawn tight and only a low lamp illuminated the room. I quickly surveyed the faces there, looking for the medium, and settled on a plump woman with a heavy, heaving bosom and closed eyes, dressed entirely in black and wearing big dangly earrings, but it was another person on the opposite side of the table who spoke up. She was a gray-haired sparrow of a thing, far different from the archetypal notion of a clairvoyant, the friendly, favorite aunt, Doris Stokes kind. Her face was skinny, gaunt even, with high jutting cheekbones and deeply sunken cheeks, her neck as scrawny as a plucked chicken's. The wrists that projected from the tight-fitting sleeves of a faded paisley dress were spindly, wrist bones prominent, and her fingers trembled slightly on the deep-red tablecloth. Dark-blue veins were clearly embossed beneath the limpid skin of her wrists and hands. She wore no make-up and her eyebrows, below an unfurrowed forehead and above a large narrow nose, were too heavy for such an otherwise fragile face. Her age in this dim light was undeterminable, anywhere between fifty and seventy, probably toward the latter end if I had to guess, and her voice was as thin as her features, high-pitched and reedy. Her heavy-lidded eyes were closed, her face pointed slightly upward as though the person she addressed was in the corner of the ceiling.

"Andrew? Can you hear me, Andrew? I can feel you're near. Catherine is waiting for a message, Andrew. Do you have a message for her?"

The plump woman who, mistakenly, was my prime candidate for medium, was now watching the speaker across the table intently, unlike the others, a motley band of varying ages and attire, who either stared at their own hands or kept their eyes closed and heads bowed.

The frail clairvoyant spoke again. "Andrew, we're here for you and wish you nothing but peace and love. Do you want to speak through me?"

Only silence followed and one or two of the sitters shifted in their chairs, either out of embarrassment or discomfort.

Suddenly, the medium's eyes opened—they were blue, almost faded to gray—and for a moment I thought she was looking directly at me. But before I could speak, she invoked the name again.

"Andrew?"

Now I looked over my shoulder, thinking Andrew's spirit might be standing behind me. There was nothing there. But I thought something might have moved somewhere in the shadows.

"It is you, Andrew, I can hear you telling me your name," came the trembling voice of the thin woman.

At the table, other eyes opened and heads turned in my direction. I returned my gaze to the shadows behind me again.

There was definite movement, something looming larger, a shadow disassociating itself from other shadows. Although impossible, I swear I felt the hairs on the back of my neck bristle. Like a slowly developing photoprint, a face began to appear, followed by the shoulders.

It was hard to focus on it at first, because the shape was nebulous, the features hazy. But with more encouragement from the medium, it began to resolve itself. Soon I was able to tell that the face belonged to an elderly man, his hair white, but his skin relatively unlined, as if the troubles of this world had not followed him into the next.

"So many," I heard the medium say. "There are so many present today, all with messages for their loved ones."

Sighs, gasps, even some moans came from the group around the table. I could feel a tension and it felt like a precursor to hysteria. I was pretty near the edge myself.

I half-thought that when the medium had remarked that there were so many present today she was referring to the sitters, but when I looked past the emerging apparition, I noticed that there were others taking form behind it. The leader was the clearest, even if on occasions the image wavered and threatened to disappear, along with his more timid companions, who continued to linger behind him.

"So many," the medium said again, with something like gratitude in her shaky voice. I turned to her once more and she was smiling, mouth open, thin lips pulled back to reveal yellow teeth. The smile failed to warm her expression; in fact, the smile was almost a rictus. "Come forward," she intoned, "we're waiting for your communication."

By now, I'd backed away a little, not wanting to get between the medium and her ethereal guests. But these looming ghosts had frozen in their manifestation. I saw faces, pale, wide-eyed faces, faces that most definitely were from a realm other than this, because there was nothing solid about them, nothing of substance, only vaporous incarnations. Bizarrely, they looked frightened of me.

They reversed their development, began to be absorbed by the shadows, consumed by them, their gaze never leaving me. I opened my mouth to say something, but I couldn't think what. Call them back? Tell them I was one of them? In that instant, I knew the truth of it: I wasn't one of them, not a ghost, not as I should be. Nevertheless, I held out a beseeching hand; wherever they were going, I wanted to go with them. But disbelief was evident on their waning faces, joining the fear already there, making me feel an abomination.

My God. It suddenly struck me that I was haunting ghosts.

"Please don't leave us." It was the desperate reedy voice of the medium. "Your loved ones are waiting to hear from you. Andrew, tell me what's wrong so that I can reassure you. We are all as one in this room and wish you no harm."

Distracted, I turned to her, and when I looked back at the apparitions, they were all but gone, just dispersing mists. Except for one.

I wasn't sure if it had stood its ground, or if it was a new spirit, freshly arrived at the séance and had not yet become aware of my presence. But that couldn't be, because he was looking directly at me.

There was something familiar about him and I suddenly realized why: he was the spook I'd noticed on the small rise at my funeral. He had been familiar then, but still I could not remember how I knew him. If alive, he would have been just past middle age, somewhere in his middle or late forties, because there was knowledge in his eyes, and experience in his features. His hair was full but almost colorless, and he wore a suit, a little crumpled, but not shabby; he also had on a white shirt with a dark tie (his suit and tie were too vague to suggest any other color than gray). I knew this man. I *knew* this man.

A warmth denied to me since my demise emanated from him. I lost my own trepidation, if not my astonishment, as I watched the specter become clearer, gray flushing to weak colors, the image itself more clearly rendered. I saw that his tie was red, his suit brown.

He smiled—at me—and the warmth engulfed me. His mouth opened to speak.

But the voice came from behind me.

"*Jimmy.*"

It wasn't his voice, for it was female, high-pitched and querulous. I looked back at the medium once again as she spoke my name three times.

"*Jimmy . . . Jimmy . . . Jimmy . . .*"

I hadn't been called that since I was a child.

"*You must listen to me.*"

Too surprised to know where to look now, my eyes went from sitters to ghost, ghost to sitters. The medium's mouth moved again and I noticed her lips were wet with spit.

"*You must go back, Jimmy,*" she said and only then did it dawn on me that the apparition was talking to me through the bird-like woman, whose hands remained flat on the velvet cloth, her end-fingers still in contact with other hands around the table. It was her voice, yet it wasn't quite the same as before when she had called to the spirit named Andrew. For some reason breath vapor was emerging from her mouth with the words, as if the temperature in the room had suddenly sunk dramatically, something I couldn't actually feel myself.

The other sitters were looking at each other with perplexed expressions.

"Who's Jimmy?" I heard one of them ask. There was a general shaking of heads, a few negative murmurs.

"I'm Jim—he means me," I said, perhaps hoping that the medium, with her sensing powers, might hear me.

It was plain that she didn't, for her head rolled round her shoulders, the pupils of her pale-blue eyes disappeared up into her head; she froze, her back arched, her scrawny neck stretched to its limit. For a moment, I thought she might topple, but her hands remained firmly on the tabletop.

"*She can't hear you, Jimmy.*" The words came from the same source, the medium herself, but I knew they were from the ghostly man behind me. Turning directly to him, I saw his eyes were still on me, the woman a mere conductor for his message. Shapes cowered at his back, the other ghosts wavering in image and, apparently, wavering with fear also; I could feel it emanating from them. I should have been the one to be afraid and I couldn't help but shake my head at the anomaly, even though I wasn't quite without fear myself.

"What . . . who are you?" I asked, hardly expecting a reply—I'd become too used to being ignored nowadays.

There was a tenderness in his smile. I saw that his eyes were blue, his hair brown but graying. I *knew* this man.

"*That doesn't matter for now,*" I heard the medium say over my shoulder, but the man's lips forming the words. *"You must go back, Jimmy. You must go back and stop him. Many others will die if you don't."*

"Stop who? D'you mean Oliver, the friend who murdered me?"

A look of dismay swept over his ghostly features. *"No. The one who lives in shadows, the one whose soul is black. You've already met this person, Jimmy, you must put an end to these murders. Find the person who has no face again."*

Somehow I knew instantly who he meant even before the medium spoke.

"The one with the scissors," she said, while the apparition formed the words.

The man who clipped news stories from the papers. The man who lived in the gloomy basement flat. The man with the horribly disfigured face. Rather, the man without a face.

"No." It was a one-word refusal from me. No way did I want to visit that grotesque again. Leave him undisturbed. Leave him to his own obsessions. Even though I was beyond harm these days, the thought of returning to that dark pit repulsed me.

"You must bring this evil to an end, Jimmy. The murder and defilement must stop."

I was confused. Mutilation. The killer who I first blamed for my death. The man with the scissors.

"But there's nothing I can do," I cried out loud. "I'm . . . I'm a ghost, like you."

"No. You're not yet that. In time, Jimmy, in . . ." The medium's voice was growing softer, the vision before me, and the cowering shapes behind it, beginning to fade.

"Your time will come, but first . . ."

The sound fading as the ghostly figure dematerialized before my eyes.

"The power . . ." his words were waning, dying, then reviving as if a volume control was being manipulated *". . . others here . . . afraid of you . . . the link . . . ting weak . . . visit you . . . one . . . time . . . this is over. Take heart . . . must be strong . . . your family . . . danger . . ."*

The image—and the voice—was gone, dissolved in front of me. I heard a muted thump and someone shrieked. Wheeling round, I saw that the medium had fallen forward, her head hitting the table. One of the sitters, the plump woman I think, had cried out at the drama.

I stared into the shadowy corner, but there was nothing to see anymore, no fading remnants, no indication whatsoever that the ghosts had truly been there. A memory came to me then, suddenly, without pre-thought. I had seen the ghost who had spoken to me before, but it was many years ago and almost buried by time. I remembered when I had crashed my motorbike at the age of seventeen. I had left my body as a result of the trauma and had observed misty figures watching my unconscious body in the gutter. And I thought of one in particular, one who had tried to speak to me, but either his power or my receptiveness was not strong enough for his words to be clear. He had seemed familiar to me then and I couldn't understand why at the time. I did now, though.

That man had been the same one who had appeared to me moments before in this clairvoyant's parlor, the ghost who had spoken to me. I understood beyond any doubt now that this was my father.

TWENTY-SIX

So that's why I returned to the horrible dingy basement flat somewhere in west London. It was easy to do, even if I hadn't wanted to go: I just envisaged it in my mind, and then I was flying, the streets below me almost a blur. Within a few seconds, I was there, in the dimly lit room that had shadows darker than the séance parlor I'd just left. The hideously disfigured man was at home.

I find it difficult to express the consternation and nausea I felt the moment I saw him hunched over his central table, because I was to see a lot worse subsequently, stuff that would revolt me even more. The bent man was feeding. But he was feeding through a straw, sucking up some pulverized mixture into the hole that should have been his face, the slurping-gurgling noise he made as sickening as the sight.

The clear plastic container from a blending machine stood close by on the table—a table whose top was still littered with old newspaper cuttings and a pair of long-bladed scissors, by the way—with only a few dregs of some sludgy liquid remaining. The rest of the murky brown porridge was in the bowl from which the hunched figure drank.

In his black shabby clothes, shoulders rounded and head bent low, he resembled a giant fly sucking through its proboscis, the shit-brown of the liquid compounding the illusion. Even though I was of no substance I wanted to vomit. Nevertheless, I stayed with him. I could imagine the flat's foul stench just by looking around at its shoddy state, the black fungi on certain parts of the wall and ceiling, the threadbare carpet, and the open cans of food left in the small kitchen's sink next door, and for the first time I appreciated having no sense of smell. It was a queer situation to be in, and I mean that by location as well as intention: I had a world outside to explore (if I could work up the "interest"), so why contain myself to this nasty hovel when I could float through the wall and visit far more wholesome and entertaining places? But I remained there, not sure why I was obeying a ghost's plea. A ghost who had mentioned my family . . . and danger . . .

The man with the scissors, the ghost of my father had said. *Bring this evil to an end.*

Was this hunched person the serial killer, then? Was he the one who had murdered and mutilated all those poor people? The killer Oliver had foolishly tried to emulate? And if not, why then had I been drawn to him in the first place, before the séance, before my father had had the chance to talk to me? This person's interest in the murders, shown by the press clippings still in disarray on the table, indicated more than just morbid curiosity. It was crazy. I was—used to be—an ordinary man, with precious little regard for otherworldly matters, even though I had the ability to leave my own body at times, so what was I to believe now? I wanted to get out of there, away from this unfortunate but disgusting creature, my conscience chastizing me for such uncharitable thoughts, while my eyes implored me to flee. Besides, I had more interest in seeing Oliver brought to justice rather than this ogre. Selfish, I know, but I couldn't get over my partner's betrayal, first with my wife, then the ultimate treachery of murdering me.

I forced myself to linger. Even when this grotesque interrupted his feeding and his body, suddenly tense, looked around at me, I did not retreat. What harm could he do to me? I was already dead. It was freaky though, those coal-black eyes staring at me as if he knew I was there. I metaphorically held my breath and his gaze roamed further, searching the corners of his foul habitat. After a while, he returned to his noisy guzzling and I sighed with relief. But why was it that on both of the other occasions I'd come here he had seemed to sense my presence? What psychic powers did he have? Nobody else had been aware of me since my death, not even my close family—not even my mother—so why this man? Just more questions to the overall mystery of my predicament.*

I would wait, I decided. I would stay here for as long as I could stand it and see what evolved, loathsome though the ordeal might be. What the hell—I had nothing else to do. So I stayed with him through the night, watched him shamble around his tiny, three-roomed flat, saw him mull over his mass of newspaper clippings. He seemed vexed when he picked up the cutting concerning my

---

*The fact that even the medium had been unable to see me created a new puzzle. She had been aware of the ghosts' presence, had spoken to the one I believed to be my dead father, and he had spoken to me through her. Did that mean I wasn't a proper ghost; even though there was no doubt that my body was dead? Hell, it had even been cremated! If I wasn't a spirit, then what was I? Neither alive, nor a ghost; at least, apparently not in the true sense of the word. I feared I might be going mad.

own terrible demise, and then became angry, striking the tabletop with the heel of his fist several times. I could only assume that he was furious because someone appeared to have stolen his thunder and, having enjoyed the pleasure (the disfigured man must have got some kind of perverted kick out of slaying and mutilation, so would have assumed the copycat killer had experienced the same), this person had put the blame on him. He read the article over and over again and, to my horror, he underlined my home's vague address with a stubby pencil. I felt a panic when I reasoned why he should do so. After a while, he sat up straight and pushed the clipping aside. He stared at the blemished wallpaper on the wall opposite, but his eyes seemed blank, as though he were not studying its faded patterns, but rather thinking inwardly, his eyes dulled as though they were matt-finished, the large cavity in his face oozing spittle and a yellowish pus-like substance that ran down his half-formed chin. I would have liked to have looked away from him, but somehow his deformity held me mesmerized. God, what had this man gone through in life? Had he been born with this deep wound where his nose and mouth should have been, or had some tragic accident occurred to render him so? What kind of world did he live in? What mental torment he must have been through. Did he have an occupation, or did his deformity force him to hide away permanently, venturing out only with his hat and scarf concealing his lack of normal features? And was it the ugliness in his face that had caused the ugliness in his soul? I almost felt sorry for him, but quickly remembered he was a killer who had chopped up the bodies of his victims.

Perhaps it was odd that never for a moment did I doubt that he was the serial killer the police were looking for, but everything about him—his interest in the newspaper clippings concerning the murders, the dark aura that surrounded him, even the black brooding atmosphere of the flat itself—indicated to me that there was something very wrong with this man and it had nothing to do with his deformity. And when he shuffled over to a corner cupboard and took out something wrapped in rough cloth my curiosity was roused further. Something, or things, clicked together as he laid the bundle on the table and unraveled it. Several long—about one-foot long—grey knitting needles lay exposed and I saw that their coated steel points had been honed into something lethal.

I stayed in that frightening and depressing place for the rest of the night, watching the disfigured man, listening to his guttural breathing, seeing him sort through his pile of newspaper clippings, avoiding contact with him as he paced the room in his dark raincoat. Occasionally, he would return to the table and pick up the accounts of my murder as if they had some special signifi-cance to him (and I realized it had, for if the police were right, this was one of the murders he did not commit). His breathing became heavier and more coarse each time he scanned the cut-out pages, and he would throw them back onto the table, his anger barely contained, only to pace the floor again for ten minutes or so, then pick the clippings up once more. It was a pattern that went on for some time and it confirmed in my mind that he really was deranged. I could only keep to one shadowy corner, ready to move each time he approached, afraid of him even though I knew I could not be harmed anymore, freezing each time he seemed to look directly at me, as if he sensed I was there. At these moments, he himself, would become very still, and his protrusive eyes would beam their curiosity and malice. I felt as though I were looking into the eyes of evil incarnate and I never held their gaze for long, always averting my face and cowering, ready to make a break for it should he advance any further.

He never did though. Instead, his shoulders would slump and he'd continue his pacing or return to the table with its wild spread of newspaper articles and dirty bowl and blender jug, which he had not yet bothered to clear away. I've no idea how long it was before he decided to turn in for the night, because I seemed to be losing track of time in some small way, but eventually he turned out the feeble light in the main room and went through to his bedroom. I had no wish to be present when he undressed—what other horrors might his naked round-shouldered body reveal—so I remained in my corner, which was now pitch black, the only light coming from the open doorway. After some thumps—probably shoes being dropped—and some groans—were other, hid-den disfigurements causing him pain?—I heard him urinating (presumably a toilet or bathroom adjoined the bedroom), then a flush. Padded footsteps as he returned to the bed, then the creak of old springs.

I listened as he grumbled to himself, once in a while his voice rising to an angry unformed roar, and eventually there came the unlovely sound of his snoring, a rasping squeezed exhalation followed by a rough droning intake of breath. I explored the rest of the flat in the darkness (the bedroom light had been turned off just before he'd climbed into bed and the only illumination came down from a street light on the pavement above the basement steps), but found nothing of importance, nothing that might reveal this man's identity. Dishes and plates were stacked up unwashed in the sink, the plastic bin beneath it overloaded with rubbish, some of which—a milk carton, half an egg shell, an empty tin of beans—had spilled onto the floor. Going back to the main room I forced myself to sit on the lumpy, magazine-strewn couch, its outline only just discernible in the weak light from the basement window. Again, I was grateful that I no longer had a sense of smell.

I suppose I fell into a deep sleep, because the next thing I knew there was gray twilight showing through the grimy glass of the window and my host was shuffling about the room. It looked as though he was preparing to leave. With dismay I realized I must have slept or blacked out for a whole night and most of the next day.

TWENTY-SEVEN

I followed him up the stone steps to street level. He wore the same dark rain-coat and scarf muffler as yesterday, only those bulging eyes barely visible in the shadow of the hat's brim. It was a drizzly and apparently cold autumn morning, for other pedestrians wore raincoats or topcoats, one or two carrying open umbrellas. I had no idea what time it was, but it felt like late afternoon. God, had I been asleep (or just oblivious) while he dressed and took meals, unaware of me as I'd been unaware of him?

His shoulders hunched even more than usual, as if shrinking into himself so as not to be noticed, he made his way along a line of vehicles parked in resident-only bays, and I followed two feet behind him, the light rain passing right through me. He stopped by an ancient Hillman Minx, a gray tank of a car that must have been manufactured in the last century's fifties. The wheel arches were rusted, the door panels pitted and scored, the windows as grimy as those in the flat we'd just left, smeared arcs caused by wipers relieving the windscreen of some of the dirt. I noticed there was a parking permit stuck to the inside of the windscreen, but when I peered closer it gave no owner's name, only the vehicle registration.

The man unlocked the car door and climbed in, so I passed through the rear passenger door and settled into the wide seat. Like his home, the interior was untidy, bits of paper and debris—a lidless can of frost spray, a battered *A to Z*, an empty milk carton, used straws—littering the floor both front and back. The leather upholstery was split in places and a soiled rag lay on the passenger seat beside the driver. The man ducked low, pushing something underneath his seat, tucking it away out of sight; I hadn't registered the fact that he had been carrying something under his arm as he'd made his way to the car, and it was this that he was concealing. Something inside the cloth-wrapped bundle clicked, a recognizable sound. He'd brought the knitting needles with him.

Before I could wonder why, he pushed the key into the ignition and switched on the engine. It moaned its reluctance to start and he made another two attempts before the engine finally turned over and settled to an uneasy murmur. Immediately he pushed the gear lever—so ancient was the Hillman that it was a column shift on the steering wheel—into first, then pulled away from the curb; it was only when we left the sidestreet and turned into the main road that I realized I'd got my timing wrong, for the pavements were busy with people, all the shops and offices lit up, the road itself crowded with traffic. It was early evening and not the afternoon. How had I been asleep so long? Why hadn't his movement in the flat aroused me earlier? Then again had I really slept that long, or was this merely another slippage in time? There was no way of knowing; I wasn't yet familiar enough with my condition to be able to tell. All I knew was that at certain times I fell asleep, or simply blacked out, so that my spirit, soul, consciousness, whatever I was, rested, or renewed itself. I did, in fact, feel a little fresher each time I "awoke" so I could only assume that even *my* state required its rest and replenishment. It seemed mundane, but I supposed that incorporeal existence paralleled normal life to some extent, the mind continuing to follow a familiar pattern. Maybe in the *unknown* you instinctively comforted yourself with the *known*, or perhaps a lifetime's habit was hard to break even in death.

As he drove on, it took only a few minutes for me to realize we were in the Shepherd's Bush area and I watched people going about their business, unaware that some strange kind of ghost was traveling through their midst. How I envied their humdrum lives, how I wished I was part of the system again, a living, breathing person with all the problems, heartaches, and joy that went with the human condition. The world I now lived in was no fun at all and I began to wonder if I was in purgatory, the stage between life and death that some religions—especially my own—told us we had to pass through before reaching our paradise (or heaven, as we called it). And if that were the case, part of my redemption might lie in preventing this monster from murdering more innocents. What the hell, I had nothing else to do with my time, and I could no longer be harmed myself, so why not go along with it? It certainly seemed important to the spirit I now believed to be my father. How I could stop the sick lunatic I had no idea, but hoped that something would present itself along the way.

My thoughts returned to the driver of this clapped-out vehicle and I studied the back of his head from the rear seat. His low snuffles were occasionally interrupted by deliberate snorts, his reaction to other drivers who irritated him with their careless maneuvering. Again, the sickness of his aura disturbed me as much as the man himself, the muddy radiation sending off dispiriting vibes that I felt must surely unsettle the living people he came in contact with. It's odd that some individuals can take an instant dislike to certain other people they've just met, which can only be put down to the chemistry between them. I now believe that dislike or aversion had more to do with the sensing of aura than any chemical reaction (maybe it amounted to the same thing, who could tell? Certainly not me); probably, the opposite was also true, attraction being just as easily influenced by a compelling aura. Maybe this was the answer to the mystery of "love at first sight."*

I think we must have been driving for ten minutes or so (not being sure of time anymore, I found this hard to judge) when the car pulled into the fore-court of a huge gray stretch of a building, and I just glimpsed the word "HOSPI-TAL" on a big noticeboard as we passed by. Which London hospital it was I had no idea, but there were two wings on either side of the main block and its façade was grubby with city pollution. My unwitting chauffeur drove around to the back of the gray edifice and eased the Hillman into a crowded staff car park. Climbing out, he took time to check on the wrapped package on the floor, pushing it back further out of sight with the guttural kind of grunt I was getting used to from him. I followed as he slammed the door shut, locked it, and shambled away. He had a peculiar shuffling gait, one hunched shoulder higher than the other, and I wondered what other things were wrong with his body. Certainly his stride was impeded in some way, although his physique looked strong, powerful, those shoulders broad if stooped and tilted, his hands and wrists large, his booted feet also big, suggesting thick legs. His face was al-most completely hidden by the woolen scarf and hat, his bulging black eyes peering out from between. Although the covered cavity where there should have been a nose and mouth was gristled and raw, seepage constantly leaking so that the night before he had been forced to hold a large soiled cloth to it constantly, I had the feeling that this was no new injury, if injury it was. He ap-peared to be too competent with his method of eating for the orifice to have

---

*Again, I remembered—I was too distraught to register anything as subtle as auras at the time—how Prim's muted radiance (although it still contained vibrant flashes within its down-toned glow) had intermingled with Andrea's, who tried to console her, their light be-coming part of a whole. It had also been visible when Primrose had sat on her granddad's lap on the day of my funeral. Unfortunately, I recalled witnessing a different kind of inter-action when Andrea and Oliver had kissed so passionately in my home later that same day: through their dulled colors, small vibrant charges had flashed from each of them.

been recently created, placing the straw perfectly into whatever receptacle lay beyond the rough edges, with no hint of pain or discomfort, sucking up the blended food with practiced ease. Several people, uniformed nurses, gave him odd glances as he passed by, but none spoke to him. I kept to his heels, wondering if he was seeking treatment at the hospital, or if he was employed there, perhaps as a porter or boilerman, any kind of job that did not involve the public. Cruel as the thought was, I felt pretty certain that his work would not bring him into much contact with the public.

He approached a double door marked "MORTUARY—RESTRICTED AREA," and pushed one side of it open, passing through and entering a long, wide and dismal corridor, the walls painted a turgid olive green, the lights in its ceiling behind wire guards for some reason, as if the corpses wheeled along this way might rise up and try to break them. I still kept close to him, walking not gliding, behind him, as though I remained part of the real world. A man wearing green overalls approached from the opposite direction, a surgeon's mask, also green, hanging around his neck. He nodded at the man I followed as he went by and was greeted with a muffled grunt that could have meant anything.

Soon we arrived at plastic doors, the kind that overlapped and were easy to push trolleys and gurneys through, and I saw that we were in a long room, floor-to-ceiling white wall tiles and overhead strip lighting giving an air of clinical cleanliness. To one side there was a whole wall filled with refrigerated steel cabinets, the door to each one approximately three feet by two. There must have been at least forty of them. Three stainless-steel tables, carts filled with surgical tools standing next to each one, occupied the concrete floor; only one had a naked body stretched out on its surface. Another man, also wearing gown and mask, as well as latex gloves, was working on the pale carcass.

"Ah, good," the masked man said, looking up. "You've got the evening shift tonight, have you, Moker?"

A familiar grunt from my man.

"Well, there's not much going on, unless anything fresh is brought in." The man standing by the dead body pulled his surgical mask free from his face. "This one's all done, so just clean him up before you put him away for the night. I understand the relatives are coming in in the morning for a last look and positive ID, so make sure you do a good job."

There was no friendliness in the mortician's tone as he spoke to the man he'd called . . . what was it? Moter? No, Moker. I'm sure he said *Moker*. In fact, he eyed the muffled man with disdain, and I was sure it wasn't because of the way Moker looked, not in these politically correct times. Moker didn't seem to be too popular, and I could well understand that. With or without his deformity, there was just something plain unpleasant about the guy.

The mortician began peeling off his latex gloves, studying the corpse before him as he did so, lost in thought for the moment. As he dropped the gloves into a pedal bin, he noticed Moker had not yet moved. He glared at him through wire-framed spectacles.

"Well, what are you waiting for?" he said gruffly. "Get yourself changed and don't forget to wear gloves tonight. I've told you enough times that all kinds of diseases can be picked up from cadavers. Now get on with it."

Moker shuffled away, going through a door that I hadn't noticed on one side of the long sparse room. I went with him out of curiosity. This was a locker room, tall cabinets set along the wall, where a youngish guy, who looked as if he enjoyed too many Big Macs, was just closing the door of one of them. Moker went to a locker, produced a key from his raincoat pocket, and opened it; but not before I'd had the chance to read the small name card on the door. "A. MOKER" it read in badly written capital letters. So, the name was confirmed, not that it would help me in any way. Why had I even bothered to follow him? I asked myself. What was I supposed to do? Not only could I not physically touch him, I could not even haunt him. He might seem aware of my presence at times, but there had been no indication that he'd actually *seen* me.

The mortician who had given Moker his instructions came in behind us holding a rumpled apron in front of him by the fingers of one hand as if it carried the plague.

"Whose is this?" he barked at both men in the locker room.

The tubby guy was shrugging on a jacket and his hand appeared from a sleeve to point at Moker.

"Alec's," he said, without a trace of betrayal.

The mortician gave Moker a withering look and pushed the offending garment toward him.

"I've told you before," the mortician reprimanded as Moker took the grubby apron. "Don't leave soiled aprons lying in the cabinet room. This looks as if it should have been laundered weeks ago."

He wheeled away without another word and Tubby Guy followed him from the room, leaving Moker alone.

I watched as he threw the apron in the bottom of the locker and took out green overalls, a long linen coat of the type worn by the mortician himself. He laid it over the back of a hard chair then unwound the choker from his neck. I flinched again at the sight of his poor ravaged face, but he quickly reached inside the locker again and took out a surgical mask, this one white, which he pulled over most of his face, hiding the hole beneath. Even so, with no shape of a nose and mouth, the cloth mask looked odd. It puffed out as he breathed, shrinking concavely as he took a breath.

Donning the overalls, he put his own coat, scarf, and hat inside the locker and closed the door. Picking up a dry sponge and cloth he returned to the main room which, apart from the body on the metal table, was now empty. Moker approached the corpse, considered it for a minute or two, examining the plain stitching on its chest and groin where the mortician had removed organs for inspection. I noticed there were labeled jars on a shelf nearby, each one containing interior body parts. A brown clipboard filled with handwritten details hung from the side of the stainless-steel table. The corpse itself had a label with more details attached to the big toe of the right foot. I heard a muted cough and glanced over to a doorway leading to a small and, from what I could see, cramped office where the person who had greeted Moker sat bent over a desk. He still wore his green overalls and was busy with more paperwork, no doubt filling out forms appertaining to the deceased. At the sound, Moker busied himself swabbing down the body and I drifted away. The dead man was pallid beyond belief, with blue stains around his eyes and lips, similar stains blemishing his skin in other places. It was an awful sight, particularly with the stitched Y-shaped wound running down his chest and stomach, and I had no morbid interest in watching Moker at work. I drifted around, peering into glass cabinets containing all kinds of liquids, powders, and creams, even body deodorants, wound fillers, and body plugs. There was an embalming machine nearby with dials and tubes attached, its large glass container filled with pinkish fluid mounted on top. In the small office next door where the mortician continued his form filling, there was a desk crammed with upright files, a computer keyboard and screen, two lamps, a telephone, and various pieces of paperwork and folders. The mortician barely had room to write. Around the walls were more clipboards bearing various other forms, framed morticians' licenses, a calendar, and some kind of printed schedule with days of the week and allotted work times inked in. I saw Moker's name entered for all that week's evening shifts.

The mortician finally laid down his pen with a grumble of relief and pushed back his chair, which was on castors. I stepped away as if the chair might knock into me (instinctive reactions were still hard to overcome), retreating into the mortuary itself, and the mortician followed me through. He didn't bother to bid Moker goodnight as he made his way to the plastic doors, and Moker, who was busy swabbing down the corpse, didn't look up from his work.

I still felt very uneasy in Moker's presence, even though I could not be seen (although it chilled me whenever Moker seemed to sense that something was with him and he peered around the room, seeking out whatever it was that disturbed him), and I would have loved to have left that place. I couldn't go though—the spirit's words at the séance had had too much of an effect on me. Maybe I was on some path toward redemption, a path that would take me from this purgatory I was in. After all, I was a Catholic, even if a lapsed one, and I was supposed to believe in that kind of thing. Besides, incorporeality had to have some effect, didn't it?

So I stuck with the situation, not having a clue as to the purpose of my vigil, but trusting that something important might come of it. The evening drew on and the later it got, the more the mortuary seemed isolated from the rest of the world. Footsteps, a cough from Moker, the dribble as he squeezed out the sponge—all sounded hollow, echoey, and louder than they should have been. I knew it was the acoustics created by the tiled walls and metal cabinets, but nevertheless, it was kind of ghostly. I suppose the hidden rows of dead bodies and the sight of the corpse that Moker worked on added to the creepiness, but I had to remind myself that I was the one doing the haunting. No one disturbed Moker in his work, nobody at all entered the mortuary that night; the telephone didn't ring, there were no extraneous noises from beyond the four walls. The silence was relieved only by his grunts and occasional harsh breathing. It was both depressing and nerve-wracking.

At last he finished his labors and threw the sodden sponge and cloth into a plastic water bucket at the foot of the metal table. He gazed at his handiwork for a few moments, then traced with his thick fingers the stitched scar that ran from chest to groin. It was a sickening thing to do and I could only wonder at the man's mentality and motive. Finally, he shuffled away, left shoulder higher than the right, and went over to a tall freestanding cupboard, from which he took a large folded white sheet. This he spread over the body, covering it from head to ankles, allowing only the feet to show. After this, he wheeled over a gurney and, effortlessly, it seemed to me, transferred the corpse onto it. He pushed it to the end of the row of closed cabinets, read the card on one, before pulling the cabinet all the way out. Naturally, it was empty and he came back to the body on the gurney and pushed it toward the exposed shelf of the cabinet. Again, effortlessly, it seemed, he lifted the corpse and laid it out on the shelf, tidily tucking the sheet around its outline so that he could close the cabinet once more. This he did, and when the shrouded body was out of sight, he tapped the cabinet front twice with the flat of his hand as if bidding the dead man goodnight.

This was cavalier at best, but what followed was far worse. My God, it was far, far worse; disgustingly so. First, he went to the plastic double door, pushing it open a fraction and peering out as if to see if the coast was clear. Then he came back to the closed cabinets and walked along them, tapping each door that was at chest level. He stopped, took another swift look at the plastic doors, then pulled open one cabinet. It slid out easily, only the low rumble of its runners breaking the silence, and I could see that the figure it held was smallish. Although the head was fully covered, I could tell by the dainty, colorless feet and the two slight chest bumps that a woman or girl lay beneath the shroud.

Moker pulled back the white sheet, slowly, as if relishing every stage of exposure, pausing as the breasts were uncovered. The surgical mask he wore puffed in and out with increased labor and I saw a dark saliva stain spread across it. The unveiling continued and I wanted to turn away from the obvious necrophilia. Instead, as if mesmerized again, I continued to stare in horror.

When, at last, the folds of sheet lay around the girl's feet—I saw she could only be in her early twenties—Moker raised his thick, and now trembling hands and ran them over her chalky-white figure. Apart from her deathly whiteness and the blueness of her lips, she looked unharmed, as though whatever had ended her young life remained hidden within the vessel that was her body; her hair was golden blonde and it lay in matted ringlets around her head and neck.

I yelled a high-pitched protest when I saw what Moker was doing and tried to grab his arms, wanting to pull him away, wanting to prevent his desecrating this beautiful but lifeless girl. Nothing I could do would stop him though and, although I was aware of my inadequacy, I could not still my arms and I beat at him, tore at him, desperately tried to force him away. His big hand delved between her thighs, which were now spread in a revealing pose, and I screamed again and again.

Eventually, I gave up and went into the small office next door. I sank into the desk chair and lay my head in my hands, covering my ears.

I could still hear the brute noises coming from next door, the animal moans of Moker as he abused the body that had been left in his charge.

But shocked and repulsed though I was by the depravity, nothing could have prepared me for the horror that was to follow later that night.

TWENTY-EIGHT

It was a long wretched night and more than once I had to force myself to remain in the presence of this monster. I kept to the little office, desperately trying to close my mind to the activity next door. Other cabinets had been opened, but I refused to think of what might be happening to other cadavers. Perhaps having finished with the girl, Moker was merely carrying out his normal duties; I could only hope. Twice he came into view through the doorway, pushing a floor mop, a metal bucket by his feet, and I supposed that not only was it his job to clean the corpses, but also the mortuary itself. Once he came into the office and I had to back away into a tight corner to avoid his touch—I shuddered at the idea of sharing any of his sick thoughts—and I remained there as he shuffled through paperwork on the desk. I got the feeling that he was just snooping rather than working, because he added nothing to the various forms he browsed through, nor did he instigate new paperwork himself. He looked into the desk drawers and I had the impression he was still prying and not actually searching for something. And strangely, all the while he wore the surgical mask over the gaping hole in his face, as if visitors might drop in any moment and he did not want anyone to see the disfigurement. I had no idea how long he'd worked in this hospital mortuary, but I thought it pretty certain that other staff in the hospital knew of his deformity. In some strange way, perhaps he was hiding it from himself: I had noticed there were no mirrors in his grubby flat, but there were bound to be in other places he visited; in fact, there was a small one in this very room, stuck on a wall at about head level, obviously for morticians to groom themselves before they went about their business. Moker, deliberately it seemed to me, had refrained from glancing into the mirror all the while he was in the office.

It was a relief when he went outside again and carried on with whatever duties he was paid to do—cleaning and sweeping mostly, I'd have said, and not just tending bodies. I stayed where I was, sitting in the chair and closing my eyes, ready to jump up should he return. Occasionally I checked the time on the round clock fixed to the wall above the desk and only when the hands ap-proached 10 P.M. and I heard Moker pouring water away into one of the mor-tuary's stainless-steel sinks, and then the clatter of the bucket and mop as they were stored away, inside a cupboard, did I guess his shift was nearly up and he was getting ready to leave.

I went back into the long white-tiled morgue and trailed him to the locker room. He shed the green overalls and put the surgical mask into his raincoat pocket. Then he wound the long woolen scarf around his neck and face, and donned the coat and wide-brimmed hat. He was ready to leave and some inner instinct told me he was not immediately returning home.

I was right: he didn't go back to his basement flat. Instead he drove to a twenty-four-hour underground car park in Bayswater.

We'd been sitting there quite some time, Moker slumped in the driver's seat, me in the back, an impalpable passenger. I hated being so close to him—I was sure that if I had the sense of smell, his stench would have been unbearable—but there was no other option. I sensed he was up to no good (finely attuned instinct again?)—why else would he sit in the darkness of the car park's lowest level, studying every person (and there weren't that many at that time of night) who returned to collect their vehicle.

This basement area was almost as poorly lit as his flat (I was getting used to dark, dispiriting places by now: the séance parlor, Moker's dingy home, Mother's front room, and now this gloomy place, the car park itself), with no CCTV cameras, the parked cars few on this level. Footsteps, when they came, sounded lonely in this deep underground space. The old Hillman was parked between two smart cars, a Mondeo and a BMW, which only accentuated the battered wreck that it was. I thought Moker's raspy breathing might carry be-yond the confines of his vehicle, so quiet was this level he'd chosen, but it could be because of my own overwrought imagination. I heard a door shut and an engine start up, then the muffled sound of wheels traveling over concrete. The noise faded away. More footsteps, these belonging to more than one person.

Two people came into view, walking down the curving ramp in our direc-tion, and Moker sank lower into his seat. It was a man and a woman, and they were arm in arm, gazing into each other's eyes, seemingly oblivious to all else.

They reached the BMW, failing to notice the dark hunched figure in the old car next to it, and the man fumbled in his pocket for his car key. Before he inserted it into the lock, the couple paused to engage in a passionate kiss, the man running his free hand down the length of the woman's back. They clung together for a little while and I heard Moker's breathing become heavier, more ragged.

The driver climbed into the BMW and the woman walked round to the passenger side; her lover stretched across and pushed the door open for her. As she passed my window I saw that she was attractive, probably mid-thirties, smart in long skirt and navy jacket. The man, I'd noticed, wore a slightly crumpled business suit and had carried a briefcase, which he'd dropped onto the BMW's back seat. The pair looked like work colleagues who had just put in a stint of overtime. Once settled in the car, they practically hurled themselves at each other, mouths pressed tight, arms never still. Their kiss was passionate, their embrace ardent; they fumbled at each other and I began to feel embarrassed. Moker kept low in his seat, but constantly peeped over at the couple, obviously aroused, but wary of being spotted. Just when it seemed that the man and woman were about to lose all inhibition, an EXIT door about fifty yards or so away opened and three men stepped through. They were loud, laughing at each other's remarks, one of them playfully punching another on the upper arm. The couple in the BMW froze for a moment, then sat up, the man fiddling with the key in the ignition as if getting ready to start up. When the three men lingered by two cars not far away, one of them looking across and spying the couple, the driver of the BMW did start the engine and switched on the headlights, muttering something inaudible as he did so. He drove off, probably to find some other secluded place for their after-work activities.

As the BMW sped by, the three men split up, two of them getting into a blue Peugeot estate, the remaining one walking to a parked Celica and climbing in. Moker straightened up as the Celica drove off, then bent forward to pick up something from under his seat, the small bundle he had stowed away earlier. As he held it in his lap and unwrapped the cloth, I heard the familiar clicking sounds and I leaned forward for a better view. Although the lighting in the underground car park was inadequate, I was able to see what he held up to the windscreen to scrutinize.

It was one of those wickedly sharpened coated-steel knitting needles.

I sank back in the seat, suddenly very afraid. Why was Moker loitering in this badly lit and isolated place? Why *was* he holding that modified wicked-looking domestic tool? It didn't take a genius to figure it out. Oh God! I wanted to get out. I didn't want to be a witness to murder! Not when there was nothing I could do to prevent it. I—

The EXIT door opened again. Moker's head snapped up. A figure, silhouetted by the light inside the stairwell, came through. Footsteps echoed around the concrete walls and pillars. The figure walked under the dull glow of a ceiling light and both Moker and I saw at the same time that it was a man. According to the newspaper reports, gender didn't matter to the killer whose rampage had continued over barely six weeks. So if Moker *was* the serial killer—and by now I was sure he was—then a solitary man in this empty place would be an ideal victim. The ENTRANCE/EXIT part of this car park was three floors up, with thick concrete ceilings between.

Moker held the knitting needle upright in his hand like a knife while he waited for the man to draw nearer. I felt him tense, heard his breathing held in check; his other hand fingered the Hillman's inside door handle. The man came closer, unaware he was being watched. He moved through an ocean of shadow until he passed beneath another overlight and I heard Moker give out a little moan of disappointment.

The man, who was squinting around through heavy-lensed glasses, was short, overweight, and balding. Little did he realize that his plain looks were to save his life that night. I didn't realize either until a little later. Moker slumped in his seat once more, leaning across the passenger seat so that he would not be seen from outside the car. The man, lucky to live a longer life, passed by about fifteen yards away and, with a "humph" of recognition, made his way toward a gray Saab several vehicles further along. I watched with relief as he started his car and drove out of the parking space, his headlights lighting up the interior of the Hillman for a couple of seconds. Moker kept out of sight until the Saab had passed and was heading up the curved ramp to the next level.

I'm not sure just how much longer we waited, but it must have been at least half an hour before the EXIT door opened again. This time a woman came out, her shape in silhouette, and I felt Moker's rising excitement. She was alone and that made her very vulnerable. She was slim and had long flowing hair which made her a definite target, for I began to understand how the killer chose his target.

We could see more of the woman now and although she was not quite as glamorous as the first glance had suggested—her nose was a little large, her jaw a little weak—she carried herself well and the skirt and slim topcoat she wore accentuated the attractiveness of her figure. Her blouse plunged open a button too far and her ankles were trim in high-heel pumps. Now Moker's excitement had him trembling.

His hand crept to the door handle once again as he watched the woman go to her car and we heard the "dweep" of her electronic door key. Moker pulled the handle slowly, deliberately, quietly, and eased the door open a fraction, checking that the woman, who was just opening her own door, had not heard the sound. She hadn't; she opened her car door just as Moker pushed his wide.

"*No!*" I shouted as I lunged forward to grab him by the shoulders. It was useless, of course—my hands merely went through his body, raincoat and all. But he did hesitate. And I withdrew sharply, as though zapped by a thousand volts, for I had *sensed* him, caught sight of his nature, and the infringement was shocking. I felt as if my soul had lurched into something unbearably evil, an existence that was devoid of all compassion and wretched in its malice. It was only momentary—for both of us apparently, because Moker sat rigid, as if stunned—passing quickly and taking some of my energy with it. Moker turned and seemed to look directly at me as he had before now, but naturally seeing nothing. Even so, it was a relief when he turned away again and pushed the door, which had swung closed a little. He was about to step from the car when the EXIT door crashed open once more and two men virtually spilled out, laughing and giggling together at some joke that only the truly inebriated find funny.

Startled, Moker immediately pulled the car door shut again and watched the two drunks walk unsteadily along a row of parked vehicles. He gripped the Hillman's steering wheel tightly with one hand and I heard him sounding off what must have been incoherent oaths. The woman, who had been about to climb into her car, glanced up and gave a disgusted shake of her head before getting in. I heard her car's engine start and the head- and taillights came on. She reversed out and swept round, honking at the men, who had taken exaggerated steps to get out of her way, as she passed them by. One of them gave her the finger, which the other thought was hilarious. Her taillights disappeared up the ramp and the two drunks found the car they were blindly searching for. That neither one should be driving in their state didn't seem to bother them. One climbed into the driver's seat and the other went round to the passenger door and let himself in. The Jaguar reversed out perfectly and headed smoothly for the incline. It was quickly gone, the driver remembering to switch on his lights just as the Jag disappeared round the ramp's curve.

Moker and I were left alone in the shadows once more.

We waited a long time.

There were still a few cars parked and some, I assumed, would remain there overnight, but no one came to collect any for quite a while and I thought my nerve—and my resolve—would break long before then. After all, I'd touched this man, I'd *sensed* him, I'd felt the harsh bleakness of his soul. I wondered if he had been born evil, or if his disfigurement—lifelong?—had made him that way. Bad as his disability might be, it was hard to justify his apparent hatred of normal human beings. And hate them, he did; I'd felt it when part of my body had merged with his. Could you be born evil? Or did you learn from environment and condition? I could hardly ask him the question.

How long was this psychopathic monster prepared to wait here for a suitable victim? Oh yes, I was doubly sure now that this was his intention—why else the sharpened knitting needles, why had he made a move toward the lone woman, if not waiting for suitable prey? But why not the first man who had come along? There had been no one else about, and previous victims had included both men and women. Also, the man had been overweight and soft-looking, hardly the type to put up a fierce struggle. It had seemed that Moker was about to go for him, but when he saw the man's face he had relaxed back in his seat again. That was when it finally dawned on me. Was it that the first guy had been particularly unattractive? In fact, to be blunt, he was downright ugly. Was the qualification for murder that the victim had to be handsome or beautiful, or at least, presentable? So was that what Moker was looking for? The woman who had come along was certainly good-looking and Moker had prepared himself to go for her, only the two drunks arriving at an inopportune moment having saved her. According to the lurid reports in the tabloids, all victims so far had been either successful or fairly successful business types, smartly dressed and, from the photos of the deceased, attractive. That was why back in the hotel room Chief Superintendent Sadler had asked Oliver if I'd been handsome! Did Moker have a grudge against good-looking and smart people? Did he envy them? Did he want to eradicate them—and, of course, spoil their looks—because he could never be like them? I was soon to learn that killing these people was only part of it; Moker's vengeful jealousy went far beyond that.

He was patient, this nasty psychopath. So very patient. Just when I thought he must surely give up his vigil, that the rest of the cars in the car park were here for the night, we both heard the clatter of what could only be a woman's high-heeled shoes coming from the direction of the curving ramp. Amplified by the low concrete ceiling and walls, the sound grew louder by the moment. She came into view.

From a distance she looked tall and slim, slimmer even than the previous woman who had used the stairway and EXIT door to access this floor, and as she drew nearer we saw her hair was long and falling in bangs around her face. She entered a pool of light and I groaned inwardly when I saw her pleasant, although not stunning, features. I knew there was a good chance she would pass the Moker test of attractiveness.

In the front seat, Moker shifted, and I noticed that the knitting needle was held in his hand once more. As before, his free hand slowly reached for the door handle.

The woman passed by the front of the Hillman and failed to notice her stalker in the deeper shadows of the old car. She wore narrow, silver-framed designer spectacles which in no way detracted from her appeal—far from it: they seemed to render her even more vulnerable. Her lips were finely drawn, her nose strong but not obtrusive. Her breasts, beneath a thin cream blouse, spread apart the front of her unbuttoned check jacket, while in her left hand she carried a plastic Safeway's bag and a briefcase (probably after working late, she'd done some late-night supermarket shopping). I noticed that she wore no wedding or engagement ring; perhaps she was a career woman with scant time for romance.

The situation was perfect for Moker: the dark, lonely location, the victim alone and unaware, her looks favorable, the shadows a welcome ally. Slowly he removed his hat. God, I prayed for somebody to come through the EXIT door, or down the ramp; I prayed for another vehicle to come down looking for a parking place. But I knew it wasn't going to happen. Circumstances were too bloody ideal for murder.

The woman, whom I judged to be in her late twenties or early thirties, headed toward a dark-colored Mazda sports car, which was isolated behind a pillar about twenty yards away. She gripped its key in her right hand, her arm extended as if singling out the car. I could tell she was nervous from where I watched, and what lone woman wouldn't be in this still graveyard of a place, parked vehicles like metal mausoleums in the artificial dusk. While the woman cautiously looked about her as she walked, Moker silently waited before quietly slipping out of the Hillman. He unwound the scarf from his disfigured face.

The prey had almost reached her car when he followed on tiptoe, soft shoes (for the first time I noticed he wore grubby cheap-looking sneakers) soundless on the concrete floor. She leaned forward to insert the Mazda's key in the lock and Moker hurried his steps, coming up behind her, pulling her round to face him, her eyes widening in horror, her mouth opening to scream, but his left hand reaching up to gag her, the hand holding the deadly thin weapon sweeping upward to strike beneath her left ribcage.

It had all happened so fast that I was still in the car, frozen there because I knew what was about to happen, only released from the stupor when the long needle sank through the blouse into her flesh.

Yet even as I sat there stunned, a memory came back to me, something the police detectives had discussed at the crime scene in the hotel: the police surgeon had mentioned that two weapons had been used on me, one an axe or chopper, and something that made a hole through the heart. A needle—a long thin needle—was the weapon used. I hadn't realized it at the time, but he was obviously talking about a common knitting needle, of which Moker had plenty. The news cuttings that Moker had collected indicated his fascination for the killings, but the collection of knitting needles in his possession had to confirm that beyond all doubt he was the guilty party.

Passing through the closed passenger door I sped toward the horrendous tableau, the woman held tight against her assailant's body, his hand no longer clamped over her mouth as she shivered in his grasp, the vicious needle pushing in deeper and deeper, its point sliding into her heart.

I ran at him, howling, wanting to tear him to pieces, but only too aware that I could not even touch him. I believe I was hot with rage at that stage, because my vision was scorched, the scene before me unclear. He held on to her, in almost a lover's embrace, their bodies locked tight. Quickly her struggles diminished so that her arms and legs began to quiver as life fled from her body. So fast, so easy. So contemptible.

She became still, only one foot occasionally twitching, and Moker allowed her to slip to the floor. Holding her shoulders, he knelt with her, his right hand still pressing the thin steel shaft into a point just below her left breast so that it entered her heart. Soon, even the twitching foot lost all movement. She was dead and I yelled in frustration and anguish.

Then I saw something rise from her still body, something that was neither ectoplasm nor vapor, but perhaps a combination of both. It was only inches high and was like some silky ethereal mist, pale enough to be translucent, rising as a wisp of smoke would from a spent match. Within a moment it was gone and I knew the woman's soul had left its host.

Moker looked around, scanning the shadows for any movement, the ramp for any approaching lights. Except for us the car park's lowest level was empty. He continued to press the honed needle in further until its flat round base plugged the wound. Surprisingly there was little blood, because the minute hole was effectively sealed; only a small bright seepage of blood ringed the needle's blunt end. Aghast—no, *mortified*—even though I'd known this might happen, I thought what a sad and brutal way to die. So sudden and so terrifying those last few seconds of her young life; but then, the consolation was that the ordeal had been so swift. I stared down at her blanched face, her mouth set in a final grimace, her eyes only partially closed behind the wire-framed spectacles, all shock gone from them.

I could hear Moker grunting, the noise as repellent as the man himself. Rising from his crouch, he picked her up easily and swung round toward the old Hillman, the body limp in his arms. I forced myself to walk along behind them, aware that further horror was to follow—hadn't he mutilated his victims?—but somehow resolved to see this nightmare through. God only knew what I could do to change things, but the spirit of my father had urged me to return to this killer. There had to be a reason.

And yes, there was further horror to follow, but it wasn't what I'd expected. In its own way, it was far worse.

TWENTY-NINE

To my surprise, Moker lifted the dead woman onto the back seat of the veteran Hillman. To my further surprise, he climbed in after her. What was this? Was he now going to violate her corpse, just as he had violated the corpses in the mortuary? Or was this where he intended to mutilate his victim? There were no dried bloodstains that I could see in the car, so it was unlikely he'd used it for that purpose before.

I sat in the front passenger seat and twisted round to watch, nauseated, frightened, but morbidly curious. Maybe I was still looking for a way to interfere, to stop this maniac.

Moker took out a large cotton cloth, perhaps just an oversized handkerchief, and stuffed it up the woman's blouse, laying it over the wound to staunch what little blood spread around the flat base of the knitting needle. Then he buttoned the jacket tight over her breasts, the cloth held against the wound, and I cringed when I saw that his bulging eyes burned with some fervor.

Even though I was there to witness what happened next, I still could not believe it.

Moker sat back in the rear passenger seat and closed his eyes, the dead body slumped against the car's opposite corner. I waited, mystified, caught up in what was taking place. Was this an extra way of getting his kicks, sitting with the person he'd just killed, enjoying the corpse's company as it grew colder? That he was a deviant of the lowest kind, there was no doubt, but this loitering with the victim beat all common sense. Certainly there wasn't much danger of being caught in the car park—anyone who did come along would be unable to see into the back of the car because of this level's inadequate lighting—but why take the risk anyway? And if he was going to cut the body up, he'd hardly do it in his own vehicle. Even with the blood beginning to congeal there would still be a terrible mess. I didn't understand and could only watch him as his breathing became deeper, the sound it made more disturbing. Soon he was sleeping and the rough-knitted muffler he'd rewrapped around his face billowed slightly with every escaping breath.

And then it occurred. At first I thought I might be imagining it, but the more intensely I gazed at Moker, the more certain I became that his image was wavering.

Something was leaving him.

I admit it, I was even more frightened than before and, because of it, I hunkered down almost into the footwell under the windscreen. I shouldn't have—I shouldn't have had—any physical discomforts in my condition, but I became cold. Very, very cold. And although I was hunched down, I could still see over the top of the front passenger seat, could still see some peculiar kind of transformation in Moker. I cowered down further, lest he discovered me somehow, and watched as his head and shoulders became blurred, as though something thin and vapory was smothering them, while a kind of nebulous mist—no, no, a kind of weak *ectoplasm*—was emerging from him so his image was indistinct behind it. And as this diaphanous cloud rose into the air, I saw that it was now taking on some sort of form. And the form was of Moker himself, but without the scarf and hat, without the grimy raincoat he always seemed to wear, without any clothes at all.

Although the image was unclear and ever-forming, I could make out the pits and scars to his body (I wondered if the old wounds had been self-inflicted), the malformed bones and surprising plumpness of his chest, and I wondered how a person could exist with such afflictions and could come to terms with such hideous defects. The substance was rising upward, breaking free of the man himself, rising like a ghost from the grave, and Moker's body was sliding sideways as if its lifeforce was deserting it. Finally, Moker's empty body slumped against the rear seat's corner. As Moker's real eyes were closed, so too were the eyes of his fluctuating self-image, but I remained hidden all the same.

The substance—ectoplasm, animus, essence, I didn't know what to call it—continued to build until I thought it might disappear through the roof of the car, but as the bare head—it had traces of wispy hair—touched the ceiling, the whole thing began to float sideways, toward the corpse in the other corner. This emanation was both fascinating and horrible, unusual and frightening, even though I'd left my own body many times in similar fashion in my past life (although I was sure that my spirit had never been visible like this, otherwise somebody would have mentioned it!). The ghosts at the séance parlor hadn't scared me as much, because there was nothing threatening about them. This was different, there was something malign about the phenomenon I was witnessing, and I felt nonexistent hairs on the back of my neck prickle, goosebumps rise on my arms. If I hadn't been dead, I'd have run for my life.

This is when it happened. This is when I saw something I never thought possible. Of course I'd read the books and watched the films about demonic possession, but only hokey or over-imaginative writers and film-makers were responsible for such scenarios, while this was a real man, albeit an abnormal one, whose soul was stealing another person's body. Death had emptied the woman's body of its soul and now a different soul was taking its place, filling the vacuum. As I watched, the vaporous issue from Moker was entering the corpse on the back seat, creeping into it, smoothly but bit by bit, nothing hurried, no sudden possession, just a steady ingress, the hazy but discernible "mist" gradually sinking into the body until the nebulous features of Moker had completely disappeared.

After a few moments—but very *long* moments—the corpse's eyes snapped open wide and looked into mine.

THIRTY

When the corpse spoke, its voice was strange, forced as if remembering the process. It was female, but there was an underlying hoarseness to the tone.

"I . . . know . . . you," she said.

I jerked back so fiercely that I went through the dashboard and landed in a heap beneath the car's engine. Stunned, I remained there for a few beats, at least out of sight of the Hillman's two back-seat occupants; then, rather than stand and be in view again, I rolled out and crawled around the Celica that was parked next to Moker's car, keeping low, afraid of being noticed, coming to rest behind the Celica's furthest front tire.

How was it possible for this woman to see me? Wait—the spirits at the séance had. In fact, most had been frightened of me. But . . . but . . . this woman's eyes had fully opened and had looked right at me. Did it mean she wasn't really dead? But that long, sharpened knitting needle straight through the heart— who could survive that? But then Moker's spirit had left him and entered his victim's body, so did that now mean he was dead? Think, I urged myself, think it through. Hadn't I once had the power to leave my own body without being dead? I was almost an expert of the out-of-body experience, but had this man Moker developed his own ability to a level where he could use a body once its true tenant had left?

I peered over the Celica's bonnet, squinting to see into the shadows of the Hillman. It was very dark, but there was movement in there. I kept low, nervous of being caught again. I heard rather than saw the rear door open and I ducked down out of sight. Cautiously I raised my head again, moving along the Celica's bodywork so that I could watch through its windows without too much exposure.

The woman was standing by the Hillman's open door. I could only see from the chin down to her waist, but I could tell she was unsteady. She raised a hand to lean on the gray metal roof, the other hand gripping the door handle. Her chest was heaving as if breathing was a strain. Was it Moker forcing the lungs to inhale? Was he inside the woman, forcing the dead body to function again? Unbelievable though it was, I suddenly had no doubts. After all, everything I had gone through recently was incredible, so what was so hard about this? The woman's spirit had vacated her dead body and Moker's own spirit had moved in to fill the vacuum, had taken possession. I was witness to it.

I kept out of sight, moving away from the Celica to get behind a concrete pillar, only standing up when the pillar was between the two vehicles and me. I risked a quick look.

The resurrected woman slowly and awkwardly turned her whole body to look around the car park. I flinched back out of sight once more, wondering if she was searching for me. Waiting for perhaps half a minute, I carefully peeked around the pillar again. She was moving her arms, trying to flex her stubborn fingers, only succeeding in straightening and clawing them stiffly. She began to walk, quite unstably to begin with, a hand brushing along the Hillman's roof for support, but her stride becoming just a little more adept with each step. I moved around the concealing pillar to keep out of sight, but still I peered around its corner.

Her right hand was now on the Hillman's bonnet, and her footsteps were still somewhat awkward, but I couldn't be sure if that was because of her zombie-like state, or because of the high-heeled shoes she was wearing. Her confidence seemed to grow though with each further step, and soon she had left the security of the old car and was walking along unaided, the shoes dragging along the concrete floor rather than clattering as they had when the woman was alive. At one point, her left knee gave out and she went down, her hands slapping against the ground and saving herself from falling all the way. She knelt there on one knee, her shoulders sinking and rising as though she were catching her breath, the knuckles of her hands pressed firmly against the concrete. She stayed that way for one, two minutes?—I couldn't be sure—then forced herself to rise again. That is, Moker forced her to rise again.

It was a graceless effort, like Bambi finding his feet for the first time, but with considerable effort she made it. The woman—this zombie of a woman— stood in the emptiness of the darkened car park regaining her breath, seemingly gathering more strength.

I began to understand that when the body dies, not everything fails at once; it takes a little while if only seconds for organs to cease functioning, and longer for muscles and tissues to atrophy, so was it possible for an alien entity to take over and make them work again? Probably, like me a week or so ago, you'd think *no way;* yet here I was witness to the miracle(?). It seemed possession was not confined to devils and demons. I understood now that when Jesus Christ had brought Lazarus back to life, He'd actually recalled Lazarus' soul, ordering it to return to its host. Who would have thought that the host body could also be appropriated by someone else's soul?

Before continuing, the dead woman looked about her once more as if looking for something. I had no doubt that "something" was me, so I remained hidden, frightened, incredulous—but inquisitive. She appeared to give up her search, although I'm sure she wasn't satisfied. She started moving again, the first few steps clumsy, ungainly, and also slow (although not as slow as those zombies in old and hackneyed horror flicks), heading toward the EXIT door that Moker had been watching for a couple of hours that night.

What the hell was she—*he*—doing? Wasn't mutilation the next item on the killer's agenda? According to the newspapers, that was the *whole* agenda. It was then I wondered if Moker, using the OBE, had entered all his dead victims this way. And if so, what was the point, what kind of kick did Moker get from it? I decided to follow. Oh, believe me, I didn't want to, I wanted to flee, get somewhere sane—like my own home. But the truth is, by now I was *really* curious.

I waited for the door to swing closed before leaving my hiding place—I don't know why I was quite so wary of being seen; after all, wasn't I untouchable? What could Moker do to me?—and went to the yellow-painted door. I listened before passing through it and heard shuffling footsteps ascending the stone steps that led to ground level. When they had faded enough for me to feel confident, I pressed through—no, I didn't even have to press this time—I just glided through the door.

The footsteps could be heard clearly now, although they were growing quieter, fading into the distance. Cautiously, *very* cautiously, I mounted the first few steps, then listened again. The foot-shuffle was barely audible, so I climbed further, looking upward over the iron rail as I went. Occasionally, I'd see the woman's hand grab at the rail as if to pull herself along, not all of the fingers coordinated, two of them poking out, straight and stiff, and I deliberately kept back, making sure there was at least one landing between us. At last I heard a door swing open at the top. She, *he*—I still had to get used to the idea that it was Moker I was following, not this poor woman—had stepped out into Queensway, a street that was always busy, with shops open day and night.

What game was Moker playing? I couldn't understand his motive. Had he done this with all his victims? Had the killer taken over each victim after death had occurred? Why had he appropriated their bodies? When I'd eaves-dropped on the two detectives' conversation outside my house, I'd heard them say that all the previous victims of the serial killer had acted in some bizarre ways around the time of their death: was I about to find out why and how? I shuddered. Just how deranged was this man? What was his purpose? To ridicule his victims? Was his mind so warped by his own deformity that he wanted to destroy the reputation of these innocent people, not content merely to destroy their bodies? Or was it simply for sexual self-gratification, commit-ting acts that he could not do as himself (whether it was because of his facial deformity, or because something else was physically wrong with him I had no idea).

Skimming up to the top floor, my mind reeling with concerns and ques-tions, I paused at the door to the street—just to try and bring my thoughts un-der control—before passing through.

There was plenty of light in Queensway, from shops, overhead lamps and slow-moving traffic, and plenty of people too. I didn't know the time.* As al-ways it was what you might call a "metropolitan" crowd, bustling or strolling the pavements, all types of people, some noisy and demonstrative, others en-gaged in their own private thoughts. The woman I followed weaved in and out of the throng, awkwardly at first, as if drunk, but beginning to pick up coordi-nation as she went. I kept to the gutter to avoid people, occasionally stepping aside for those pedestrians who joined me there for speed. One-way traffic slowly passed me by from behind, but naturally was never a threat; metalwork and wing mirrors went straight through my left side.

Up ahead, the woman stopped and seemed to be accosting a man who was probably just past middle age, an American tourist by the look of his loud out-fit and the camcorder hanging by a strap around his neck. I caught up in time to hear him say: "No thank you, dear. I'm happily married."

---

*It was peculiar how everything I would normally expect to be there (as far as I, myself, was concerned) indeed was, from my wristwatch to the handkerchief and keys in my pocket, even though I had no use for any of them. I could only assume that in the out-of-body state I saw everything as it was supposed to be, as if these inconsequential accessories that were personal and familiar to me afforded some small comfort. I'd have felt both embarrassed and intimidated if I were naked, even though I could not be seen, so my own mind gave me clothes, those I had been wearing on the night of my death. The other things were necessary for credibility. I'm sure I could easily have changed what I was wearing if I had set my mind to it, but what would be the point?

She rudely brushed past him and he turned around to watch her incursion back into the crowd. With a bemused shake of his head, he resumed his own journey.

Next, she stopped a black guy, a big man, smartly dressed, somewhere in his late thirties. I was too far behind to catch her words—maybe they were softly spoken, the hubbub around us easily drowning them. The tall guy looked her up and down, then laughed aloud. He didn't say anything, but just pushed by, shaking his head and continuing to laugh.

"Crazy bitch," I heard him say as he passed close to me.

Other people were turning to stare and I assume they thought she was drunk because of the unsteady way she progressed along the pavement, bumping into some pedestrians, swearing loudly at others so that they quickly dodged out of her path. Just before she reached a brightly lit newsagent's selling Arabian journals and magazines, three sallow-complexioned gentlemen came out, voices raised high in their own language, laughing together and generally in a cheerful mood. The woman strode up to them and once again said something I couldn't quite catch. I caught just enough, though, to understand that she was propositioning all three.

At first they gawped at her in surprise, obviously taking in her smart business clothes and appearance, before looking at each other. Two of them burst out laughing, a cackling sound that somehow managed to be insulting to the woman, but the third studied her face and body with interest. He murmured something to the other two, which initiated some nodding of heads, their laughter dissolving into wide lascivious grins. The first one took the woman's arm and said something softly into her ear. I presumed it was in English, because she instantly hung onto one of his companions' arms as if about to totter. She found herself supported by the two, one on either side. They led her away, a happy foursome, two of them jabbering excitedly, the Arab who'd replied to her proposition more reserved, although plainly eager. I kept to the gutter, almost abreast of them, dodging pedestrians who stepped off the curb to avoid the group, a sick feeling in my stomach.

Was this why Moker had taken over the woman's body, to indulge in sex with strangers, to debase her, soil her? But why? What was the point? To live vicariously through her for a short while? I was sure my first thoughts were right as I recalled the television and newspaper pictures of the previous victims, all of whom were smart and successful career people.

Moker wanted to *be* them, if only for a short while. And he wanted to enjoy what was probably impossible for him, because of his awful facial disfigurement, *through* them. He had possessed the fresh corpses for a while—did the bodies finally lose all strength and motion, was their after-death condition a very temporary situation?—only to degrade them, shame them, perhaps even to enjoy them. Only when he was satisfied—physically as well as mentally?—did he leave their bodies in some lonely place where he could return to mutilate them without interruption.

The four people I was following, three Arabs and one dead woman, suddenly changed direction and, using a busy zebra crossing close to a big corner store, crossed the road. I trailed behind.

The men were dressed smartly, two of them in light summer suits despite the obvious autumn chill, the third one, the serious one, had on an expensive-looking leather jacket. All wore good-quality shirts and ties and their shoes were highly polished. They might have been brothers, so similar were their features, although one of the suited men was a little overweight, his paunch overhanging his belt. His hair was sparser too, a light-brown shiny pate beneath carefully groomed hairs, which caught reflections from the lights spilling from the shops and the big store. On the other side of the road, they diverted into a sidestreet, and I noticed they had stopped talking now. Nobody was laughing anymore, either.

The woman's legs suddenly gave way and she almost fell to her knees, but the men gripped her tightly, hauling her up again and supporting her, their faces now grim, angry even. The one in the leather jacket snapped at her and I heard her burble something incoherent. She plodded along between two of them, her motion still unsteady, but not as bad as a moment ago.

Few pedestrians walked this sidestreet, although traffic still made its way toward Queensway where it was as busy as ever. This area of Bayswater was always vibrant, whatever the hour (except for the very early hours of the morning), but the further we moved away from the main thoroughfare, the fewer people we saw. The three men had quickened their step now, almost dragging the woman along. They crossed a narrow sidestreet and one of the men gesticulated, pointing toward the darkness at the end of it, but the one in the leather jacket shook his head and growled something in their language.

I was quite close to them, guessing their intent, but unable to do a thing about it. They soon reached another narrow sidestreet and this time Leather Jacket nodded and indicated with his head. He probably knew the area well.

How could this be happening? I repeatedly asked myself. The woman was dead, her heart had been stopped by a long sharp knitting needle. How was it possible for her to walk and talk, how could Moker manipulate her so? I could only reason that once the soul, the spirit, the vital spark of life itself, whatever, left the human body, it still took some time for it to run down completely. It was as if a dead battery had been replaced by a working one. Absolutely crazy, yet here was I, witness to that craziness.

There were no moving vehicles in this little street, only parked ones, and the further we went, the blacker it got. Several of the overhead lamps were out of order, and this was why there were so many inky shadows.

The group reached a junction and one end of it was a cul-de-sac, unlit shops on one side, darkened commercial buildings on the other. The woman was dragged in this direction and she did not resist, the slowness and awkwardness of her pace the only reason for leading her. When they reached a recess that was the entrance to one of the commercial buildings, they pushed her into its pitch-black shadow.

She tripped over the wide stone step and once again they hauled her to her feet, this time roughly. I moved in closer, knowing what was going to happen, wanting to help the woman—*her*, not Moker, the man inside her; he knew what *he* wanted—desperately thinking of what I might do. If I'd been flesh and blood I'd have waded right in, three of them or not. But I was just . . . *nothing!* I couldn't scream at them, I couldn't touch them. Dear God, I couldn't even *frighten* them.

The leader of the pack wasted no time. His hand went straight up the woman's tight skirt, the triangular split at the side helping his wrist hitch up the material. I was used to the bad light by now—either my eyes had grown accustomed to it, or in my out-of-body state I could see more clearly than before—and I saw the other two men—the other two animals—pulling at her jacket. One paused for a moment to unzip his flies and release his aroused penis, a squat fat thing that should have been an embarrassment, and then Leather Jacket followed suit, the fingers of his right hand still busy beneath the skirt. The woman was laughing, an eerie hollow sound in the darkness, her head back against the metal door behind her. She twisted her face from side to side, her eyes half-closed, pupils hidden by the drooping upper lids.

Leather Jacket, his member standing proud from his trousers, yanked at her panties and tights, and they came down to her knees. His right hand disappeared again and her upper body fell forward, then shot back against the door, the back of her skull smacking against the metal. Still she laughed, an insane roar that seemed hardly human, and the two other men ripped open her jacket to crush her breasts under feverish hands.

By now their leader had hitched up the skirt to her waist and was attempting to thrust himself inside her, his knees bent, one hand on her hip, the other guiding his swollen penis. His two companions were becoming frantic, pulling at her blouse to expose her breasts. The bloody wad of material that had helped stem the flow of blood from her dead heart fell to the ground.

I heard Leather Jacket, who had found his way into her, exclaim something in Arabic, probably a curse, as he wondered why he was suddenly becoming wet. He pulled away from her without withdrawing completely and touched the dark running stain that was soiling his white shirt. I'm not sure if he could see the blood in the poor light, or if he smelt it, but he seemed to know immediately what it was. The blood had not yet had time to cool or begin to congeal in her veins and now it flowed copiously, overwhelming the needle's round blunted end, running down her front, between her spread legs, soaking her panties and torn tights, spattering onto the stone step beneath her.

Leather Jacket pulled away completely, his penis catching the blood flow. He made a sharp disgusted sound and instantly struck out, slapping the woman's face hard. A moaning kind of laugh came from her and the two Arabs on either side quit their rough, fumbling fondling and stared at her. Then they looked toward their leader and angry words were exchanged between them all.

I could just make out their expressions in the darkness and they were ugly, maybe as ugly as their souls. One studied his hands and saw that they were darkly stained with what could only be blood. He struck out at her, and now his bloodied fist was clenched, the blow a hard punch. She tottered against the Arab on the other side and he angrily pushed her away, back into his companion, who punched her again, catching her upper arm. Whether she—Moker—felt any pain, I've no idea, but her low laughter became sharper, which seemed to annoy the Arabs even more. They started to flail her body with their fists, the leader, his penis still in evidence and still hard, stepping back to kick her. The first kick hit her knee, which buckled, the other two assailants whacking her as she went down. When they discovered that their nice light summer suits had become bloodied, they really lost it. They began pounding her, kicking her as she sank into a corner of the recess.

I tried to intervene, tried to grab the leader, whose vicious kicks were aimed at her head and shoulders, but my efforts were in vain—as I knew they would be. I won't tell you the names I called them but they were very politically *in-correct*. I think I was more disgusted with them than they were with this gibbering bleeding woman. Okay, I knew the woman was dead and that it was the deviant Moker who was taking the hammering (did *he* feel any pain? Not by the sound of her sniggering and delighted shrieks) but somehow respect for the woman before she'd become this *thing* remained with me. If only she would stop taunting them their violence might stop. Unfortunately, inside her Moker was enjoying himself too much.

She cowered on the doorstep, but only under the pressure of their attack, not because she was afraid. The deranged sniggering that came from her revealed that.

Finally, she was flat out on the concrete, lying half on her side, knees held together by the bunched panties and hose, but ankles and feet spread wide. Her skirt had dropped enough to cover her pubic hair; blood continued to dribble but not pump from her wound. The three men kept kicking her prone body.

They stopped only, it seemed, when they had exhausted themselves. They muttered to one another as they stared down at the woman, who was still moving and still mocking them, although her sniggers had become quieter and punctuated by short silences.

Leather Jacket barked at the other two and, after looking at him in surprise, they grinned. The leader and one of his companions were already exposed and it seemed that their violence had strengthened their erections even more. The third paunchy man unzipped himself and the other two laughed and pointed when they saw that he was flaccid. He grumbled something, I don't know what, and prodded the woman sharply with the toe of his shoe. The only reaction he got was another snigger.

I already felt sickened by their treatment of the woman—they must have assumed she was either drunk, drugged, or a nutter; she certainly didn't look like a hooker—but what happened next forced me to reel away in utter disgust.

Standing over the fallen woman, Leather Jacket began to pleasure himself using his hand. The other two moved in closer and followed suit.

I went to the other side of the narrow cul-de-sac, shaking my head and cursing these men for their vileness, refusing to watch, but reluctant to leave the woman. But even when I didn't look I could hear the grunts and moans of the Arabs as they masturbated over her.

Their noises quickly reached a crescendo as first one, then another, reached climax. They didn't even bother to curb their cries. I tried not to listen to their sighs and their mutterings in Arabic, only turning back when they started laughing again. They were gesticulating at the third man's limp organ as he frantically worked at it. He swore at the other two—at least, it sounded like a curse—and they laughed all the more. The flustered Arab gave up and took his hand away, leaving his flabby penis dangling.

He appeared to have a bright idea, for he suddenly chuckled. Saying something to his companions, he took hold of his penis again, this time in both hands, and made straining noises. The other two urged him on enthusiastically. It took him less than a minute to start urinating and he aimed the stream directly at the woman on the step, drenching her exposed thighs, her jacket, her face and hair.

I was shocked by the degradation, the sordidness, and I backed further into the shadows, filled with rage and despair.

I wanted to kill.

THIRTY-ONE

Her three abusers had gone, but I lingered. Soul-destroying though the whole squalid business was, I remained curious. And angry. What was Moker's intention now that the once presentable woman—she'd been an executive type, I thought—lay defiled and bedraggled in a pool of piss inside the recessed doorway? He had humiliated her, brought this presumably respectable woman down to gutter level, and it occurred to me that this was part of his purpose, to possess his victims (there was no doubt in my mind that he had put his previous victims through similar humiliation), degrade them, and make them carry out acts they would never have considered in their normal lives. I guessed it was all part of his revenge on society, a society that probably had always turned away from him. I had no idea of his background or history, but I was willing to bet his early life had been in various institutions, perhaps even in hospitals where they had tried to fix his face (if its present condition was *after* surgery, what must it have been like before?). His childhood must have been torment, his young adulthood torture. Had he always been a loner, or was it only when he became a man that he was an outcast? Did he have a family and had he been rejected by them? I knew so little about Moker.

But don't imagine I was beginning to feel sorry for the guy; I couldn't, not with that pathetic bundle lying in the doorway opposite. Moker was evil. His very presence somehow *exuded* malevolence and I had felt that from the first moment I'd discovered him. Hell, even his aura was nasty. He was evil and he had to be stopped. No matter that he was grotesquely deformed, either from birth, or through some horrendous and freakish accident: he was a killer without mercy.

He had to be stopped, but I didn't know how.

I stayed in deep shadow, watching the dead body, thoughts, doubts, tumbling through my mind. The three men had been laughing and clapping each other's shoulders as they departed the scene, and I loathed them for what they had done. But I loathed Moker more.

Just when I felt I'd waited long enough and was about to approach the re-cumbent body, something stirred. At first, I thought it was the woman herself—I was sure she had moved—but as I peered closer, I realized I was mistaken. Once again I backed away, retreating into deeper shadow. Without doubt, I was afraid of the monster who had possessed his victim. As before in the underground car park, a nebulous shape, a configuration that was transparent, was slowly evolving into something recognizable, and even in the darkness, and despite its limpid nature, I could tell it was Moker leaving the body.

The gauzy form thickened, took on more solidity, and began to arrange it-self into something more human—except, of course, for the face. The body of flesh and bone beneath him was completely motionless, a lifeless corpse once more, as Moker continued to rise. There was no awkwardness to him now; his emergence was even graceful. I shrunk further back, almost passing through the glass of the shop door behind me. As I realized this I took another step backward so that I was now on the other side of the glass, and inside the shop itself. There was the usual uncomfortable feeling for a nanosecond, a kind of claustrophobic thing followed by a sense of being at one with the glass, ab-sorbed by its molecules, nothing overwhelming, just a natural transition spoiled only by the fear I had for the thing that was out there in the street.

The vision that was Moker stood upright in a fluid movement, and glanced back down at his victim. Although in shadow, he was clearly visible to me, not quite in solid form, but giving off a slight glow in the darkness. I wondered if I would look the same to him. In fact, his reappearance in this form caused me to wonder about his ability to float out-of-body. Was it the same ability that I possessed? It had to be—it could be nothing else. But he had left his physical self so quickly and effortlessly. Perhaps it was the very nature of the man him-self that made it possible, the curse of loneliness giving time for the perfection of the pursuit of leaving his own body.

And what better incentive to leave his own wretched form than his own physical imperfection? What better motive than living as someone else for a little while, someone fit, attractive, wealthy—respected? (And in his twisted mind, who better to shame and humiliate—his victims the very type he had al-ways envied, later wanting to destroy their faces and bodies to satisfy his own vengeful hatred of them? He despised them for the qualities that he, himself, had never possessed and so his final retribution on them was to render them in his own likeness by way of a chopper.)

How Moker had discovered he could leave his own body at will, there was no way of knowing, but there was no doubt he had developed the gift to a fine degree. And again, how he had learned to enter deceased bodies and possess them, there was also no way of knowing. But he did work in an environment of corpses, in a mortuary.

My conclusion was that Moker had put in the hours. To me, the OBE was an occasional habit; to Moker, it was both a release and a means of revenge. He'd obviously become adept at it.

His dimly luminous shape remained immobile as he continued to look down at his poor victim. Then he shifted and looked about him. For a tense moment I thought he might discover me hiding in the shop but, although his eyes lingered for a long second on the shop's doorway, his attention moved on.

After a while, he himself moved on and, for a reckless moment, I wanted to chase after him. I wanted to destroy him. I wanted to prevent him from doing this same thing ever again. But he terrified me and I held back. Besides, I didn't know if I could make contact with him in our state of being. That was my excuse anyway.

I did have another idea though.

Moker had long departed before I ventured out of the shop. Before crossing the street to the doorway where the urine-sodden woman was sprawled, I checked to my right, making sure the killer wasn't about to reappear. I waited nervously, ready to flee. The street was empty. I crossed over.

I examined the dead woman, checking that she hadn't, by some miracle, started breathing again. No, she really was dead.

I wondered if her killer's plan was to return in his car using his physical form then mutilate the body here, where it was dark and quiet, with little chance of being disturbed. Maybe that was how he always did it: kill, possess, leave the dead victim somewhere isolated, return and chop it; or maybe he would load the corpse into his car and take it elsewhere to mutilate. Whatever, I knew the nightmare wasn't over, that he'd be coming back to finish the job, and that I didn't have much time.

I wondered if I could pull it off.

After studying her for a few moments—her lip was cut, her cheekbones black with dirt from the undersoles of the three Arabs' shoes when they'd kicked her, her previously smart business suit drenched with blood and piss— I squatted down next to her (I suppose in some way I was trying to get the *feel* of her). I squeezed into the gap (yeah, no need to squeeze in my form, but I did anyway) behind her on the step and, taking a deep pointless breath, I melted into her.

And it worked, I seemed to fit.

But only seconds after I was enveloped by her flesh, the fading memories rushed at me. I experienced her life, just flashes, only moments in time, but it seemed to cover everything, from birth to death. I guess even after death, a residue of precious life remains in the brain and even in the flesh of the body. Like those old radios and televisions whose energy faded rather than stopped immediately when switched off, so this was an ebbing of power rather than a complete cut-off. Now, it seemed to me as I immersed myself into this cooling corpse, energies—at least, her *memories*—lingered in the substance of her form.

My own mind sapped up the remains of the woman's lifetime experiences. It wasn't focused enough to be overwhelming, but it was startling.

Images, sensations, thoughts: they poured through me.

A huge bright red ball with yellow spots, bigger than me, the observer, it seemed; absolute joy—a man, somewhere in his early thirties, I thought, although he seemed very old, giggling as he pushed me on a swing; it was a long time ago and this was my father and I was his little daughter (there was no question, no mystery, it was just as it was), and wonderful happiness spread through me, but it quickly left, a harsh sadness taking its place as the man was gone—a woman now, an unhappy strict woman, pleasant face, yet a severity to her eyes; mother, the dead woman's mother, and there was love, but it was not the same as before; the woman was older, gray-haired, and she was angry, raising her voice, at me, and dislike weighted heavily on the love; but it seemed that in death, my death, for-giveness was granted and I ached with longing—still pining, the regret of having lost my father so many years ago—

Although I was experiencing the remnants of the dead woman's memories, my own feelings continued to intrude, for my own mind was ensconced in this host of flesh and stilled blood, and I wondered if Primrose would mourn me for years to come. An image of my father came to me too, but he was like a stranger.

—a slim pink doll, a Barbie or a Wendy (the resolution was not clear enough)—a puppy dog, me calling its name: Rumbo—a boy, a surge of love here—the sea, a wonderful calm sea that was green then blue—a jolt, an accident of some kind, an arm in pain, soon gone—guilt, guilt, guilt, more sorrow, visions of a man, an indistinct person, a woman behind him, and I knew that he was my

*lover and the woman was his wife, deep, deep grief, a terrible wrench of emotions,
the affair soon over—the sea again, beautifully warm and calm—*

I soaked up tiny segments of the victim's life just before they faded, before
they finally left the storehouse of flesh, bone, and tissue.

*—the mother again, love still present, but also a stronger dislike—bad times,
black times, it all came to me, some moments witnessed as through a kaleidoscope,
while others were individual and sharply defined, some fleeting, others lasting
mere seconds that felt like long periods—thoughts, energies, flowed through, but
fading, fading all the time, dwindling, waning, as if growing weary themselves—
now an office, a workplace; computer screens, faces, mixed emotions, snap visions
that somehow were complete—an apartment, simply but tastefully furnished, a
warmth for that place, and now a black-and-white cat called Tibbles—people,
friends—leaving the office—*

And then it all changed: darkness entered, slowly at first until it was almost
absolute; it brought with it fear . . .

*—and terror, heart-freezing terror—a lonely walk down into shadows, a sense
of danger—the car, very near the car—shambling footsteps from behind—all
these last sounds and images felt with a resurgence of power—pain, terrible pain
and screaming fear!—the darkness strong, peaking before starting to drain
away—fading, wasting away—until there was only light . . .*

Inside her, I reeled under the pressure of it all, some of her terror left with
me. I willed myself to be calm, aware that if those last sensations had gone on
any longer I would have fled the cold flesh that now bound me. I felt myself
trembling, even though that wasn't possible. Her death had been horrible and
the suffering had continued even after the heart had stopped.

I steadied myself. I was in a void; nothing else of the woman was left. The
body was without any trace of its previous owner.

It was time for me to subjugate it. I prayed for it to be possible.

I settled my mind and it was surprisingly easy to do. Despite everything I'd
been witness to that night, despite my fear and anxiety, I soothed my own consciousness by repeating the exercise I had used to travel outside my own body.

Deep, deep breaths (pretend breaths now, obviously), long, long exhalations.
Addressing each part of my non-physical form, starting with the absent toes
and moving up my nonexistent legs, then invisible groin, working my way
through my impalpable belly, chest, shoulders, arms right to my indiscernible

head, willing them all to relax. Then, instead of commanding myself to move out of my physical form (usually by concentrating on one specific spot near the ceiling of whatever room I was in—mostly the bedroom—and willing my inner self to go there), I forced myself to become part of the vessel I now inhabited. That in life I'd been much bigger than the unfortunate woman seemed to make no difference—I still had to "fill out" her human shape. I felt myself flow into her, strangely expanding rather than shrinking, sensing myself into her muscles and bones and organs. Occasionally, a fragment of her memory would return, but always too weak to linger.

My fingers slipped into hers. My stomach and chest moulded themselves to the inner side of her skin. Bit by bit I took over her shape, feeling my way in, and suffering no discomfort as I did so. Earlier, it had taken Moker practically no time at all to possess his victim, but he'd had more practice than I. Briefly I wondered if this was how demons possessed certain afflicted human beings (I'd never believed in demonic possession before, but these days I'm more susceptible to all manner of possibilities).

Once I felt myself totally absorbed, I endeavored to move her right hand. I slipped out of her.

Drawing my own hand back again and sliding into her fingers as though they were the digits of a glove, I took more deep breaths and concentrated even harder, thinking of myself as at one with her.

Her hand shifted just a little.

Eventually, taking over the dead woman's body proved relatively easy (although controlling it was much more difficult). It was a matter of "thinking" myself into what was in essence a vacated property, a kind of Zen thing, if you like. As I mentioned before, it was a matter of being "at one with her," not quite taking over the lifeless flesh and blood, but becoming part of it; not wearing it, but being it. Because I'd had practice at projecting my inner self to other places outside my "shell," it wasn't that difficult for me to project myself into the other person's body. Difficult to explain, and not that easy to do; but if you already had the knack, it helped.

Now being inside, "fitting" the new body, was all well and good, but getting it to obey my will was something else. I got used to moving the right hand first, then the arm up to the elbow. Getting a reaction from the rest of the body was a little harder, but perseverance paid off. Remember, I was still very shaken, so it took a lot of effort just to calm myself; controlling somebody else's body needed full concentration. It came though, the ability to govern came gradually at first, and then with a rush. The trick was not to try *too* hard but to relax and just sink into it.

Sitting up wasn't so bad, although the alien body felt heavy and cumbersome, but rising to my feet was almost impossible. You see, living inside your own body, adapting to its growth over the years, you're not aware of its weight so much, but occupying somebody else's is like trying on a suit of armor—armor that's made out of lead. You have to get used to it, and even then motion is awkward. Moker had obviously become skilled at it with practice, but even when he had possessed the woman's corpse, movement had been a little stiff and graceless.

First problem, though, was vision. Everything was blurred through the victim's eyes and I remembered she had worn glasses, which were now missing, obviously knocked off during the vicious attack by the scummy threesome. I used both clumsy hands to feel around the concrete step and, although the fingertips were numb, I felt something move. It took a little while to pick up the glasses—it was like wearing thick gloves without individual fingers—and I dropped them more than once. Eventually, I got them over the nose and managed to fumble the side arms through the hair and over the ears. One of the lenses had cracked, but vision improved, not as much as I had hoped, but enough to enable me to find my way around.

I was a mere novice, but I was determined to succeed. I had a plan.

Using the brick wall of the recessed doorway for support and balance, I slowly hauled myself up, rising to my (her) knees first, raising one leg so shin and thigh were at right angles to each other, then, digging my (her) fingers into the indentations between bricks for extra support, I used all my willpower and the woman's waning strength to stand. (Fortunately for me, she had lost her shoes in the fracas with the three men, so I didn't have to worry about high heels). I made it, but instantly fell back against the metal door where I stayed for several minutes, legs spread and firmly rooted to the wide doorstep, the rest of me (her) trembling. With a whole lot of effort, I managed to adjust the woman's clothing, dragging up panties and hose, buttoning (almost impossible, this, but I persevered) the jacket.

I felt dizzy, as though I was too high off the ground, the feeling you get when you ride a bike or climb onto a horse for the first time. And when I pushed myself away from the door and tried to walk, my legs felt like long stilts.

I fell off the step and had to go through the whole process of rising once again. It was almost but not quite like learning to walk for the first time (I suppose an amputee who has been given prosthetic legs must go through a similar procedure) and, believe me, it wasn't easy. I stumbled and fell twice more before I reached the street junction.

However, although my gait was clumsy and somewhat perilous, my arms waving in the air for balance, I soon began to get used to walking. By the time I reached the main thoroughfare of Queensway, I resembled only a hopeless drunk.

The journey through the London streets was horrendous. Luckily it was late night, and once I'd moved out of the Queensway area, the sidestreets became darker again and virtually deserted. The few people who did pass me by must have thought I was either drunk or drugged by the way I lurched along and used walls where I could for support. Heads turned, a few people crossed over to the other side of the street before they reached me. A group of young guys laughed at me, yelling insults and suggestions of what we all might do together, but they soon lost interest and went on their way when I ignored them.

One person, an elderly, scruffily dressed man, approached me and asked if I was all right and if he could assist me in any way. I don't know whether it was my blood-drenched clothes, my battered face, the stench of urine coming from me, or the way I babbled and gurgled as I attempted to reply, that deterred him. Possibly—probably—it was all of these things. He backed off and I stumbled onward.

It was quite a hike and I wasn't sure I was going to make it. When the body dies it doesn't take muscles long to start atrophying, so I was becoming weaker by the minute. The fact that blood had stopped coursing through the arteries was neither here nor there—I wasn't alive, so I didn't need it—but the fact that it was settling into my lower legs and feet made it feel as if I were wearing lead boots. Also, the increasing coldness was rendering the corpse evermore stiff. By the time I reached the police station I was moving like Frankenstein's monster.

All through the journey I had been trying to speak, something that brought me extra stares from infrequent (fortunately) passers-by. To them, not only was I drunk and disheveled, but I was crazy also.

The idea was to be able to talk coherently when I got to my destination: I had a tale to tell and a name to name. This was an extra hurdle though, and far more difficult than making the body walk. It took a while to produce any noise at all, and then it was only a raspy whispering which sounded something like *"Unurrrrgahh."* Not very good, but the best I could do to start with.

I kept trying to pronounce certain words, simple ones at first—"cat, sat, mat," that kind of thing, but all that came out was: "ca, sa, ma." I persisted though, struggling to walk, striving to talk. And although in my out-of-body state I had lost all sense of physical feeling (passing through walls and the like were mental sensations), I felt a distinct chill enveloping me. It was like wearing a heavy suit that had been left outside on a frigid winter's night. How long before rigor mortis started to take over? I wondered. Usually it started about forty-five minutes to an hour after death, I seemed to remember from somewhere.

I plodded on, sliding a hand along walls for balance, hanging on to lamp posts along the way, summoning up extra willpower to cross roads where there was nothing to grab hold of should my knees buckle, unable to avoid traffic (mercifully, there was very little), so forcing myself to stand stock-still while cars and the occasional bus maneuvered around me instead. Abuse was hurled at me, horns were tooted, but I was oblivious. I only had one thing in mind and that was to reach my goal before flesh and bone gave up.

Having lived in the city all my life, I knew where to find the local police station and my mind was sharp enough to recognize roads and streets. How long I'd been traveling, I had no idea: it could have been an hour or only half an hour. Whatever, the effort was draining my resolve.

I saw a big flyover up ahead and it gave me hope, because it meant I was close. For a short while my rambling gait—somewhere between Liam Gallagher's swagger and Ozzy Osbourne's shuffle—actually quickened, but it couldn't last long. Against my will, I slowed down and one foot began to drag. And then I saw the building I was looking for in the distance and the sight of it gave me fresh determination. I stepped off the curb, almost tripping in my sudden haste, but managed to recover before falling; it was a particularly ungainly moment, my arms bending in all sorts of ways. Someone whistled at me, then laughed, but no one came to my aid, and perhaps that was a good thing.

Still attracting curious stares (there were a few more people on this main road) I stomped ungracefully toward my goal. Reaching the other side, I had difficulty in raising a foot to mount the pavement. My toenail scraped the curbstone to find the higher level and I leaned forward so that my weight was on that leg, then dragged my other foot after the first. It didn't work out so well—I lost my balance and toppled over onto the pavement. Luckily, I didn't go all the way down, ending up sitting on the ground, one hand against the stone, my legs spread sideways, knees bent. I remained in that position for a minute or two, trying to regain my composure and psyching myself for the effort it would now take to get me on my feet again.

That was when I caught sight of the last thing in the world that I wanted to see.

Coming toward me on the opposite side of the road was Moker's old beat-up Hillman, its sidelights shining like warning beacons. I knew whose shadowy figure was behind the wheel and I groaned. With the groan I swore out loud and at least the word was fairly coherent (to my own ears at least).

Moker obviously hadn't seen me, for the vehicle was coming straight ahead without slowing. Now instinct should have made me hide my face, maybe roll myself into an inconspicuous ball, but making somebody else's body react sharply was not so easy. For some reason I ended up on all fours like a dog, my head raised and facing toward the approaching car.

Moker hit the brakes as soon as he saw me and in that instant I realized that he'd been cruising the neighborhood searching for me. He must have collected his car from the car park (no doubt using the quiet side EXIT/ENTRANCE to reach it) and returned to the secluded cul-de-sac where he had left the woman's battered corpse to find it gone. What a shock that must have been for him.

So he'd come looking for his prize, perhaps wondering if the Arabs had carried it off—or perhaps even suspecting another spirit had somehow stolen his right. And now his search had proved successful. He'd spotted me. And I was helpless.

THIRTY-TWO

I struggled to get to my feet again (okay, it was the dead woman's feet, but to keep on mentioning that gets tedious) but could only fumble around on the pavement, my legs becoming stubbornly obstinate. The Hillman, which had not been traveling very fast in the first place, slid to a halt. Masked by hat and scarf, Moker looked out the side window at me.

I scrambled around in panic, but my legs refused to obey me. Each time I attempted to bend a knee the leg declined to fold. Moker was looking about, no doubt making sure the coast was clear for him to bundle me into the boot of the car, when an Audi arrived behind him. The irritated driver tooted his horn and yelled at the obstacle in his way, and Moker looked back at him; either surprise or anger might have been on his face if he'd had a face. He unwound his side window, not a speedy process in the old Hillman, and indicated for the other driver to go around him, but fortunately for me, the guy was the obstreperous kind and saw no reason why he should have to go out of his way to avoid another vehicle that was wrongly parked in the middle of the road (it was a very wide road, but that wasn't the point). He continued to thump his horn and swear at Moker.

Moker had obviously decided that it would be easier to move than engage in a haranguing match, because he drove on, pulling into the curb on his side of the road. I took the opportunity to try and get up again, but without much joy: my legs kept collapsing each time I tried to kneel. Out of the corner of my eye I saw Moker starting the first move of a three-point turn and I groaned in frustration.

Suddenly, I was gripped under the arms by strong hands and hauled to my unsteady feet. A big woman with butch, short blonde hair and no make-up came around from behind me, one hand hanging onto my arm to prevent me from falling again. She wore a dark jacket with dark slacks, the collar of a pale-blue shirt spread over the neck and lapels of the jacket, its long tips pointing toward the nipples of wide and ample breasts.

"You all right, dear?" I heard her ask in a surprisingly high voice given the masculinity of her build. Her only adornments, I saw, were a pair of large, round and dangly earrings.

"*Muh . . . ma . . . yeh-es,*" I managed to reply.

Although her face began to waver in front of me, my vision beginning to fail, I still caught the look of disgust she gave me when she noticed my state and smelled the blood and urine (and other stuff!) on my clothes. She began to back away, not through fear, I guessed, but from revulsion. I was aware that I was not a pretty sight, nor very well perfumed, but I held up a pleading hand to her anyway. She continued to back off and I couldn't blame her: I wasn't the finest figure to come face to face with, especially at that hour (well, any hour, really).

"*Hel . . . hel . . . me . . .*" I muttered, but it was no good; she turned on her heel (sensible brogues, actually) and walked away from me.

More beeping of horns sounded and I slowly craned my neck to look back at Moker. Seemed he'd become a nuisance to other drivers, for he was sideways across the road, blocking the paths of two more vehicles, one of them a late-night bus. They were causing quite a racket, although the noise suddenly dwindled in my borrowed ears. Oh shit, now my hearing was going.

I began to walk, following the big woman who'd just become a blur in the distance by now. She soon passed the front entrance of the police station I was aiming for, and I thought it a pity that she hadn't popped inside to report a battered madwoman on the loose.

I moved one foot in front of the other, one in front of the other, one in front of the other, concentrating hard as I tried to say the words.

"*Un . . . an . . . funt . . . of . . . udder . . .*" Practicing all the way, forcing my stiff legs to move. "*Un . . . in . . . funt . . . o . . . udder . . . one . . . in . . . front . . . of . . . udder . . .*"

I repeated it all the way until it began to sound like a chant. A red bus passed me, the bus Moker had held up, then a car, and I knew it would not be long before he came alongside me like some curb-crawling creep. I tried to hasten my step, but almost tumbled over with the extra effort. Take it easy, I told myself, think hard, one foot in front of the other, but don't rush it. Not far to go . . . oh God, so why did it seem such a long way away?

"*One . . . in . . . front . . . of . . . udder . . .*" Bloody hell!

Soon there though. Not that far. Where was Moker? I wasn't going to look. To look meant stopping and forcing my head round. Would take too long. Besides, eyes becoming too blurred. Halos around streetlamps. Cold, bloody cold inside this refrigerated carcass. Almost there, I think.

I was speaking as I went, keeping up the practice because if I couldn't talk coherently once inside the police station, then this whole mission was pointless.

Uh-oh. Car coming up from behind. I knew who it was without looking but, as it would only take a sideways glance, I looked anyway. I thought I could hear the sinews and bones of my neck grinding against each other.

There was Moker, wide-set bulging eyes gazing out at me from the open side window. I couldn't be sure if it was surprise or panic in those frightening eyes. Maybe a mixture of both. I swerved aside, because I realized that if I could see his eyes so clearly, then I was too close to him. A big hand came out of the window to grab at me, but I'd just about put enough distance between us.

What must he be thinking? That he hadn't entirely finished the woman off? But surely the beating from the Arabs should have completed the job? Or could he penetrate the hide of flesh and see me beneath it? He had, after all, seemed to sense my presence before.

No time for me to ponder such things. He was drawing the crawling car to a halt. Beginning to open the driver's door . . .

But I was there, I was outside the entrance to the police station. Oh no, steps to climb! Two sets of steps to climb!

I called on every last ounce of willpower I had left. Had to make it, had to climb. One—step, two—step . . . Was he behind me? Oh God, he had to be. It would only take a moment to leave the car and run across the pavement, catch hold of me before I'd even climbed the third step.

"Fee—feb . . ." I said aloud, expecting to feel rough hands on me, hands that would drag me away, back into the Hillman, the back seat or the boot.

"Four—feb . . ."

Why couldn't I feel his touch? Why was he taking so long?

"Fife—feb . . ."

More steps, at the bend, keep going, one step, two step, three, four, keep climbing, pull on the rail, lift one leg after the other . . . God, so heavy, filled with quick-drying cement . . . but keep on, not far, not so far—

I was there, I was at the top! I swayed in surprise. The double doors were in front of me, although the light shining from inside was getting dimmer. I knew that it was not the fault of the lights themselves, but because the eyes I was using were gradually closing down. I noticed a shadow inside, a man with a huge elongated black head and I suddenly understood why Moker hadn't left his car to come after me: it was a policeman wearing a helmet, standing on the other side of the glass, and he was pulling one side of the door open for me. He must have watched my stumbling ascent of the stairs and my pursuer had noticed him at the last minute. Moker had probably driven off before I'd even reached the last step.

The policeman—God bless his pointed head!—was waving me through and inspecting me more closely. I was aware of him snapping his head and shoulders back sharply, no doubt because of my unpleasant odor.

His voice was muffled because of my growing deafness, but I heard him call out: *"Visitor for you, Sarge!"*

I fell against him, and I think his reaction was to push me away, but a sense of duty prevailed. A strong hand gripped my arm and I heard him say as if from another room: *"Christ, what happened to you?"*

I was too busy preparing the words I was about to speak to answer his question. Regaining my balance, I lumbered away from him toward the front desk counter where I could just make out the top half of that night's duty officer.

I collapsed against the counter and said, *"Fumbod . . . murded . . . moo . . ."*

THIRTY-THREE

I didn't have much left to give.

The body was growing heavier and colder. The knees were buckling. The sight was fading. I heard only white sound in the ears, and then nothing. The chin was sagging, the eyelids drooping, starting to close. There was precious little time left and so I summoned all the will I had, which wasn't much.

I said to the duty officer: "I wish . . . to . . . rep . . . report a murded—a murder. Mine. The . . . killer . . . is called . . . Al . . . Alec . . . Moker. He murded—murdered . . . the others . . . too . . ."

Then the woman's body gave out.

THIRTY-FOUR

I'd left her lying on the floor of the police station's long, brightly lit reception area, surrounded by uniformed men and women, one of whom—the duty officer himself—was trying to resuscitate the corpse with mouth-to-mouth and heart massaging. No point in hanging around as far as I was concerned: I'd given them the murderer's name, and I only hoped they'd understand what I'd said. Bit of a waste, otherwise.

Leaving the body was far easier than entering it. I just kind of pulled myself from it, picturing myself somewhere near the room's ceiling, the way I used to when going out of body. Instantly, I was away from the still woman, looking down at the scene from a corner. I didn't linger. The woman was well and truly dead and there was no way they were going to bring her back.

I pictured Moker's rotten dingy flat and in a flash I was through the police station's wall and gliding across town toward Shepherd's Bush. In no time at all, it seemed, I was there, floating down the basement steps and passing through the paint-chipped front-door.

The place was empty, but something told me I would not have to wait long. And I was right. I'd already scouted the grubby rooms again, looking for I don't know what, just curious, I guess, as to how this monster lived. Most of the food in the dirty kitchen was in tins, the rest in packages. A well-worn food blender stood on the small counter by the sink. There were no photographs anywhere, which may have been reasonable as far as Moker was concerned— would he really want to look at mug shots of himself?—but there also were none of family or friends (friends? Was it likely? Maybe it was a little cruel of me to think so, but I thought he could only be an outcast, a pariah). There was a calendar on the kitchen wall, and a date was ringed on that month's page. Although I'd lost track of the days, I was fairly certain that it was today's date that had been marked—it seemed about right—and I wondered whether, if I had the power to turn back the leaves of the flip-over calendar, I'd find other murder dates indicated. I felt sure I would. The interesting thing was that no other date in that month was ringed, which seemed to me to be further evidence that Moker was not the one who had recently killed me.

Scuffling footsteps outside on the steps, and I knew the beast had returned to its unwholesome lair. I sank back into the darkest shadow I could find.

A key scraped into the lock, the door swung open with a tired creak, and the slouched black shape that was Moker entered. Disgusting snufflings came from behind the thick woolen mask as if he'd had to walk or run some distance from his car and was out of breath. He slammed the door shut behind him and leaned back against it, his chest heaving as he fought to calm himself. Had I managed to panic him? When he saw his victim lumbering into the police station had he realized somebody else had taken over her body? I was sure he had caught sight of me in the car park when he was in the out-of-body state and before entering his dead victim; yet he hadn't seen me when I was first inside this flat, although he had seemed to sense my presence. So did that mean he could only see me when he, himself, was out of body? Maybe I'd soon find out.

Slowly the serial killer unwound his scarf and dropped it to the floor. His trilby hat followed and, once again, his true horror was exposed to me, the hole in his face deep but, at least, shaded. If anything, the aura around him had increased both in foulness of color and malevolence. A strange mewing sound came from him as if he were trying to express himself and it grew in volume as he advanced toward me, swinging his arms in front of him, hands grabbing at the air.

I cringed away from him, confused by his attack, now unsure whether he could see me or not. But he stopped short, his head turning toward the opposite corner. He went for it, arms flailing, and gave out a hollow and ill-formed kind of roar when his fingertips felt nothing but the air itself. Nevertheless, I dodged around the table with its untidy heap of newspapers and cuttings, keeping it between us.

Moker shuffled through to the kitchen area, turning on its light as he entered. A few seconds later he was out again, turning a sharp right and bursting into the bedroom. The light came on and I could hear him raging and throwing objects about. That he was searching for me, I had no doubt, and I only felt slight relief in the knowledge that he could sense me but still not see me. Storming out of the bedroom, he came to an unsteady halt on the opposite side of the table, his grotesque head continuing to point this way and that. A couple of times he stared so forcibly toward me that I was sure I was visible, but on each occasion his attention was quickly diverted elsewhere.

The grim aura around him seemed to bristle with small shards of angry brightness, like sparks from bare cable. His chest rose and fell, and his sore, husky breathing was distressed, as if he were about to sob, drool and spittle glistened at the ravaged edges of his facial malformation. Finally, his body movement—the twitching of his arms, the heaving of his upper body, the restlessness of his head—ceased and he stared down at the littered tabletop.

A step forward brought him to the edge of the table, and he leaned over it to begin searching through the newspapers, knocking some of them onto the floor with violent sweeps of his arms, rummaging through the remainder for something specific. He soon found what he was looking for.

It was the news story of my murder, naming me as another suspected victim of the current serial killer. He stared at the black-and-white picture of me; then at the smaller one featuring Andrea and Oliver, with Primrose in the background. The first finger of his hand found the thick, pencilled underlining. Even though the type was upside down to me, I knew exactly what was underlined. Obviously, the newspaper didn't give my complete address, just the general location: south Woodford.

Moker went to the tall cupboard set against a wall, his breathing still hoarse, his chest still exerting itself. The cupboard had an old-fashioned swivel catch that he flicked upright with a finger and the door all but burst open, a jumble of papers and detritus tumbling out in a mini-landslide. He dug his beefy hands into the pile that remained inside and dragged out two large telephone directories that were at the bottom of the heap. I saw that one was a London listings while the other one was a Yellow Pages. Both were in well-thumbed condition, and I wondered why Moker would have them. There was no telephone in the flat, and even if there were, Moker would have been unable to use it. He couldn't talk, he could only make noises.

He brought the London book back to the table and set it down, swinging the angle-poise lamp over it and switching on the light. If I'd been my normal self, I'm sure I would have broken out in a sweat when he began thumbing through the pages, because I knew what he was looking for. Moker had probably stolen the directories from a neighbor's doorstep, a common enough occurrence in blocks of flats where British Telecom just dumped the listings outside people's homes, but it didn't explain why he needed them. It had to be that he used them only for looking up addresses, as he was now.

I watched in dismay as he reached the Ts and I wanted to tear the book from his hands, and rip it to shreds with my own. He ceased leafing through and began running down the names. His finger slowed, moved more deliberately, came to a stop. I saw my own name under his fingertip.

That was when we both heard a car screech to a halt on the road outside. Then another car, coming to a swift halt, tires squealing. Doors slamming. Heavy hurrying footsteps . . .

THIRTY-FIVE

I had to admit it, Moker was no slouch when it came to running away. Oh, his movement was clumsy, his stride more lumbering than graceful, but his getaway was fast. We'd both heard the footsteps outside growing louder on the pavement, and even as they reached the stairway leading down to the basement flat, Moker was pulling on his scarf and hat, winding the former around his ruined face like a mask and snapping the hat's brim down to shade his eyes. The heavy raincoat came next, shrugging it on, none of these procedures taking more than a few seconds.

There were moving shadows outside the grimy window as he tore a page from the telephone book and folded it. He was shoving the page into his raincoat pocket as he made for the door leading into the small kitchen. Heavy banging on the front door now, voices announcing, "Police—open up!"

I clenched my fist and hissed, "Yes!" as I saw more legs descending the outside steps, but when I looked toward Moker he'd gone. I went after him, running myself even though I could have just glided along, and was in time to see him disappear out the kitchen's back door. More banging on the front door, the lock being rattled. The voice again: "Open up! Police!"

If only I could let them in, I thought to myself, hovering between front room and kitchen. If only . . . Silly to think about impossibilities. I had to make up my mind what to do next: follow Moker, or wait for the police to break the door down? Back at the police station, they'd obviously taken the "dying" woman's last words seriously. I/she had given them the name of her attacker/killer, her appearance giving the words credibility. When they discovered the leaking wound to her heart, the knitting needle still in place, they would have been bound to investigate. A swift computer check of the electoral roll would have soon provided Alec Moker's address. That had been my plan and it seemed to have worked. At least I'd caught their attention.

But now Moker was fleeing and for the moment I'd lost sight of him. I sped through the grubby kitchen and out the back door where there was a small concrete yard full of junk—a rust-stained fridge, cardboard boxes, a piece of rolled-up lino, just the normal throwaways that mount up when communal flat dwellers find it too much bother to dispose of their bits and pieces legitimately. Moker was just disappearing over a five-foot-high wall at the end of the yard.

I knew where he was going and it filled me with horror.

I followed him over the wall to find myself in a secluded church garden, a small and neatly kept oasis with trees, shrubbery, flowerbeds, and a trivial amount of flat lawn. It was surrounded on all sides by tall buildings, old houses probably converted into flats, and the rear edifice of the church itself, its spire looming over all, a mocking finger that pointed heavenward—mocking to me, that is. Moker was galloping along a narrow flagstone path with that peculiar gait of his, ducking into the passage between church wall and thick shrubbery. When I reached it I saw a single tall gate at the far end which Moker was just shuffling through. I cursed the gate for not being locked.

A streetlamp lit up his slouched figure as he turned to his right. Then he was gone and I moved swiftly to catch up. Through the shadowed passageway I went and I was soon out into the light of a broad but quiet road that must have run parallel to the one in which Moker's flat was situated. Vehicles were parked along either side and I noticed the old Hillman among them: Moker was standing beside it, fumbling in his raincoat pocket for the keys. Presumably he always parked some distance from his home for reasons of his own, or there had been no empty spaces nearer to his flat. Tonight it had been Moker's good fortune that parking in central London was always a problem.

He found his car keys and unlocked the Hillman's door, although it took him a couple of attempts to guide the key in. His nervous excitement—excitement of the unpleasant kind—was evident in his aura, for under a nearby street light the weird halo was still sparkling, but now short explosions of grayish light flew from it. There were also new colors in the aura, which, until now, had remained malevolently dark apart from the earlier angry eruptions. Mauve and deep blue were the main hues present, although red blushed through them all at irregular intervals. None of these shades was vivid though, all were somehow muddied, impure, foul-looking.

By the time I had reached him he was sitting inside the car with the page torn from the telephone directory held before him at an angle so that it caught the light from outside (presumably the Hillman either had no interior light, or it was broken—or Moker wasn't risking being spotted). I peered through the side window and saw his finger moving down the Ts again.

He was looking up my address once more.

I could have hitched a ride with him, but I wanted to reach my house first. I had no idea of how I would warn Andrea that an unexpected—and very unwelcome—guest was on the way; my only thought was to be there before he arrived.

It seemed that Moker had always sensed my presence, but it was only when he, too, was in the out-of-body state that he could *see* me. It may have been for a brief moment, but Moker had known my face earlier, and later, back at his flat, he had checked it out with the newspaper photograph. Now he was on the way to my home, his mission . . .? To extract some distorted idea of revenge? To punish me for telling the police the identity of the woman's attacker which, hopefully, and without too much brainwork, would connect him to the other serial murders? Or because I was the only one who knew of his special powers? It didn't matter which—he was a sick madman and he was going after my family.

I willed myself through the empty streets and roads, taking long, low leaps so that I was almost flying, pushing myself off the ground with my hands each time I sank, just as I had in dreams. The chill inside me had nothing to do with temperature; it was because of the fear that gripped my soul. I wanted to scream in frustration, wanted to confront Moker before he reached my house, but all I could do was propel myself along and pray that Andrea wasn't home, that she'd taken Primrose to a friend or relative just to be away from the news-hounds and even well-wishers who might mistake interference for sympathy. Yet somehow I knew she would not leave home if only for Prim's sake; our daughter would need familiar things around her, for when life is upheaved by tragedy, a small comfort can be taken from the familiar, from the things you know and feel comfortable with—things that are still *there*. Prim would need time to adapt and, more importantly, to accept, and taking her away would not help. No, Andrea would not leave our home with Primrose; not for a while, anyway. I just hoped my wife had locked all doors and windows before she went to bed tonight.

My journey seemed to be taking forever, although I knew I was making good progress. There was hardly any traffic around—not that it would have bothered me—and the pavements were deserted save for some lonely night-worker or two or revelled-out revellers. I had no idea at all of the time, but I could see that most of the houses and all of the shops and offices were in darkness.

I remembered the number of times I'd chastized Andrea for leaving a window, upstairs or downstairs, slightly ajar, or the back door locked but unbolted, and I prayed that my absence would spur her to take proper precautions. She must be feeling vulnerable without me and that thought only emphasized how useless I would be to her now.

At last—at long, long last—I was gliding up the road leading home. And despite the late hour, the lights were still on.

I paused at the gate. Oliver's silver BMW was parked at the curbside and I didn't know whether to feel elated or angry. At least Andrea and Prim were not alone. But why should Oliver be here at this hour?

Maybe Moker would do me a favor and murder him.

I quickly pushed such worthless thoughts from my mind. Even if Oliver had killed me, pretending it was the work of another, he would be able to protect my wife and daughter. And it was my daughter I cared about most.

I passed through the gate and went up the path to the front door. I took a deep and unnecessary breath before moving through it.

I could hear their voices coming from the lounge—Oliver's and Andrea's—speaking low so all I could hear from where I waited in the hall were murmurings. The lounge door was open and, foolishly, I was tempted to linger outside and eavesdrop, as if I might be seen should I enter the room. I rebuked myself before slipping through the doorway.

They were together on the sofa. My best friend and my wife. Close, inclined toward each other, knees almost touching, Oliver with a casual arm over the back of the sofa, Andrea leaning sideways toward him, her hand on his knee. She was gazing into his face, but his eyes were cast downward, focused on the small space between them.

Andrea wore one of my old high-necked FCUK coffee-colored cardigans, unzipped over a black exercise vest and charcoal gray sweatpants. Her feet were bare on the plush carpet.* Oliver was dressed as if having only just returned from the office: light twill trousers, loose beige jacket over a burgundy sweatshirt. His brown ankle boots were suede.

Anger boiled inside me, but I had the sudden urge to see Primrose, check on her, make sure she was safe and sound. I left the room and took to the stairs, climbing them as if I were a normal human being rather than a lost specter.

The door to her bedroom was partially open—we never closed Prim's bedroom door at night in case she should call out, stirred by some threatening dream. We also listened for wheezy breaths, a sign that one of her asthma attacks was about to start. I slid through the gap and foolishly tiptoed toward her narrow bunk bed as if I still had the power to disturb.

Her flower-patterned duvet was down almost to her waist, a sign of restless sleep or that the room was too warm. One little arm was bent so that her hand, and particularly her thumb, was near to her face; the other arm stretched down her side, the hand on top of a ruffled sheet. Her hair was curled around her cheek, almost hiding her profile. How I longed to lie down beside her and cuddle her.

A soft nightlight—a happy pink elephant lit up from inside—threw its comforting but limited glow into the room and, as if by habit, I checked the small gaily painted cabinet that stood next to the bed. Beneath the Winnie the Pooh lamp was her puffer. I remembered when the family doctor had first prescribed the Ventolin inhaler for Prim's asthma, and how it broke my heart to watch her place it within easy reach on the bedside cabinet every night, as comforting to her—no, more so—as the white teddy bear, Snowy. You know, all children are precious, but your own are beyond value. To watch them suffer illness from time to time is a torment that most parents have to endure, but to know that the illness could be life-threatening, well, that's sheer torture. Even the fact that asthma was a common malady among children these days—at least three other kids in her class were afflicted by it—made it no less tolerable.

I bent down to kiss her cheek, wishing I could draw back her curls with my fingers and, although I made no physical contact, she stirred in her sleep. Her head turned and her eyelids flickered for a moment, but never opened. The

---

*Even at the time I wondered why I noticed such irrelevant details and realized that since I'd left the dead woman's body everything had become more clearly defined, my already enhanced perceptions now heightened to an incredible degree. I guess death and danger will do that whatever your state of existence.

movement surprised me and I pulled back a few inches so that I could observe her. The restlessness did not last long; she soon returned to deep slumber, her narrow chest rising and sinking evenly. Her movement though had disturbed the blankets and the top half of a colored photograph still in its frame was uncovered.

I closed my eyes to hold back the tears. Even though in the photo only my head and shoulders and the top of Prim's head were in view, I knew which one it was. Andrea had taken the shot at least four years ago when I was pushing my daughter on a playground swing. I was laughing as I held the swing's seat in which Prim was locked, ready to give it another almighty push so that she would sail "high into sky," as she put it. Although most of her face remained concealed, I knew that she was laughing happily, only a tiny bit of fear—no, it was more excited apprehension—in her eyes, a long strand of hair—red in the sunshine—loose down her face, almost dissecting it. My increased sadness was both because I would never live such wonderful moments again and because Prim felt the need to have my picture in bed with her, like the inhaler, close at hand.

But then rage began to override my emotions. Oliver was to blame for my death; Oliver was the one who had lost my daughter her daddy; Oliver was the "friend" who'd stolen my wife. I stood up, blinded by tears that brimmed unshed in my incorporeal eyes, raging at the duplicity of it all. Oliver. We'd shared so many good times together, hard times too, building up the business, bouncing off each other with creative ideas, sharing either celebratory or consolatory drinks depending on whether accounts were won or lost. At times we'd been like brothers—no probably closer than brothers, because there was no sibling rivalry between us—and we complemented each other as a team, he the garrulous but smooth and convincing talker who could charm clients as easily as he could charm women, and I, the quiet but plain-speaking one who was just a little shy in front of both clients and women. A great team with no jealousy between us, not a common thing where copywriter and art director are concerned, when invariably the politics of protectionism (toward ideas as well as status) raises its ugly head. Or so I had believed.

All those years, those good exciting years, he must have envied me for winning Andrea as my wife, even though he, himself, had ruined their previous relationship. Envied me so much that he had plotted to take her back for himself. All those years of deceit . . .

These black thoughts swept through me as I stood at my daughter's bedside, the melancholy of a few moments ago overwhelmed by a boiling hatred against someone who had taken not only my wife, but my life also. With one last look at Prim, feeling a love for her that softened only the edges of my anger, I stole back out onto the landing. I heard Andrea's voice as I came down the stairs.

"What do you expect of me, Oliver?" she was saying. "Jim has been dead for no more than a week and you think I can just dismiss him from my life?"

"I'm not suggesting you should, or even could, do that." Oliver was talking in low, reasonable tones, the way he used to persuade clients our ad or campaign was great even if they themselves were not quite swept away by it. "But I want to end the deceit, Andrea. I want us to be together all the time."

Oh, he wanted to end the deceit. Well that would be easy enough with me out of the way.

Andrea again, rising frustration in her voice. "You don't understand how much I loved him, how I miss him now!"

Loved me? That was hard to get my head around. How could she betray me if she loved me so much?

"You loved us both, I accept that, Andrea. But be honest with yourself—you love me more. You always have."

"You never made it easy for me. You would never leave me alone."

"Jim and I had a thriving business partnership. I couldn't just clear out, it wouldn't have been fair to him."

"Did you hear what you just said? You were screwing his wife and you thought it would be unfair to split up your business partnership? I can't believe you ever saw things that way."

Nor could I. Oliver wanted it all ways. He wanted my wife and he also wanted the success and revenue that our partnership brought him. Unbelievable.

"I couldn't leave *you*, Andrea. I tried, I tried to forget about you and all we had together, but it wasn't possible. I loved you too much then and I love you too much now!"

"Keep your voice down. I don't want Prim to wake up. She's been through enough already."

Oliver spoke in a whisper, but by then I was close enough to hear. I was just outside the door.

"It's because of Prim that we have to be together again," he said.

His words were followed by a silence. I waited.

"It isn't right for you to bring that up. Not now, not when I'm going through so much pain." Andrea's voice was quiet, but it wasn't a whisper. I heard the sofa creak, as if one of them had changed position.

Oliver's voice again, still in a whisper, but an edge of . . . what? Regret? Humility? Neither was really his style, yet there was a new tone to his words. Could have been sadness. "I know it's too soon, but I do have a right. You know that."

Another silence, longer this time and, still rooted to the spot outside the door, I imagined Andrea searching his face. Perhaps she, too, wondered what he was implying.

After a while, she said, equally as quietly: "It was the cruellest thing we did to Jim."

Pointlessly, I held my breath. What could be more cruel than cheating on me all these years?

"It would have destroyed him if he'd known," Oliver replied.

I began to feel that dreadful inner chill again. Where the hell were they going with this? What did Oliver mean? Surely nothing could hurt me more than their betrayal?

"You're talking nonsense, Oliver. Even we don't know for sure."

"Stop kidding yourself. We checked out the dates a million times. Jim was overseas on a photographic job when she was conceived. The timing works out perfectly, but Jim just thought you'd given birth a little prematurely."

What? What was he saying?

"We still can't be certain." It was a defensive protest.

"We've always known. Look at her hair—it's the same shade of brown as mine. She's even got my freckles around the side of her nose. Mine have faded over time, but a few are still there."

It was true: Oliver had a small spattering of light freckles on his face, so light, in fact, that they were almost unnoticeable.

"But it's her eyes that give her away. Oh, they're like yours, but they're more like mine. Each passing year she gets to resemble me more and more."

"Stop it. I won't listen! Now's not the time."

"The time has never been right, has it, Andrea? It was never the right time to tell Jim the truth."

"I would never have left him. I would never have let it ruin our marriage."

"Eventually you would have had no choice. And then Jim would have despised you."

I heard Andrea sob. I half-collapsed against the wall, my shoulder sinking into it.

"Please don't say any more." Andrea's sob escaped her.

"You—we—both have to face what has always been there between us, and it goes beyond mere love. It means responsibility, Andrea. Primrose is my daughter, and now I want to be a proper father to her."

I was stunned. No, I was shocked, shattered. Completely. Nothing had ever hit me so hard. Not even when I discovered Andrea had been unfaithful to me all these years, or when I discovered my best friend was suspected of killing me. Even finding my own dead and mutilated body had not hit me in quite this way. *Nothing* that had gone before—in my *whole* life—had ever touched me like this. It wrenched the heart from me.

I sagged against the hall wall, broken, bent by the deepest despair I'd ever known. Next door, their conversation continued, but I was too numbed to take it in any more, my mind filling with images of my little Primrose, the one person in this world who gave me unconditional love, the light that countered all darkness, my daughter whom I loved above all others, above life itself. I sank to my knees and gave out a long moaning wail that no one could hear. If my tears had been a reality, they would have dampened the wall I rested my cheek against; if my strength had been real, I would have seriously harmed, if not killed, the man sitting beside my wife and speaking of the worst betrayal of all.

I don't know how much time went by before their words began to register with me again, but eventually, they infiltrated the great fog of confusion and pain that had engulfed me.

Andrea was speaking. "Why do the police think you murdered Jim? Why you, Oliver?"

"Because I was the last person to see him alive. That person is usually the prime suspect in murder investigations especially when the police can cook up a motive. The Press certainly had a field day when I was taken in for questioning."

"But why didn't you tell the police?"

"What, that I came straight here after my argument with Jim at the hotel? That I was here making love to you?"

"That you were screwing me while my husband lay dead in a hotel room?"

"Making love, Andrea. Please don't use that kind of language about what we have. And we were making love, the two of us, together. It's always been mutual, hasn't it?"

A brief silence followed before Oliver spoke again. "Besides, being here doesn't mean I couldn't have committed the crime beforehand, or I couldn't have gone back to the hotel and killed him. I didn't stay long, remember? You were worried Prim might wake up and find us both down here. Now I wish I had stayed, but the point is, I didn't want to involve you in any scandal."

"My husband was hacked to pieces and you were concerned about tarnishing my reputation?"

I heard a short humorless laugh from Andrea.

"Something like that," said Oliver. "I don't want to use you as an alibi either, especially as it might not help my case anyway. In fact, it might make it worse for me. I love you, Andrea. Surely you understand my reasons."

The faint sound of weeping.

"And you love me." It was a simple statement from Oliver. "You always have. You never stopped loving me, but you didn't want to hurt Jim."

"No, I didn't want to hurt him, but I kept on seeing you." She sounded bitter and cynical.

"Even when you married him nothing really changed between us."

"I tried, I tried to forget about you. You were such a bastard to me and Jim was so caring."

"I did my best to forget about us too, Andrea. I honestly wanted to stop loving you. Unfortunately, I couldn't pretend for very long. I gave in to my true feelings. And eventually, so did you."

"I couldn't help myself. I missed you so much, despite your cruelty. I thought my love for you would fade in time, but it never did. I could only cope with my life by seeing you again. I should have been happy with Jim, and then Primrose, but it was never complete. Part of *me* was missing."

"Then don't let guilt spoil everything now."

"Now that we're both free? You honestly believe I can put my feelings to one side just because he's gone? It isn't possible. He was a good man, a loving husband, and a wonderful father. He deserved more than that."

"You have the right to be happy again, Andrea." Ollie's sincere client voice again.

"I would have been happy with Jim. I *was* happy with him."

"But a moment ago you said something was missing from your life . . ."

"Because I still loved you? That was the missing ingredient I could have managed, Oliver. I'd have got by if only you'd kept away from me."

"All those wonderful times we had together. You can't ignore them, you can't pretend they didn't happen."

"In hotel rooms, your car? In your flat? Sneaking around, telling lies. I *despise* them."

"You gave yourself to me completely. You wanted me as much as I—"

"*No!*"

"—*as much as I wanted you. We're still in love with each other, don't you see that?*"

For a while there was no response. Then: "How can you be so callous? How can you say these things knowing my husband—*your* best friend—was brutally murdered only days ago?"

"Because I'm speaking honestly and you have to listen to me. Okay, we can give it a while, that's probably for the best anyway. But I'm not going to let you get away from me again. We don't have to live a lie anymore, we—me, you, Primrose—can become a real family."

"I had a real family."

"Please believe me, I don't want to sound harsh. But you'll have to face the truth some time. If I thought you didn't want me, I'd get out of your life for good. But we both know how it really is, don't we?"

Smooth-talking, convincing Oliver. How I detested the bastard.

There was some hesitation before Andrea said, "No. I do love you, Oliver, but you have to understand . . ."

"I do. Honestly, I do understand. I'm aware of how difficult it is for you. It's the same for me, you know."

"How could it be? You were only his so-called friend."

"I still loved him."

"You betrayed him!"

"We both did. And there's nothing either of us can do to change that. Look, you need time to grieve, and I'm prepared to wait if that's how it has to be. I won't give up, though. I'll be there for you whenever you need me. Is that okay with you? I'll stay away for a while, but sooner or later—it really depends on you—I'll come back."

I heard more muffled weeping.

"You should go now," Andrea said between sniffles. "You should go home."

"I have to go to the agency."

"This time of night?"

"Sydney's working overnight to get the books ready for audit and examination. Blake & Turnbrow have the right to check them before the merger can progress."

"You're going through with it—the merger, the buyout?—even though Jim was against it?"

"It's the right move."

"Doesn't it give you another motive for murder? The police are aware that Jim was fighting it."

"I'm prepared to risk that. My idea has always been to build up a small but lucrative agency, gain some blue-chip or at least prestigious accounts, then sell for a large amount and perhaps get out of the business altogether. Big agencies have always liked swallowing up the smaller fry, especially if their creativity is exceptional, as ours is."

"Was. You've lost Jim."

"I always had the best ideas. Jim was just the art man."

In the hall, I couldn't feel any more devastated than I already felt, but a seething anger was pushing its way through once again.

Andrea came back at him. "You know that's not true. You were a team—Jim always came up with wonderful campaign ideas."

"Okay, we both know that, but Blake & Turnbrow don't. Sydney and I have had numerous meetings with their people that Jim knew nothing about, and others that pressure of work prevented him from joining. The art director is always the last in the chain as far as preparing for presentations is concerned. I think the other agency assumes I'm the driving force behind our creativity."

"If Jim had only realized how devious you really are . . ."

"That was one of his faults, wasn't it? He always trusted people, always thought the best of them. You see, Jim had two main faults. The first was that he was gullible; the second that he wouldn't admit it, especially not to himself."

"And this is meant to make me love you more?"

"It's all for you, Andrea. You and Primrose."

If I'd had any doubts about Guinane having killed me (see that? I couldn't bring myself to call him Oliver or Ollie anymore) they had all gone by now. How had I ever believed in him? How had I ever thought I truly knew him? I mean, here was a scumbag who'd wanted to wreck my business life, who had planned to steal my wife, and now, perhaps worse of all (yeah, worse to me than screwing my wife, because *she* had played a voluntary part in that), he wanted to claim *my* daughter as his own, so what would be so hard about murdering me? Oh yeah, he did it all right. Tonight my ex-partner had revealed things about himself that I would never even have guessed at a week ago. God, give me the means, give me the means to hit back, to avenge myself. Vengeance might be Thine, but hey, throw me a crumb, let me help out just a little bit.

I forced myself to listen on.

"Why tell me all this now? What's your point, Oliver? You can't make me feel any lower than I do already, so why make me finally see exactly what you are?"

He sounded anxious, yet there was still that arrogance in his voice. "Because I want honesty between us after all these years of deceit. I want you to know how much I'm prepared to do for you."

"For yourself, you mean."

"No, so we can have a good future together. You, me and Prim. I've had enough of the rat race, darling, I want out. With the money I'll make from the merger I can leave advertising behind me. We'll have time for ourselves, Andrea. No more deadlines for me, no more distractions, no more stress. And of course, eventually my inheritance will come my way and it should be quite substantial."

"I'm not impressed, Oliver. But thank you for helping me make up my mind. It's over. I want you out—*now!*"

"You've tried to end it before. More than once."

"It's different this time. Jim's death has made me see what a bitch I am. And what a two-faced swine you are."

"You'll feel differently when the grief is over and you can think clearly again."

"I don't think I'll ever be over it."

"It wasn't our fault, Andrea. Not yours, not mine. His death was an act of fate and had nothing to do with us. You'll see that eventually."

"I'm beginning to wonder about that. The police suspect you, Oliver, and I'm wondering just what lengths you'd go to to get what you want."

"Don't lay his murder on me, Andrea. At times this week I've felt his death was meant to be, that with Jim gone everything can be as it should."

"You know what? At last I'm seeing you in your true light, and it isn't very pleasant. Go and see Sydney at the agency, cook up more of your greedy little get-rich-quick schemes. Just leave me—and Primrose—alone from now on."

Another creak of the sofa and I guessed Guinane was rising to his feet.

"Okay, I'm going," I heard him say. "I know you'll change your mind about us. Sooner or later, you'll see things clearly."

"Just go, Oliver. It's over, don't you understand? We're finished."

Footsteps crossing the carpeted floor. Guinane appeared in the doorway, no more than two feet away from me. I wanted to throw myself at him as he paused there and turned to look back at Andrea.

"I'll call you tomorrow," he said.

Her voice was cold. "Please don't."

He watched her from the doorway for a moment, but from the expression on his face I don't think Andrea returned his look.

Finally, he said, "I'm there when you need me."

With that he whirled around and made for the front door.

I still wanted to hurl myself at him. I wanted to kill him.

And then I remembered.

Suddenly, I wanted him to stay.

Because Moker was on his way.

About ten minutes later there was a knock on the door.

I don't know why Moker didn't ring the bell; perhaps he thought using the knocker above the letterbox was more portentous, more scary, who knows?

I'd gone into our long lounge—it extended to the back of the house since a dividing wall had been taken out—and watched Andrea on the sofa as she wept quietly.

She looked dreadful. Her dark hair was unkempt, her face sallow, sickly looking. The rims of her eyes were red and looked very sore, while the skin around them was puffy. She seemed frail, as if she had neither eaten nor slept well for a week, and she was hunched forward on the edge of the sofa, elbows on knees, twisting a sodden handkerchief in her hands.

"I'm so sorry, Jim," I heard her say in a voice that was weak, full of sadness and regret.

For a moment, I wanted to go to her and hold her tight, comfort her with forgiving words, but the thought of her duplicity prevented me (not that it would have been possible anyway). At last aware of all those years of deception and adultery, I raged inwardly, and my pity was limited. Had our *whole* marriage been a sham? If—I would have screamed my thoughts had I had a voice that could be heard—if Primrose was Oliver's daughter, then his and Andrea's affair must have revived itself shortly after we got together, even before we married, so what was wrong with me, how had I failed her? I loved Andrea as much as any man could possibly love a woman, yet it wasn't enough for her. Dark images of the two of them sneaking around, making love in the daytime, when I was always on photo or film shoots, at night when Andrea had made some excuse of having a girls' night out, staying with one of her closest friends because it was so late—all those thoughts rushed through my head. Guinane and Andrea naked, together, Guinane touching my wife's body, entering her. *Fucking* her. The thought, like the word, was brutal. Brutal and ugly.

But it was the shock of learning the truth about Primrose that subjugated all else. That had finally busted me.

I loved her so much and the thought that she was not truly my daughter broke my heart, my will—my *soul*. This child whom I'd adored since first she had slid oh-so-easily from Andrea's womb, all sticky and bloody, but the most beautiful sight I'd ever seen. How nervous I'd been because it was all so new to me, I'd never had someone who would depend on me so much, and how gratifying fatherhood had come to be.

If I were still alive and Guinane suddenly announced to the world that he was Prim's true father and even took blood tests to prove it, I would fight tooth and nail to keep her as mine. I would never love her any less, to me she would always be *my* daughter, and I was sure that to her I'd always be her daddy.

I could only look down at the wretched figure of Andrea as she quietly wept and curse her for what she had done to me.

Andrea's bowed head came up and she looked toward the open lounge doorway.

"Oliver . . .?" she whispered.

Her sad, tear-stained face took on some kind of firmness, a hard glint narrowing her dampened eyes.

"No," I heard her say in a voice that was angry as much as remorseful. "I told you, it's over."

Three sharp knocks again.

Andrea rose from the sofa and took weary but determined strides across the carpet. She passed right through me and I suddenly felt a mental anguish that was almost a match for my own. It was as if a cloud full of misery, regret, with anger gnawing at its edges, had enveloped me. Only fear—fear for her—sent me after her.

I raced around her as she reached the lounge door and held up my hands as if to block her way.

"*No!*" I screamed into her face. "*Don't open the door, please don't open the door.*"

Once again, her distress engulfed me, but this time I was ready for it and let it slip through without burdening myself. I went with her, screeching in her ear all the way to the thick oak front door to our house.

"*Don't let him in! For God's sake, don't open the door!*"

Then it all became like a slow-motion dream: *She's hesitating, as though she's heard me, but she couldn't have, because she's taking another slow, oh so slow, step closer to the door, and she's lifting an arm, her hand reaching for the latch, and I'm screaming at her—don't do it, Andrea, please don't let him in!—and*

her wrist is twisting as she says Oliver's name, and now my wife, my widow, is
pulling the door open, stepping back to allow it to swing wide . . .

And Moker was standing outside on the doorstep.

His scarf no longer hid his face; it was draped around his shoulders, the ends dangling past his waist. He still wore the hat and he held a sharp-pointed knitting needle in one hand.

This must be his method, I realized, for I've witnessed it before, in the underground car park. He stuns his intended victim by showing them his ghastly face, paralyzing them with fear for a moment or two, giving him just enough time to plunge the knitting needle up into their heart, his other hand covering their mouth to stifle whatever screams might come.

There was darkness behind him, but light from the hall revealed the shocking visage, the deep crater that should have been a face. Swiftly, he moved his hands, one to strike, the other to smother, but Andrea took a step backward in horror, and before Moker could move forward, she turned and ran through the doorway to the lounge.

I tried to stand in his way, willed myself to be solid, but it was hopeless. He walked right through me and for an instant my soul was filled with a complete blackness. I shuddered.

Then Moker paused, looked back for a second as though he had been made aware of my presence. The moment was all too quickly gone and he turned his grotesque head to seek out his quarry. Andrea tried to shut the lounge door behind her, but Moker held up a hand and pushed back, so viciously that Andrea was sent reeling backward. When he lumbered after her into the lounge, she was on one knee, struggling to rise, her breath taken in short panic-stricken gasps.

I rushed past Moker, with only a shoulder passing through him, and tried to lift Andrea, always forgetting I could not influence anything in my old world.

"Get out, Andrea!" I yelled at her. *"Get out of the house! Don't let him get near you!"*

It was worse than useless—it was a waste of time. I wheeled around and threw myself at Moker again. Once more the total blackness. And once more he stopped, the sharp point of the steel knitting needle pointing upward. He looked this way and that, his large dark eyes confused. He had felt me, just for a moment. He'd experienced something that was close to my own experience, a sensation of fusion with something else; something alien.

It was quickly gone, because I staggered out on the other side of him, but the delay was enough for Andrea to get to her feet again. She ran round to the back of the sofa, keeping it between herself and the monster who stalked her, forcing herself to look away from him to search for anything that would help her, anything she could use as a weapon.

I did the same, scanning the long room for any object she could use to defend herself. I saw the heavy poker leaning against the side of the stark white fireplace toward the other end of the room. Nothing more warming to the soul than a real fire with real flames, I'd always insisted, and was now glad that I had.

"The poker, Andrea! Get the poker!" Maybe I expected that by shouting at her, the thought itself might be put inside her head. And perhaps it had worked, because she made a sudden dash toward the poker.

She screamed as she ran, and maybe it was partly to rouse our neighbors and not only because of fear. I had never regretted living in a detached house before, but I did on this night. Nobody was near enough to hear.

Moker lumbered after her like a zombie on speed, aware she had no place to go and making peculiar snorting noises. Although there were patio doors at the far end of the room, which led out to our largish but unspectacular garden, they were always kept locked, the key hidden in the drawer of the long sideboard that stood opposite the fireplace. Keys were only in the lock when the doors were in use on summer days or evenings, and the chances now of Andrea getting to the drawer, retrieving the key, and unlocking the doors before Moker got to her were zero.

Thank God she was going for the poker. Only she wasn't. Instead she ran past the fireplace and made for a Grecian bust mounted on a plinth.

I realized what she was going for and cried out, *"No, you'll never make it, he's too close!"* (Stupidly, I just couldn't get out of the habit of acting like a normal human being.) Naturally she didn't hear.

Earlier in the day, Andrea had obviously been on the phone, taking it from its charger, usually kept on an elegant stand in the hall, and had wandered over to the lounge's big door-windows to look out at the garden while she talked, something she invariably did when she knew the conversation was going to be lengthy, and I saw the receiver precariously balanced on the top edge of the plinth. It was that she was headed for, not the statue, but there was no way she would have time to call the police. Maybe she intended to dodge around Moker, keeping her distance while she dialed.

Moker's clumsy stride quickened and yet again I plunged into him, anything to slow him down. The blackness swallowed me up, but this time there were vague images filtering through, images of dead people as far as I could tell, dead people whose corpses were badly damaged, great gashes in their flesh, limbs almost severed. This time, despite those awful visions that were trying to resolve themselves, I tried to stay inside the killer rather than pay a fleeting visit; my purpose was to slow his advance with the distraction, give Andrea the chance to escape the corner she'd backed into.

The ruse worked only for a couple of seconds. Moker seemed to shrug me off and went for Andrea again. She threw the phone at him and it struck his head. It must have hurt a little, because he stalled, one beefy hand going to his forehead.

Quickly taking advantage, Andrea ducked under his free outstretched arm and headed back down the room. Unfortunately, Moker made a surprisingly fluid move and tried to grab her shoulder. He'd overbalanced though, and fell to the floor. But as he did so, that outstretched hand snagged Andrea's ankle.

She screamed as Moker hauled her back to him, his own body shifting forward as though he intended to smother her with his weight. Andrea squirmed and wriggled, kicked out with her other bare foot, but all was futile against his superior strength and tonnage. He crawled over her legs, pinning both of them to the floor, his left hand gripping the loose folds of the coffee-colored cardigan that used to belong to me. Now she was whimpering as he snatched at her hair and pulled her head back, bending her spine the wrong way.

He was making those awful gurgling-snuffling sounds as he stretched her, either through excitement or rage, God knows which. Probably both. I thought her back would break as he continued to pull at her, and I frantically but futilely beat his head, my fists merely sinking through long but sparse hair and skull.

"*Oh, please, God, help me, help me. Let me make him stop!*"

I was pleading to no effect and I knew it. There was nothing else I could do. Occupying his body wouldn't stop him, even if it confused him for a second or two. His body pinned her lower body to the floor as, one hand cupping her chin, he drew her back further, and further.

The sharpened needle in his other hand was poised to strike.

And that was when yet another shock made me wail in despair.

In all the panic and confusion I'd almost forgotten about her, and now here she was, her little face white with terror.

Primrose stood there by the sofa in her pretty yellow ankle-length nightie, bare toes sunk into the thick carpet, her wide eyes bewildered and afraid. Her lungs pumped against her chest as she struggled to breathe (it's just as hard for an asthmatic to expel air as it is for them to draw air in), the first signs of an all-out asthma attack. In one tiny and delicate hand she held Snowy by its paw, its white feet dragging on the carpet.

Her words were broken into separate parts because of her breathlessness.

"Leave . . . Mummy . . . alone!" she cried out.

Andrea painfully managed to squeeze out a warning, her back still arched, her head restrained by the hand under her chin. "Run, darling, run away!"

That coarse guttural snuffling came from the hole in Moker's face as he held Andrea there on the floor.

He became still as he stared at the daughter I had believed was mine.

I rushed past the monster and foolishly tried to gather up Primrose in my arms. It was like clutching at empty air and in my desperate confusion it was as if she were the immaterial one, not me. I groaned in frustration and yelled at her to get out of the house, run next door, wake the neighbors, anything but stay here at the mercy of the lunatic who threatened her mother.

A partly stifled sob came from Prim, an abrupt sound caught in her struggle to draw breath. I glanced at the free hand by her side, hoping to see she had brought her inhaler with her. She hadn't, but right now, that wasn't the priority.

"*Run, Prim, run away!*" Andrea screeched more forcefully this time, but our little girl was frozen with fright.

Tears welled in her tawny-brown eyes (even in that predicament I realized they were more like Guinane's than mine or her mother's) and her chest rose and fell in judders. She wouldn't move, she *couldn't* move.

I turned to face Moker, putting myself between him and Primrose as though I could protect her. The killer was still staring at her—looking through me!—a curious cast in those black eyes of his. I think it was the glint of anticipation.

Andrea, whose eyes were bulging as they were forced to look down her cheeks at Prim because of the angle of her head, gave out a piercing scream, one so high-pitched and shrill that it must have passed far beyond the walls of the house.

Moker was distracted only for a second. His merciless eyes flicked down at Andrea and he pulled her head back a little further out of pure masochism I'm sure and I feared her neck would snap. In the blink of an eye he had changed his grip and sank his fingers into her hair, then he pushed down fast and hard, smashing her face against the floor. Even though the floor was thickly carpeted, the smacking sound was explosive, and blood instantly burst outward, spattering the beige carpet around her head with bright red blots. Andrea made no sound, but lay there motionless, perhaps even dead.

"Oh dear God, don't let this happen," I prayed.

And when Moker slid the needle into a pocket, then shambled to his feet and started toward Prim, I said it again, this time aloud even if only I could hear the words.

"Oh dear God, please *don't let this happen!"*

Moker came closer, Andrea's unmoving body recumbent behind him, her arms and legs splayed.

"Don't you touch her!" I yelled into Moker's absent face. *"I'll kill you if you touch her!"*

All to no avail, of course, even as it would have been if he could hear my threat.

I whirled and dropped to my knees in front of Prim. "Primrose, you must get out of the house. You must run away right now."

I spoke fiercely but firmly, and hoped the sheer power behind my words and very concentrated thoughts would somehow get through to her. Her round eyes were looking upward at the approaching monster, her lower lip trembling as a strained wheezing came from between her lips.

My own eyes, blurred with tears of frustration, desperation—sheer *hopelessness*—must have been as wide and terrified as hers. I threw my arms around her small thin body as if to shield her, but big hands reached through me and wrapped themselves around her narrow shoulders. Snowy dropped to the floor.

"Mummy," Primrose whimpered quietly, and two large teardrops spilled over and began their irregular descent of her cheeks. "Daddy . . ."

The killer's hands moved over her shoulders and their fingers curled around her throat.

THIRTY-EIGHT

Moker had picked up Primrose by the neck, his arms outstretched at shoulder level. But as she dangled there, her tiny feet kicking empty air, the face that had been pallid before beginning to turn red, the carpet started to undulate.

I was raining impotent blows on Moker, having tried to enter him again, but horrifically I began to experience part of his own sick pleasure, and that was too much for me to bear. Now I continued to beat at him because there was nothing left that I could do—I just couldn't stand by and watch him kill my Primrose!

It was Moker, himself, who first became aware of the thick beige carpet rippling from one end of the room to the other as if a wind was caught beneath it. Pressure on Prim's throat must have eased momentarily because she drew in a strangulated breath as he looked down and around him. Following his gaze, I also glanced down and was astounded at what I saw.

The carpet appeared to be flowing as each and every individual woolen fiber of its pile stood erect. We seemed to be at its center and the movement, which could be seen as a growing shadow, had a rippling effect like the gently spreading wave circle when a stone is dropped into a still pond.

It was an expensive carpet, plush and wall-to-wall. It wasn't shag-pile by any means, but it was *deep*-pile, so that feet would sink into it almost as if into fine sand, a luxury Andrea and I had treated ourselves to after a year of walking on exposed but stained and highly varnished floorboards.

But now there was something wrong with it. Now it seemed to have come alive. Now the carpet had turned nasty.

Although preoccupied right then, Moker had nevertheless become distracted by the phenomenon, because the radiating carpet strands had nearly unbalanced him and, still astonished, I realized the fibers must be as hard as nails. Andrea's unconscious body, which lay in the other half of the room close to the fireplace, suddenly stirred as a thousand or so stiffened fibers straightened under her body, lifting her slightly. She tried to raise her head, blood from her busted nose spoiling the carpet, but the effort was too much and she slumped down again, a short muffled cry escaping as fibers pricked her cheek.

Moker was still fascinated by the carpet's movement, a kind of shiny wildness in those black eyes of his, his victim held aloft but forgotten for the moment. The distraction had also briefly diverted me.

The closed curtains began to wave as if caught in a breeze, even though the windows behind them were shut. A delicate figurine that sat near the center of the long sideboard suddenly streaked across the room to smash against the white-brick fire surround. Moker stared at the myriad pieces as if expecting the little statue to put itself together again. There were hefty, tall, white-marble candlestick holders on each end of the sideboard and one began to wobble on the flat surface. The agitation caused a rumbling sound before the ornament slowly rose into the air, the candle it held tilting, then falling back onto the sideboard. The marble holder hovered at about head height as we watched and then, without warning, it shot down the room toward us.

Out of instinct, I ducked, but Moker's reactions were not so fast. The heavy object struck full in his disfigured face. A rough, snuffling cry escaped him and he dropped Primrose onto the bristling carpet. I fell to my knees beside her and quickly examined her face. The redness had gone from it, but a bluish tinge had crept into her new pallor, another serious warning that an asthma attack was under way. The rise and fall of her chest was shallow, but I was pleased to see at least breath vapor leaking from behind her lips, which meant she was breathing. Wait a minute! Breath vapor? What was that all about?

No sooner had I asked myself the question then I felt the chill.

In my state of spirit, the room's temperature should have been of no consequence. Yet I had become cold, a deep frigidity seeping through my nonexistent bones, filling my interior, chilling my blood, cooling organs that I no longer possessed, *freezing* me! I felt the hairs on my forearms prickle—God, I felt the hair on my head stiffen! And when I looked across the room at Moker, who was leaning against a wall holding his forehead, I saw frost in his sparse lank strands of hair and billows of steam escaping the hole in his face.

It seemed that he, too, was now aware of the room's iciness, because he slowly straightened, taking his hand away from his head (I was disappointed to see that the missile had not broken the skin—there was no blood—although he was marked and likely to have a very nasty bruise there), and this time he scanned the whole room. Now I thought there was a glint of fear in those killer eyes.

Andrea was still not moving at all. Was she unconscious or dead? Small amounts of white frost speckled her hair also, hair that seemed full of static.

What the hell was going on?

A color photograph—Andrea, Prim, and myself, Prim just three years old and smiling deliciously, taken when on holiday in Naples, not in Italy but on the Gulf of Mexico—heavily weighted by its silver frame, flew off the mantelpiece and thudded into Moker's back, so that he swung around again.

An elegant but empty vase that sat solo on a tall stand beside the front window hurled itself across the room and smashed against Moker's kneecap, inducing a grunt of pain from him.

The recessed ceiling lights suddenly oscillated between bright and low, then back again, as if some unseen hand was manipulating their dimmer control, the change becoming quicker as the sequence continued to repeat itself. But this weak strobing effect had nothing to do with their control switch, because the independent glows from two lamps at either end of the room, one floor-standing, the other, smaller, lamp on the sideboard, were following the ceiling lights' behavior.

A large black-framed painting—a limited edition Rothko print, three unequal slabs of color piled one on top of the other—dropped to the floor with a crash, landing upright, the glass cracking from top to bottom with only a few jagged shards breaking free, before the whole thing toppled face-forward onto the petrified (literally) carpet.

Moker looked around him as if stupefied and clouds of vapor billowed from his funnelled face.

Once again I became conscious of the coldness: it was as if a huge icy hand had gripped me inside, its fingers now curling round my heart. Even though I didn't exist in the physical sense, I felt my limbs stiffen, my back and neck freeze up. The door to the lounge slammed shut, the sound like a shot from a cannon, making me jump; it flew open again and there was no one outside in the hall to have pulled it. The door slammed shut once more, the sound shattering, its crash causing the remaining paintings around the room to fall. This time the door rebounded off its frame, then casually swung open. One of the paintings covered by non-reflective glass had landed face-up about a yard away from me and I noticed the glass surface was completely frosted over, the picture beneath a vague pattern of faded pastel colors. Further along the lounge the fireplace implements clattered into the hearth and seemed to vibrate there, as though trying to levitate. A straight-backed chair near the coffee table toppled over as the silent whirlwind ruffled curtains and either moved books and magazines or riffled their pages. The lights, which for a while had remained constantly low, dimmed even further and it was as if the night outside had broken in.

More objects—CDs rattling in their rack, other framed photographs, a long-handled pewter candle snuffer, small but valued ornaments collected over the years, those same disturbed books and magazines—all swept across the room to hurl themselves at the bewildered and, I hoped, frightened killer, who could only gape at the maelstrom as the missiles bounced off him.

It was then that the shapes began to emerge from the darkness.

Blurred phantasms at first, that was all. Elements that did not quite hang together filtering through the dusk. Discarnate conformations, shades that as yet had no definition. All in motion, weaving as if in some exotic but ethereal dance as they assembled themselves.

Ghosts.

A kind of snorting gasp came from Moker, and his black eyes were fixed on the flittering haze that was closer to me than him. Even without a face, his body language alone revealed his alarm: he trembled violently as he cowered against a wall and the hands he held high to shield himself from further projectiles shook as if he were several stages into Parkinson's disease. His heavy eyebrows were crusted with ice crystals and hanging strands of his hair looked brittle enough to snap. I thanked God that the lunatic had forgotten about Primrose.

The swirling mists rolled like fog in his direction, configurations within constantly resolving themselves only to fade again and lose distinction from the mass. But I was sure that I recognized one chimera among the many as the gray mutable shroud purled past me, a ghost that had haunted me long ago, as well as more recently. It was my father and I sensed beyond doubt that he was here with these other ghosts to help me. How was that possible? I had no answer right then, because I didn't even know how *I* was possible.

When the now boiling mass crowded in on Moker he tried to beat them off with his hands, but because they had no genuine substance, his efforts were worthless. The mists hardly stirred under his frenzied swipes, although they continued to create shadowy forms within, all of them ambiguous, no single entity dominating the others. There seemed to be a horde of them as they enveloped Moker.

Although they appeared to fall on him with vigor, ultimately they were no more effective than Moker himself was in warding them off. Sure, they tugged at his long raincoat, stabbed spectral fingers at his face, but they had no power to inflict injury,* save for hurling various inanimate bits and pieces at him and even then, that stuff appeared to have no real force behind it. No, it was sheer terror that drove Moker to his knees.

For a short while the unearthly manifestations grew stronger, although none became solid as they engulfed the serial killer. Gratified, perhaps cruelly so, I sought out individual faces and diaphanous but clearer figures among the spectral host, none of which I recognized, save for the one who had been my absent father in the physical world. He was apart from the others as though he were overseer to the attack. Right now, he was observing me. His was the only image that did not falter and, although he wasn't smiling—the situation was too desperate for that—his expression was benign.

I could only wonder what he had brought with him to my house this night. Cohorts? Angels? Soldiers of God? I had no idea and there was a time when I would never even have considered such things. I just felt thankful that they were on my side. At the séance, the spirits had been separate, individual entities, but tonight they were integrated, unified, as if their collective purpose enhanced their power. I knew very little about the supernatural, or paranormal, but I reasoned that the fading house lights and the deep chill in the atmosphere were because the spirits were drawing energy from the "real" world, this one, the world in which humans live and breathe; they were tapping intangible forces that existed unperceived around us, perhaps also feeding off the psychic energy of the people present in the room. These thoughts passed through my mind swiftly as I looked into the face of my dead father, and maybe it was he who had put them there.

---

*Remember this: GHOSTS CANNOT PHYSICALLY HARM LIVING PEOPLE. Okay, they can cause insensate objects to fly across rooms, but those same objects will not even scratch their target; ghosts can make heavy furniture move, cause teacups and windows to rattle, even will some things to levitate, BUT THEY CANNOT PHYSICALLY HARM ANY LIVING PERSON. Of course, they can scare you to death, induce heart failure, even send you insane with fear by their haunting, BUT THEY CANNOT PHYSICALLY HARM YOU. Try not to forget it.

A guttural yelp from Moker grabbed me back and I saw him cringing on his knees, one shoulder pressed against the wall as if he were trying to push himself through the plaster, while the ghosts vainly flayed, their blows having no true physical impact. Yet he cowered there, blubbering and flinching as though he actually felt their relentless punishment and I guess it was his own terror and the *expectancy* of their blows that fixed him there. I knew that soon he would wise up to it.

And he did.

His whole body was quaking when he tentatively raised his disfigured head, and I couldn't tell if it was because of the room's Arctic temperature (his black raincoat had a light dusting of frost over it and, when he moved, the stiffened material crackled) or because he was so afraid. Cautiously, he craned his neck to face his incorporeal bullies.

I felt rather than saw Primrose stir beside me and when I looked down she raised an arm from the floor and restlessly threw it across her chest. She was not quite unconscious, but was close to it. Prim lay on her back, the carpet rigid and unyielding beneath her, her eyelids twitching as if she had left one nightmare for another; her breathing was shallow, labored, short harsh wheezing gasps coming from lips that were becoming discolored. The underside of the bare arm she had moved to her chest was stippled with scores of tiny red indents as if it had rested on a bed of blunt close-set nails, and I worried about her other arm and exposed legs. But my prime concern was for her breathing. A major asthma attack could kill, and if she didn't use her Ventolin inhaler soon, this might easily develop into one. She might even need an epinephrine injection.

Panicking, I whirled around to see if Andrea had recovered yet. Through the agitated mist-shapes, I saw that her inert body lay in exactly the same position as the last time I checked; the only difference was that blood beneath her face had soaked a little more of the carpet (the carpet itself bristled like the raised hackles of a dog, the vibration continuing to create ripples around the room). I prayed she wasn't dead, both for her sake and for Prim's.

Moker caught my eye again. He was pushing himself to his feet, his back and hands flat against the wall behind, ignoring the entities that flailed him without effect. They seemed more frantic now, as if their impotence had enraged them. Moker swept an arm through them like a man might wave a cloud of midges away from his face.

The fog paled even more and the overhead lights and the room's lamps brightened a fraction. The ghosts were losing sway, their own failure somehow diminishing their strength and, as if understanding their weakness, Moker took a step forward, his arms swinging before him so that the closer parts of the mist licked and curled upon themselves. The vision that was my father rejoined the nebulous throng and the serial killer turned in my direction.

But it was Primrose he was interested in.

On my knees, I sagged forward, as if in supplication. I was in deep despair.

The ghosts hadn't quite finished with Moker though.

The shapes that had become almost indiscernible in what was now a haze began to draw together to form a compact whole. Their shade intensified to a deeper hue, and they grew more substantial, more concentrated, so that once again they gained Moker's respect. He had already started to move toward Primrose when he paused to watch. His eyes gleamed as though mesmerized.

I was more concerned about Prim's condition. I was almost overwhelmed by despair when I saw how fast she had deteriorated—her breathing sounded torturous as her small lungs fought to draw in air and the bluish tinge was more apparent. Without much hope I swung toward Andrea again, but now I couldn't ignore what was happening near the center of the room.

There was hardly anything left of the floating haze, because much of it had been gathered by the black storm that was forming. This Delphian formation was revolving like a miniature tornado, moving faster and faster so that soon it was spinning.

Moker gaped at it (and with that great black excavation beneath his staring eyes, it really was a gape). The lights dimmed once more as if the brightness was being sucked into the blackness, and the chill inside me intensified, even though there was no "inside me"; I felt like a block of ice, coldest at the center. Moker's shivering became extreme, a kind of repetitive juddering, each jolt like a sudden seizure. I checked Primrose, afraid now that she might freeze to death, but there were no ice particles in her curly hair, nor were there goosebumps on her bare arms and legs. I wondered if her semi-consciousness was a factor, her psychic energy untapped and, if so, I hoped it would be the same for Andrea, who appeared totally unconscious (please don't let her be dead, Lord).

The strange fusion of ghosts was about five feet in height, its sides too irregular to measure (widest part roughly three feet, thinnest about two) and looked almost solid as it hovered a few inches above the floor, its spin increasing by the moment. Objects that had flown across the room only minutes ago seemed attracted to its gyration, although they only shifted or twitched where they lay. The carpet, however, went berserk, sections of it lifting (particularly the area directly under the maelstrom) as though a wind had found its way into the house's airbricks and beneath the floorboards to rise with some pressure through the thin cracks between boards. One corner tore itself off the tack rail and curled toward the center storm, flapping there like a loose tongue. The carpet's pile weaved circles like iron filings attracted to a playful magnet, too far away for them to take the leap, but close enough to encourage them to try. Dust specks that no vacuum cleaner could capture rose in circles, tiny whirlpools themselves, competing with the mother one.

And still Moker was gripped by the main phenomenon: transfixed, confused, fearful . . .

. . . Until this primary maelstrom became thinner and sleeker, resolving itself into a curious matt black pillar that was perfectly rounded, quivering with what I could only guess was pure energy. It thrummed as if it were machinery of some kind and the loose things in the lounge became even more agitated. Abruptly, without warning, it shot across the gap between itself and Moker and plunged into the dark pit of his face.

I suppose it was as close to a scream as Moker could raise, and the eruption swelled throughout the room, a frightened screech that had no proper form; it was a prolonged and raw ululation, an animal cry that echoed off the walls. He collapsed onto his hands and knees and howled—a minor sound compared to the attempted scream—as they came in contact with the carpet's hardened fibers. Now he whimpered, a high-pitched agonized mewling as though the blackness inside was poisoning his system, or had clamped onto vital organs and was squeezing the life from them.

I thought that the battle was nearly over. I thought that Moker would flee from the house, run from his tormentors, and forget about Primrose and Andrea. There was still the problem of Prim's asthma attack, but at least there would be a reprieve, more time for Andrea to wake up—*if* she could wake up—and bring the life-saving nebulizing inhaler to our little girl. I thought there was a chance.

But I was wrong. Oh boy, I was so wrong.

The lights began to brighten again. The carpet pile lost its vibrancy and relaxed to its normal state, leaving millions of dust motes swarming in the air like pygmy midges. Fallen stuff became immobile once more. Only a few inconsequential wisps of the haze remained to drift lazily in the air. The room was almost calm . . .

. . . Until Moker gave one shocking, protracted belch and expelled the blackness he had swallowed only moments before.

It had lost its sleek form and billowed out like smoke from an industrial chimney, its curling edges dissipating into the atmosphere. More of it was disgorged as Moker began to retch like a dog that had swallowed too much greasy fat with its meat, and each time he heaved, less and less of the smoky substance spilled. His body shuddered with every expulsion and soon only weak gray trails emerged from the void in his face to join the other fuller drifts. The frost in the serial killer's hair and raincoat lost its whiteness as it rapidly melted, and I felt the deep coldness within me soften its grip. Somehow I understood that the ghosts had used up all the energy they had been able to filch, their united manifestation losing strength, gradually fading.

Moker, still on his hands and knees, but no longer retching, slowly raised his head. And looked toward Primrose.

Her chest quivered each time she tried to gasp a breath and there was only whiteness like thin slivers of snow between her half-closed eyelids. Her little fists were clenched tight and each time she tried to draw air her chin trembled. She was so pale, her skin looked bleached, making the telltale blue tinge even more evident. Soon she might be at the stage where only pure oxygen could save her.

The room was hushed when Moker started to crawl toward us.

For a horrifying moment, I thought Prim had stopped breathing altogether, but she had only paused to regather her strength, her body continuing to work even without conscious imputation. And with her next strained rasping inhalation, the room exploded into life again.

Noises came from everywhere at once—from the walls, the ceiling, the floor—as if the ghosts, unable to possess Moker, had appropriated the house itself. Behind the curtains the windows rattled, the curtains themselves fluttered, and all the fallen objects—the marble candlestick, the ornaments, framed photographs—became agitated once more, dancing where they lay, some rising inches into the air, while others, smaller items such as figurines, an ashtray, the pewter candle snuffer, flew at Moker, who continued to crawl on hands and knees, but this time they fell limply against his head and shoulders. Glass that had cracked in picture frames now shattered completely, shards sprinkling the carpet whose fibers stirred but now failed to come erect. The big-screen TV in the corner behind me switched itself on with a startling blare of voices and a burst of confusing color, immediately switching itself off again. An avalanche of soot gushed out of the fireplace, its dirt clouds rising and spreading around that end of the room, mingling with the revived mists in which vague shapes struggled to reform. I heard a moaning grow into a muted wailing that told me the ghosts were failing to regain their strength.

They rolled over him, chimney dirt recruited so that he appeared to be moving through a wind-tossed smoke; yet they still had no power against him, they could only pester, harass, but not hinder him.

And Moker knew it. He hardly noticed what was happening around him, not even the glass splinters that flew from the broken picture glass to glance off his head and the heavy raincoat he wore. The serial killer had only one objective, and she lay struggling for air beside me.

For a short while, the havoc and the wailing increased.

Moker ignored it all.

And maybe because he ignored it—after all, they had invaded his body only to be defeated by the black vileness of his unclean soul (I learned this later), so he already knew their influence was limited—the dwindling of their power quickened.

He drew closer and, seen through the troubled dust and fog that tried to smother him, he resembled some fabulous but repulsive beast of prey, a nightmare creature that deserved a whole page to itself in the *Complete Book of Monsters and Demons*. Things continued to fall uselessly against him, the dreadful wailing of souls in despair went on, the room was dense with churning clouds, but Moker came on unconcerned.

As if sensing the approach of something evil, something terribly threatening, Prim's eyes flickered open wide and instantly filled with horror when she saw Moker looming over her. (I realized then that she had not been rendered semi-conscious by the asthma attack, but that she had fallen into a faint when Moker had tried to choke her.) Her mouth opened wide too, but she could not catch her breath to scream.

Frantically, she tried to push herself away from the horror, using elbows and heels of her bare feet, but Moker easily grabbed her ankle and pulled her back to him.

The wailing around us rose to a plaintive howling, but the voices were distant, as if the assembled ghosts had been drawn back unwillingly to their proper place, where humans were only a memory. A new kind of chill flooded through me, one that numbed and debilitated, caused by final despair.

Primrose was shaking with terror, but she gamely kicked out at him, tried to scrabble out from the shadow of his intimidating bulk. Saliva drooled from the gristle-edged opening of his face, tiny bubbles interrupting the long silky stream that pooled on her nightie to dampen her tremulous chest beneath the thin material. He rested one big hand on her slight shoulder to pin her to the floor, then reached inside his raincoat pocket with his other hand and drew out the long sharpened knitting needle.

The mists were thin, depleted, but I could still hear those anguished cries though now they were far, far away as if the ghosts were gone but the portal between worlds was not quite closed. Soot still infested the air and a few tenuous ribbons of vapor floated lazily, but these were just meaningless remnants of what had gone on before.

Moker held the long gray needle at an angle against Prim's slender body, just below her left ribcage, its point pressing upward into her nightie, indenting the light material without piercing. Primrose had closed her eyes against the bad dream.

Out of sheer reaction, I threw myself between them, hoping I could deflect the weapon, I guess, but knowing it was hopeless. I fell through them both to sprawl on the floor beside them.

I crouched on my knees, my face low, almost touching Prim's as if I could whisper comforting words, perhaps something like it would only hurt for a moment and then she would sleep to wake and find herself in a better place, a *wonderful* place.

Moker's grip on the long thin needle tightened. His thumb closed over the flat, button end. His knuckle whitened.

He began to push.

I screamed.

And Andrea brought the poker down brutally hard on Moker's bowed head.

THIRTY-NINE

The sound that the heavy iron poker made as it caved in the monster's skull was sickening—but sickeningly good. Sweet and right. Pleasing. Justified. It was the noise a chocolate egg filled with goodies might make when dropped from a great height onto concrete, a kind of heavy, dull cracking thud.

Movement, noise—all quickly faded to nothing.

He seemed paralyzed. He bent over Prim, whose eyes stayed closed, her breathing still shallow, strained, the needle poised beneath her ribs. Not a single utterance came from the yawning pit that substituted for Moker's nose and mouth—no gurgling, no snuffling, neither inhalation nor exhalation. His eyes protruded more than ever; they had become sightless, lackluster, without shine. Blood began to bubble from the new chasm in his head where the iron poker remained embedded. He was either dead, or as good as. He himself didn't seem to know which.

There was a total stillness to the room . . .

. . . Until his head jerked as Andrea wrenched the poker free again.

Now blood spurted from the deep wound like a miniature red fountain when the pressure was released. It started to flood over his head, spilling down onto his forehead, masking one eye, trickling into the pit below it.

Andrea struck again, same place, same force (I remembered reading somewhere that on occasions women can produce supernormal strength to protect their child; one woman had lifted a car on her own when her toddler was trapped beneath it), and a faint sigh filtered through from another dimension.

Once more, the poker was pulled free, and still Moker's body stayed upright, and once more the poker was brought down with a force that drove its blunted end down through his forehead.

This time, Moker toppled over sideways and the poker remained in Andrea's hand, wrenched free from the smashed egg of his skull. She threw it down so hard it bounced on the carpet.

Even as the dead man sprawled beside Prim, one of his dirty sneakered feet trapping her ankles, Andrea was down on the floor reaching for her daughter with both hands. But she swooned suddenly, one of her hands flattening against the floor to steady herself; full-consciousness was not quite ready for her yet. She closed her eyes, opened them again, took a deep breath through her mouth, frowned at the taste of blood. She leaned over Prim again and lifted her by the shoulders, then held her tight against her own body. Prim's face buried itself into Andrea's neck.

I moved closer to them both, an arm passing around Andrea's shoulders, a hand stroking my little girl's back. (Yes, I still thought of Primrose as my little girl. Seven years couldn't be wiped away like chalk from a slate.)

"Her inhaler, Andrea!" I yelled. *"Fetch her inhaler, quick as you can!"*

Andrea's nose was a pulpy mess, blood pouring from it, running copiously over her lips, spilling down her chin, onto her black exercise vest and cardigan, a huge amount of it which suggested her nose was broken. When she opened her mouth to call Prim's name I saw that three front teeth were chipped and her gums were bloody. Prim failed to respond and Andrea held her away so that she could examine her face.

Small spittles of blood sprayed on Prim's cheeks as Andrea gasped, then hugged her tight again. A sudden tortuous intake of breath told us both that Primrose was still alive and, without further ado, Andrea lifted her from the floor and rushed from the lounge with her daughter in her arms, fragments of picture glass crackling under her bare feet. She ignored the pain they must have caused, but she wobbled when she reached the lounge door. She took another breath and began climbing the hall stairs.

I followed and within seconds we were in Prim's small bedroom, so bright and innocently cheerful in daylight, but now menaced by shadows for which the feeble night-light was no match. Andrea quickly remedied that by flicking on the main light switch with her elbow. She hurriedly set Prim on the narrow bed with its cheerful flowery quilt and held her there in a sitting position while a free hand snatched the blue puffer from the bedside cabinet. Maybe it was the lifting and being carried that revived Primrose—or perhaps some inner sense told her she was safe in her mother's arms—but her eyelids fluttered open and her lips moved between strained gasps for air as she tried to form words. By the time Andrea held the puffer up to her face, her eyes were wider— *and looking directly at me.*

"Daddy?" I heard her whisper.

Andrea appeared not to have noticed. She held the inhaler in front of Prim's mouth, index finger on the depressor at the top.

"Open, Baby, open your mouth," she implored, a tremor in her voice.

Prim's eyes went to her mother's and she did as she was told.

Fine droplets of mist sprayed into her mouth and she gulped in air.

"Again, darling, again," her mother urged.

The procedure was repeated several times and gradually Prim's shoulders ceased their shudders and the rise and fall of her chest began to take on a steady rhythm. Andrea's tension seemed to ebb away, even though she must still have been very frightened by all that had happened. I think she was putting on a brave face for our daughter's sake.

As Prim's breathing calmed, she looked once again over her mother's shoulder. Disappointment showed in her eyes.

I stared back at her with what I hoped was a loving smile, just in case she might see me again.

She didn't. Her sweet pale face scrunched up in puzzlement. "I saw Daddy, Mummy," she said when her breathing allowed.

Andrea held her close, but not close enough to restrict her breathing, "Hush, Prim," she said softly, soothingly. "Everything's all right now. The bad man has gone away. He can't hurt you anymore." Her voice sounded as if she had a serious head cold.

"But Mummy—"

"I'm sure Daddy was watching over us. I think he was there protecting us."

Was she merely saying this to comfort Prim, or did Andrea believe her own words? There was no way of knowing, but maybe it was the latter. I like to think so.

It gave me comfort.

As I left them there on the bed, clutching each other, Andrea gently rocking Prim to and fro and making soothing nasal sounds, holding a dozen or so blood-soaked tissues to her nose, a fierce emotion was edging my love for them—yes, my love for them *both*—aside. The emotion was bitterness. And . . . anger.

I had lost so much on the night of my death and now I'd discovered I'd lost even more: I'd lost something that I'd never truly possessed anyway. The final reality was harsh, overwhelming.

And it was Guinane who had caused everything bad that had happened to me. By coveting my wife and stealing my daughter. By betraying me as a friend and business partner. By murdering me. And by murdering me he had caused the monster to visit my home, to threaten and terrorize the two people who had meant more to me than life itself.

Guinane was to blame for everything.

I entered the lounge. It was quiet and perfectly still, but resembled a battle-ground after the battle. The floor was littered with broken or bent debris with fragments of glass, with scattered CDs, with overturned furniture. Even the television screen was filled with a great white, burned-out blemish.

Among it all lay the battered corpse of Alec Moker. His body was without aura.

The room was bright with light and the ghosts had returned.

They were pallid. Almost insignificant. Still weakened. My father was among them, perhaps more visible than the rest because there was contact be-tween us. He smiled at me as those around him waned.

I wondered if they had found the strength—as feeble as it was—to come back because their adversary was dead but they needed to witness the outcome for themselves. None was dancing on his body I noticed.

I stopped on the other side of Moker's corpse and my father smiled at me. The warmth I felt from him, the unbounded love, was akin to my feelings for Primrose.

As he joined his companions in their fading, I looked down at the crumpled bulk that had been Moker.

Fluid from his damaged head was spreading over the beige carpet, sinking into the flattened pile so that it would never be completely beige again. There was no movement at all from him, no death spasms, no voiding of liquids other than the blood itself. Maybe he smelled of death and excrement, I couldn't tell. There was no twitching of fingers, no sudden lurches of feet. Oh yeah, the wicked witch was dead all right.

Yet with death, there came something else. The final and irrevocable act of all those who had lived in this world: the soul's departure from its host.

That time had come for Alec Moker.

As I took a step toward the corpse, something about it began to change.

At first, I thought the body was stirring, and my metaphorical heart skipped a metaphorical beat. It couldn't be. Moker was well and truly dead. Nobody could have survived that kind of punishment to their skull, not even a creature like him. Yet he was moving.

No. I was wrong. Something was *emerging*.

The body remained still. But something was rising from it. Moker's soul was taking its leave.

Moker's *black* soul, it was like the darkest shadow among other shadows.

The vanishing ghosts opposite drew back, my father's among them. Their fading images were fearful and some seemed to shrink before the rising darkness. Their alarm was contagious and I took a step backward myself, reluctant to be close to the thing on the floor. The atmosphere became full of weight, full of foreboding, and there was a pre-thunderstorm charge in the air. I heard faint whisperings from the ghosts as they gradually fled the scene and I sensed their revulsion of this malign animus that was the very essence of Moker himself.

It was a sickly thing, foul and murky, like the stagnant waters of a deep, forgotten well. It appeared to rage within itself; yet it cowered also, as if it knew its own malevolence was beyond redemption and its fate was beyond all contrition. For the first time I understood what was meant by "a lost soul."

The sludgy darkness continued to rise from the dead body, the vague shapes beyond it almost gone, only their low whispering remaining. It began to take on a form. Moker's form. Filling out, shaping first a head, and then the shoulders, but always obscure, muddied, unclean. I backed further away as it loomed, until I was almost at the door. I could have been preparing to flee; at that moment, I wasn't sure.

Features slowly emerged—the big hands, the eyes that no longer gleamed, the ears. Finally, the gaping hole in the face. It seemed that even in death, Moker was not without his affliction.

There was no longer any harm to it: somehow the malevolence had been absorbed. And even as the notion came to me, that this thing was to be pitied, the squalid replicate began to break up, falling away in tenuous pieces, dispersing and dissolving like the mist before it, and I watched until there was none of it left. Watched until Moker's unrepentant soul had become nothing.

Only myself and the dead body were left in the room. The ghosts had departed, Moker's damned soul had ceased to exist. All was quiet and calm. I prayed that my home would evermore be so.

There was no noise from upstairs, but I assumed that once Prim was reasonably reassured, Andrea would call the police from our bedroom phone. I felt sure she would not venture downstairs until they arrived, and my plan had to be carried out before that happened.

I went over to the still—the empty—body on the carpet. The blood formed a deeply rich halo around its head. Abhorrent though it was to me, I forced myself to my knees, then lay over it. There was no resistance: I sank into Moker's corpse as easily as immersing myself in water. But nothing had prepared me for the horrendous and debased sensations that swept through me. I saw the victims Moker had claimed, observed their injuries even as the attack was taking place, experienced the exquisite lust and perverted joy that the killer had felt, as well as the thrill of danger that went with the slaying, the sexual gratification that always followed the murders. Yet underlying all this depraved glory was an abject misery, an agony of suffering that had been Moker's constant companion, a vile wretchedness that had been with him all his life. In this remembrance of recent events, the sick exultation outweighed the bitterness, but I knew the latter had always prevailed and that only for short passages of time it was vanquished.

Within this formation of flesh and bone, I cried out, the awfulness and the sordid pleasure almost too much to bear; but I needed this body, needed Moker's corpse, for my own purposes, my own revenge. Retribution was my guiding force now.

I brought my own thoughts to the fore, maintaining images of Prim in my mind, in an effort to override Moker's memories. But, in truth, it was only thoughts of retaliation that quelled the riot of loathsome impressions. With all the resolve I possessed, I pushed the atrocities and the glory they aroused aside and concentrated on ruling this newfound vessel. I willed myself into every part of the body, its structure, the arteries, flesh, subjugating them so that they would become mine, if only for a brief time.

Slowly, ever so slowly, I moved the fingers of one hand. Then the hand itself. Then the other hand. An arm. It was working: for a little while Moker's body could be mine. I heard footsteps thudding across the floor overhead and guessed that Andrea was in our bedroom and heading for the phone. I wondered how long it would take the police to get here.

I had to move faster. I had to get Moker's body onto its feet. I pushed the shoulders up off the floor, then drew up a knee. It took great effort, but I managed to lumber to my/Moker's feet. I stood there unsteadily, swaying as I got used to the alien body. Taking a tentative step forward, I almost fell, just managing to correct myself before I overbalanced. Another step and it was not too bad. If I concentrated hard, I could make it. The problem then would be whether I was capable of driving a car. Another step. Fine. It was working. I was getting close to the open doorway.

But I remembered something and I turned back, awkwardly retracing my steps. Carefully, I bent down and retrieved the knitting needle from the floor.

FORTY

I left the front door open behind me. Frankly, it was too much trouble to turn around and pull it closed; I'd entered Moker's body only moments before and it would take time to get acquainted. I paused to use one of the long scarf's dangling ends to wipe away the blood covering one of Moker's eyes and when I took the next step forward it was all I could do to prevent myself from falling off the doorstep.

I coped, but movement was stiff, awkward, just as it had been with the woman's body before. In life, Moker had had a curious style to his walking and in death it was even more strange and ungainly. The feet shuffled more than ever and the body swayed from side to side like the proverbial drunken sailor. A zombie would have had more grace.

As I made my lumbering way down the drive, which was partially lit by lights from the hall behind me and the street lights ahead, I felt the cold night air bite. I should have been almost oblivious of the cold, but instead it struck deep into the hole in my face—and the newly created vent in the top of my head—chilling the flesh inside and touching me, the body's new controller.* With some difficulty, I wound both dangling ends of the long scarf around my lower face, shielding the gaping hole from the chill.

I staggered, stumbled my way to the curb outside my property, nearly falling twice before I reached it. There was Moker's ancient Hillman, parked almost directly in front of the house. Even though my state of mind was somewhat dazzled by the adjustment it was having to make—controlling another person's reflexes and movement, as well as tamping down the remaining dregs of Moker's

---

*I had wondered if the damage to the brain (all those grayish lumps flowing with the blood!) would upset the body's mechanism—the chemical signals sent through the system, the sinews that worked the bones—but it seemed that the mind, and thus the will, could manage without all of the physical driving force, the body's engine, if you like. A metaphysical engine had now taken over Moker's corpse, and while alien to its host, I hoped it would have the power to help me finish my task.

memory—I was aware enough to search for the car keys in the raincoat's deep pockets. The fingers were numb, barely able to feel anything at all, but I could tell there were no keys present in either one. Then probably, with luck . . .

Yes! I'd reached the old car and peered through the nearside window to see that the keys were in the ignition. Blood trickled into my eye again and I clumsily wiped it with one of the scarf ends. Next bit might be tricky. Driving a car while using someone else's body wouldn't be easy, but at least the roads should be virtually deserted at this time of night—or this time of the morning. What time was it? I wondered. One, two o'clock? It didn't matter and trying to read the tiny digits on a wristwatch—if Moker wore such a thing—seemed like too much effort. It was unimportant.

That was when it struck me. The first memory. Like a bolt of lightning out of the blue, so vivid it seemed more like a hallucination.

Prim's horrified little face, beneath me, me hovering over it, and then it was Andrea, fighting me, spittle shooting at my face, then Prim again, her chest quivering as she struggled for air, me holding something, the knitting needle, gray, deadly sharp—

I collapsed to the pavement and it was gone, the vision abruptly checked, the scene washed from my mind. My hand scrabbled at the Hillman's bodywork, fingernails grating against painted metal as I sought to pull myself up. On my knees, one hand pressed against the window's sill. Sliding against the side of the car as I straightened my knees, hands applying pressure to lift myself, then my whole body leaning there as I tried to recover the strength I'd just lost. It must have taken a minute or two for me to compose myself, to regain the determination to dominate this freakish vessel.

It took a couple of attempts to grip the door handle firmly enough to open the door, but finally I managed. I clambered into the driver's high seat and settled myself. I stared in dismay at the controls. Of course, I'd forgotten. The gearshift was on the steering wheel column. Only once had I driven with a gear stick like this, and that had been a long time ago in America. Still, once you can ride a bike . . .

Still perturbed by the memory flash, I bent low, a shaky hand reaching for the key in the ignition. The engine failed when I turned the key and I pumped the accelerator pedal with a heavy foot as I tried again. Luckily, the engine caught—the Hillman had had a couple of good runs that night, so the engine hadn't cooled completely—and I slumped back in the seat. Difficult bit, now. Driving the bloody thing.

Left foot on the clutch, I lifted the gearshift beneath the steering wheel into first, then eased up the clutch pedal while pressing the accelerator. The engine roared and the car jolted. The engine stalled. Oh shit, this wasn't going to be easy. Just before I performed the whole routine again, I remembered the handbrake. I hadn't released it. I did so slowly, because it wasn't only the car I was trying to get used to, but Moker's body as well. After switching on the engine once more, I danced clumsily with the floor pedals. On reflection, I think it was only because the Hillman was still familiar to Moker's body that I managed to drive the old heap that night. I found that the less I thought about what I was doing, the more those borrowed hands and feet were able to take over. In a way, it was like driving on autopilot and I was grateful for that. I guess from time to time we all do things automatically, and to a certain extent, this was what was happening now.

The first maneuver was to turn the car around so that it was facing the right direction. I swung the wheel and pushed down on the accelerator—

—*the underground car park, the smart woman wearing glasses turning toward me, surprised then horrified, opening her mouth to scream, a wonderful feeling of exultation rushing through me as I pushed the long thin needle upward, beneath her breast, into the heart—*

The Hillman smashed into the side of a vehicle parked on the other side of the avenue. *Oh, sweet . . . !* Had to reverse, pull the car back. Had it made a terrible noise? I didn't care if my neighbors were roused from their comfortable slumber—so long as I got away first. Okay. Calm down, take it steady. Reverse. Where the fuck was reverse? Oh yeah, down, had to push the lever down. Whoops. That was second gear. I remembered. No, had to pull the lever out first, then down. That was reverse.

Following my recollection of column gearshifts and also relying on this body's own instincts, I reversed the car back across the road until the rear wheels hit the curb, swinging the steering wheel to my right as I did so. A light came on in a bedroom window opposite.

Gears grinding, I shifted to first, and put my right foot down hard. The Hillman shot forward and its wing scraped along the side of another vehicle parked at the opposite curb, taking off a wing mirror as it went—

—*a dark, lonely street, wet with rain, a man coming toward me, unwrapping my scarf, waiting for him to draw near before revealing all, the man hesitating, footsteps slowing, the first hint of concern on his handsome face, then the look of utter terror taking over as the scarf fell loose, turning to run, but not quickly*

enough, first a big hand spinning him back round, then the needle striking up-
ward, piercing material, skin, flesh, finding the heart, and pure glorious joy—

Uhhh! The memory was almost painful, the shock of it making me jerk
the steering wheel so that the Hillman scraped along another car parked on
the left-hand side of the road. *God, can't I control them? Can't I hold back the*
memories and the perverted pleasure that came with them? Had to get a grip,
had to push extraneous thoughts aside. *But could I?* After all, this was not *my*
body and whatever recollection it held could not be tamed by me, the usurper.
Had to make myself immune to them. I still had control over my own mind,
didn't I? Sure I did.

The roads were pretty empty, as was the main thoroughfare when I turned
into it. I'd have to drive carefully, concentrating all the way, do my best not to
get distracted—*Oh God!*—

—*a cemetery, an old one with Gothic tombs and large angels, weather-worn*
slabs everywhere, and there was the woman, alone laying flowers on the grave of
some departed loved one, and here was I, moving among the stained crosses and
angels with spread wings and mausoleums with boarded doors, stalking the
woman, who was well turned out, attractive, long dark hair, getting closer to her,
unwinding the two ends of the scarf, ready to pounce, bringing the murder tool
from my pocket as she turns her head and sees me, and pure delight at the terror
on her face, those beautifully startled eyes that already know she's dead, then the
exquisite delight as the needle sinks in, through the satin material of her blouse,
just under the lower ribs, pushing—no, sliding, for very little effort is required—
the long needle through the flesh, piercing then slipping right inside her heart, her
scream muffled by a big hand, and she falls across the grave of the one she is there
to grieve for, then the touching, the lifting of clothes, pulling down fine panties,
pushing inside her with trembling, excited fingers . . .

The scene was so strong, so very lucid, filling my mind so that the car
swerved across the road, mounted a pavement, and almost crashed into a lamp
post. I shook my head, trying to clear it of pictures, nasty, depraved images,
and they swiftly faded so that only the road was before me now.

Guiding the car back on to it, I tried to control my own mind, to shield it
from the other's thoughts, and for a short while I was successful. I steered the
old Hillman in as straight a line as possible along the broad, lonely road, my
way lit by amber street lights, the shadowed windows of shops and houses on
either side like eyes witnessing my progress. Flashing blue lights appeared in
the distance, police cars or ambulances having turned into the main road

from a junction, and I took no chances, pulling over to the curbside, the rubber of the left-hand wheels squealing against the stone. I pulled up behind a white van.

I'd been wise to do so, for two police cars, sirens wailing, followed closely by an unmarked vehicle, shot past on the other side of the road. Heading for my place? I wondered. Surely not. They couldn't have reacted so fast to a phone call from Andrea, could they? Police response to call-outs these days was unreliable to say the least, but maybe it was a quiet night for them. Maybe they were speeding to some other call, there was no way of knowing and I wasn't about to go back and check.

Something else nagged me as I sat stiffly in the driver's seat staring at the back of the van in front, blood drying around one of my eyes. Then it hit me. Just as well I'd pulled over before the police cars reached me—I'd forgotten to turn on the Hillman's headlights. I leaned forward to do so, my hand—Moker's hand—scrabbling around the dashboard, searching for the appropriate switch. I found a likely suspect, pressed and—

—*a pitch black alleyway, somewhere in the city, a figure leaning back in a doorway, someone waiting there, waiting for someone, waiting for me, the short hatchet—a hatchet, not a butcher's chopper—in my hand, taken from the oversized raincoat where a large, deep pocket had been sewn in to accommodate it, lifting it high as the body waited, already dead—and empty—standing there as stiff as a board, freakishly held up by the wall and legs that were locked in rigor mortis, lifting the hatchet, the thrill of bringing it down hard on the dead man's head, continuing the chopping and the cutting as the body toppled and fell to the ground, and going down with it, smashing and slicing, cutting into the cold carcass, destroying it beyond recognition, leaving behind on the wet floor of the alleyway a mound of chopped meat and naked bloody bones—*

Had I occupied my own body, I know I would have thrown up right there in the car so repugnant was the memory sustained within the tissues and cooling flesh of this monster, but even so, my own mind reeled with shock and it was not entirely due to these invasive visions alone; no, it was the glorification that went with them, the overflowing happiness as the hatchet had struck again and again, the lazy spurts and dribbling of thickening blood, the disassembling of the human structure—the complete destruction.

This time something lingered after the vision had dissolved to black, not a continuation but the isolated memory of Moker's final act of desecration. No wonder the police had not seriously connected my murder with the other serial killings, because there was one more gross defilement that had not been evident in my case.

Moker always left his victims in quiet, concealed locations, places that he could return to as himself, inside his own body, to carry out the mutilations without being disturbed; lonely sites where he could squat over the demolished body and defecate into the bloody pit left by the removed heart.

It was just as well there was so little traffic about at that time of night, or else my erratic driving would probably have caused a serious accident. As it was, I struck parked vehicles along the way, knocked over a bollard on a pedestrian island and for a time, when my concentration was at its weakest, traveled for almost a mile on the wrong side of the road. It was the memories somehow detained by Moker's entity, his being, released at irregular and uncontrolled intervals, finally shed only after they had been recalled one last time.

—*working with cadavers in the morgue, washing them, cleansing them, so they were fit for burial, the private obscene moments with them—*

—*faces of men in expensive suits, wearing silk ties and crisp shirts, surgeons who hid their natural repugnance with professional aloofness (although not all succeeding too well) as they peered into the hole of my face, the shaking of their head because there was nothing they could do to rebuild, there was not enough there for reconstruction, the operations to re-form at least a workable orifice, the pain suffered, the hope denied—*

—*looking at myself in a mirror, but me as someone young, in jeans and baggy jumper, the anguish, the despair, the bitterness—the anger! The smashing of mirror, any mirrors, anything at all that reflected my image!—*

—*the maiming of small animals—*

—*the stares from people, the screams of children, the undisguised or ill-concealed disgust of women, of girls, boys—*

—*the misery, the emptiness—*

—*then glorious flight, freedom from this marked body, invisibility, the dreams that were not dreams but true escapes, the journeys away from myself that were a discovery that changed everything—*

Here I was, Jim True—or the spirit of Jim True—inhabiting another person's shell, remembering that person's life, the pain, the wretched misery, the surprising and new joy, while driving toward my own destiny, or what I perceived to be my destiny.

—walking the streets, people glancing at me and freezing in their tracks or quickly looking away again, searching for a place, a particular house, finding it, knocking on the door, the wild-haired woman with the pinched features and ashen skin standing at the open door, looking out, seeing me, the mother who had abandoned me, screaming now at the sight of me, the disfigurement her only recognition, slamming the door, shrieking at me to go away, go away!—

Had to shut the thoughts out, had to fix my focus on the road ahead, concentrate on steering the car, hardly bothering with the gears once it was in third, the effort of using the stiff column shift too much.

—catching a bee in an empty jam jar, filling it with water through a small hole drilled into the lid—

So many memories, rushing to expunge themselves, no chronological order to them anymore, a boy one moment, a man the next, but one common thread through all the ages, one consistent theme: *rejection . . .*

Fortunately, most of my journey was by way of broad main roads, the minor ones unnecessary, otherwise driving would have been even more difficult, with less leeway for swerving and avoiding parked vehicles. I ignored traffic lights, reluctant to shift through the gears, and again my luck held, no other traffic crossed in front of me.

—fitting the mask, the white surgical mask, concealing the affliction even though the disguise was further cause for curiosity or ridicule. Keeping the ugliness to myself. For street wear, even in the summer months, the long scarf, wrapped tightly around the head so only my eyes showed, often the surgical mask beneath this, then the hat, which cast shade over my eyes because even these were unsightly, too black, too protruding—

I'd driven this route many, many times but although it was familiar to me, I had to fight hard to remember which turns to make (so heavy was the Hillman that changing down for corners was unnecessary as long as I maintained reasonable speed).

—children, a classroom, a playground, full of them, gawking in fear, whispering to friends as they pointed, some of them sniggering, later to laugh outright, call me names—

—rejection—

—loneliness, time spent in dim rooms, bitterness the only companion—

Steady as a car flashed me from behind. Slowly I lifted one of those big hands, the other remaining gripped on the steering wheel, touched the scarf to make sure it was still in place, still hiding the deformity, as the impatient driver put his foot down and sped around the lazy Hillman, glaring across his passenger at me as he passed. He gave a derisive little toot of his horn, rear lights disappearing into the distance.

—the dreams, many of them horrible, depressing, but others that were wonderful and the realization that these generally were more than just dreams, that they were flights from the body, journeys of the spirit which took me to familiar places, but where I could not be seen, where my grotesqueness was hidden by invisibility, where even to myself there was nothing at all—learning that these flights were not restricted to night-times alone, that they could be controlled, sleep, itself, the only invariable, the essential requirement, and that could be learned, could be governed just as the journeys themselves could be governed—

—so many places traveled to, so many homes visited, so many activities spied upon, so many bedrooms—

—and always the glorious sense of freedom—

—the impossibility of rejection—

—and always the misery of returning to life as it truly was, the loneliness, heartache, the resentment—

—but eventually, the miracle of dominating the dead, of using corpses for my own gratification and for revenge—

—the first experiment, the first freshly deceased body, witnessing its lingering soul finally leaving its vessel, for a certain psychic ability had always been with me, perhaps nature's compensation for the physical affliction, watching the soul lift itself from the corpse, like steam from a pot, but perhaps less clear, leaving a vacancy behind, or so it had occurred to me at the time, and on a whim, escaping from my own body in the otherwise deserted mortuary, letting it sleep in a chair in the empty little office attached to the tiled room where the cadavers were kept, lying down in the cold shell of flesh and organs that were already corrupting, raising a dead arm stiffly, awkwardly, rigor mortis in its earliest stages, elevating that reluctant arm, then the other one, then, although with more difficulty, the legs, one at a time, finally sitting up and looking around, viewing the last fleeting memories that were stored both in the brain and body itself like faded tape—

—repeating the experiment, over and over again, until it was time to take it to its logical—logical to me, that is—conclusion, the procurement of other, fresher, bodies, to live, if only for a very short time, as that person had, no, as whatever that person was capable of—

Oh God, it was unbearable. The sickness here, the evil within. I almost collapsed against the steering wheel, only the knowledge that I was drawing near to my destination preventing me from doing so. What other memories of this man Moker did I have to suffer? I didn't think I could take much more, not if they were like those already remembered.

But there was one last memory to be recalled before it was erased forever and perhaps, in its way, it was the most disturbing of all because it was the very beginning of his hatred of normal people.

—chaos, images rushing through with no order and proper recognition—

—until everything slowed, everything resolved itself into one final and perfectly clear recollection—

—darkness becoming lighter, redness then too much brightness, shapes moving around me, feeling myself lifted, a separation, a snapping of something that had connected me to existence itself, the terrible, the awful, feeling of isolation, the sadness of losing something even though I didn't know what, then the sounds around me, noises that sounded like intakes of air, familiar because it had seemed always to be with me, except this was sharp, unpleasant, not cozy and reassuring anymore, and those shapes, bright, white, leaning toward me, another blurred form coming into my feeble clouded vision, and there was something familiar about this, something nice and warming—

Another flashback, one already experienced, interposing itself for only a moment, a snapshot of the woman whose home I had searched for and found, the mother who had screamed—*go away, go away!*—before slamming the door in my undisguised face.

—rejection—

—absolute rejection—

And then, no more, the last memory unfinished.

I pulled the car over in a violent swerve, no longer able to bear the weight of these memories that were not mine but belonged to someone who had known only misery throughout his life.

Despite everything I knew about his deeds, despite the evil that was as much part of his nature as love is of most others'—despite that, I lay my head on those large hands that rested against the steering wheel and wept. I wept for Alec Moker.

FORTY-ONE

The irony wasn't lost on me as I wiped tears from those bulbous eyes with the sleeve of the raincoat: I was weeping for Moker with his own tears.

Rationally, it seemed foolish to feel pity for someone as wicked and as perverted as Moker, a necrophile who had murdered and mutilated four people—who had tried to kill my own wife and my little Primrose, for Christ's sake!—but that was what I felt for him. His whole life had been despicable, from birth to manhood, he'd suffered shame and humiliation, hopelessness and loneliness; and perhaps worst of all for Moker—rejection. Total rejection. Rejection even by his own mother. Wouldn't that be enough to warp any person's soul, that and the physical disfiguration that was its cause? Yet I could not wipe the picture of Moker kneeling above Primrose, the sharpened knitting needle ready to sink into her small heart, from my mind. It still shocked me, still filled me with a burning anger: but pity for him loitered behind the anger. Who could live a life such as his and remain normal? Mentally normal, I mean. Who would not develop a distorted view of life itself under those same circumstances? But maybe Andrea had been right when she had called me gullible, because there are many in the world who suffer even worse afflictions than this killer, victims of constant pain, people with terrible abnormalities, paraplegics, men, women, and children who need machines to help them breathe—the list is endless—most of whom strive to live as normal lives as possible, without overt bitterness, without rancor, *without resentment of others*. Why the hell should I feel sorry for a monster like Moker? I shouldn't. Yet somehow, I did.

When the weeping had stopped and my eyes were dried, a realization occurred to me. I had "remembered" through Moker the killing of four people. Four people. I hadn't been among them. Not that I needed it, but this was final proof that Oliver Guinane was my murderer. Bitter resentment and insanity were Moker's excuse, but what was Guinane's? Envy and greed? Yeah, envy and greed. He envied me my wife—and child. He wanted to make a huge pile of money out of something I didn't support. Pretty basic, really.

But why he had chopped off my genitals was a mystery.

I looked out the side window up at the gtp sign, our agency's logo, neon-lit over the glass front doors. Guinane True Presswell. That name was going to vanish when the so-called "merger" went through. Some accounts might move, but many of our existing clients would be content to come under the wing of such an internationally successful advertising agency as Blake & Turn-brow. Oh, a certain amount of new presentations would have to take place, a lot of client lunches would have to be undertaken, as well as corporate days out, but no doubt the freshness and glamor of it all would win most reluctant clients over. It was the nature of the game.

Although these thoughts ran through my mind now that Moker's memories mercifully appeared to be spent, they were trivial, totally unimportant as, in the grand scheme of things, all such matters are. At that moment, I focused on one thing alone.

Clumsily pushing down the handle, I opened the car door and lumbered out. With effort, I peered up at the building. The top office lights were on, the low stone balustrade of the mock balcony on the fifth floor silhouetted by them. Sydney's office, and next door, the one I shared with Guinane. And Guinane's silver BMW was parked right outside our building, just behind Sydney's Merc.

It took me several attempts to get my finger—Moker's finger—to press the lift button for the fifth floor. For some reason, conducting small tasks with some-body else's body proved more difficult than making the bigger moves—it hadn't been easy to pick up the killer's deadly knitting needle from the floor in my home and slide it into one of the raincoat's deep pockets, as it hadn't been easy buttoning the dead woman's jacket earlier that night. Walking, getting in and out of cars, even driving was relatively easy compared to opening doors and pressing lift buttons.

Fortunately, the plate-glass doors of the agency were unlocked, so one side only needed a shove for me to gain access.

The street outside, dampened by a light drizzle, was deserted, which was unsurprising at this late or early hour, whichever way you cared to look at it. My feeling, and it was only a guess, was that it was around one or two o'clock in the morning. The small lift came, its door slid open. Feeling weaker by the moment, I shuffled inside, awkwardly thumped the fifth-floor button and leaned back against the rear wall, hands resting on the waist-high interior steel rail, allowing them to take some of my weight. I wasn't sure how long I could use this body before its system finally ran down completely, but the woman's corpse earlier had got me from Bayswater to Paddington, so I should have some time left. Of course, I hadn't walked from my house to the agency in the center of London, but the sheer effort of concentrating on driving, hindered by the constant sudden replays of Moker's memories, had somehow wearied *me*, let alone the body I had borrowed. My knees were not far from buckling and my upper body felt too heavy, as if I were carrying weights in the raincoat's pockets. It was even hard to keep my head up; the neck felt too decrepit to bear such a load. Had to cope though, had to use whatever was left to carry out my little task.

The lift came to a halt, although I didn't feel it and only realized I was on the fifth floor when the doors slid open. The mini-reception area (the main one was on the ground floor) and corridor were unlit, only a faint glow radiating from an office further along. Walking woodenly from the small lift, I waited in the reception area for a while, listening for any sounds, anything at all. The three partners' office suite was at the far end of the corridor and nobody there would have heard the lift arriving. At least, I didn't think so, but at this time of night (or morning) the rest of the building was silent, so the sound might have traveled. I hoped it hadn't: it was important to catch Guinane by surprise. I'd use the knitting needle to kill him.

So quiet. So very quiet. I'd worked enough late nights in my time to be used to the loneliness that comes to offices when most employees have packed up and gone home for the night, switching off lights and leaving behind a sepulchral kind of quietness. You might get a lot more work done without the usual interruptions, but eventually the eeriness starts to get to you and you wonder if you're the only person left on the planet. That's when you give someone a call—wife, girlfriend, business associate, it doesn't matter who, just so that you hear another voice.

On this night, the agency was filled with that quiet eeriness—more so than ever, you might say—but who could I call? What would I say? It's me, babe, but not as you know me. If only I'd had a proper mouth to say the words. Andrea didn't need to be freaked out anymore tonight. Besides, I didn't regard her as my wife now; he'd destroyed that. And it seemed I could no longer regard Prim as my daughter either. That was the *really* hard part.

I shuffled onward, occasionally reaching out a hand to the wall to steady myself, knocking askew one of the several framed advertising awards the agency had won, most by Guinane and me, a couple by one of our talented junior art director/copywriter teams. Our Walk of Vanity, we called it, but all the awards seemed absolutely worthless to me now. Although I didn't need to breathe air anymore, I was conscious of the involuntary snuffling sounds coming from the cavity of Moker's face, half-raspy, half-sibilant, and I did my best to control them. Unfortunately, it wasn't a controllable thing and I could only hope the sound was loud to me alone.

Halfway down the corridor, the murmur of voices came to me. I stopped to listen.

Was it only one voice I could hear? I took a few more steps, Moker's grubby sneakers scuffing the carpet. It *sounded* like one voice, a kind of monotonous low-key drone that now and again was interrupted by . . . ? A groan? Somebody groaning? Had Guinane hurt Sydney Presswell? Was Sydney next on his hit list? With both partners gone, Guinane stood to make a lot more money and, if he had it in him to murder me, then Sydney would be no problem.

I edged further along the corridor, this time forcing myself not to hurry, afraid I'd be heard and so lose the element of surprise, which I would need if I were to get close enough to Guinane to push the needle into his chest. It's funny how in zombie movies, the zombie is always endowed with superhuman strength, whereas in reality (if we can talk reality here) the undead's muscles and sinews would have atrophied and lost most of their power. In Moker's debilitated—debilitated by death—body, I was weak and becoming weaker by the moment. Soon, the body would collapse—just as earlier, in the police station, the woman had finally expired—and would be useless to me. I could not afford to let Guinane see me coming; I had to strike before he had a chance to defend himself. Carefully, I placed one foot in front of the other, waited a beat, did the same thing again, making my way down the carpeted corridor at snail's pace, keeping as quiet as I possibly could.

The voice—and the groans—became louder as I approached the end offices. Soon I was able to make out the words being spoken.

FORTY-TWO

Sydney Presswell's office was empty, although the lights were on. As Moker, I was standing at the darkened corridor's junction with another, shorter, corridor, and opposite, but a little to the right, was the open doorway into Sydney's place of work where company files and records were kept and where the agency's financial accounts were balanced so diligently. It wasn't unusual for our bookkeeper to be working late, although I could never quite understand his fascination for figures and balance sheets; mercifully I didn't have to, nor did Guinane—Sydney relieved us of such stultifying but essential tedium and we were glad to let him. Oh yeah, that's how stupid we both were.

The voices came from the large office next door, to the left of the junction, which Guinane and I, as copywriter and art director, shared so that we could work on ideas together. The door to this was ajar so I couldn't see much of the interior, the opening no more than a foot or so wide. Although the angle also meant that I could not easily be seen, I stepped back and pressed against the corridor's wall so that the corner of the junction concealed me completely. Trying to keep those guttural noises I was making down to a minimum, I listened.

". . . pity you caught me searching through your desk when you showed up tonight, Oliver. Pity for you, that is, because as far as I'm concerned, it suits my plans very well. Jim was always a stumbling block, but you . . . well, you were just a bloody nuisance."

A low murmuring then, almost a grumble. From Guinane? Had to be.

Then Sydney once more: "I must have hit you a little too hard—you've been out of it for some time. I did want to explain a few things to you before . . ." His voice trailed off, leaving an implication hanging in the air.

I peered round the corner of the corridor in an attempt to see more through the partially open doorway and ducked back swiftly as a figure passed across the gap. It was Sydney, pacing the floor, something long and silvery gripped in one hand, its upper length resting in the open palm of his other hand. With my back braced against the corridor wall, I waited and tried to muffle the snuffling noise that came from the aperture of Moker's face with my hands. Although I'd only caught a brief glimpse, I suddenly realized what the silvery thing he had been brandishing was; a three-foot long unmarked steel rule, the one I used for cutting card and paper. One side was flat, blunted, while the other was slightly angled to provide a keen cutting edge for a Stanley knife blade or scalpel. Although flat at each end of its length, it resembled—and I'm sure could be used as—a saber or heavy sword. Whatever, I was always aware it could be a lethal weapon in the wrong hands.

"You know what I was looking for, Oliver?"

Despite the circumstances, Sydney's voice was modulated, restrained, the kind of monotonous tone that used to make my eyelids heavy the moment the first balance sheet figures were mentioned.

Only a mumble came for Guinane.

"I was looking for more letters," Sydney went on. "Those very private letters Jim's wife has been sending you over the years. I discovered the first one a long, long time ago and have kept tabs on them ever since. Rather a passionate lady, Andrea, although I could have done without the guilt trip she laid on you both. Tried to stop your affair many times, didn't she? Only you wouldn't let go. But why keep those letters in your locked drawer, Oliver? Oh, by the way, I have extra keys to every drawer, cupboard, and filing cabinet in the place. Very handy for my kind of snooping. But why, Oliver, why keep the letters in the office? Tell you what I think. I think you got some kind of kick reading them while your friend and partner sat opposite you without a clue. Wasn't that the reason? Yes, I really do believe so."

"*Bastard!*"

At least this was coherent, but Guinane failed to follow up with anything else.

"You see, all those late nights I put in were not just spent doctoring the agency's accounts. No, I was spying on you and Jim too. I can't tell you how much I despised your cozy relationship. I was always the outsider, the boring bean counter, while you and he *were* the agency, you were the creative team that brought in all the suckers. I've always been in a weak position, which is why I had to watch you both constantly, make sure you weren't conspiring against me."

I almost banged the wall behind me with the heel of my fist. What was he on about? The company was called gtp, for Christ's sake, Guinane True Presswell—he was always an equal partner. We never conspired against him, he was an important part of the team, the shrewd one that kept our feet on the ground, who dealt . . . with . . . all . . . the . . . agency's financial affairs . . . The words slowed down in my mind. Apart from searching our desks and, no doubt, our files too, what else was Sydney involved in?

"Oh yes, you were the glory boys, the winners of clients and awards. Me? Just a third party, nobody important. As I said, bean counter. Did either of you consider I had an outside life? Did you? Did you know I've been divorced twice, the third one on the way? And each divorce cost me dear, as the next one will. And did you know I gamble, Oliver? Oh, I love to gamble. Horses, casinos, even dog tracks—I love 'em all. Have you any idea what it costs to maintain such a lifestyle? And then there's the cost of cocaine. That's the great irony. Jim thought only you had a problem with drugs—we discussed it many times behind your back. How do we get you off them, would you agree to rehab? Should we even confront you with the issue, would it damage the partnership? In fact, I was the one who pointed out to Jim that you were back on the coke again. And all the time, neither of you realized I was a heavy user myself. Though, unlike you, I know how to control it. Question of metabolism, and you must have the wrong kind. An expensive habit, all the same."

I heard a mirthless chuckle and it came from Sydney as he paced the floor. From Guinane there was only more mumbling, a weak kind of protest, I think. What the hell was wrong with him?

"I could never let either of you know that I had financial difficulties, of course. If I had, the first thing you'd do is check the books, or have an independent auditor take a look at them, and no way could I allow that. I'm running too many scams with the company's money, see? Couldn't have some snooper inspecting the accounts. No, I'd probably end up in prison. Want to hear about some of my little deceptions, Oliver?"

If he didn't, I certainly did. I peered around the corner again and looked toward the open door across the corridor. I didn't know if it was his placid intonation, or the unexpected revelations, but I seemed to be fascinated with these revelations of Sydney's. Why was he confessing these things to Guinane? And what had he done to him? Our financial director—our *bean counter*—passed the narrow gap in the doorway again and this time he slapped the steel rule against the palm of his hand in the way that teachers used to brandish their canes before the corporal punishment ban.

"I hope you're listening, Oliver. It's a relief to get this off my chest after so long, so I'd appreciate it if you paid attention."

He stopped his pacing for a moment and I could see most of him in the opening. The blunted steel blade flashed in the overhead lighting.

"I had had money troubles since—and before—I met you and Jim True, but I kept them well hidden. Jim was easy to fool and you—you, Oliver, didn't care anyway. You two left the financial side of the business entirely in my hands and accepted my word on everything. You were both too in love with your own creativity to bother about money. So long as it was coming in regularly, and the amounts afforded you grand lifestyles, you didn't worry about boring things like balancing the books, checking invoices, chasing clients for money owed. I wasn't complaining, because it allowed me so much leeway. I have deals with printers—and you know how much print work we put out each year—photo-setters, art studios, even one or two photographers. They put in an inflated invoice and we share the difference between real costs and imagined costs. It's worked out very nicely over the years and nobody has ever complained—least of all our clients who have no idea whatsoever about such charges. They'd be shocked if they knew the profit margin on all these services."

He moved out of view again, resumed his pacing. By the way he tilted his head when speaking, I was aware that Guinane was not on his feet. Not even sitting in a chair.

"Apart from travel, hotel, lunch, and dinner expenditures, there was no end of ways I could milk the company. Entertainment, company cars—one for my soon-to-be ex-wife, incidentally—phone bills, all lost in the agency accounts. gtp even paid for my drug habit, how's that grab you?"

Another mirthless chuckle. Another low groan from Guinane.

"But the real kicker, the scam that brought in the most for me, was the setting up of another company, one that neither of you knew about. And it was so simple. All I had to do was add 'Limited' to gtp. When certain checks came in for gtp, I only had to write 'Limited' after the name, and then pay the money into my own secret company bank account. I had to be cautious, naturally, couldn't let huge amounts go missing, but over the years the scheme—sorry, the *scam*—has been highly profitable. Sweet, don't you think? Actually, I've been quite brilliant. Never too greedy, you understand, always keeping within certain limits, but oh so lucrative."

Slowly, creeping inch by inch, I made my way across the corridor's junction, hoping I'd timed the move so Sydney wouldn't pass the open doorway and see me. If I made a noise, a scuffing as I dragged Moker's feet across the carpet, I don't know; I think Sydney was too wrapped up in his boasts to hear anything beyond the room he was in. I could feel myself—I could feel Moker's body—growing weaker by the second as vital functions within the flesh that were only kept going by my own will wound down.

"And then Blake & Turnbrow, one of London and New York's biggest and richest advertising agencies, came along with the intention of swallowing up gtp. Jim always knew in essence it would be a takeover, and you were in denial—or you had your own agenda. But you both thought it was Blake & Turnbrow's idea, so impressed were they with our work and client list. Well, to tell you the truth, Oliver—and that is what I'm doing tonight, telling you nothing but the truth—it was I who put out the feelers initially, I was the one who approached them. In a surreptitious way, of course, through a contact I had there. I let them know we wouldn't be adverse to talks."

A muted *thwack* as he slapped the steel rule against the palm of his hand again. From where I now stood, I couldn't see Sydney anymore but I glimpsed Guinane. He was on one knee, a hand and elbow flat on the desktop, the knuckles of his other hand pressed against the floor for support. His head kept sagging as if too heavy to support. A trickle of blood ran from his hairline to his cheek.

"A risk for me," Sydney continued, his shadow cast out into the corridor for a moment, "but the money we three would be paid makes all my cheating over the years seem petty, small change. Of course, because I'll be the only one left of the partnership after tonight, my financial reward will be even greater. Are you interested in the risk the situation presented for me, Oliver? It doesn't matter if you're not, because I'm going to tell you anyway. I hope you're not too groggy to take it all in. Did I hit you too hard when you surprised me at your desk? This piece of metal makes a dangerous weapon, wouldn't you agree? I only used the blunt side so that there wouldn't be too much damage, because that wouldn't suit my purpose at all."

I edged nearer to the open door, my legs beginning to droop under the weight they were carrying.

Sydney continued, "Now, where was I? Oh yes, the 'merger.' Being one of the smartest agencies in town as well as the most profitable, Blake & Turnbrow would want to know exactly what they were getting and whether or not my forecasts for the next few years were exaggerated. 'Due diligence' it's called. They will send in forensic accountants to inspect our books and look at our cost structure to make sure we are already operating efficiently. They'll search for skeletons in the cupboard, tax or VAT fraud, that sort of thing, of which, as a matter of fact, we're entirely in the clear—I'm neither stupid nor so greedy as to take such risks."

I heard him stop pacing.

"It was bloody hard work," Sydney said, "and I'm sure you noticed that I've been putting in even more overtime and weekends lately. Tonight, I finally put everything in place and as long as I'm around to answer any queries their team might make, everything will be fine. Teeming and lading, the allocation of future money against old debts, will take care of any discrepancies, so the books will look up to date. They're bound to find little things that are not quite right, but they'll consider them unimportant in the grand scheme. Blake & Turnbrow is too eager to take possession to let slight errors affect the buyout."

When he spoke, Guinane's words were sluggish, slurred, but they could be understood. "Why, Sydney? Why did you do this to us?"

"I've already explained. I'm in great need of money. The people I gamble with are a little impatient and a bit short on understanding; as are my ex-wives who are complaining about slow alimony payments. Buying cocaine in today's over-inflated market doesn't help the situation either. No, I'm rather desperate at the moment."

He paused, as if reflecting on his next words.

"That's why Jim had to die. He was in the way, he wanted to block the takeover. Fortunately, I had an acquaintance in the police force who unwittingly gave me an idea. One that's been working out rather well, as a matter of fact."

"You . . . you killed Jim?" Guinane was obviously beginning to recover from the blow on the head. Sydney must have grabbed the first heavy object that came to hand when Guinane walked into our office—the steel rule sometimes kept on my desk.

"Oh yes. I thought you'd realized that by now," I heard Sydney say. "Detective Constable Danny Coates is my second wife's brother, now my ex-brother-in-law. We'd always got on despite the bitch his sister turned out to be, and we've kept in touch even after the divorce. Like me, he enjoys a flutter on the horses, as well as Blackjack and roulette. We frequent the same gambling clubs, as a matter of fact. He's also not adverse to the occasional coke wrap I supply him with from time to time."

"Sydney . . . look, let me get up. Let's stop . . . all this." Guinane's speech was still slurred and he sounded as if he was in pain, maybe concussed.

"I thought you wanted to hear? You know, it's quite cathartic to get it off my chest, especially when you won't be able to repeat it to anyone."

"What do you mean?"

I heard noises as if Guinane was trying to get to his feet, but even as I peeked through the gap I saw him slump to the floor again, only saving himself from going all the way down by gripping the edge of the desk.

Sydney's voice was soothing, yet it chilled me. "Hush, now. Be patient, Oliver. You want to hear the whole story, don't you?"

Sydney appeared in the gap, his back to me. He was looming over Oliver, the metal rule held by his side, ready to strike.

"Yes, my cop friend gambles too much and has a penchant for cocaine. Not a fine endorsement for law and order, is it? Unfortunately, that's the world we live in nowadays. Nothing's clean anymore."

Satisfied that Guinane was still weak and too dazed to be a problem, Sydney walked away, out of my line of sight. I crept closer to the opening, aware that it was becoming more and more difficult to maintain control over the body I occupied. If I was going to make a move, it would have to be soon, yet I had to hear more; I was still absorbed in these revelations.

"My ex-brother-in-law is chuffed to be detailed for such a high-profile case, the search for a serial killer who mutilates every victim. So much so, he can't stop talking about it when we meet up for a spot of boozing and gambling. Bragging, I suppose you could say, because it made him look important. That's why the plan to get rid of Jim True grew so easily in my mind. I could do the deed and make it look like the work of the serial killer. Jim would be put out of the way, no hindrance to the takeover. And who would suspect me of the crime? All I needed was the right opportunity, and you provided me with that, Oliver, when you rang me last Sunday night to tell me you and he had fallen out and you'd left the hotel. Leaving Jim alone. I was becoming pretty desperate by then, and your phone call was just the prompt I needed."

"You couldn't have . . ." There was shock and dismay in Guinane's voice.

Sydney responded quickly, almost angrily. It was the first time his mood had tightened since I'd been listening. "Oh yes I could! I took my time after your call—forgive me for not backing up your story to the police, but by the time they asked me if you'd called that night as you'd told them, the plot had moved on. Now where was I? Oh yes, after your phone call I chose a suitable weapon—one of those short chef's choppers from my kitchen that was not quite like the murder weapon used in the previous serial killings, but which served my purposes perfectly—blabbermouth DC Coates had told me about the real weapon. Incidentally, I got rid of it in the Thames the same night. I went to the hotel and used the keycard to your suite—you remember, I acquired a key for myself when I booked you both in, so that I could come and go as I pleased, check on your progress from time to time. I let myself in and, as I'd hoped, because it was so late, past midnight, found Jim asleep fully clothed on his bed. I think he'd hit the whiskey bottle after your bust-up. And my, what a deep sleep he was in. You might have thought he was already dead, so shallow was his breath. It made him a nice easy target. I wore gloves and one of those terrible, old, gaudy shellsuits I thought were the height of fashion in the eighties and which I'd never thrown away, so blood wasn't a problem. Any that splashed onto my face I washed away in the bathroom. I'd brought the shellsuit and gloves along in my briefcase, the chopper too, and that's where they were returned to after the deed, just in case anyone saw me leave. Oh, and of course, the other weapon came in the briefcase too, but that was left at the scene of the crime. Danny Coates told me about the knitting needle—seemed to think it was common knowledge anyway even though it had been kept out of the media, by mutual agreement. You could easily have learned of it through one of your journalist friends. And by the way, another mistake the police think *you* made was to use the knitting needle on Jim *after* you'd killed him with the chopper. Their forensic expert worked that one out. That was just another thing that led them to believe a copycat killer was the perpetrator."

"You're insane," Oliver said thickly. (See how I'd reverted to "Oliver" in my mind. I still hated him for what he'd done to me with my wife and how he'd stolen the most precious thing in the world to me, my daughter Primrose, but he *hadn't* killed me, he hadn't quite sunk *that* low. Because of his predicament right then, I almost pitied him.)

"Not really," Presswell replied. "Let's say years of resentment and my hopeless financial situation came together at a crucial moment. You know, Jim didn't make anything as much as a moan when I cleavered his head. I find that quite surprising, don't you?"

Oliver was right: Presswell was insane. Nobody normal could speak of such a horrendous act in the matter-of-fact tones he'd returned to. I felt sick, not physically, because I was inside someone else's body, but spiritually sick, sick in my mind. It had been Sydney Presswell, not Oliver, all along. Butchered by my own business partner and friend. I might have laughed if my sense of humor hadn't left me some time ago. This was the deviant madman who'd cut off my genitals and left them in a pile. How sick was that? I shuffled even closer to the opening, my ruptured face almost at the edge of the door. My killer's back was to me.

"Suitably," he continued, as if enjoying his own confession, "the hotel was like a morgue when I arrived and, because I used a staff entrance at the back, not even the night porter saw my coming and going."

"I don't . . ." Oliver began with some difficulty. "I don't understand why they immediately suspected it was me."

"Because you were the last person to see Jim alive—always the first suspect, that person in this kind of case—and you'd been arguing with him in your suite—an extremely heated argument, they were told by the night porter. When they heard about the conflict between you two over the takeover by Blake & Turnbrow, they became even more suspicious of you. Then when I told DC Coates about your ongoing affair with Jim's wife—well, I think that really clinched matters for them. You wanted your business partner out of the way because he objected to the takeover that would make you rich and also because you wanted his wife. Pretty strong motives as far as they were concerned. And by the way, I mentioned you were heavily into drugs." Presswell was hovering over Oliver, the heavy rule held like a club. Threatening.

"You tried to make it look as if it was just another serial killing, but although you'd found out about the murder weapon, you were unaware of one other vital element in those crimes, something you could never have arranged even if you hadn't been. How could you know of the victims' crazy behavior before they died? Only the police directly involved in the cases knew that the three previous victims had acted totally out of character before they were killed. They had degraded themselves after leading perfectly respectable lives. The Press never found out, it was a factor that was completely hushed up. Oh yes, *I* knew, because my ex-brother-in-law wanted me to think he was a very important policeman who worked only on A-list crimes, and he loved to let me in on inside stuff, things he thought made him a big man in my eyes. The copycat killer—*you*, Oliver—made an important mistake because he hadn't full knowledge of the crimes. The previous victims were under duress, perhaps their families were under threat if the intended victim didn't comply with the killer's instructions. Or they were being blackmailed. Or hypnotized. All kinds of theories have been put forward, but the police cannot know for sure. What they are agreed on is that the killer is a very sick person with no apparent motive. But *you*, Oliver, you have a couple of motives for killing Jim, and as far as they're aware, you might be scheming, but you're not sick. Even chopping off Jim's private parts had some peculiar logic—he was sleeping with the woman you loved. That's what makes you different from their target and why this murder is not like the others. Even the murder weapons were used in the wrong order."

There seemed to be more humor in his laughter now, but the hysteria that was only hinted at before had become more noticeable.

I saw Oliver try to rise to his feet, but Sydney struck him again with the rule, using only the flat side, bringing it down hard against Oliver's scalp. Oliver yelped, then groaned and collapsed once more.

He was still conscious though, because I heard him say, "I'll . . . tell them . . . I'll tell them about you . . ."

Still in view, Sydney leaned over him. "You won't be around to tell them anything. Are you really so stupid that you think you're going to live through the night? That I was confessing all this to ease my conscience? Huh! You really are a first-prize idiot, d'you know that? All brains and no sense, as my dear mother used to say."

He straightened, and carried on talking as he did so. "I have to admit I've been working half on instinct all this week, improvising as things went along, but tonight you've given me the perfect ending. Tonight you die, you see? And you leave behind your confession. You knew the police were on to you, you were full of remorse over killing your best friend, so you took the only honorable way out."

And your lover had thrown you out, I could have added but didn't.

Oliver had grabbed the edge of the desk with both hands and was trying to pull himself up. Sydney ignored his efforts, although he now kept the steel rule raised over the struggling man.

"Let me give you the whole scenario, Oliver. You came here tonight, your last place of refuge, as it were. Nobody else was around. No, not even me. I was at home tucked up in bed—as I was that fateful Sunday night. Yes, I'd worked late, but had left before you arrived. You typed your confession on your computer and left it on the screen, no hard copy necessary. You've been screwing your best friend's wife for years, you and he had business differences, and in a fit of rage you killed him. Naturally, I'll type all of this for you and I'll use my handkerchief over my index finger so the only fingerprints on your keyboard will be yours alone. I'm told computer suicide notes are popular these days. No handwritten signature necessary, which is particularly helpful to me in these circumstances."

I could feel any power I had left over Moker's body swiftly ebbing away. I had to make my move, but couldn't just yet: Sydney's exposition to a man he thought would shortly be dead was not quite finished.

"Why, Sydney?" I heard Oliver ask. "Why do this after all the years we've worked together? Surely nothing's worth killing your friends for."

"You still don't get it, do you? Neither of you ever realized the pressure I was under. Well fuck you!"

You know what? That shocked me. Hearing Sydney Presswell swear shocked me. Ridiculous, I know, considering he'd just confessed to years of embezzlement and, worse, my murder, and hearing Sydney—*Presswell!*—say *"fuck"* absolutely shocked me. You see, I'd never heard him curse like that before, not once, not ever, even when we argued over some company matter or other. In fact, I can't recall Sydney ever getting angry before. Or cross. He'd always been mild-mannered. Not docile, I don't mean that, but he'd always been the perfect gentleman, the most even-tempered person I'd ever known.

Now he'd said the *f*—word and that clinched everything for me. Sydney—see? I couldn't even call him Presswell for long—was two people, it seemed: the nice, quiet, soft-toned accountant, and respected colleague, and the scheming killer who leaned over Oliver now. The *"fuck"* confirmed it. Sydney was completely crazy.

His voice was raised; he was almost shouting at Oliver.

"You creative people are always complaining about tight copy dates, lack of time for presentations, overnight layouts and copy ideas, all that crap! But never did you understand the pressure I'm under, and I don't mean the kind that goes with the job! I'm in deep shit, Oliver, and it's been coming to a head for some time now. I don't just mean greedy ex-wives and kids' school fees. I owe serious money to people who don't like to wait too long for payment. Money I haven't got. That is, I haven't got it right now."

I practically jumped out of the body I was occupying when he brought the metal rule down hard on the desktop.

"But all that will change once the deal has gone through. I've already been asked to stay on as a financial consultant at a higher salary, but the real reward will be the partners' bonus from Blake & Turnbrow and the large secret commission I'll receive for brokering the deal in the first place. You and Jim were never supposed to know about that, but I guess in the words of the late, great Buddy Holly, it doesn't matter anymore."

Somehow I was even more scared now that his voice had resumed its normal, placid pitch.

"So, what's to be done with you, Oliver?"

Sydney made the question sound reasonable. Mr. Nice Guy again.

He answered his own question. "It's actually very simple. You have to die, of course, but then I'm sure you already knew that. So it begs the question. How are you going to die? Again, the answer is simple. You're going to take a high dive."

Another moan from Oliver, a kind of despairing protest.

"Your confession is taken care of—or it will be in a few minutes' time. All that needs doing is the deed itself. I suppose I'm going to have to drag you over to the windows, aren't I? No chance of you helping me with that? I thought not."

I heard him walk across the room, his voice fading slightly.

"I warned you about these floor-to-ceiling windows with that pointless balustrade right outside them, told you both they were dangerous when opened, but you loved the elegant style too much to care. Now you're about to learn how *seriously* dangerous they are."

The sounds of bolts being drawn, a catch turned. Then a fresh breeze pushed at the door I was hiding behind, narrowing the gap. A scuffling noise came from inside, Oliver moaning protests again, a soft dragging sound.

Oh dear God, the moment was here. I had to do something and do it quickly.

I dug a hand into one of the raincoat's deep pockets, stiffened fingers feeling for the knitting needle I'd put there. My fingertips were numbed, but I forced them closed around the thin weapon, gripping the needle as best I could, slowly drawing it out, afraid I might drop it.

With my other hand, I shoved at the door, sending it wide. I held the needle out in front of me, the lethal tip pointed upward.

But strength was quickly draining from the body I possessed. The knees were giving way, the raised arm was trembling.

I'm losing it, I thought. *I'm losing control!*

Sydney Presswell was halfway across the room, Oliver limp in his arms, the copywriter's feet dragging over the carpet, the French windows open wide before them.

Sydney heard my heavy shambling footsteps. He looked back over his shoulder, saw me, and astonishment stretched his bland features.

FORTY-THREE

But as I stood there in the doorway, the knitting needle's point quivering in my unsteady hand, I knew I no longer had the strength to attack. Moker's skin felt like a deep-sea diver's suit, his head like the metal helmet. I felt my own spirit struggling to free itself of the useless body, to discard it like an unnecessary layer. In a few short moments, Oliver would be thrown over the low balcony outside the windows and I shouldn't—no, I honestly *couldn't,* despite what he'd done to me—let that happen. He'd sold me out, stolen my wife, and had cheated me out of the daughter that should have been mine. But he hadn't *killed* me. Sydney had done that. Greedy, resentful Sydney Presswell, mild-mannered, easy-going Sydney. Embezzler Sydney. Perverse Sydney. Killer Sydney! And I'd grown too weak to prevent him from killing someone else! Oh, Jesus God, please help me! Give me that last ounce of strength or willpower, whatever it takes to stop Sydney throwing Oliver out the window!

But it was no good—I had hardly anything left. Astonished, surprised, he might be, but there was no fear in Sydney's eyes, and certainly no shock.

But it was that lack of shock that gave me the idea. And the idea was inspired by the real serial killer.

I had to make Sydney so afraid of me he'd be paralyzed if only for a few seconds, like Moker's victims. It might just give me enough time to stab him with the needle, but in the neck, an easier target than his awkward-to-get-at heart.

I tore at the scarf around my face—no, my arm was too dysfunctional to move swiftly; more accurate to say that I worked at the scarf with my free hand—to get it loose and reveal the deformity that Moker had borne all his life, the facial aberration that had frozen the people he was about to kill for a few crippling seconds.

And in a way, it worked, although in Sydney's case, fear was not a factor. No, revulsion had replaced the astonishment, disgust at this deformed creature that, for the moment, was interfering with his grand plan. Then something else flickered behind those rimless glasses he wore. Was it recognition? His eyes had left my face to stare at the nasty-looking weapon I held toward him. The sharpened knitting needle. Had he made the connection?

And I think it was this also that sent a fresh pulsing through Moker's corpse. I don't know, I'm not absolutely sure about these things, but I thought that maybe whatever remnant of Moker's psyche was left behind inside his battered brain, or even inside the flesh of his body as a whole, had stirred up memories of a lifetime's rejection, years of being an outcast, because of normal people's revulsion of him. *The same revulsion that was behind the fear in Sydney's eyes.* Did flesh and blood absorb such soul-rending emotions? Was everything that happened to us throughout our lives recorded, somehow embedded into our very substance? I've no idea, but the angry surge now pouring through Moker's body could not be denied.

Another thought: maybe the anger that brought strength with its flow naturally came from myself, my own spirit. Hadn't I wept for Moker earlier? Hadn't I experienced the emotional pain he had felt all his life? Was my sympathy for him, my *empathy* for him, my *anger* for him, empowering my own last reserves of willpower? Had Sydney's undisguised revulsion at the grotesque who stood before him triggered a reaction shared between myself and whatever was left of Moker? I can only guess at the answer.

This returning vitality sent me rushing across the room at Sydney.

Oliver dropped to the floor when Sydney let him go and raised his hands to ward off my attack.

The knitting needle was held high in my hand and I brought it down just before I cannoned into Sydney, aiming for his plump neck but missing, the sharpened point piercing his cheek, an inch below his left eye, my clumsy but fierce momentum pushing him backward, either the pain or the surprise provoking a shrill shriek, his fear and revulsion turning to horror as he pedalled back, my force and his own panic sending us toward the open windows.

I dug down with the needle, ripping his cheek, and now he screamed, a full-blooded sound, a frightened cry of conviction, this from a man I'd never known to show strong emotion. Blood spurted from his face to join the crusted blood on my forehead as I pushed with strength that was already waning once more, driving us both through the tall open windows onto the foot-wide false balcony outside.

An odd thing happened when we tottered there on the brink of the sixty-feet drop to the shiny wet street below. Sydney, with the back of his knees pressed against the stone balustrade, looked directly into my—into *Moker's*—eyes. The moment froze, became meaningless as far as real time was concerned in the way such important moments often do.

Just for that ceaseless instant, his pale-gray eyes widened and I thought I saw recognition in them.

Maybe his guilt, with oblivion or hell a breath or two away, caused his mind to superimpose my real face onto one that was largely absent, because I'm sure his mouth and his voice started to shape my name, the fright in his eyes swapped briefly for a question.

"Ji—?" I'm certain he was about to say, but overbalance tore him away from me.

The half-formed query—if I'm correct in judging it so—swelled into a ferocious scream that withered to a self-pitying wail just before he hit the ground.

The soft mulchy—mushy—crunch that came back at me was awful to hear.

FORTY-FOUR

I swayed there on the phoney narrow balcony, any power I had left finally depleted, and the light drizzle soaking the head and hands of a body I'd borrowed for a while, one I'd never have liked to own full-time. A breeze flapped the lapel of the raincoat I was wearing, a breeze whose evidence I saw but couldn't feel.

I felt empty, vacant, as bare as the shell I occupied. I thought that whatever memories Moker's cooling flesh had sustained after his soul's departure—or whatever chemicals in the brain that governed such things and which took just that little bit longer to expire after the body's death—were finally spent. This shell, this vessel, this *host,* had no significance anymore, except to those who would view it later and recoil at its ugliness and injury.

It had no importance to me either. Nor had anything else in this world. Maybe.

I leaned forward, knees against the stone balustrade.

I had no further use for Moker. I wanted out. At least his carcass had helped prevent another murder. Pity Moker, himself, hadn't earned that small redemption.

It was *too* cold inside this body now, *too* vacant. I could almost feel its flesh corrupting around me. I wanted my freedom.

I leaned even further out over the shiny deserted street, knees no longer hard against the balustrade, then followed Sydney.

Falling in the dark. Body lazily tumbling over. Descent slow. So slow you'd believe that meeting the ground might not be so inevitable. But it is. Of course it is. It just takes longer than you would ever imagine.

And I'm suddenly afraid, even though I know I can't be hurt at this journey's conclusion. I'm already dead, so how can I feel pain? Besides, this isn't even my body. Maybe it's the shock I'm afraid of. Or maybe my mind is informing me that when you drop from a great height onto something hard and unyielding there's going to be a lot of hurt. Probably only for an instant—depends on how far you fall—but, like the drop itself, that instant might last a very long time.

Also, something else awaits me in that moment *before* journey's end. Moker's final memory—and yet his first.

And I've been here before, but then I was interrupted by my own distress.

—chaos, images rushing through a freshly created mind—no order, no recognition, until everything slows, resolves itself, becomes calm and a clear recollection—

I understand. This is Moker's original memory. His birth. I continue to fall, sailing down on my back, arms and legs splayed.

—darkness becoming lighter, redness and too much brightness, unformed shapes moving in front of me, floating, but not how I've floated before in the womb, huge rough hands beneath my slimed and bloody body, a separation, a snapping of something, the link that fed me, the sudden awful feeling of loss, a sadness, my first, then sounds around me, not like the constant thud-up *that had always comforted me, that had gone now, was replaced by these harsher noises I don't like very much, and those blurred moving shapes, bright and white and pink, one looming larger than the others, warm stickiness being wiped from my body, unpleasant sounds, gasps, a sudden rigidity to the arms that hold me, an unhappy emotion that somehow transfers itself to me through that hardened grip, causing me unhappiness, more pink shapes, scarcely defined in my early unfocused vision—hands—reaching out to me—*

—passed over to someone else, a wonderful feeling, a sense of comfort and safety, a pleasure that was common and continuous until a short time ago—wonderful to have it back, even though it's not quite the same, not as secure as before—

—A terrible noise, sudden, high, frightened, a scream—

—and a new scene intrudes on the altering reverie, a flashback from a time that's yet to come—a woman I know although I haven't seen her for many, many years, the woman who gave birth to me, standing inside an open front door, a haggard woman whose prematurely wrinkled skin is yellowish, her wiry gray-streaked hair straggly, her clothes unkempt, and she looks at me with horror and contempt and slams the door in my face—my poor, poor face—and I hear her screeching on the other side of the closed door—

—go away!—

—go away!—

—and I'm returning to my birth setting and I'm being handed over to that same woman, younger now, tired but pleased—except she's looking at me in the same way she would look at me years later when I'd gone searching for her and she had screamed and screamed when she had discovered me on her doorstep, the one she'd birthed all those years ago, the child she had tried to forget, the one she should love as any mother would, as any mother should, as any mother must *love her own—but instead she was screeching, screeching—*

—go away!—

—go away!—

—and now that same screech, only this is the first time, just after I am born, the screeching terrifying me although I have no conception of why it should—the disturbed sounds around me that I don't even know are voices because I haven't experienced life yet, but something in the sounds increasing my anxiety—already I don't like this new world, already I'm becoming bewildered—frightened—and that screeching is shattering forever the contentment I had known in the womb—

—take it away!—

—take it away!—

—and already I have learned rejection.

I smashed into the ground beside Sydney and even relaxed bones shattered. The back of Moker's head, which had impacted first, cracked like an egg—like a real egg this time, filled with runny yolk rather than chocolate goodies—and I felt the brain mash, some pieces of its matter scattering across the tarmac. Interior organs jumped from their moorings, most rupturing, others squeezed flat. The lungs that must have gathered air through the irregular funnel-shaped face on the way down before the body flipped over burst like overinflated balloons. But the worst thing was the *noise* of hitting the ground, that same mulchy-mushy-crunch that Sydney had made, except I heard it from the *inside,* where it was louder and more scary, and the squashing of substances and the snapping and grinding of bones could be felt (no, there wasn't any pain involved).

The collision almost jolted me from Moker's body, but I kind of bounced—or reverberated, to be more accurate—before settling into it once more. I sensed there was nothing left inside, no more memories and no more functioning.

Now, in every way, it was an *empty* shell; and it was time for me to discard it. I sat up and the carcass remained where it was.

Next to me, Sydney's head was just pulp—unlike Moker, he'd landed face first—and strange yellowish stuff oozed out with the blood. One of his legs stretched out at a comical right angle from his hip and a hand rested against the back of his neck, the palm and clawed fingers curiously turned upward, his elbow twisted. I think his stomach must have split open, because a big pool of blood was spreading over the rain-soaked street beneath him. It expanded in spurts, as though the heart was still pumping, but it quickly became a steady flow, indicating the last weak dregs of life had finally given in.

I stood up and stepped out of Moker as if I were stepping out of a beached canoe. Yet I couldn't leave him right then and I'm not sure why. His body was of no more use to me and revenge had been delivered—not that I felt any sense of satisfaction or achievement, by the way, only a feeling of great sadness and completion. Oh, and pity, a deep pity for the unfortunate man who was Alec Moker. I remembered the flashback, the instant memory just before his body struck tarmac, the moment of his birth, a beginning that was so traumatic, so devastating, that it had never been erased from his subconscious, even though it happened when he'd only just been born and such an early event should never have been registered, let alone remembered so many years later. (I wondered if everything that happened to us during our lifetime was neatly stowed away somewhere deep beneath the layers of our mind, never to be lost, never to die, but perhaps recalled at the moment of death. Didn't happen with me, but then mine wasn't what you'd call a regular demise.)

I turned as a harsh light came from the other end of the narrow street. A car was approaching at speed, headlights on full beam. Then police sirens, two more cars screeching round from a sidestreet at the other end, racing toward me, the darkness and rain somehow giving their sounds even more urgency. Tires squealed as all three police vehicles slid to a halt on the street's slippery surface.

FORTY-FIVE

A uniformed policeman leaped from his car and ran the few yards to the two broken bodies lying in the street, while on the other side of me the two detectives I knew as Simmons and Coates (the latter Sydney's ex-brother-in-law no less!) left their Volvo and hurried toward the corpses without quite the same urgency. Other uniformed figures were emerging from the patrol car, a Vauxhall Cavalier, that had stopped behind the Volvo.

"Jesus fuck," the detective called Coates said in a dismayed whisper as he looked down at the two busted men at his feet. There was no need to take the pulse of either of them to verify they were dead.

The uniformed policeman had made the mistake of taking a small torch from his pocket and shining it on the heads of the two dead men. The light wavered as he suddenly turned away as if to throw up. Simmons gripped the policeman's wrist and held the torch steady so that he could get a proper look at the corpse.

"That one must be Moker, the lunatic we're looking for," he said quietly. "That damage to his face wasn't caused by it hitting the deck. There's no blood coming from it for a start and the face is just how Andrea True described it. What about the other one? Oliver Guinane, you reckon?"

"I don't think so," Coates' voice was hesitant, his initial dismay graduating to shock. "Even belly down you can see he hasn't got Guinane's curly brown hair. I . . . I think I know who this is." He pointed a shaky finger. "See the smashed glasses lying in the blood by his head?"

"So?"

"I think it's my contact in the agency. Sydney Presswell, company manager and financial director. Used to be my brother-in-law until my sister divorced him a few years ago. I'm sure I recognize that gray-check suit—he wears it a lot. He's the guy Andrea True said Guinane was going to see tonight."

Both men, and some of the policemen who were now milling around, peered up at the lights near the top of the building.

"Right," Simmons said briskly, pointing first at the uniforms, then toward the building's fifth-floor balcony, lights from the room behind throwing the balustrade into relief. "I want three of you up there right away. That's obviously where these two took a dive from. See if there's anyone else around. There should be a man called Oliver Guinane about somewhere. Yes, that's right, the one we hauled in for questioning about the death of his business partner, James True. For all we know, he might be responsible for this as well." He nodded at the corpses on the ground. "So go careful just in case. If you find him give us a shout."

He turned toward the officer who had gagged a few moments ago. "You. Get on to control, tell 'em we need SOC set up ASAP. Better get the medics in, too. There's nothing they can do, but we'll need an ambulance to take the bodies. And listen, I want both ends of the street sealed off for now—we can minimize the area once the essentials have been taken care of. Get moving."

The uniformed policeman headed for his striped white patrol car, just as a Transit van pulled up behind it. More uniformed men piled out of the police carrier.

Simmons caught the elbow of a policeman close to him and pointed to the Hillman parked outside the agency. "Search that old heap over there, break in if it's locked. It's the car we've been looking for."

"Looks to me," said Coates, whose face was pale in the glare of headlights, "by the position of their bodies, that they might have come down together. Maybe they were having a ruck and it spilled out over the balcony."

"Yeah, could be. But why would Moker go for Presswell?"

"Guinane must have been the target, but Sydney got in the way, or maybe tried to save his friend, or he could have been the only one in the office. It was no secret that we'd taken Guinane in for questioning about James True's murder, so maybe Moker thought he was the copycat killer and didn't like it. Andrea True said Moker arrived at the house shortly after Guinane had left, but maybe Moker got there earlier and listened at a window."

"Heard Guinane telling his girlfriend where he was going next," Simmons continued for him, although his tone was dubious.

"I reckon that's it. We know now Moker was the serial killer. Hadn't managed to get Mrs. True and her kid, so went for other bait."

Simmons shook his head as he pulled his raincoat up against the rain. "I dunno. Doesn't make sense to me. How could he know where the agency was?"

"We found those phone books in his flat. He'd got the address beforehand, probably days ago when he first read about Guinane in the papers. Don't forget, the agency's name as well as Guinane's was underlined in thick pencil in those articles about him being a suspect. Same as the location of True's house."

The two detectives had obviously been able to go through the cuttings more thoroughly than I had, even if it had only been a quick search.

Simmons clucked his tongue against the roof of his mouth. "Nah, doesn't work for me. It's too pat. I want a proper look into this Sydney Presswell's background, your brother-in-law or not."

"Ex-brother-in-law," Coates insisted.

"In every sense now. Look, there's something going on that doesn't sit well with what we know. I want more background on Guinane, Presswell and True. Especially Presswell though, because he's the one who's been feeding you information about Guinane. I mean, really putting Guinane in the shit."

"Okay, but—"

Both men looked toward a new car, a dark Jaguar saloon that has just drawn up behind the other police vehicles.

"Oh-oh," said Coates resignedly. "The governor's here."

"Yep, and he's got Commander Newman with him," said Simmons. "Word's obviously got upstairs about our breakthrough."

Should be interesting, I thought, as I loitered close by, a wall behind my back so that I was out of the way of the busy policemen (not that it mattered, of course, they'd never know they'd bumped into me apart from a brief moment of disorientation). How the hell was *anyone* going to make sense of what had been going on?

The two senior policemen came toward the apparent crime scene, walking briskly and acknowledging the salutes of officers who were making themselves look even more busy. The taller one was Chief Superintendent Sadler. The shorter man (although only comparatively shorter because Sadler was so tall) wore an important-looking crisp, dark uniform and sported a neatly clipped beard. This one acknowledged his men with a sharp flick of the brown leather gloves he carried toward the rain-speckled visor of his cap.

When they reached the two detectives, Sadler introduced them to the uniformed policemen. "DS Simmons and DC Coates."

The senior officer gave a curt nod of his head. He addressed Simmons.

"Give me a quick rundown on the main investigation and how it ties in with this." His gloves indicated the two figures at their feet. "I gather they *are* connected in some way?"

"We heard about the woman who collapsed and died earlier tonight at Paddington Green after naming her attacker," Sadler said to his two detectives. "The wonder is how she ever made it to the station in the first place with her injuries."

"That's right, Sir," agreed Simmons. "She arrived there with a knitting needle straight through her heart."

"Carry on from that point," Commander Newman said impatiently.

"Because of the murder weapon involved, Paddington Green got on to the Yard's major incident room, the one dealing with the recent spate of serial killings. As luck would have it, DC Coates and I were there on overtime and we scooted over to the nick as soon as our receiver passed on the information."

"She was already dead when you got there?" queried Chief Superintendent Sadler as he scrutinized the bodies on the ground, a sour expression on his lean face.

"That's correct, Sir. Incidentally, she had many other marks on her body, indicating her killer had roughed her up beforehand. She must have put up quite a struggle and there was no mutilation. We figure she'd managed to escape before that could happen."

"And you say she named this person Moker as her attacker." It wasn't a question from the police commander but an affirmation.

Sadler spoke. "That's right. She wasn't all that coherent apparently—not surprising after everything she'd been through—but fortunately the name itself was perfectly clear."

Simmons picked up again. "Locating Moker's address was easy enough. No previous form by the way. Our computer found it on the electoral roll and Swansea supplied the make and number of Moker's vehicle. We assumed there'd be a car involved because our killer would have had to have some kind of transport to transfer previous victims from one place to another for the mutilation. It was the break we were waiting for—a fresh killing. Could've been another copycat, of course, but this time we thought we were really on to something. In all, there were three 'Mokers' in the book but two lived out in the suburbs and we were keen on the one from inner London where all the murders were committed. We sent men out to the other addresses just in case, but our main attention was on the Shepherd's Bush address. We knew our instincts were right the minute we entered Moker's empty flat."

"You had a search warrant, I take it?" Commander Newman asked sharply.

"Requested over the phone, delivered while we were there, Sir."

I think neither of the two officers wanted to ask if that was before or *after* they'd entered the flat.

"We didn't make any mess getting in though, Sir," Coates quickly put in, as if reading their minds. "The window was only latch-locked and a credit card quickly took care of that when we got no response to knocking on the door. A constable climbed in and opened up for us. We can always say the door was open in the first place if it's a problem."

The commander stared at him for a second or two and, as an observer who didn't like the grubby little detective, I enjoyed Coates' discomfort.

"Let's hear the rest, Simmons," Newman said, redirecting his gaze.

"Yes, Sir. Well, although it was unfortunate that we didn't catch Moker at home there was enough evidence in that place to know we'd found our serial killer, and forensics are going through the flat with a fine-tooth comb as we speak."

Commander Newman gave an encouraging nod of his head and Simmons went on.

"We found newspaper clippings of every murder and mutilation so far, including James True's. We also found a whole bunch of knitting needles stashed away in a cupboard, some of them already sharpened and all the same brand as the murder weapon."

"Well done," Newman acknowledged, slapping the leather gloves into the palm of his hand. "Now how does it tie in with all this?" This time he nodded down at the dead bodies on the ground.

"Yes, I'm not too clear about what you told me over the phone," put in Simmons' immediate boss, Sadler. "You said Moker turned up at this James True's house."

It was odd being referred to in this way when I was standing only a couple of feet away (I'd moved away from the wall to get closer to the group).

With Coates chipping in every so often to let his superiors know he was in the picture, Simmons quickly explained how they had found news clipping showing pictures of Andrea and Primrose, and then had noticed the missing page in the telephone book from the T section. They'd immediately—and quite smartly, I thought—put two and two together, so they sped to my home in force and found a distraught Andrea and Prim. With what they'd learned from Andrea they had put out a fresh APB for all units to step up their search for Moker's Hillman which, in the event, was spotted by an officer on fixed point outside a VIP diplomat's house, who called in the information. The Hillman was only two streets away from the agency and that was when Simmons and Coates suspected (again, quite astutely, I thought) Moker had gone after Oliver Guinane, the man who had tried to appropriate his, Moker's, crimes.

It was Sadler who interrupted the flow. "Is this man Guinane inside the agency now?" The tall man glanced up at the lights on the fifth floor and, reflexively, the commander did the same.

"Not sure, Sir. I sent some men up there a little while ago to look, but they haven't reported back to me yet. I was about to go up there myself, just before you arrived. Thought I'd better put you and the commander in the picture first."

"Right. Good. Let's all—"

The policeman Simmons had ordered to search Moker's car appeared at the detective's side carefully carrying an object in one hand, a large handkerchief, preventing contact between it and his palm and curled fingers. I moved even closer for a better look, peering over Coates' left shoulder.

It was Sadler who spoke to the PC, who seemed reluctant to interrupt his superiors.

"Uh, small chopper, Sir. I suppose you'd call it a hatchet."

"You found it in the Hillman?" Simmons leaned forward with great interest.

"Yes, Sir. Under the driver's seat."

Moker's mutilation tool. I'd forgotten all about it. Oh thank God he didn't bring it with him into the house . . .

"I told him to search Moker's car when we got here," Simmons said to both the commander and the chief superintendent.

The loud wail of an ambulance; we hadn't noticed its approach. The sound cut out as its driver waited for a policeman to hold back the blue and white tape that had already been strung across the street at both ends.

Our attention returned to the nasty little weapon in the constable's hand.

"Didn't have to break into the vehicle, Sir," the young policeman said to no particular sir, displaying the hatchet proudly. "It was unlocked and it didn't take long to find this. Lots of blood on it, even the handle. Newish and old stains. Looks as if it's never been cleaned."

Simmons grinned broadly and, although now I couldn't see his face from behind, I'm sure Coates was grinning too. Sadler allowed himself only a small smile.

"Well done, constable," the commander said to the young policeman (What was he? Twelve years old? His head was too small for his helmet). "Extremely well done." (Spoken like a leader of men.) "Bag it and give it to forensics when they turn up. What's your name?"

"DC Kempton, Sir."

"Once you've passed it over to the bods, carry on with the search of the vehicle, see what else you can find. And get someone to help you, I want two men on the job."

"Already taken care of, Sir," Simmons put in quickly, but not defensively. "The other man's continuing the search as we speak."

Commander Newman gave a satisfied nod of his head.

"Sir!" the young policeman said smartly and took his leave. He marched off toward a patrol car, no doubt to collect a plastic bag big enough to hold his prize.

Simmons, and probably Coates too, were still grinning.

"Well I think the hatchet, together with those knitting needles you found in Moker's flat, ties it all up rather neatly," commented Sadler as if in praise of his two detectives.

"Except for this other man lying here," said Commander Newman to spoil the fun. "What did you say his name was?"

"Presswell," Coates quickly told him. "Sydney Presswell. We think he might have got in a tussle with Moker. Syd—Presswell was probably trying to save Guinane from Moker and they crashed through the window and over the balcony."

"We'll know more if Guinane *is* up there," Simmons said helpfully. "He might be hurt, maybe unconscious."

"Then we'd better find out," said Newman, slapping the gloves into the palm of his hand again like a punctuation mark to the detectives' report.

I'd almost lost interest by now. The facts were clear as far as I was concerned and I didn't need to know any more. They'd find Ollie semi-conscious in our old office and no doubt he'd fill them in the details for the police when he was able to. He would tell them about Sydney's foolhardy confession—Sydney thought he was talking to a man who would be dead in a matter of moments— and they'd check out our devious bloody bean counter—yeah, I really did think of him like that now, although I hadn't before—and discover all the little discrepancies in the accounts which foxy old Sydney wouldn't be around to explain away, and they'd delve into his background thoroughly, find out about his debts, his gambling, his alimony payments to two high-maintenance ex-wives, a third one coming up. The drugs. They might—no, they *would* search his home after Oliver had spoken to them—and find his stash. Or maybe one of his exes would rat on him for revenge—it's impossible for a wife not to know her husband is doing drugs. Of course, all that wouldn't necessarily make him a killer, but he'd lose all credibility as a fine upstanding man. They'd dig even deeper and would come up with something, I was sure about that.

Ollie? He wasn't guilty of the crime of murder, but he was guilty of other things where I was concerned. I could never forgive him but, hey, suddenly I didn't care as much. I seemed to be moving away from emotional things like anger tonight. Oddly, I couldn't even hate Sydney for cheating and murdering me; I just thought he was a very sick man. God, I even felt pity for Moker.

Imagine remembering your mother's rejection at your own birth! Followed by rejection for the rest of your life! Born to be reviled or spurned by the ignorant few—few, but still too many!—driven crazy by your own disfigurement. (It seemed that if anger was slipping off the board, then compassion appeared to be growing stronger.) I felt sorry for the poor, poor guy who had tried to kill Andrea and Primrose, sorry for someone who'd already murdered four other people, used them, then chopped three of the bodies to pieces, and it beat me, I couldn't understand why. Probably because I'd had glimpses of his life literally from the inside, experienced his sorrow and pain. But then, I'd also felt his excitement and sick joy for those terrible things he'd done. I'd felt the lingering shadows of his black soul—the whole of which had repelled those good souls who had sunk into his foulness in a vain attempt to influence the man. There was nothing worthy there, only wretched darkness and cruel malevolence. Could evil ever be absolute? Nothing there to glimmer in the umbra? I'd never thought so before, but now I wasn't so sure. Maybe Moker's soul would have been evil whatever the state of his body.

Anyway. Time to move on. Nothing left for me to hear, I had the answer I'd sought. Have to return home, see for myself if Prim and Andrea were okay. My wife—who'd deceived me. My daughter—who wasn't truly mine. Oh Hell—!

What did it really matter? I still loved them both. Yeah, even Andrea. Our marriage may have been a lie, but there'd been good times, great times. (Maybe love was growing stronger too, moving in to fill those gaps from where the negative vibes were absconding.) And nothing ever—ever—would diminish my love for Primrose. No, that couldn't change.

So. Time to go.

I started to drift away down the street, oblivious to the rain and the bustling uniformed figures around me. Started to drift away, but something stopped me, something said among the small group I'd been eavesdropping on. Something said by Coates.

"She should've stuck to knitting scarves," Coates had said.

Commander Newman, who had taken a couple of strides toward the gtp entrance with Chief Superintendent Sadler by his side, stopped short and turned round to Coates and Simmons. The two detectives were following so close behind they almost bumped into the senior officers.

I turned to look at Coates as well.

"What did you say?" the commander demanded, his expression severe. Sadler looked puzzled as he took in the detective constable.

"What did you say, man?" Newman glared at Coates with steely eyes.

"Er, we found a whole pile of badly knitted scarves when we searched the flat. Long ones, all dark. A few balls of wool and more knitting needles. She must have had an obsession for needles."

Sadler cut in. "What the bloody Hell are you talking about Coates? Who's this *she*?"

"Her, Sir." Coates looked confused as he pointed back at the dark shapes lying in the street. "Moker."

"Moker?" It was Newman again, his eyebrows arched, but his jaw set firm. "Do you mean to tell us that Moker—" now he was pointing at the bodies, "—*Moker,*" he repeated, "is—was—a woman?"

"Uh, yes, Sir." The detective constable was distinctly uncomfortable. "I thought you knew. Alexandra Moker. That was the full name on the electoral roll and driving license. We found tampons in her bathroom but not much other woman's stuff though."

I was stunned. I stood rigid, light rain falling through me. Moker had been a woman. It was unbelievable. Did it make any difference? Yeah, it did to me. Somehow it made the misery she'd had to bear all her life even more poignant. Call me a sucker, call me old-fashioned, but I'd always had a great respect—and a soft spot—for women, young or old, fat or thin, pretty or—or not pretty; I'd always *cherished* women. Even my mother had not managed to change my regard for them. To me, women were vulnerable, they needed protection. Not politically correct these days, I know, but they'd always be the weaker sex (physically, I mean, not mentally, not even emotionally) to me. I'd always open a door for one; I'd always give up my seat for one. Believe it or not, I used to stand up most times a woman or girl entered the room. An anachronism? Maybe I was, but I'm not around anymore to be called names. Besides, nearly every woman or girl I'd ever known seemed to appreciate my regard for them.

So that probably was why finding out that Moker had been female hit me hard. God, what had life been like for her? And had her physical appearance driven out *all* her femininity? I mean, just the way she walked! And I thought she was just plump when I saw her naked chest! What was God's great plan for her? My spirit—literally—my spirit sagged. I couldn't move so had to listen to Coates as he continued.

"Those telephone books, by the way," the detective was saying. "We wondered about them when we searched Moker's flat. You know, without a proper mouth there could hardly be any two-way dialogue, plus there wasn't a phone in the flat anyway. James True's wife—widow—told us Moker never said a word when she attacked her and her daughter, she just made kinda grunting noises and snorts."

Sadler, no doubt still digesting the startling news of Moker's gender—I'm sure there can't have been many female serial killers in the annals of crime—spoke curtly to Coates. "What's your point?" he snapped.

Simmons came to his colleague's rescue. "We also found unposted letters in the flat. Poison-pen letters, no two alike, every envelope addressed differently and to both men and women. We reckon she chose them from the telephone books and got some kind of perverted kick out of sending them. They were pretty horrible. Sick, I think you'd call them. You know, sex stuff."

Neither Newman nor Sadler wanted him to elaborate and Sadler made it clear. "Enough of that for now. Let's get into the building and see if Oliver Guinane is inside. He might be lying dead for all we know."

Without a further word from any of them, all seemingly lost in thought save for Coates who began to whistle quietly, they made their way toward the agency building. As they entered the glass doors of my old agency, I saw one of the cops Simmons had sent in earlier coming from the lift. He saluted the commander and began telling the group something, a finger jabbing upward as if to indicate the top offices. I hoped they'd managed to bring Ollie round. I also hoped he wasn't badly hurt.

Although I'd turned to watch Newman and his detectives enter the building, I still hadn't moved from the spot. Maybe I was bewildered by what I truly wished was the last revelation in a very traumatic week.

Moker. Alexandra Moker. A woman. Even when I'd used her body for my own purposes I didn't have a clue. Was there supposed to be a difference, should a cuckoo spirit feel the physical variation between a man or woman without sight of those differences? I honestly had no idea, and right then it was of no great importance to me. I just wondered why I'd so naturally assumed Moker was a man.

I remembered the mortuary earlier that day—God, was it the same day? All right, it might be after midnight, but it was still today's night as far as I was concerned. When, alone in the mortuary, Moker had molested a female cadaver, did that mean she was a lesbian? But then she had commandeered a young woman that evening and gone off with the debauched men for sex. There had also been a previous female victim. My guess was that her sexuality meant nothing to her because there had probably never been an opportunity to make love with either male or female. Despite her necrophilia, I still felt pity for her.

It occurred to me that my confusion over her sex was for a far simpler reason. When she had arrived at the morgue, her boss had asked whose grubby apron had been left in the corpse room, and her co-worker, who was about to leave, had pointed a thumb over his shoulder at Moker and replied; "Alec's."

Only he hadn't said "Alec's" at all. He'd replied "Alex," short for Alexandra. That's how I'd made the mistake in the beginning; also I'd *expected* the serial killer to be a man, as had the police themselves. She even *walked* like a man!

My melancholy gave way to numbness. Moker had been a monster in every sense of the word. But her life had been miserable, her *birth* had been hideous. No excuse for the odious things she'd done, but . . . but . . .

I would have wept for the woman called Alexandra Moker that night. But lately, I'd wept too much.

FORTY-SIX

After returning to Primrose and Andrea and making sure they were okay—they were both asleep in Andrea's and my bed, front door securely locked, a policeman keeping guard on the doorstep, the bedroom door locked too—I wandered. And have wandered ever since.

Literally as a lost soul, I drifted through the city, day and night. I observed people, almost living their sorrows with them. I eavesdropped on conversations and heated debates, even watched couples making love (no pervy sexual thing for me this last one, because sex or desire no longer played any part in my make-up; rather it was a personal wish to see men and women bonding in the most intimate way possible, a need to feel their commitment to one another at its strongest—yet too often all I sensed was their lust). I think I was just searching for love in this sad old world of ours and, yes, I did find it and it wasn't rare. It was in most people, young and old—*especially* in these two extremes, in fact—and in those of middle years as I had been. Sounds corny, I know, but it was a great comfort to me.

I experienced everything in a fresh and new way, and every detail was of interest to me. It was the same feeling you get immediately after you've recovered from a serious or debilitating illness, only this was a hundred times more intense. I sat in parks and watched people, muffled up in the cold, pass by, momentarily sensing their feelings, their thoughts. I was especially fond of watching children in school playgrounds, because their unbounded zest for life when they were playing touched me deeply. If only you could see their colorful and vivacious auras.

Some animals sensed me, others didn't. Cats were particularly sensitive to my presence whereas most dogs became confused, often afraid. Birds deliberately ignored me when I sat on park benches, coming close to peck at insects or any breadcrumbs they might find, yet never invading my space. It was as if they were aware of me, but it was of no concern to them, I was neither a threat nor a means of more food.*

One day, I dropped by Westminster Cathedral. It must have been a Sunday morning—I'd lost *all* sense of time by then—because a High Mass was in progress. When I walked out later I found I was relieved of the guilt, baggage—never a burden, but ever a nag—I'd carried around with me as a pathetic Catholic (in common with many other Catholics) for far too many years. I'd discovered that pomp and ceremony were not essential to belief, although the ritual and symbolism were necessary for many and *essential* for some. Individual or collective worship were both right—naturally a combination of both was the ideal because neither one precluded the other—and a person was free to choose without persuasion or dictates by those who has set themselves up as conduits to God.

I don't know how I realized this, it was just a reverse epiphany that suddenly cleansed my mind and lightened (enlightened?) my soul. One moment I was unsuccessfully aligning myself with the other worshippers and respectfully following the service, trying to get closer to God for obvious reasons, the next it was as if a great gray cloud had been lifted. Suddenly I knew that my way, and the way of millions like me, was okay. God was accessible to us all without intermediaries.

(However, there was one lovely thing that happened during the church service. Every worshipper's aura spread to their neighbors' and when the priest held high the little round wafer called the Host, all the auras joined together as one. The golden brilliance was too pure and dazzling to look at directly and I had to cover my eyes. More vivid than the sun, it was wonderful to be in its presence. It's a pity it isn't perceptible to the living.)

---

*Incidentally, animals also have souls. I've watched them leave the bodies of dogs and cats run over in the streets (happens a lot in the city) or when they die naturally (cats nearly always find some secluded spot to die in, whereas dogs like to have their owners close by). And their little souls don't rise up into the "heavens," but, like ours, they evaporate just moments after leaving the dead body (if they don't, if they drift away rather than vanishing, then a new ghost has been created). Yep, there are ghost-animals too. It's the same with people, which is why ghosts always seem melancholy—they're lost, you see. Other ghosts, like my father (I learned all this from him when he next came to me), come back from another dimension, but only to visit and never for very long. Anyway, it was he who explained how animals and human souls vanish rather than rise as if on a journey to the sky. The only exceptions, he told me, were birds, whose small spirits did float skywards, but only because that was what they knew best.

I continued to follow people home to see how they lived, haunted one or two bars at night, and generally drifted from place to place. I never visited another séance parlor again; I knew they would make me feel uncomfortable after that last time. Because it would torture me so, I also stayed away from Andrea and Primrose for a while, my mother too, but for different reasons.

Another day, taking a break from my roving, I hung around a picturesque graveyard, maybe with the idea of meeting some friendly ghosts. (I was never tempted to visit the crematorium's "place of rest," because there was no grave, just a tiny plaque with my name on it, among many on a wall, the ashes in a closed recess behind. Nothing sentimental there then.) I found a bench by a gravel path deep inside the cemetery and sat looking out over the many headstones and tombs, angels with high wings and outstretched arms, white crosses stained by lichen, one or two plots well tended, many others sadly neglected. With its Gothic mausoleums, markers and occasional monuments, the place had a quiet brooding atmosphere, which I found peaceful rather than sinister.

It was here, while hoping for a little peace and quiet from the harsh world outside, with the sun high in a clear azure sky, that my father came to me for the last time.

He was standing beneath an old oak tree whose thick leafless branches still managed to cast him in shadow. How long he had been standing there, I couldn't be sure, for only when I sensed that eyes were watching me did I glance in his direction. At first, he was merely an insubstantial shadow among others, but as my gaze became more intense, his form took on a clearer definition, although his lower legs and feet remained invisible.

I didn't move, I just stared back at him, wondering if I should join him beneath the oak. After a while, it was he who came to me.

By the time he reached me, he was fully formed, so much so that he could have been a normal man who'd stopped for a chat. He stood on the gravel path that ran between the plots, smiling down at me, and he wore the same clothes as on the previous occasions he'd appeared to me: old-fashioned double-breasted suit, too creased to be smart, and plain white shirt, dull, red tie. For the first time I noticed his shoes, brown brogues with swirls of tiny neat puncture patterns decorating the upper leather; they were slightly creased also, but at least polished.

"Hello, Jimmy," he said in a pleasantly gruff but quiet voice.

The sun was behind him, his white hair a halo round his head; it was difficult to see his features.

"It's you—Dad," I said for some reason. Of course it was my dad.

"Yes, it's me. Can I sit with you for a little while?"

I shuffled my butt toward the arm at the end of the wooden bench, making room for him. The past times we'd met had been traumatic, the last one particularly horrendous. But today, in this morbid but tranquil setting, I felt completely at ease with him.

"This time I can hear you," I said, only now appreciating the fact. "You can speak directly to me."

"You're closer to us."

I didn't ask him to elucidate. Instead, I thanked him for helping me when Moker had attacked my family.

"We were weak," he replied regretfully, shaking his head. Looking at him in the clear light of day (his image wavered only occasionally) I could see our resemblance. Perhaps he was how I would have looked eventually if I hadn't died.

"I brought many souls with me," he went on, "in the belief that our collective force would defeat the poor beast." He sighed unhappily. "Unfortunately, when we stormed into the body, the soul there was so foul, so malign, we couldn't stay. It was too overwhelming, too frightening—too corruptive. I'm sorry I fled with the others, but we were combined, there could be no separation from them."

"You bought us time, that's the point. Enough time for Andrea to recover and take her best shot with the poker."

My father smiled again. "We were still there, although our usefulness was spent. We tried to give your wife strength." His expression became serious. "But you know, what you did afterward was very foolish."

"You mean taking over Moker's dead body?"

"You could have been tainted by the evil left inside him."

"If there was any, it helped my anger at my ex-friend. Maybe it enforced the hatred I felt for the friend I thought I had."

"Murder is never a solution."

"D'you understand what Oliver Guinane did to me?"

The ghost nodded. "To want revenge is still wrong."

"Huh! Seems to me I was deceived most of my life. His betrayal with my wife tipped me over the edge. I'd reached breaking point. And let's be frank here—you were the one who started the ball rolling as far as betrayal was concerned. You walked out on me and Mother when I was just a kid."

"I explained everything in the letters I wrote to you, letters your mother never let you see."

We were interrupted by an old lady we hadn't noticed coming along the path. She was slightly crooked and somewhere in her late seventies drawing toward eighty, and wearing an old coat with a scraggy synthetic fur collar that drowned her meager frame (probably it fitted her well before she started to shrink). Held tight against her shapeless chest was a potted plant. As she drew level with the bench, she gave my father a cheery smile that revealed perfect porcelain teeth above bare lower gums.

"Nice day," she greeted him in a croaky voice that was as cheerful as her incomplete grin.

My father smiled back and gave a small acknowledgment with his hand. She trundled on her way, perhaps to visit and chat to a late husband, or maybe a dearly missed friend. Perhaps she wanted to tell them she wouldn't be long.

But I was puzzled. She could see my father, but she couldn't see me. How's that for irony? He was more dead than I was, surely? I mean—what was the expression they used? Oh yeah—he had "passed over" whereas I was still earthbound, so didn't that mean he was more dead than me? Shouldn't there be some kind of priority? I shrugged it off.

My father seemed to have enjoyed the brief encounter with the old lady, but the half-smile left his face when he turned back to me.

"Son, you saw the letters your mother kept from you for years when you were growing up. I wrote to you regularly after I left even though I never received replies. I never gave up, but eventually I died."

"You still deserted me—us," I reminded him.

"No, I didn't, I didn't desert you. Your mother made me leave."

I shook my head. "I don't believe that."

"I'm sorry, but it's true. You must have realized over the years that she wasn't . . . well, she wasn't quite right in the head."

I thought of the evening I'd found Mother ripping up photographs of me and destroying letters from my father that I'd never been allowed to see, let alone read. And that was because I, too, had left her by dying. No rational person would ever react in that way, and especially not with such venom, such loathing.

"She could be a bit cranky, sure," I said.

"Perhaps you're in denial. Sons should love and respect their mothers, no matter what. Before you were born she was already making my life impossible with demands and strictures. I had a decent job, but she was never happy with what we'd got, she always felt she'd lowered her own high standards by taking me on as a husband—high standards that had never existed, incidentally. She was from a very humble background, her mother and father good plain people, her father a postman, her mother a part-time cleaning lady. It was only when they died within months of each other that your mother started to take on those grand airs. I suppose there was no longer anyone around to remind her of her working-class beginnings."

He sighed, lost in memories for a little while. "At one time she was courting a reasonably wealthy young man, an assistant manager at a big chain store, his family quite well to do. But he broke off with her after a year or so, found someone else apparently. But it was that year with him and all its possibilities that aroused those airs and graces in her. She took me on the rebound and regretted it almost immediately. I won't embarrass you about the physical side of our marriage; I'd only comment that her pregnancy with you was a surprise to us both."

I remained silent. Truth is, I had nothing to say.

"When you came along I'm afraid she became even more difficult to live with. Now nothing was ever good enough for either of you. She disliked the house we lived in, felt the area was too working class, and she wanted to make plans for you eventually to be taught at a private school. I did my best, Jimmy, but it was never good enough."

His image faded briefly as though regret had weakened whatever power it took to maintain a visible presence. Then it returned like a developing Polaroid image.

"Eventually, your mother became impossible to live with and I was forced to give her an ultimatum: accept what we had, *appreciate* what we had, or I would leave and take you with me." He gave a small, dry laugh. "It was as if I'd lifted the lid off her madness. Oh, I don't mean she became certifiably insane, but her hysteria was terrifying. She screamed at me to leave immediately, she never wanted to see me again, that *I* would never see my son again. She threw herself around, deliberately fell against furniture so that she was bruised and cut. It was our next-door neighbors, people she felt were her inferiors and not worthy of speaking to, who called the police. They thought she was being murdered. They were concerned for you also. You were just a toddler and you were frightened; you all but screeched the house down."

He told me this with a bitter smile that disturbed his pleasant features and

I tried to remember but couldn't, even though the incident must have had a traumatic effect on me at the time. Maybe it was so upsetting for me that it was stowed away somewhere deep in my subconscious and maybe I thought my father was to blame so that it tainted my feelings toward him for evermore. Mother had certainly poisoned my mind against him over the years and perhaps that terrible day was when the foundation of resentment was laid. I'd been much too young to understand the situation; all I knew was that Daddy had upset Mummy and I must have hated him for that. Hadn't he, himself, just told me that every son should love and respect his mother?

"The police came and, naturally, I was the villain of the piece. I had hoped that eventually things would settle down, we'd continue in the same unsatisfactory but steady way. Far from it. Your mother's attitude grew worse day by day and, in the end, I did exactly what she'd constantly told me to do: I left."

He gave another sigh, his head was turned toward me again and in his face I saw not just misery, but deep grief. "I had no choice. She would never have let you go, and I knew that by staying myself, her condition would only grow worse. In the end, I left for the sake of you both. Life had become impossible. I'm sorry, though, Jimmy. I did try to keep in touch, but eventually I was worn down by it all. All I could do was write you letters."

I was quiet, absorbing everything he had told me. All those wasted years, for many of them despising a father I thought had abandoned me, and that followed by disdain, then finally by cold detachment—he had ceased to exist as far as I was concerned, and that was *before* I'd learned of his death.

"Can you forgive me, son?" Grief had been replaced by pleading in those faded blue eyes. "After I died I tried to stay connected with you, but that's almost impossible once a person has passed over."

I suddenly recalled a certain face among a crowd of onlookers, all of whom wore expressions of alarm and concern for the young man who had just been knocked from his motorbike, his leg cruelly twisted, blood seeping from beneath his crash helmet to run along the gutter where he lay. There was no fear on my father's face that day, only compassion.

Here we were now, two ghosts sitting in a graveyard, one a veteran, the other a novice (I didn't understand the difference between us, but I didn't feel like a proper ghost). Father and son. Reunited. Together again, but only in death. I was grateful at least for that, and I think if we'd both had substance I would have hugged him; or I'd have asked my father to hug me.

Instead, and perhaps to cover that childlike yearning, I said: "But why didn't you try to see me away from home? Why didn't you find me when I grew older?"

He shook his head remorsefully. "I did that once. I went to your school and waited for you to come out. Unfortunately, your mother saw me first and threatened to call the police. She said she would hurt herself like before and blame me. She told me it would make her very happy to see me locked up in jail."

Jesus Christ, I thought. I'd always known Mother could be a bitch, but I had no idea of how wicked she was.

"In my letters to you," my father went on, "I was always suggesting times and places where you and I could meet but, of course, you never received them. The years went by and then, one day, I decided to hell with the consequences, I would come to your home, just knock on the door and introduce myself to you. She might rant and rave, call the police, but at least you would know I hadn't forgotten you. I was determined it would happen, no matter what. Unfortunately, I died of a stroke before I had the chance."

I took it all in, no longer confused, a certain emptiness, never acknowledged but always with me nonetheless, had suddenly been appeased. If it hadn't been for more recent revelations, I might even have felt whole again.

"I think I'm beginning to understand," I said, then added, "Dad."

His smile was different from before. It was as if he'd finally found something he had sought for a long, long time, both in life and in death. His smile was pure, untainted by anguishes of the past.

"You know, there have been other deceptions in my life," I told him, unable to return his smile. "Knowing the truth of our situation means a lot to me, but these other . . . these other . . ."

"Deceptions, you said."

"Yeah, I guess it's the right word. My mother, my wife, my best friend, my business partner—even the person who means everything in the whole world to me, the little girl I thought was my daughter."

I slumped forward, elbows on my knees, hands covering part of my face. "I just can't get it right in my head," I said. "I can't seem to take it all in." I'm sure my expression was a mixture of sorrow and anger when I raised my head and looked sideways at him. "Was nobody true to me?" I asked as if he might have the answer, or at least, make sense of all that had happened.

He spoke softly. "By all means blame your mother for her cruelty to us both, but temper your anger with pity."

Yeah, I thought. *I can do pity nowadays. Hadn't I felt pity for Moker? Christ, Moker! Even the cold-blooded killer wasn't, as he—she—seemed!*

"She isn't responsible for her mental problems. In her mind, I had left her. She hadn't forced me to go. After that, she was always afraid of losing you too, and that's why she turned your mind against me. But, of course, eventually you did leave her—you got married. And then you died. That has shattered her, she feels she has nothing left."

"But Andrea and I didn't want to cut her out of our lives, she made the choice herself."

"For her, in her fragile mental state, it was the right choice to cut *you* out, or at least begin the process. I'm sorry to say this, but it was the right choice for you both. She would have tried to destroy your marriage."

I gave a little shake of my head in frustration, then leaned back on the bench.

"You have to accept what she is, son. With acceptance comes forgiveness, and forgiveness is important to you right now."

I didn't follow up this last remark: my mind was still busy with other deceits.

"You know my wife was unfaithful to me throughout our marriage?"

He nodded. "It wasn't entirely her fault. The other man was different to you and he has a power over her that is strong yet inexplicable. You'll think it strange, but your wife loved you in her own way."

"So that's okay then."

"You've every right to be bitter, but it's a sentiment that's of no use to anyone. All this anger of yours is only delaying your own progress."

Again, I failed to follow up; in my mind there were only visions of Andrea and Oliver together, living happily with Primrose.

"Her lover—my best friend and working partner—is Prim's father." I gazed across the cemetery, unwilling to show him the full intensity of my fury—of my *jealousy.*

"To Primrose, you will always be her father. No matter if she learns the truth when she becomes older, she will still consider herself your daughter. Don't underestimate the child's devotion to you."

"In time she'll forget me."

"With time her love will only be more assured. She'll grieve for you now, just as your wife grieves for you, but eventually the hurt will pass for them, to be replaced by a memory that won't ever be spoiled."

"I just . . . I just don't know whether I can believe you."

"Then go back home and see them once more. Only once, mind you. You wouldn't want to haunt your own family." He smiled again, but it wasn't catching. "If you stay with them, then their mourning will take longer to resolve itself. They won't see you, but your presence will be there and they will sense something that they can't understand. It will only make their pain harder to bear."

"I don't think I can do that," I told him dejectedly. "I can't just turn my back on them."

"You must. Go back once and it might help you accept."

"I don't want to accept. I *can't* accept!"

"Before long you'll grow tired of your own melancholy. That's when everything will change for you."

"Okay. I still love Andrea and I'll always love Primrose."

"And that's precisely what will help you overcome your bitterness. In your present state you'll soon begin to experience pure love. Love without jealousy or passion, without partiality or bounds, an unselfish love, because it won't be burdened by need. Anxieties will soon disappear."

"I could never forgive Oliver for what he did to me."

"No, but sooner or later you'll accept it. I hope for your sake it will be sooner."

"Forgive him?"

"Forgiveness follows acceptance."

"You sound like a priest."

He laughed aloud. "Where I come from we all do. It's something we have to resist." He became serious again. "You mentioned one other person who deceived you."

"Sydney. Sydney Presswell. He was the agency's business partner and accountant. Sydney did more than just deceive me though—he was the bastard that killed me."

My father nodded as if he already knew.

"He also stole money from the company and engineered a takeover bid that I was against. Seems he's been fiddling the books for years." I breathed a resigned sigh. "I used to like him. Didn't always agree with some of his methods and business proposals, but I always thought he was a stand-up guy. That's the kind of idiot I am—*was.*"

"Gullible?"

I looked at him, about to object, then thought better of it. Wryly, I said,

"Yeah, that's about it. Sydney had been cheating on us for years, but Oliver and I, well we didn't have a clue."

"No wonder you feel nobody was ever true to you."

"Paranoid? Doesn't mean they're not out to get you." An old joke that failed to raise a chuckle between us. "But you know what? I couldn't care less about Sydney anymore. Weird, I know, because not only was he a crook, but he took my life away, too. I don't feel hatred and I don't feel forgiveness. I just feel kind of numb where he's concerned."

"That might be because he's dead."

"And I killed him. Retribution, I'd call it."

"Is *that* how you feel—you've avenged yourself."

I thought about it for a short while. "Well—no. Like I said, I don't feel anything at all."

"That's good."

"Is it? Doesn't seem right to me. He turned out to be a complete sham, who even tried to get someone else blamed for my murder."

"But you've accepted it."

"I don't know, I wouldn't quite say that. Let me put it this way: the murder and the embezzlement are bothering me less and less with each day that passes."

"You're getting yourself ready."

I looked at him sharply. "Ready for what?"

"Ready to leave this all behind you."

It didn't come as a shock. "So I really am dead? There's no reprise, no coming back, not even as someone else?"

He shook his head, and he seemed pleased.

"You've lost your body."

"Couldn't I . . . couldn't I find another one?"

"They're all taken. You'd have to be born again to gain another and that would put you in a different time and place. You wouldn't even remember this life."

"I could live with that," I assured him.

"I'm afraid the choice won't be yours. There's much more to learn on the other side, you see. Much more."

"Oh." I didn't bother to hide my disappointment. "So how do I get to this 'other side?' I feel useless here."

"You're making progress all the time."

"I am a ghost then."

"Not quite. In your present form, you're a transient spirit."

"I thought that was the same thing."

"No."

"My body's dead, so why do I have to hang about here?" I protested.

"You weren't in your body when it died. Fortunately."

"Fortunately? How so?"

"It enabled you to do something before leaving this world. Something important."

"Kill the killer."

"She was corrupted."

"But her face—"

"Her soul was not deformed to begin with. Only her own resentment and wickedness changed that."

"Where is she now? I saw her soul leave her body. I was kind of hoping she'd become extinct, you know, become nothing."

"Not punished?"

I shrugged. "She was a woman. For her—I mean her soul—to be totally snuffed seems reasonable to me. She'd been punished enough in this place. I didn't think she should suffer anymore."

"They were right about you. Gullible. Perhaps it's no bad thing though. It shows a certain innocence of heart."

"So tell me."

"Alexandra Moker's soul? Nothing ever becomes extinct. Let's just say her soul won't be around for a very long time."

"I see. No one's punished throughout eternity."

"There are exceptions. Fortunately for poor embittered Alexandra, she wasn't one of them."

"I don't think I want to know what it takes to be totally canceled."

"Very wise, Jimmy."

"Can we get back to me, my situation?"

"Your departure will be a gradual process. You have the opportunity to learn more about the world you've lived in, and that gift isn't given to many."

"Lucky me."

"It'll be worth it. First though, you must follow my advice."

"Accept the bad things in my life?"

He nodded. "Go back. Be impartial. Learn."

Right then, I couldn't think of anything more to ask, so we just sat quietly.

FORTY-SEVEN

I did some more roaming before I returned to my old home and my mother's dismal flat because I was reluctant to follow my father's advice immediately, too aware that being close to Primrose and unable to communicate would hurt and frustrate me even more. Aware, too, that I had to let them go, I shouldn't haunt them, that it might be the last time I'd see Prim and Andrea. I knew how emotionally painful it would be.

So I drifted for a while.

Time began to mean less and less to me and I experienced those "blackouts" more and more. I'd awake, if that's how it could be described, usually in a different place to the one I'd occupied before the unconsciousness. At first, this was disorientating, but eventually I got used to it. I realized I had always become very drained just before it occurred even though I was only in spirit, and I assumed that the "blackouts" were nothing more than falling asleep, unexpected though they were, and gave me the chance to replenish myself.

More than once I bumped into lonely ghosts on my wanderings, but they appeared either perplexed by me or frightened, as if I were the ghost and they were human. They scooted away, or evaporated, leaving me alone again.

I visited more churches, because I found their tranquillity was good for meditation, and I was meditating more and more as time went on. Night revealed some of its mysteries to me, the activity that continued throughout the sunless hours. I understood why ghosts, visible or otherwise, were more active when the land was dark: it was because at night the streets are emptier and generally people slept, so there would be minimal contact between the dead and the living. It seems ghosts are very shy and often, but not always, aware that they are in the wrong place. As I mentioned, none wanted contact with me and I began to feel like some kind of pariah as far as they were concerned.

Even as I examined, explored, or just observed, I could feel myself waning, not growing weak exactly, but feeling more and more disassociated with the world I knew, somehow growing disconnected from it. Still I delved, still I was interested in everything around me, but not as keenly as before.

I called in on hospitals, often visiting intensive care units to watch souls depart from recently deceased host bodies. Some were happy to go, while others were glum, perhaps confused or disbelieving, a few not even aware that they were dead. There was always a special joyous radiance about the happy ones who accepted their passing, as if they already knew they would find peace and contentment, whereas the souls of those who failed to realize their situation, or who would not accept their death, were dull, gray, listless, and lingered by their corpse far too long. But none of these latter egressions matched the awfulness of Moker's.

Incidentally, never again did I attempt to insinuate myself into a freshly dead body. The idea was now abhorrent to me and I wondered how I'd managed twice before. (Early on, I considered usurping someone's living body permanently, to share their life, to be of substance again, but had rejected the idea almost immediately for three reasons: one, having two minds in one head would surely lead to insanity; two, it would be extremely difficult; and three, it would be wrong, very, *very* wrong—it would be theft.)

I learned a lot during that period of discovery and assessment, reaching understandings I never thought possible. Life, itself, began to make some kind of sense to me at last.

And day by day (I judged time only by the activity before and around me, the risings of the sun and moon, the day's lengthening shadows; if I were to stand inside an empty pitch black room I'd have no idea of passing moments whatsoever; however, this wouldn't be like my recurring blackouts, because my thought processes would continue to work and thoughts are no judge of time) I became just a little more detached from the world, gradually withdrawing, it seemed, from the existence I used to know.

I figured I should return home before it was too late.

I visited Mother first: I wanted to get it out of the way. It was daytime when I arrived, but only twilight in the front room because of the drawn curtains, with a gap of barely a couple of inches in the middle for light to infiltrate the room. She'd lit candles, five or six of them, two of those on the low coffee table before the lumpy armchair I seemed to have grown up with.

Mother sat in the armchair, leaning forward, the wrists of her clasped hands resting on her knees. Unlike the last time I saw her, she had made some effort to tidy herself up. Her gray-brown hair was brushed and heavily lacquered, the beige blouse she wore beneath a light pink cardigan was neatly pressed, as was the long, pleated skirt she wore.

There was sorrow in her eyes, but no puffiness around them and no redness to the eyelids; it seemed her crying was done. I moved round to her side and saw what she was staring at.

On the coffee table, propped up by something behind and with the two candles acting as sentinels on either side, was a color photograph held together— it was in four rough-edged sections—with clear Sellotape. It was the picture of me on the day I'd left art college; my young, wide, smile was marred by the rip down the center of my face, but you could still see the happy anticipation in my eyes, the eagerness to get on with the next exciting stage of my life. Lit by the candles' soft glow, the assemblage resembled a small shrine in the restful gloom and it occurred to me that this might have been Mother's intention. Certainly there was no anger in those sad eyes that were taking in my beaming image, nor could I detect any more self-pity. Instead, there was a softness I hadn't noticed for many years; since I was a child, in fact.

Had her demons finally left her in peace after all these years? I wanted to believe so, but Mother had always been unpredictable. This might be a new, but temporary phase she was going through. I could only hope its influence would not be too short.

I felt my old, uncomplicated love for her returning, a child's natural blind devotion, and I decided to leave before memories tarnished it. Aware she could never feel the touch, not even the whisper of a breath, on her cheek, I bent low and kissed her anyway.

Holding a mental picture of my house, I allowed myself to travel there by thought alone, which was a wonderful means of transport. Swift, too.

I'd expected to find Andrea on her own and had intended to wait for Primrose to return from school. When I found both of them there I realized it must be a weekend, probably a Sunday by the feel of it. Andrea was resting on our bed, and Prim was next door in her own bedroom, kneeling before the yellow and pink doll's house we'd bought her for her last birthday. Prim was absorbed in organizing her "little people"—small, plastic men, women, children, and animals, who inhabited the make-believe world she loved to escape into—around the wooden building's various rooms, her own imagination giving them life and story.

Having first established where they both were, I went back to my wife. I gazed down at her lovely face as she lay on the bed and saw that the large wad of gauze held by Elastoplast, which had covered her damaged nose when I had returned to the house after Sydney's death, was gone. Her face was gaunt and her eyes were damp with unreleased tears. I hoped that they were the last, that she'd finally cried herself out and this was only a moment of weakness, the worst of the grieving having run its course. And yes, I knew she had grieved terribly for me; the dullness of her aura told me how depleted by sadness she felt and I could sense the wretchedness of her spirit itself (I'd become very adept at such sensing lately).

As I watched, she closed her eyes, not to sleep, but to lose herself in a memory. Somehow I knew it was of me.

I noticed what she clutched in her arms, pressing it to her breast. It was one of my old sweaters, its color a deep blue. A framed photograph stood on the bedside table, a place it had never occupied before. A family shot, a fairly recent one; me with one arm thrown over Andrea's shoulder and hugging her tight to me, my other hand resting flatly against Prim's chest, pulling her close between Andrea and myself. All of us were laughing and, as I remembered, not just for the camera—we were at Disneyland, Paris, and had spent most of the day laughing.

Perhaps, before, some of the reluctance to return home was, in part, because I feared Oliver might be there. But he wasn't. There was no impression of him either. Again, this came from Andrea herself. I sensed nothing of Oliver (and I told you that my perception, or if you like, my intuition, had become acute) and I hoped he was now absent from her life. Maybe the shock of my death had cleansed her of him; maybe guilt had made her realize how deceitful they had been together, and that love cannot flourish on guilt. Could be that Andrea had finally seen Oliver in his true colors—a lying, vain, cheating coke-head. Again, I hoped so.

And I also hoped that, in time, she would forgive herself. I wanted her to find happiness in the future, not misery or loneliness.

I leaned over and kissed her forehead.

Lastly, I went to see Primrose.

She was still playing with the doll's house and her tiny plastic people when I entered her bedroom and when she unexpectedly looked over her shoulder,

I thought she could see me. There was no expression on her sweet little face though and, just as quickly, she returned to her game.

I went over and sat on the floor next to her. I watched her profile as she arranged her little fun world and spoke the tiny people's lines for them. I used to be fascinated by the playlets she made them perform while I surreptitiously watched from behind a newspaper whenever she set up the whole production downstairs in the living room. Her inventiveness since the age of five had always amazed me, each performance turning into a simple morality tale—plastic children (the same size as the adults) becoming lost, those same kids stealing, then repenting and becoming good once more, the father figure arriving home late from work yet again and missing his dinner, but promising not to work so hard anymore (I wonder where she got that one from?). It's always wonderful to watch your own child grow and develop physically and mentally, and I was a sucker for it.

And now this would be my last opportunity to be entranced by her (don't ask me how I knew, I just sensed it was so, and as I've said, my perception was becoming pretty sharp). I was sure my father was right when he said that by hanging on, "haunting" them, I'd interfere with their healing process, because part of them would not accept my death and subconsciously they would sense my presence. The mind sometimes absorbs ethereal elements that it will not always relay to the brain; such messages or unrealized perceptions are never lost though, and their influence can often be felt.

I noticed Prim, like her mother, had a photograph by her bedside. But this featured just the two of us, Prim and me, cheek-to-cheek headshots, our grins perfectly matched.

I sat with her for some time (I knew it had been a while, because when I glanced out the window, the sun was much lower in the sky). It had to be now, I thought. Staying any longer would only make it harder to leave.

Trying to dismiss the heartache that was threatening to undermine my resolve I bent forward on my knees and put my arms around Prim, careful not to encroach her small body, and touched her soft cheek with my lips.

I kissed her and she suddenly jumped. I withdrew sharply, not wanting to frighten her. She looked directly at me for a moment, but then her gaze went beyond where I knelt. She turned her head, to the left, to the right, and then behind her. For a little while, her expression was one of bewilderment and then, her tawny-flecked eyes shining, it changed to one of amazement.

"Daddy?" she whispered in awe.

Unchecked tears spoiled my vision. I knew she could not see me, nor would she hear me if I spoke. Nevertheless, I said, "Yes, Prim, it's me, Daddy."

No recognition in her eyes, no sign that she had heard my voice. As I knew there wouldn't be—I was not a proper ghost.

She frowned and looked around the room again. She moved off her knees and sat on the floor, her ankles crossed as she pondered. There was still puzzlement there on her innocent face but, thankfully, no alarm.

Then she smiled and looked at our picture by the bed.

I smiled too.

FORTY-EIGHT

So that's my story. I hope it's been of some interest to you.

Maybe, when you awaken from your out-of-body dream, you'll have forgotten everything I've told you. I know I forgot dreams sometimes when I was alive.

The point is: do you believe me? Well, ask yourself why would I lie? I've spent too much time with you to waste on gibberish—it was dark when we met by chance and now the sky to the east is growing lighter. It doesn't matter anyway. You can trust me or not. It's up to you.

You might also ask yourself why this storyteller died but his soul did not go to its proper ordained place like most souls? I'm still a little puzzled by that myself, but this is how I see it.

For one, my soul was not in its body when I died—when I was *murdered.*

Two, there was some work for me to do in this world before I left it. I had more murders to prevent, because Moker's killing would have gone on and on until she was caught. That's why I found myself in Moker's basement flat at the beginning of all this. It seems a Higher Source—at least, that's what my father called it the last time we talked—a Higher Source guided me there. The rest was up to me.

And three, my unusual status gave me the opportunity to learn about myself and about life. I suspect many other souls get the same chance before they move on but, of course, the living wouldn't know it. In my incorporeal form—my astral state, if you like—without flesh and blood, and all the hang-ups that go with that, I was pure mind with no physical distractions. The sensory gift we all have, but few of us use, was unfettered, my psyche was liberated. *Is* liberated—it's an ongoing thing.

I've begun to understand and appreciate just a little about life on this planet. Not much, but way more than before. I won't bore you with the "love is all" cliché, although that plays a big part in the understanding, and an even bigger part in our next stop. I'm assured—by my father—that it's going to be something wonderful, but that's all he said. No, we're here on this earth to learn *acceptance.* Yep, that's right—*acceptance.* Acceptance of everything that life throws at you. All the good, all the bad—*everything.* Doesn't mean you don't work—or fight—to defeat it or make the bad things good, but sometimes we have no control at all over it. That's when you *have* to accept; you have no other choice.

My father told me acceptance leads to forgiveness, which is vital for progression, according to him, but I don't believe it's quite as simple as that—for us, anyway—and not as easy. Believe me, I *know* it isn't easy. I think acceptance *can* lead to forgiveness, but it's too hard for most people. How do you accept a tyrant, a child molester, a rapist—a murderer? I had to accept that last one, although I did my best to stop the killer. But it doesn't matter to me anymore. I can be objective—forgiving—because I'm no longer part of it all. Because ultimately, in the grand scheme of things, the tribulations in this life are not so important, not compared to what happens next, the wondrous things that will come to each and every one of us.

What's helped me begin to understand is this gradual disconnection with the world I've always known—the place you're living in now. Jealousy, deceit, anger, acquisition—it's all trivial as far as the big picture is concerned, and it fades into insignificance when you're totally free of those imperfections yourself. That's why I've forgiven Andrea, Oliver, and Sydney. My mother too. As for my father, it seems there was nothing to forgive. I've accepted the emotional pain they caused me. It isn't easy, nor that simple, but the more my presence here wanes, the easier and simpler it becomes.

The only person I've not yet fully forgiven is myself, because I had some of those imperfections or faults I mentioned. But I'm working on it.

You know, even Alexandra Moker should have accepted her disfigurement, but unfortunately it—and the lifetime of rejection she suffered—corrupted her mind and soul. I think she'll get another chance though, but it's only a guess.

I don't expect to be around much longer. But that's okay. I've seen a lot. I've finally taken excursions into the countryside and even though I'm becoming more distant from this world, the true beauty of nature took my breath away (metaphorically speaking, yet again!).

I've spent ages in art galleries, really *looking* at paintings and sculptures, really *absorbing* them and, for the first time, truly appreciating the artists' intent.

I've explored famous old buildings and some spectacular new ones, museums too, gaining insights into other times, other civilizations.

I went to the palace to see the queen again—she wasn't in the first time. Very tedious, not the kind of life you and I would like, I promise you.

I've sat in parliament and, believe me, most MPs are just as lazy and self-important as we think they are.

One dark and beautiful night I tried to reach the stars, but never even got as far as any helicopter might fly. Something pulled me back and I knew it wasn't gravity; it was as if I'd reached my limits and my own will would not take me further. But I saw stars and planets as I'd never seen them before, zillions of them, each one a separate dazzling jewel.

I've seen over our world from a new perspective and I can assure you, it's more fabulous than you could ever imagine.

Now time's running out for me.

I can feel myself slowly vanishing, my mind gradually becoming disenfranchised from this place. Look at my arm. It's almost transparent. And by the way you're squinting at me, I suspect the rest of me is disappearing too. It's okay. I feel ready to leave.

Am I afraid? My destiny *was* daunting to me, but that's not so anymore. In fact, I'm eager to go on. There are many more answers on the other side as well as more mysteries. I know, because not only have I become acutely sensitive to this world and its meaning, but I'm already beginning to perceive something of the next. I think it's going to be incredible.

It's been good to meet you and get so much off my chest. It'll help me forget the hurt. You're the only one I've been able to communicate with in my wandering, so thanks for listening. Ghosts, yes, but not out-of-body spirits like you. Besides, they never wanted to chat. I glimpsed Moker before and she glimpsed me, but it wasn't the same as this. There was no contact. Incidentally, I feel I ought to warn you to beware of the OBEs—look what happened to me—but I know you have no choice. Just don't journey too far away from your host body, okay? And if you can, always leave it somewhere safe.

You know, my feelings of being drawn away from this life have been growing stronger even as I've been speaking to you. I think my departure is more imminent than I expected.

Take care of yourself and remember what I said about acceptance. It can resolve many things. And again, be cautious in your spirit state—you're leaving your body very vulnerable. Don't abuse your gift, use it only for good things or not at all. Learn things and treat your body like the temple it is. Treat it with reverence—it's more valuable than you know. Oh, and I hope you didn't mind my little digressions from the main story. Just thought you might be interested. Besides, I haven't had the chance to talk like this for quite a while.

Okay. Got to go now.

More things to see before it's too late. More things to understand.

Take good care of yourself. Don't neglect your body. Appreciate it.

Hey, you're fading too. Your body wants you back. Try and remember this—it might just help.

Take good care.

See you eventually . . .

In another pla—